A Heart's Charade

Copyright © 2025 by Jill Ann Mai

All Scripture quotations unless otherwise indicated are taken from the New International Version of the Bible.

All rights reserved. This book or any portion thereof may not be reproduced or used in any manner whatsoever without the express written permission of the publisher except for the use of brief quotations in a book review or scholarly journal.

First Printing: 2025

ISBN-13: 979-8-9889628-2-3

For more information about the book or author, please visit www.jillannmai.com

This book is dedicated to Charles "Speedy" Wagoner, an anchor for me and for so many in my family.

A Heart's Charade

Jill Ann Mai

Chapter 1

Paris, France 1776

Charlotte watched from the Hôtel de Beauvais window at the man driving his cart on the street below, her mind quite made up on a decision she foresaw not being well-received. Her sister would forgive her. The captain over her charge, probably not. But she didn't care. She had a debt to repay. And even Captain Nicholas J. Edwards wouldn't sway her otherwise.

She clasped the letter that had come all the way from Massachusetts between her fingers, dread and devotion at odds within her. To her chagrin, devotion won out.

Her aunt's business was on the line, after all. And Aunt Sylvia had become like a mother to her over the past year. Well, almost like a mother. Of course, her aunt was quite different from her own mother. For one, her aunt was alive.

"We're leaving in less than an hour and you've barely packed anything."

Charlotte turned from the balcony window to see Abigail entering the Parisian-tailored room. Her sister's eyes pointed to the two pieces of luggage sitting on the Persian rug—one packed and bound, ready for its departure, the other not. The accusation had been generous on her sister's part. Charlotte hadn't packed a single item.

"I'm not going."

"What do you mean you're not going?" Abigail paused in the middle of retrieving one of Charlotte's chemises.

"Things are getting worse in Portsmouth. Some men calling themselves patriots have been throwing bricks at the windows tied to messages conveying further threats. It seems flinging mud and scraps at our aunt's carriage is no longer sufficient enough."

"But why? Aunt Sylvia has taken a neutral stance on the war. She's not a loyalist." Her sister stood from her kneeled place on the rug, her palm faced upward as if expecting something to be put into it.

Reluctantly, Charlotte handed the letter over. "No, but her best friend, Madame Allewood, is. And I don't imagine our aunt's attendance to parties at the Allewood's estate where British officers are invited is helping."

"Parties? You mean like the ones you attended last year? I remember you mentioning some of the king's men were there when we got back."

It was true. She had. While her older siblings were under Washington's command in Cambridge last year, her aunt had used the liberty in Portsmouth to formally introduce her into society to both blue and red coats alike.

But that was at the onset of the war, when the majority of opinions were still being decided on whether the idea of an uprising was worth the conquest. Now that a year had passed, those opinions couldn't be more fixed and tensions never higher.

Her sister returned the letter, Charlotte's hands shaking as she folded the correspondence, enraged at what this war was doing, even among friends.

"Yes. Aunt Sylvia and Madame Allewood are just trying to keep the peace. Not just with each side, but with their friendship too. They've always been very close."

"It sounds like some people don't see it that way. Still, it seems rather rash they would destroy property. What if someone had been near the window?"

Charlotte shuddered to think of it while also doing her best to bury what was better left concealed from her sister with a tight lip. This hadn't been the only incident. In fact, their aunt voiced in her letter they'd been escalating since Washington's victory in Boston the previous fall. It was only mere suspicion, but Charlotte had an idea as to why.

Aside from their aunt, the Thatcher family wasn't exactly in good favor when it came to the war either. True, her older brother and sister had been a part of what they were now calling *a fight for liberty*, but Abraham had left the fight and Abigail had married a Royal Navy officer.

Their father's desire at the onset of the conflict to stay neutral had tipped his two eldest children into the fire of patriotism, but now it seemed the heat had abated. Their allegiance to either side of the war was neither hot nor cold and no one seemed to like lukewarm devotion. Charlotte didn't have the heart to tell her sister they were calling their family "deserters" back home.

A pain in her stomach surfaced, a reminder of the family she'd left behind in the colonies enduring such hardship while she sought refuge elsewhere.

"That doesn't make sense to me." Abigail shifted, her mouth in a grimace with Charlotte's unmentionables still in one hand, their aunt's letter in the other. "Those parties started months ago. So, why are the threats now? Why not back when you all were still going to Madame Allewood's estate? Wouldn't that make more sense?"

"I have an idea why." Charlotte took in a deep breath, letting it out again, the past year coming back with a vengeance. With it, everything she'd lost. "Mother."

"Mother?"

Shock spread across Abigail's face, but Charlotte was nearly certain of it. "All of Portsmouth knew Mother was sick. Aunt Sylvia never wavered on calling Dr. Jenkins at any notice of something wrong. He was constantly over, especially at the end. I think they waited until Mother . . ."

Abigail gasped, the undergarment dropping to the floor. "Charlotte, surely not. I can't believe . . ." Her sister's voice faltered, her body doing the same into a floral upholstered settee in the room they'd shared while staying in Paris.

But Charlotte could believe it. She'd *seen* it. The war had divided friends, even families. In a way, she'd admired her aunt for clinging onto her friendship with Madame Allewood, wondering if life might have been easier to sever their close ties. Or if not easier, most surely, safer.

A heaviness took over Abigail's normally animated features that made Charlotte think her sister had considered the possibility. And as if mimicking her expression, Abigail sunk deeper into the couch. "At least they had the decency to let her pass before starting their rioting. Though, it's still so awful."

"I wish that was the only bad news." Charlotte's jaw ached as she worked to bridle her frustration over a war she'd come to Paris to escape only to find that war had followed her an ocean away. "Aunt Sylvia says no one is buying. The colonists are unwilling to purchase lumber from our late uncle's company because they don't trust her loyalties and the English want the lumber at a fraction of its worth."

"I don't see our aunt being too pleased with that."

"Not at all, which is why I won't be joining you in London, not just yet anyway." Her eyes fell to their aunt's letter again. "Aunt Sylvia wants me to meet with a formal acquaintance of hers here in Paris—a Monsieur Vicomte de Vantinelle. After everything she did for us last year, especially with Mother, it's the least I can do."

Abigail's green eyes dimmed, perhaps recalling all that had happened in the past year. She nodded, eyes brightening again as if an idea had taken root. "Do you want some company? I can stay with you here in the city until you're done. I'll even come with you to meet Monsieur de Vantinelle. Garrett wouldn't mind, I'm sure of—"

Charlotte gave an adamant shake of her head, quite aware of the wedding vows she'd seen partaken only months prior to their trip across the Atlantic. "It's a big day for him, Abby. You should be there."

"I know, but I can't help thinking leaving my younger sister in Paris alone might not be the best idea."

"Then let me put your mind at ease." Charlotte joined her sister on the settee, taking Abigail's hand into her own, her grasp gentle, but firm. "You're not leaving me here. I've decided to stay of my own accord."

"But Paris is different from Massachusetts, Charlotte, It's not like home."

That was the point. Paris was nothing like the farm Charlotte grew up knowing. It was far better. At least of what she had seen of it. The problem was their detour to the French city lacked the entirety of what they were able to see—one attraction in particular her aunt boasted about and encouraged a trip to: The magnificent palace of Versailles.

Irritation worked its way through her. Why their captain had been so obliging on all her other demands . . . or, rather *urgent requests*, while so opposed to the very spot on top of her itinerary, left her feeling a little more than obtuse. No matter. At least now with the extra days—making her aunt's entreaty of meeting with the nobleman priority of course— Charlotte was determined to take advantage of the unexpected gift.

The matter decided, at least in her own mind, Charlotte put her other hand on top of Abigail's, working to convince her sister of the notion she was unwilling to budge on. "Look, I don't see my meeting with the vicomte keeping me here for more than a few days. London is only a five-day journey from here. Finding passage over shouldn't be difficult. I'll see you in a week's time."

Despite the effort Charlotte had put in her optimistic tone, her sister's lips pinched tight, but she didn't argue. Not that there was any point trying.

"Fine." Abigail sighed. "I know when you've set your mind to something, there's not much I can say to change it. Just be careful."

"You mean as careful as you were when you charged into danger by joining Washington's camp last year?" Charlotte gave a wry smile, happy to bring the reminder of the event at this particular moment. "That shouldn't be too difficult."

Her sister offered a look of reproach, but it produced little effect. Abigail had done her own part as far as the war was concerned and although Charlotte wanted as little to do with the conflict at home as possible, she had a great debt to repay. She wouldn't be swayed otherwise.

"Pardon, madame, mademoiselle." A French porter dressed in livery came through the open double doors of their room, his English on the near of perfection. "The carriage will be leaving soon and Monsieur Ward is downstairs." He eyed the two trunks, then Charlotte's chemise—her undergarment still laying sprawled on the floor. Despite the rush of heat that came to her cheeks, the man's face held his usual fair complexion. He picked up the trunk that was packed and ready before exiting the double doors of the room.

Charlotte jumped to her feet, grabbing her unmentionables, and stuffing them back into the armoire. "You better not keep your husband waiting. You want me to see you off?"

"Not if you want to stay in Paris." Abigail relinquished a terse, but teasing smile. "I have a feeling our captain isn't going to agree that leaving you here was the best choice. Just be happy he's ahead of us in Calais getting the ship ready to sail. Otherwise, he might just carry you down to the carriage himself."

Charlotte met her sister's expression with protest. "I'd like to see him try."

Though she doubted very much that their captain was the carrying type when it came to women. The man's morals were annoyingly impeccable due to naval upbringing. Still, she didn't want to leave Abigail in the middle of a potential conflict she'd made the call on.

She wrinkled her nose, not liking what she was about to offer. "Then again, maybe I should come. I can talk to him, perhaps even convince him to leave me here is to his benefit."

"His benefit?" Her sister's brow perched tall. "How do you mean?"

Charlotte crossed her arms, as if to challenge the man in question even if he wasn't there. "Well, for one, I won't go quietly. Tomorrow might be a big day for Garrett, but it's also one for our captain. I don't care how many times he's attended English court. Any day you meet with the king of England is a big day for anyone. I doubt he'll want to worry about what trouble I'm prepared to give him on top of it." She raised her chin a little higher, smiling. "I'd be happy to tell him as much, if you like."

"You better not." Abigail laughed, shaking her head. "It's too long of a trip. You might lose your chance to meet with the vicomte. Besides, Garrett will be with me. Between the two of us, I'm sure we can handle Nicholas."

Charlotte had no desire to argue, especially when Abigail was right. Their captain's respect for her sister didn't go unnoticed, and his ties to Garrett were as close as hers were to Abigail's. It was plain enough his feelings of regard didn't extend to her, but she didn't care. She knew plenty of men who felt the same way toward her. Apparently attractive enough to capture their first glance, but in not too short of a time her tendency for *having too much of an opinion as a woman*, as her father put it, sent all of them running, sometimes within minutes of her opening her mouth.

No matter. She was still young and in no need of a man, especially one that couldn't handle a little zeal, and definitely not one that was sure to get in her way of meeting the vicomte.

Sending her sister and Garrett off with a warm farewell, Charlotte watched the carriage pull out of the oval-shaped courtyard. She let the vehicle bump down the cobblestone street and fade from view before making her way to the post office. Her aunt's letter conveying her agreement to help would likely take weeks—perhaps months—to reach her. But that was fine. She hoped by then her next correspondence would be deliverance of good news.

When she arrived again at the grand townhouse, she went under the arched portal of decorative keystone, the gateway taking her back into the Hôtel de Beauvais. She was going to return to her room for a cup of her special tea and plot her conversation with the vicomte, except there was a problem that stood directly in her path.

Chapter 2

"What do you mean my room is taken?"

A muscle twitched at the base of Charlotte's chin where a dimple formed when she was upset. Her mouth fell open as she stared at a smart-looking woman with black hair pinned neatly into a bun at the nape of her neck.

The hotel liaison stood over the black-and-white checkered floor before the spiraled staircase—a barrier to the room Charlotte had occupied for the last two weeks. The woman's hands were folded calmly together, a trait that irritated Charlotte, who felt anything but calm at the unforeseen circumstance.

"I'm sorry, mademoiselle, but we were under the impression you left this morning with the rest of your group for London. Your room has since been occupied."

"Occupied?" Charlotte's voice rang out louder than she intended. The few people in the common room stared, a mixture of alarm and disapproval in their expressions, but she didn't care. She meant to get to the bottom of this.

"That can't be." Her gaze lifted to the room she and Abigail had occupied while in Paris before returning to the woman blocking her path. "But what about my luggage? I left it in the room. Surely someone saw it?"

"Oui, your trunk was seen. When the carriage departed and we did not see you, we presumed you to be in the vehicle and your luggage left behind by mistake." The coolness in the liaison's tone wavered, as did her expression. "I am sorry, mademoiselle, but I've already forwarded your belongings to the London address given to me."

Charlotte could hardly blink. No luggage. Not a change of clothes or even a fresh shift for the night. She'd have to make do with the one underneath her dress.

She checked her reticule, glad she'd decided to set a little money aside from the rest of her baggage, but it wouldn't go far. As for her meeting with the vicomte that was due later in the week—? Well, her simple robe l'anglaise of burgundy and simple cotton would also have to suffice. All of that she could make do with, but there was one thing she would unquestionably still need.

Sensing the mistake had been genuine and wishing to brush the inconveniences she might have conveyed aside, Charlotte offered the woman a non-begrudging smile. "It's all right. Another room will be fine."

The woman frowned in a way that was unmistakably apologetic, Charlotte bracing herself for the bad news. "Again, I am so sorry, mademoiselle, but we are all booked for the night."

"I see." Not bothering to hide her irritation this time, she sighed. "Well, I'll still need a place to sleep. What about any recommendations?" Her fingers tightened around her reticule, remembering the small sum in her purse. "Something a bit more modest, perhaps?"

The woman's chin tilted down to Charlotte's bag. She nodded, seeming to understand. She abandoned her post in front of the stairs to retrieve a quill, apparently trusting that Charlotte wouldn't make a dash for the newly occupied room. After scribbling a small note, she presented the paper. "Here. This is one you could try."

"Merci." Charlotte noted the address before placing the paper in her reticule. She eyed the gilded clock on the ornately marbled mantel. Three o'clock. This time of year, that gave her two hours before sunset—before Paris went dark.

Charged with a mission to find a bed for the night, Charlotte left the townhouse and took a cross street where she passed a market full of food vendors—their produce displayed on carts, tables and stands.

The smell of baked bread tingled her senses, her stomach growling in response. The boulangerie.

Hunger gnawed, a sharp reminder she hadn't eaten since her trip to the Hôtel de Postes. She couldn't afford to waste time, but the smell of the French bakery was a pull she couldn't resist.

Walking as she ate, she followed the hotel liaison's directions while the flaky layers of the croissant satisfied every inch of her hunger. She had torn into her next bite when her body jarred to one side, sending a curl across her face that had come unpinned with the abrupt altercation.

"Pardon," was all that was said as she watched a boy run past her, trailed by another who also bumped into her and offered the same apology.

Still in mid-chew, she had no time to offer any sort of salutation, or even just to say the accident was no trouble. By the time she swallowed down the bread, the two children were gone.

Taking a moment to gather herself again, she pinned her hair back into place before turning a corner on the street. That's when she saw it.

Through a glass pane, a table of neatly lined lace was displayed to confirm the sign that bore the shop's name on the side of the building. Dentelle. French for lace.

Charlotte stopped. Her fingers touched the side of her neck where her fichu rested around her shoulders, the lace serving as a reminder of a past she wished she could change.

She peered deeply into the glass to see a young woman with hair almost as dark as ebony add a piece of lace to the table inside the window. When she lifted her chin, brown eyes met Charlotte's and though having no certainty on the reason, something cognate in that moment struck between them. The woman waved for her to come inside.

Needing little prompting on the next course of action, Charlotte fully embraced the invitation she couldn't resist.

"Bonjour, mademoiselle." The woman who waved her in approached her, smiling. "Is there something you like?"

Sensing only a warm invitation in the woman's tone, Charlotte took her time to peruse the space. Though small, the size of the shop was sufficient for the need lacemaking supplied.

Two chairs sat in a corner across from each other—pins and a spool of thread on top of one. She walked over to another table; its function used much like the table in front of the window to display lace. Her fingers ran lightly over the interwoven thread, instantly catching the differences. The pieces were not as extraordinary as the ones on the table by the window, not the shop's best.

They were certainly good—perfectly suitable for whatever the buyer wished if one didn't look too closely, but since Charlotte learned more about the craft last year, she *had* noticed.

The base netting was wide on some pieces and not as tightly woven as the ones she'd first seen approaching the store—their designs also more blocky, less intricate. They were somewhat in conflict to the other pieces of more fine craftsmanship draped elegantly from shelves showing off scalloped edges, delicate patterns, and to her, an art of unrivaled finesse.

She knew that she had taken her time to answer the woman's question, but she sensed an artist might appreciate an answer that wasn't impromptu. "I see a lot of things that I like."

"Oh, you are English!"

Charlotte looked back at the lacemaker, only now realizing how close in age they seemed to be. The woman's almond skin was as fresh as her own fair complexion. Her tone mimicked more surprise than judgement. Yet, a warmth spread to Charlotte's cheeks at the reminder that she still had a lot she needed to learn. Aunt Sylvia had started giving her French lessons last year, though small things like ordering bread from the bakery and sending a letter came easy enough, Charlotte could always tell by a cock of the head or a pitiful smile, she hadn't conveyed her thoughts quite right on certain occasions.

She made a cursory gaze around the room, wondering if it was a word or pitch she'd mispronounced and knowing she'd have to do better when speaking with the vicomte. "I'm from the Americas." Setting that problem aside for later, she eyed the different pieces of lace, not bothering to hide her appreciation. "And they are all exquisite."

The woman beamed, Charlotte already finding something kindred in her overall manner.

"Thank you, mademoiselle. That is nice of you to say. A lot of work goes into each piece."

"And time."

"Yes, that is also true, but something so beautiful cannot be rushed. It must be done with great care."

A piece of wisdom Charlotte couldn't agree with more. And she had the experience to back that truth up. It had taken her ten hours to complete just a square centimeter when she'd first started her own lace design. With practice, she became faster, though realizing a fundamental truth—making lace was not about speed, but of precision, detail, and beauty.

For someone who liked to get to the point, it was those very characteristics that made the art form both inspiring and infuriating at times. Abigail was the one who'd always been meticulous with a needle and had the patience of Job. And though slow and steady wasn't *her* speed, Charlotte did have an eye and an appreciation for beautiful things . . . just like her aunt.

Gratitude filled her over the hobby that she and her aunt had busied themselves with during those long months her sister and brother were in Cambridge last year, and for so much more. As the war in the colonies continued to press on, so did the boycott for luxuries from England. But Aunt Sylvia refused to let the efforts of the war prevent her and her niece from the finer things life had to offer. If Sylvia Davenport wasn't going to be able to buy her lace, she would make it, and so that's exactly what they did. Together.

"I see you have a fichu made of lace." The woman's brown eyes appeared drawn toward Charlotte's shoulders, her gaze appraising. "The style is a bit different than what I'm used to creating. Is it French?"

Charlotte shook her head, though honored that this woman even considered her scarf to be at such a level. "My aunt and I made it together. I designed the pattern and worked on the stitches for the background, and she did the rest." She shrugged at her vices, though couldn't help but feel a sense of pride with the accomplishment, especially for her. "I can manage a little sewing, but I'm afraid I have an intolerance to patience."

"You designed this?" The woman's fine, dark brows raised, more out of delight than scrutiny, the optimistic response causing Charlotte's stomach to flutter with a hint of pleasure.

"Yes." Charlotte took the laced shawl from her shoulders, handing the fichu to the lacemaker for a better look. "The flowers are supposed to be roses. They were a favorite of my mother's."

The center of the scarf was solid linen, while the edges were simply scalloped. Charlotte had envisioned the way the roses would be arranged, but it was Aunt Sylvia's genius with the needle that brought them into being.

"The advantage of lace is that its beauty will last far longer than the flower you have modeled it from." The woman traced her fingers carefully over the floral design, her voice softening yet holding purpose. "Even nurtured, in too short a time the flower withers away, but lace will last. That is why I do it." Pride casted a smile before a small laugh came forth. "Well, I have to do it for the money and for my family, but the craft is also something I can do that could outlast me if taken good care of—passed down generations, perhaps." She handed the scarf back to Charlotte, nodding her approval. "It is very good. The queen herself would think as much. She loves both elegance and florals and you have captured both, mademoiselle. You should be proud of your work." Her eyes twinkled as if almost winking. "My name is Louise, by the way, one lacemaker to another."

"Charlotte, and thank you." Charlotte draped the fichu back over her shoulders and tucked the shawl into the front of her bodice, her gaze wandering about the room again. "Did you make all of them?"

"My mother and I. Lacemaking has been in my family for four generations." Louise's neck lengthened in a way that captured both pleasure and satisfaction. "My mother's pieces usually sell the quickest. These are some of hers from last year." She led Charlotte back over to the table near the window at the ones in full display to the public eye, signaling which pieces she meant with her hand. Her expression fell. "But she says mine will soon catch up."

"I would also say it is not a race, Chérie."

Charlotte's gaze veered to the shop's doorway where an older woman who shared the same dark hair and olive skin as Louise entered. Under the woman's arm was a loaf of bread. Having just come from the bakery, Charlotte could see and smell the loaf was different from the ones in the baker's shop this morning. The bread looked dry and a small patch of white not resembling flour lay on the baguette's side.

"Not if you want your lace to turn out right." The same kindred smile Louise had given Charlotte earlier touched the older woman's cheek as she looked at the young woman with a love Charlotte recognized from her own past.

"Maman, is that our din . . .?"

Louise's mother's face fell, Charlotte not missing the look of stern warning that replaced it. She wrapped the bread in a spare piece of cloth, putting the loaf aside on a counter and turned to Charlotte, her hands folded in a business-like manner. "Has my daughter shown you something you like, mademoiselle?" Her smile returned, though more reserved than the one she'd given Louise. "I have some pieces over here that would make an excellent addition to the sleeves of your dress."

Of course she liked the lace. "They are all exquisite, madame." But Charlotte got the feeling there was more hoped for beyond the pleasant inquiry, especially when she considered the old bread Louise's mother brought in. The image of the flaked croissant she'd had earlier now felt sour in her stomach. She wanted to help, but the expense of such finery was something she simply could not afford, even if her luggage wasn't on route to London.

"I'm sorry. I wish I had more to spend. I'm afraid I don't have enough in my allow—"

She stilled. Her allowance.

Empty hands started to tighten, but around . . . nothing. Where was her reticule? Her breath stopped short. Again, her fingers grasped for something, only meeting air. Her chest squeezed, realizing she hadn't noticed her bag's absence since the bakery.

She took a quick scan around the room to make sure, but no. Her bag wasn't here. A constriction in her chest came again, the full realization that her money was gone rearing up inside. Her heart raced beneath her fichu as she put her hand on top of her stays, willing the rapid beating inside to slow down.

"Charlotte?" Louise's face read concern. "What's the matter?"

The room blurred. Louise and her mother stepped toward her as if they might somehow intervene, but Charlotte shook her head, putting her arm out in front of her to hold them at a distance. And for good reason. There was nothing they could do. The medicines the doctor gave her were on their way to London. She was supposed to take them every day, but right now without them and without the money to buy them, that was impossible. She'd have to let the awful event run its course.

Her heart continued to accelerate for a minute or two, and though time felt like longer, experience told her otherwise. She sucked in a short breath as the beating inside her chest finally began to lag.

She forced a jagged breath out, then another, commanding her body to obey. Slowly, the tightening in her chest loosened.

Louise ran up to her, Charlotte realizing she'd given up holding out her arm, now limp at her side. "Are you all right?"

"I . . . am . . . now," she managed. With another controlled breath, Charlotte was finally able to straighten. The worst was over . . . for now.

"What was *that*?" Near panic in her expression, Louise took hold of Charlotte's arm.

They were *episodes*. That's what the doctor back home called them, anyway— "a condition," he said, "no doubt inherited from her mother." It was as if with her last breath, her mother left the illness behind for a better world while the wretched condition remained, finding a new home in her.

Charlotte didn't struggle as Louise ushered her to one of the two chairs she'd seen in the dentelle. She was always weak in the aftermath, even as she hated that result.

"They happen on occasion, but nothing to worry about. I'll be fine."

Louise frowned like she wasn't so sure.

"I have medicines for them given to me by my doctor back home. I simply haven't had the opportunity to take them today." Charlotte slumped in the chair, catching a shared glance between mother and daughter.

"Are you sure, mademoiselle?" A mother's concern held in the tone of Louise's mother. "I could send Louise for the doctor to meet you at your lodgings."

"Thank you, but that won't be necessary." Feeling her countenance somewhat restored, the reminder of what she lacked for tonight brought her to her feet again, even if unsteady. "Besides, I don't have a place to—"

"You don't have a place to stay?" Louise beat her to the answer.

"Not yet—" Charlotte put up a finger as if making a dot in the air, her breath still catching up. "But I was on my way there when I stepped into your store." Though her reticule now gone along with the paper the hotel liaison had jotted the location down with it, Charlotte had committed the address to memory. She relayed as much to the lacemaker women. Neither looked pleased by the information.

Louise's mother shook her head. "It is getting late, mademoiselle. That is a long walk for the streets of Paris, especially at night. You'll need to hire a coach."

The answer wasn't a welcomed one, Charlotte's limited funds serving as a reminder again. "I'm afraid that won't be possible."

Questions lingered on both faces of the two women, but not judgement.

"Then you must stay with us." Louise intercepted Charlotte at the dentelle door. Though no doubt Charlotte's own age, the younger woman declared the invitation with a girl-like enthusiasm. It was only after she'd made the suggestion when she looked to her mother, the action highlighting the youthful display.

The smile returned to the older woman's face, full of warmth. "We rent the apartment upstairs. The space is not much, but you are very welcome if you need a place to sleep."

***

After a meal consisting of a thin, broth soup and the bread Louise's mother had brought into the store, Louise had taken Charlotte to the only bedroom of the apartment.

"You can sleep here." Louise gestured to one of the two beds in the room, both modestly, but neatly made.

It didn't take Charlotte long to figure out the number of beds were now outnumbered by people with her stay.

"Where will you sleep?" She turned to Louise who had gone over to an oil lamp in a nook by the door, striking a piece of flint against steel.

"Over there with Maman." Having lit the lamp, Louise raised the light source toward the other bed that was only mildly big enough to fit one person, never mind two. "We can send for your things in the morning."

Charlotte gave a huff, glancing at a nearby window in the room. "Unless you're planning to retrieve them from London, don't bother."

Confusion knitted Louise's brow while Charlotte curbed a groan, too tired and irked to admit she'd lost more than her money and accommodations. "Never mind. I'll worry about them later."

"Maman says you can stay as long as you like." Louise put the oil lamp on the table situated between the two beds. A pungent smell of animal fat began to fill the room. "I just hope you don't mind the candlelight. Sometimes I work on the lace at night to help keep up with demands. This past year has proved more difficult to make sure the pieces are completed on time when our customers want them. By the time I sketch the patterns, I am already behind. Maman tries, but sometimes it's just too painful for her."

The ache in Louise's expression was one Charlotte had seen earlier in the store. The frown she wore when commenting about her own needleworking catching up to her mother's seemed misplaced—like the improvement in her skill was not something wholly welcomed. Now, Louise was giving her a hint as to why.

Not meaning to, Charlotte's gaze fell back to Louise's fingers, thinking of all the work they were expected to do and catching the rough skin on her fingertips even in the dim light. Then the thought struck. "Her hands?"

Louise nodded, a pain in her eyes Charlotte knew all too well. "She tries to hide it, but I can tell just bending her fingers is even too much for her. The pieces I showed you earlier were from before." She went over to a small chest, pulling out a piece of lace still attached to a needle from one of the drawers. "This one is of more recently."

Not wanting to offend this woman she was starting to feel a connection with, Charlotte curbed back a gasp. The piece reminded her of when she first started learning to craft lace, her needlework loose and sloppy. There were no curves of any kind within the pattern as if the maker could not bear to attempt to try them and the few highlights accomplished were too thick to be called delicate. The mangled thread was more of an expression to one's suffering than devotion to perfection—not at all like the ones Louise showed her in the store and not even the ones that were less remarkable on the table away from the window. Certainly not at all like someone who'd made lace all their life.

Fitting the fragments together like the complex interweaving of linen thread, Charlotte began to understand the progression. Those on the table belonged to Louise's mother whose condition, based on what Louise had shown her just now, was getting worse.

Louise seemed to read her thoughts; her expression conflicted as if her admitting her mother's problem was somehow a betrayal. "I never say anything, but I don't have to. We both know our customers would not take kindly to such work."

"I'm so sorry, Louise." Charlotte bit her lip, wanting to offer comfort but not knowing how. "Is there anything that can help—that can be done?"

"Oui, I was able to purchase something from the apothecary last year and her hands were better." The light Charlotte briefly saw in Louise's eyes dimmed as she looked at the recent designs of her mother. "Even still, our customers noticed the imperfections quite readily. Maman refused to keep taking the medicine when I could no longer keep up with the demands needed to afford it. She says if we can't make the lace on time, then we'll lose our customers. And if we lose customers, we might very well lose our bread altogether, especially with the price increasing since the past two years of poor grain."

The loaf tucked under Louise's mother's arm came back again. If things didn't improve for her new friend and her mother fast, moldy bread would turn into no bread at all.

Something lodged in Charlotte's throat. She was touched by what these women were doing for her—giving her shelter for the night and a bed of their own to sleep in. She could clearly see now that her staying here, even one night, came at a cost—one she didn't know if she could repay. And even if she'd managed to secure her bags from London again, whatever she could give financially didn't seem like enough.

"Can I ask you something?" Louise returned the lace fragment to the chest, closing the drawer softly. "When you were talking about your scarf, you said the roses were a favorite of your mother's. What happened to her?"

Charlotte worked the knot still stuck in her throat down, emotion welling up inside. "She died last year."

"I am sorry, mon amie. I cannot imagine losing my mother. She is all I have."

"What about your father?"

"He died three years ago from sickness." Opening a drawer to the table that sat between their beds, Louise pulled out the early beginnings of a lace design containing tightly woven stitches mixed with open areas still needed to be filled in.

Charlotte watched her friend unknot a needle attached to a piece of fine thread to continue where the pattern left off.

"I'm sorry too."

"It seems we've both lost people we love." Louise exhaled, her face turning upward to fully meet Charlotte's again. "How long will you be in Paris?"

"That depends." Charlotte scooted under the thin sheets with the shift in topic. "You don't happen to know a Vicomte de Vantinelle do you?"

"A vicomte?" Her new friend's lips pursed as if in thought before she gave a series of small nods. "I only know the name. We have never formally met, but I hear he is well-respected among the noble community. He comes from one of the traditional noble families." Her eyes glowed in the light. "Is that who you're meeting is with?"

"Yes, but only as a substitute for my aunt. I have an extended invitation to a party he'll likely be at."

"A party? C'est merveilleaux! You will be in a room full of Paris's aristocracy, no doubt. I always wondered what that would be like." Louise's tone floated through the air, carrying a dream-like quality as her needle went back to work.

Charlotte furrowed her brow. "I thought you sold lace to the aristocracy. Don't you see them all the time?"

"They are our customers, that's true, but they never come themselves to the dentelle, only their servants." She shrugged, her fingers moving in a delicate dance while the precision of her work appeared unaffected by the course of their conversation. "We don't mind. Maman and I are just happy for the buyers."

Her new friend's hopefulness tugged at Charlotte's heartstrings, and even as she read the faith in Louise's expression, Charlotte couldn't help but think of what she didn't say.

Louise's work was certainly praiseworthy—definitely desired—but how long could she go it alone like this? What would happen if she couldn't keep up?

Charlotte peered over to the chest containing the needlework of Louise's mother and conviction struck, the truth hitting with vengeance. She *wasn't* keeping up. If she was, they'd be able to afford her mother's medicine and Louise had already disclosed that wasn't the case.

Charlotte pressed her lips firm, wondering if the call she felt stemmed from God or someplace else. All Louise needed was a little something to get out from under the trampling foot of poverty. But how? It took time to draw the patterns, after all—time Louise could use for needleworking the lace and time Charlotte could make use of until her deal with the vicomte was settled.

A fluttering in Charlotte's stomach encouraged the words to flow freely. "You know, I think I have an idea that might help us both." Laying on her side to face Louise, Charlotte propped her elbow against the uneven mattress. "As I mentioned earlier, I wouldn't be of much use with the needlework, and it would only be while I'm here, but I could try to sketch some patterns for you. That might save you a little work so you wouldn't have to do them yourself."

"Sketch patterns?" The needle in Louise's hand stopped in the air. "You would do that?"

"I most certainly would." Her word, something about herself she valued and didn't take lightly, was as binding as a contract. And the way Louise's eyes lit only bolstered Charlotte's confidence behind the offer no matter where the idea generated from.

"That would be fantastic." The light that had sparked in Louise's eyes quickly faded. "But I'm sorry. I cannot pay you for them."

Though the money would have been nice, especially with the rest of her funds with her suitcase back in London, that wasn't going to dissuade her.

Charlotte waved her hand as if the lack of payment were of trifle consequence even when it wasn't. "It'll be part of my rent until I can make further accommodations. The only reason I'm still in Paris is to meet with the vicomte. While I'm here, I might as well make myself useful. I don't have the money to parade about in the city anyway." She stopped. She didn't mean to let that last part slip about the parading, especially when she knew Louise couldn't afford to do such things.

Whether it was her confidante's eager acceptance to the offer or an innate ability to forgive, Louise let the comment fall away completely as if it hadn't come out at all. She took hold of Charlotte's hand, clasping it as if in a sisterly embrace. "Well, in that case, I will take you up on that agreement."

Their agreement wasn't the business deal Charlotte needed to acquire for her aunt, but it was a business deal nonetheless, and she felt a sense of accomplishment over the small feat.

She settled further into the linen sheets, hoping tonight's success might prove likewise with the vicomte later in the week. She watched Louise continue her needlework, Charlotte's eyes growing heavy with the steady movement of her friend's fingers. With each small stich, the world blurred into a heavy-lidded sleep.

"Au fue!"

A scream from below shattered the quiet. Charlotte bolted upright—her heart, only just calmed—leaping back into her throat. "Did I just hear . . .?"

The needle dropped from her friend's hand. "Fire."

Chapter 3

Nicholas turned his compass in his hand, his grip tightening with each pivot of the motion as he waited for the hotel liaison to scroll through the list of guests. He couldn't believe it—or could he?

"I'm sorry, Captain, but there is no one by the name of Charlotte Thatcher here." The man behind the counter shook his head, the queue tied at the nape of his neck following the motion.

"Are you sure?" Nicholas felt his neck tense against the collar of his uniform. "This was the address given to her by the woman at the Hôtel de Beauvais. She said it was the only recommendation."

The man in front of him straightened from the ledger slowly as if in silent challenge. "That may be, monsieur, but the woman you are looking for is not staying here. And if she is as spirited as you described earlier, I think I would've remembered her."

That, Nicholas had no doubt. Charlotte had a way of making an impression one wasn't likely to forget. He eyed a scrap of paper alongside the liaison's list of guests. "Would you mind?" The man followed his gaze, seeming to understand. He nodded before allowing Nicholas the use of a quill also. "This is where I'll be lodging while in the city. If anything changes, please let me know."

"Misplaced someone, have you? I'd have to say I'm a little surprised. I thought Nicholas Edwards would be more careful."

Nicholas half expected the snide comment to come from Garrett, rousing him like a brother might, but his best friend was still in London. And now that Garrett had been restored to a lieutenant, he and Abigail were awaiting their next orders there. Though, a place like Paris, where many visited and so close to home, Nicholas was hardly surprised by the English accent.

He turned around from the liaison's desk, his bewilderment met with a cheeky smile on the other man's face. But not just any man. The features from his boyhood when Nicholas remembered him remained intact—the wide-bridged nose, the square chin. Only his corn-colored hair had darkened into a light brown over the years.

"Lewis." Nicholas had no trouble recognizing him from a time he could hardly believe existed—a time before the Royal Navy took over his life. "What are you doing here?"

"I'm glad to see you too after all these years." Lewis Talbot feigned a frown as if he'd been slighted, but Nicholas could hear the laughter in his voice—his trait for always finding humor in any given moment in his youth following into manhood.

"Sorry." His shock gone, Nicholas curved a smile he hadn't felt earlier, returning the compass from his grandfather to his coat pocket. "It's good to see you." He offered his hand, his childhood friend giving his arm a hearty shake. "How's Anne?" He'd read their marriage announcement in the London Gazette almost five years ago. Had it been that long?

"She's good—with our firstborn back in Cairnhaven." A mixture of pride and gratification entwined in a smile. "A girl who already has her father wrapped around her tiny little finger if you can believe it."

"I hardly can, but my congratulations to you both. I'm sure Anne is delighted."

"Over the moon." His head made a semi-circle in the air as if to emphasize his statement. "And I dare say she'll have the child ready for London society before she reaches ten."

"Yet here you are in Paris while the women in your life are back in England." Nicholas angled his chin downward to eye Lewis despite his friend having been ahead of him in years. "What brings you to France?"

"My nephew." Lewis raised his chin, grabbing the lapels of a navy coat. "He's on his Grand Tour and I have the privilege to chaperone." The same kind of gratification over his wife and daughter resurfaced.

Nicholas trailed his gaze beyond Lewis further in where polished stone flooring opened up but saw nothing of a young man who might be only a few years younger than him. He shifted back on his childhood friend, mirroring Lewis's chiding from before. "It seems like you've *also* lost someone."

Lewis bellowed a laugh, drawing his attention to a French courier who'd entered through the doorway and handed off a stack of prepared letters for mailing. "I'm afraid I can't relate to your predicament. Stephen is with his French tutor working on his lessons. He didn't have much time to acquire a good vocabulary prior to our travels, but I'm told he'll be fluent by the time we leave for Switzerland in a month. That should please my brother before our time in France has ended, I think."

The door opened again as the mail courier exited through, Lewis's gaze trailing the man leaving before bringing his attention back to Nicholas. "I was actually on my way out when I saw you. Why don't you join me? You don't seem to be having any luck here anyhow. Who knows, maybe we'll discover a clue to your missing woman."

Catching the jabbing way he'd said, "missing woman" like an attachment had been bound between he and Charlotte—something mutual—Nicholas bit the inside of his lip.

Nothing could be further from the truth. His only tie to Charlotte was his responsibility to bring her to London, but with the trouble to find her in a city as big as Paris, even that was fraying at the knots.

Other than the Hôtel de Beauvais, this place had been his only lead. He didn't know where else to look. Even if Lewis was wrong about his relationship with Charlotte, at least he was giving him something to try.

He walked in step with Lewis as they made their way toward the Seine River and eventually through the Tuileries Gardens. On the Grande Allée—the central path—noblemen and women dressed in their finest promenaded along between the impressive space lined with clipped hedges and rows of trees.

"Captain, huh?" Lewis pinned is eyes on the gold lace that rimmed the lapels of Nicholas's naval coat, a new addition to his uniform with his promotion. "I heard you did well for yourself. Your father is proud, no doubt."

The back of Nicholas's shoulders tightened. Where Lewis seemed convinced of a father's pride, Nicholas wasn't so sure.

"I also heard he's in the war with the colonies."

"He's been in Nova Scotia since Washington overtook Boston in March. I got the impression he's had enough of the riots and rebellion while we were still in the city. Other than that, I don't know much more." Nicholas wet the inside of his palette where the taste of something metallic had surfaced. "And what about you?" The man clearly knew more about Nicholas than what Nicholas knew of him. But judging by what he knew of Lewis's past compared to his current dress—a quality broadcloth coat and his current travels, his friend had also done well for himself. "I thought you were working the mines in Cairnhaven."

"I was for a while. My brothers are still there trying to make their way." Shaking his head, Lewis exhaled slowly as if almost out of pity. "I decided to move to London and take my chances with the city. More work, more opportunity." His eyes moved to a distant row of trees where two men held a private conversation then back again. "After several odd jobs, I was able to procure a benefactor that put me through law school. That's what I do now."

"So . . ." That gleam in his eye returned, telling Nicholas their conversation about Charlotte wasn't over just yet. "This woman you're looking for—don't tell me you're on your honeymoon and have lost your betrothed." He gave a wry smile. "That doesn't sound like a good start to a marriage."

Nicholas scoffed. The man was getting the wrong idea. There had been an initial attraction—he could admit that—but any pleasant thoughts ended there, and for good reason. He followed protocol and order. She was as predictable as the wind. Not to mention stubborn. Weeks aboard the same ship had taught him that much. Now she'd become a thorn in his side.

"She's a friend and she's supposed to be in London with the rest of my party I left there." Nicholas didn't bother hiding the annoyance in his tone. "I'm back in Paris on duty, but I'm also here to check in and see how she's doing."

"Supposed to be, huh?" Lewis gave him a sideways glance that reminded Nicholas of the days when they were kids. "As in, she doesn't fall in line like your men do at your command?" He chuckled, continuing to lead them down the Grand Allée. "It sounds like you haven't been exposed to many women while in the Navy, then?"

He had, actually. Officers' parties on land were never lacking in women, but not worth the time required to invest in them. Granted, many were beautiful—even showing interest in his regard, but Navy life under the authority of Captain James Edwards left no room for romance.

Nicholas rolled his shoulders back, trying to release some of the tension over a war inside that had birthed at his youth. "Let's just say this woman isn't like most I've met."

"Oh? She must be something to have you worked up." Lewis's comment drew attention to the strain Nicholas felt in his jaw.

Nicholas hadn't seen the man in years, yet Lewis could read him so easily. Apparently, Nicholas was losing his touch.

"Oh, she's definitely something."

"And to think I'd see Nicholas Edwards pay attention to anything but the Navy." Lewis shook his head. "That's what you were always set on anyway when we were kids."

Nicholas bit the inside of his cheek. He'd only been set on the career because he'd had no say otherwise. Though if he didn't succeed this time—it meant the end of the life he'd ever known.

They exited the Tuileries, walking again on the uneven streets of the city until Lewis stopped in front a building—one of many that looked like it had been squished between two others. A sign hung above the doorway. L'imprimeur.

"I have an errand in here I need to take care of."

Nicholas's brow pinched. "You have an appointment with the printer?"

"The vendor on our street ran out of papers the other day." His hand moved haphazardly, signaling an annoyance Nicholas hadn't predicted. "Something about a fire on the Île de la Cité."

A fire. The word struck an alarm inside. That was news to him too.

Lewis motioned to the printer's shop again, a quick smile covering the frustration he'd led onto seconds ago. "I like to keep updated on what's going on around the city. Perhaps the printer will have a copy of that day, or I can persuade him to make me one."

They had seen peddlers on the way over, which made Nicholas wonder. "Why not just try another street vendor or coffeehouse? They probably carry a few older copies."

"Maybe." Lewis shrugged, gesturing to the building they'd arrived at. "But we're already here. Besides, you could always put in an ad for a missing person." That cheeky smile returned. "That's one way to find your woman."

Though choosing to ignore that last comment, Nicholas did consider the missing persons ad—if to get no one else's attention, surely Charlotte's. But that was assuming she had found lodging elsewhere—that she was all right. The fact she hadn't arrived at the boardinghouse made him cautious enough to consider the proposal.

"Yes, Louise, that's perfect. Now, your work can be better viewed from the street."

Nicholas was about to enter the printer's shop after Lewis, his mind on the notion of the ad, when he heard the distinct female voice—an obstinance about the tone ringing familiar.

He turned toward the noise that somehow caught his attention even amidst the other pedestrians, carriages, and places of business. A smile of satisfaction brimmed. He'd found his mark.

***

Nicholas opened the door to the shop labeled "Dentelle" and went inside.

"Bonjour, monsieur." A woman in humble dress approached him with a friendly smile. "Is there something you want for yourself?" He sensed a kindness in her tone as she seemed to survey the lack of lace cuffs on his sleeves that were popular with the French nobility before resting on his eyes again. "Or perhaps a wife back home?"

He frowned, not because of what she said, but because of his miscalculation. He glanced around the room finding plenty of lace, but no sign of the woman he thought he'd heard minutes ago outside. "I'm sorry. I thought someone I knew came in here."

The young woman drew back, her dark eyes wide as if just now realizing something. It was when he caught her gaze locked on the whole of his uniform that he understood.

"An officer."

He made a customary bow, the gesture coming easy in his trained years against her surprise. "Yes, Miss. Captain Edwards of the Royal Navy." He straightened again.

"Captain Edwards." Another voice rang out, though this one haughty at the mention of his name. He turned in the direction the sound came and felt the smallest sensation of relief. So, he had been right.

"I see you're here to rescue me." Charlotte stood further in the room with her hands on her hips, looking anything but pleased to see him.

He stiffened, hearing the sarcasm in her tone. *Rescuing* wasn't exactly the term he'd use when he pictured having to drag her back with him by the ribbons of her petticoat.

"With all due respect Miss Thatcher, I'm not here to rescue you. You made that point clear on the voyage over from the colonies, you'd rather me not. I'm only here as a courtesy to your sister and to bring you back to London when it's convenient."

"Convenient?" Her neck tilted the slightest while she gave him a bemused smile. "For you or me, Captain?"

He heard the challenge clear enough in her tone, but he wouldn't be bated. This wasn't the place to argue, and he had orders to follow. He would be making the call from here on out. "There's an obligation I need to take care of here in the city first. We'll leave promptly after."

She put a hand to her hip. "And is this obligation of the same nature to the ones you had while we were touring Paris the past few weeks?"

He nodded, though not liking her sudden perusal. "It is." He wasn't about to tell her the obligation was the same one he'd been pursuing only to be turned down each time. "Until then, I can acquire you a room and you can see more of Paris if you'd like while you wait. I'll even hire a guide for you."

"Thank you, Captain." She smiled, though insincerity was plain in the gesture. "But I won't be waiting, and I'll be too busy to be perusing about the city." She raised her chin. "I have work to do."

"I know." He sighed. "The nobleman. I'm aware." He wanted to add, "no thanks to you," but the tension between them was already high. Instead, he made her an offer. "The party's tonight if I'm not mistaken. We'll go meet with this businessman your aunt is talking about and then you—"

"We?" She stopped him with a sideways look. "You mean you as my chaperone?"

Her blue eyes were daring, like the plan was ridiculous when the idea was the most reasonable thing in the world. Then again, he was learning Charlotte was less of a fan of reason than pure bold action.

He frowned. "Don't tell me you were planning to go it alone tonight."

She crossed her arms. "And what if I was?"

The woman was intolerable. Nicholas mustered every lesson he could remember on gentlemanly decorum from the Naval Academy, but none came to mind with how to master a woman who stood in complete opposition to him.

She put up a hand as if making a motion for him to stop, preventing his mind from venturing further down the negative pathway he had started. "Before you get worked up, I have my reasons."

"Which are?"

"Most notably, that." She pointed to a gold button on the lapel of his coat.

His eyes narrowed, but more out of not understanding than agitation this time. "My uniform?"

"If I remember my history correctly, France lost to the English in the last war. That wasn't that long ago. Tensions are still high and egos are still bruised, no doubt." She shook her head. "The last thing I need is an English soldier to remind them and ruin my chances from the moment we walk in the door."

He considered his uniform and how easy of a fix that was to resolve. "I can change my clothes, you know."

"Yes, but you can't change the fact you're a Royal Navy captain through and through." Her tone held no compliment. "I can't be seen with an English officer while trying to conduct business with a Frenchman. What if the vicomte has qualms over the last war? What if he served in it? I can't take the risk."

Nicholas's teeth clenched. Even if he didn't like the result, the argument wasn't a bad one. In fact, it wasn't that far off from what he presumed to be the French king's reason for not permitting him an audience. There was a certain relationship between the two countries and that wasn't the friendliest of terms.

"It sounds like you have it all figured out." He hadn't meant for his tone to sound as riled as it did but tracking her down had cost him an entire day—one he could have made better use of. It was too late in the day to go to Versailles. He'd have to wait until tomorrow.

"Fine." He turned around, wanting to charge for the door, but expectations of both his father and the organization he affiliated with prevented the action. "Good luck tonight, then." His boots took controlled steps past tables of lace. "Now that I know you're all right, I'll leave you to your shopping."

"Oh, she is not a customer, monsieur."

Nicholas froze in his exit, having forgotten he and Charlotte hadn't been in the shop alone.

The woman who'd greeted him when he first entered came over. "She's helping us."

"Hardly so. I'm working on a few sketches to compensate for time, that's all." Charlotte beamed a smile, but by the way she looked at the woman who'd made the announcement and what he knew she clearly thought of him, he could sense her satisfaction stemmed from something more than recognition.

"Forgive me." Charlotte moved the hand from her hip to where the top of her dress met fair skin. "Captain Edwards, this is Louise." She gestured to the young woman who'd spoken to him upon his entry. "She and her mother own this fine shop and rent the apartment upstairs. They've also provided me with accommodations for the last few days."

That answered the question of where she'd been staying. Though by the modest conditions of the shop, it didn't seem like the lacemakers had much extra to supply in accommodations. That probed at another question. He still had her luggage. What else was she making do with?

"As you can see, their lace is of exceptional quality and fine craftmanship." Charlotte bellowed the last line like she was selling the lace to a potential customer.

He didn't know anything about lace, only that he'd noticed Charlotte wearing a shawl of the thread around her shoulders from time to time. Right now, the delicate piece was missing, leaving her neck exposed. Her yellow tresses of hair swept against the column below her chin and his gaze lingered longer than protocol allowed. He snapped his focus to the lace he cared nothing about.

Her eyes widened before she revealed a smirk that let him know he'd been caught. That was fine. The moment was fleeting. He willed his resolve, using his father as his guide: stone-cold, proud, and firm.

"Something you see that you like, Captain?"

"No, not at the moment."

She frowned, but he ignored her displeasure, looking for something to write on. He settled for a piece of parchment and a fragment of charcoal.

"Here's where I'm staying. Like I said before, there's a room for you too." He held out the note that contained the address and curbed a smile, knowing how much this meeting meant to her and at the gamble he was about to take. "In the chance you might be in need of your bag for tonight, I'll have your trunk there. Then you and I can attend the party *together*."

She stared at him for a moment. The way her nostrils flared told him she'd caught his meaning.

"Thank you, Captain." The note, now in her possession, disappeared into a tight fist. "But as I mentioned earlier, your company is not warranted for tonight. Although, I would prefer to have my belongings."

"I'm sorry, but that's not part of the deal, Miss Thatcher." Though hearing an edge in her tone, he relinquished a smile he couldn't seem to prevent at her expense.

She narrowed her eyes. "You surprise me. I didn't take you to be a man that made such deals." She'd made the comment as if insinuating a mark against his character when all he was trying to do was to get her to cooperate.

"Perhaps you don't know me as much as you think you do." He pointed to the note in her hand, noticing the crushed paper. "If you change your mind, you know where to find me."

His smile peaked. "And your luggage."

Chapter 4

Pulling a piece of thread taut, Charlotte bit the thread with her teeth before securing both thread and fabric in place. Oh, how she wished she could wear the robe à la française she'd had in mind for tonight. She'd worn the rose-colored dress before to a party at Lady Allewood's estate—one of a few she'd been able to attend before her mother's condition grew more concerning. That had been her first true party, a debut—her aunt's way of her coming out into the world, so to speak. And she'd been more than ready for the new adventure.

Sighing, she smoothed out the dress she had been wearing for the past week. That was more than what she could say now, still having no possession of her luggage. She'd done her best to blot the stains from Paris's muddy streets that had accumulated on her hemline—a product of last night's rain. But in the end, she had to turn the fabric to hide the dirt.

She still couldn't believe what Nicholas had done. The nerve. Holding her bag hostage in exchange for accompanying her to the party tonight. The move was out of character for what she'd witnessed of him so far—a man who was the epitome of naval code and decorum, walking with impeccable balance on its imaginary line.

With no mirror to be found in Louise's apartment, Charlotte opted for the window, using what she could discern of her reflection as her guide. Maybe there was more to Captain Nicholas Edwards than his life's devotion to the Navy, after all. The thought gave pause, producing a pleasant effect even as annoyance brimmed.

Despite her misjudgment of Nicholas, she was certain bringing him tonight was a mistake. The man still had the Royal Navy coursing in his veins. She could handle the situation, but she wasn't willing to put her aunt's and possibility her own future at risk by taking any chances.

Her heart fluttered, the beat inside her chest echoing like the past she'd left behind. Scenes played out in her mind, all of them happening so fast. Her mother was weak, but well enough one day, then bedridden the next.

A tear made a pathway down the side of Charlotte's cheek, a part of her wanting to cling to when her mother was alive.

She stared beyond her reflection in the window, reminded by urban streets and densely packed rooftops of where she was and why she was here. That time was over. She had work to do. Aunt Sylvia had given her a second chance to become a part of the world she had introduced her to in the first place—a world far outside that of Massachusetts and away from where war and death still festered.

As if to reinforce the idea, Charlotte wiped away the tear. There was no use dwelling on the past when her aunt, alive and well, needed her here in the present.

She pinned up her hair like she had at the party at Lady Allewood's—curls at the top of her head with a single, thick strand laid over her shoulder. Picking up her aunt's letter in the chance the correspondence proved useful, she placed the letter into the pocket of her skirts.

"Good luck for tonight." Louise was downstairs working on the lace pattern Charlotte had seen her with on her first day at the dentelle while her mother rested in a chair beside her, pricking a different design in a piece of parchment. Floral motifs were being filled in by candlelight when Charlotte's carriage arrived in front of the shop window.

To walk would've saved on cost, a wise enough decision given her recently limited funds, but to arrive on foot wouldn't look good in the eyes of her host or a businessman like the vicomte. Not a good first impression for trying to strike a deal.

Having paid the carriage driver, Charlotte stepped out onto a courtyard flanked by two adjoining buildings to the main mansion. A servant dressed in scarlet and gold livery opened the door and led her into the residence's salon where a large, gilded mirror towered over the marbled fireplace mantel, extending proudly to the ceiling to meet with equally gilded cornices.

Working to steal back her breath from wherever the air had left her upon entering, she refrained from gasping like a little girl. Aside from the Hôtel de Beauvais, this was the first time in her stay in Paris to partake in the interior of such a lavish Parisian home.

Her aunt's estate, the picture of Massachusetts colonial wealth, held little comparison aside from a lovely chaise and a writing table outlined in gilt-bronze edging Aunt Sylvia had acquired from her trips to France. A much smaller version of the three gilded mirrors she'd already seen since entering the grand townhouse hung above her aunt's mantel while the walls she saw now trimmed in gold were nowhere to be found in Portsmouth.

Charlotte swept her gaze across the room of the salon, her eye drawn to wallpaper that covered the top paneling. An idealized landscape in a lush countryside with exotic plants and wildlife depicted a contrast to the busy city the mansion resided in and was nothing like the simple painted walls of colonial Massachusetts. The images around her, so new and real were fantastic and—

"Do you play?"

Charlotte turned to the female voice, catching a scent of jasmine in the air beside her where a woman in a coral satin gown approached.

Somewhat startled from her moment of appreciation, it took her a moment to understand what the woman meant.

Most of the guests were engaged in conversation in small, intimate groups, but a card table was set up in the center under a dangling chandelier. She had seen enough games at the Allewood's estate last year, and though watched up close, never partook. But if the vicomte was at the table, then tonight she might.

"Depends." Charlotte viewed the players looking enlivened by the game they partook in while others stood around to watch. "What are they playing?"

"Vingt-et-un."

"Twenty-one?" Charlotte's gaze shifted back to the woman beside her, only now truly seeing the woman with the astonishment she deserved.

The woman gave a poised smile and the way she carried herself—there was an elegance about her that somehow resonated without her needing to utter a word at all—a quality of French womanhood that must've taken since childhood to perfect.

The woman's older, yet delicate chin raised, her powdered brow also raising as if re-evaluating Charlotte in a different light. Her smile deepened. "You're from the Americas, then? An Englishwoman?"

Charlotte was going to correct her—to say she wasn't related to the land mass next door to France, keeping the idea her English ancestry might not be in her favor tonight. But with the end of the war still uncertain in the colonies, that detail remained undetermined.

"Actually, that is currently under debate." She pitched the woman a smile, not wanting to get off on the wrong footing when she had barely stepped in the door. "But yes, I'm from Massachusetts. Charlotte Thatcher."

"A pleasure to meet you, mademoiselle." A small smile played on the woman's neatly rouged lips. "I am Claudine."

The tension in Charlotte's shoulders eased now that their conversation was off to a good start. "Are you the hostess?"

"No, but I know the gentleman that owns this house very well. In fact, I am privy to his acquaintances that were to be at this gathering tonight." Something in her smile had changed as her hands came together.

Charlotte doubted the change was noticeable from an outsider's perspective, yet she could feel a shift in the trajectory of their conversation.

"You see—" Claudine continued, her tone soft, yet holding a firmness. "The host has no wife, so naturally as a friend, I helped with the invitations. There were two foreigners listed." She tipped her chin discretely in the direction of the crowd playing cards. "One is there at the card table and the other is not here."

Charlotte swallowed, catching the woman's meaning and drop in tone. But she'd expected this—questioned for who she was at a party she had no acquaintances at.

"Yes, I know." Reaching inside her skirt pocket, Charlotte produced Aunt Sylvia's invitation.

"I'm here in Sylvia Davenport's stead." She lengthened her spine, handing the invitation to Claudine. "She's my aunt."

"You are Sylvie's niece?" Claudine's hazel eyes held her with further scrutiny before examining the note, although the familiar way this woman had addressed her aunt held promise. Maybe she wouldn't be thrown out before she had a chance to speak with the vicomte.

"Yes. the one already here in Paris, anyway."

"Oh, mademoiselle, then you are welcome." A friendliness took over Claudine's tone again as she led Charlotte to a velvet upholstered couch in the same color as the servant's livery. "I do love to hear her accounts of what's happening in the colonies. The place seems so wild and humble compared to life here." She leaned in close as if Charlotte were now a confidante, all but erasing the tension from earlier. "Tell me, why has your aunt sent you tonight instead of coming on her own accord?"

"She's in the colonies helping the rest of my family, and of course, taking care of her business." Charlotte didn't want to dive into the details of her mother's death and her aunt's role in trying to keep her family together. "I suppose since I was already here, it was easier to have me come in her place." Which presented a question that needed no reminder. "Do you happen to know where I can find a Monsieur de Vantinelle?"

"The vicomte?" A refined smile touched Claudine's painted lips again. "As a matter of fact, I do."

Charlotte followed her gaze to the crowd of gamblers.

"He is over at the card table as one of the spectators." Her smile was replaced by a tightness in her features, her lips firming. "But I must warn you, if you believe in conducting business with him tonight, you are quite mistaken."

Charlotte drew back, the very reason she was here met with advice that she should refrain from her plan?

Normally, she might've scoffed at the very notion, yet even though she couldn't say why, she treated Claudine's prediction with care. "What do you mean?"

"The vicomte will be in no mood tonight for negotiations, especially from someone from the colonies."

"But that's the reason I'm here." The *only* reason in fact.

"Nevertheless, I would encourage you to wait until a more opportune time."

A more opportune time? Charlotte looked back at the card table and the man she doubted she'd ever see again if not for her aunt's invitation. No, this was that opportune time.

"Thank you, I appreciate the advice. But I'm afraid I'll have to take my chances." Rising from the couch, Charlotte could already see Claudine didn't agree with her decision, but she was set on what she'd come here to do.

"Monsieur." Charlotte approached the man Claudine had pointed out and who had moved on from spectating the card gamblers for a separate conversation with another nobleman. She peaked her mouth into a smile, one she hoped was charming.

"Do I know you, mademoiselle?" To her credit, he returned the gesture while taking a decorated glass from a man carrying a tray full of amber-colored liquid.

"No, we've never met, but I'm here specifically to see you." She declined when the servant offered her a glass of the same liquid as did the man the vicomte had been speaking with. "My name is Charlotte Thatcher. I'm from the colonies—Massachusetts to be exact."

"You have made quite a trip to see me, Mademoiselle Thatcher." He gave a smirk while taking his second sip from the elegantly decorated glass. "Tell me, how is the war going between the redcoats and the revolutionaries?"

Though she could hardly be surprised by the topic, her body stiffened, nonetheless. "I make a point to stay out of the war, monsieur. Believe me, I'm much happier here in Paris, enjoying life of the Parisians than the awful conflict back home."

"Sometimes conflicts are necessary, mademoiselle. This side of heaven we are hardly expected to find peace."

It was the other man who spoke, his queue less powdered than his companion's and his coat, though of high quality, less embellished. But she didn't agree. She couldn't—not on the topic of war. Not when the state of her countrymen, once civil, was now at such despicable odds.

She couldn't ignore the massacre in Boston at the war's onset and the bloodshed of every battle thereafter, nor the smallpox she'd witnessed first-hand last year on her brief visit to Cambridge. And certainly not her family's livelihood, now on the brink of survival.

"I agree that conflict is a necessity at times—" Charlotte addressed the vicomte's companion, holding no doubt in her mind. "But war is a waste of lives in my opinion."

"A waste of lives?" The bluntness in her tone was met with a darkened face and steadfast eyes by the man she'd addressed. His hands clamped over what she now noticed to be a mahogany cane in front of him. Though his face held a subdued refinement, his knuckles were white against the handle. There was a fire in his eyes, the flame directed at *her*.

"I can only imagine war is the last alternative when no civil agreement can be made. Much like you and I, Mademoiselle Thatcher. For I cannot believe it is a waste of life to lay down one's own for his country." One of his hands departed from the cane's handle, allowing him to stretch to his full height. He turned on his heel, Charlotte watching as he crossed the threshold of the salon and into a different room.

"You'll have to excuse him."

She turned back to the other male voice beside her—the one that truly mattered, seeing the man's glass of the amber-colored liquid nearly depleted.

"Despite his noble upbringing, sometimes the man has his rude moments."

Rude wasn't the word she'd use. The man was clearly angry—at her. She'd known she'd been direct in her opinion, but she hadn't anticipated to receive such a stark rebuke over the topic. Even so, that didn't matter. She was here for another reason; one she'd promised to uphold.

"Monsieur le Vicomte, there's something I'd like to discuss with you, on my aunt's behalf if I may."

His brow, neatly trimmed, narrowed. "I'm sorry, mademoiselle, but you have made a mistake. I am not a vicomte."

The resolve she had for this conversation went slack. "You're not the Vicomte de Vantinelle?"

"I'm afraid I am not." Though his tone contained a fraction of an apology, his expression remained good-humored. "My name is Laurent Girard."

"Girard?" Her eyes widened before the image of her aunt's invitation came into view. "You're the host."

"Oui." He gave a slight bow then motioned for a servant to come over. "And despite my friend's behavior, you are most welcomed this evening." A smile confirmed the comment as he sat his empty glass on a silver-plated tray.

Though glad to have met the evening's host, she couldn't help but consider who else she'd just met. "If you're not the vicomte, then . . ."

Charlotte's thoughts flew back to her conversation with Claudine. She'd been certain in her direction, following the woman's motion to the man at the card table. Her toes curled inside her boots—the man who was *not* alone.

Like the threads of Louise's needlework, fragments slowly came together to reveal an overall picture.

"I'm afraid Monsieur le Vicomte is the gentleman that was with us a few moments ago and the one you undoubtedly offended."

A muscle in her forehead tightened, seeing amusement in Laurent's expression, though feeling none of her own. Of course he was. Not this man that she got along with, but the one she had crossed that her aunt intended to strike a deal.

Charlotte veered her gaze, looking for the man her aunt had laid all her hopes on and seeing he had broken into a conversation with Claudine. The man was already looking less riled until—his eyes caught hers and indignation returned.

Seeing no other option, she hoped time would improve his mood toward her to be able to try again before the evening closed out. Until then—

She turned back to her host. "So do you have any advice for winning your friend over?"

"You mean the vicomte?" Laurent gave an uninterested shrug while he followed where her line of sight had been to the noble in question. "The man has had a bad stain of English blood in his life. And I'm afraid the cut runs deep, especially from the west."

"The west?" She squinted her eyes, knowing full-well what resided there, but not understanding what her homeland had to do with the vicomte. "You mean the colonies?"

"Oui, mademoiselle. I'm not certain you could win the man over if that is what your aim is to achieve." Amusement lit his expression again. "Why, I suppose the only chance you have to redeem yourself in the vicomte's eyes is to become French."

Become French. The notion was a jest, of course, but even in the teasing the idea held a sliver of optimism—optimism she needed if she was going to gain any ground with the Vicomte de Vantinelle. She could only deduce that the vicomte's quick anger was induced by the fact the man she sought out held a dark association to the information Laurent had provided concerning her homeland.

"I wish you bonne chance, mademoiselle." Her host's tidings of good luck were weighted with a hint of sarcasm, but that was all right. She'd take the challenge if it came to that. He gave a chuckle along with another bow before moving on to mingle with his other guests and leaving Charlotte to consider the possibility.

Perusing the grand salon, this time Charlotte paid more attention to the persons in the area than her evaluation of the room's impressive furnishings. The men in their powdered wigs, tied back in neat queues with silk-fashioned frocks. And oh, the women—with their high powdered poufs and silk gowns containing beads, bows, and frills that left her style more than a little wanting even if she'd had the dress she'd intended for tonight.

Charlotte searched the room, fully aware that her person of interest had changed since she'd entered the grand townhouse.

Claudine was still in conversation with the vicomte. Between the clamoring of other exchanges in the room and the distance she'd decided to keep, Charlotte couldn't distinguish the dialogue, but the vicomte seemed more at ease, his darkened face returned to its natural hue and his eyes lacking the anger she'd last seen when he looked at her.

And why wouldn't he be? The woman next to him was stunning—but not just in the way she looked; her skin powdered, absent of any natural sheen brought on from daily life. Nor was it the matching coral plumes to her gown, but more of a certain way she carried herself—a stately grace about her that captivated the eye. Charlotte had never been to the French court, or any court for that matter, but she imagined the woman could impress any king if given the chance.

Charlotte smoothed her dress at her sides as if the motion might magically change her current ensemble. It didn't. Even with the mud stain pinned and hidden underneath, her current dress wasn't the fashion of Paris, and aside from the few French lessons she had with her aunt, Charlotte had no idea how to fully embrace French culture, at least not in the way a vicomte was used to.

Claudine must have felt her staring, the woman's eyes shifting from the vicomte to meet hers briefly, offering a faint smile that only encouraged the idea Charlotte felt brewing to the surface. She needed a guide, a tutor. One that was the very image of French nobility, and she knew exactly who that was.

Chapter 5

"You say all those in French court do this?" Charlotte sat stiff, her back straight against the silk embroidered seat despite her mind being somewhat askew. A large sheet wrapped around her, protecting her dress—a delicate shade of pink and white—along with all its trimmings. The gown was as extravagant as the price tag that came along with it, or so she imagined, never owning anything quite so fine. Nor did she still since the robe à la française was on loan from Claudine.

She had wasted no time in approaching Claudine with her request for help. Not knowing if the French woman would reject her plea, Charlotte was thankful she hadn't. Her only guess as to why her plan had been accepted was Claudine's high regard for her aunt.

A man with a powdered wig stood on a stool behind her to reach the top of her head, which had nearly doubled in height. He wrapped a piece of hair over a cushion before pinning strands into place. She winced, the long pin—one of many—unforgivingly digging into her scalp.

"All that is anyone." Claudine walked around her in a fashionable dress of rich cream. Her slow pace gave Charlotte the impression she was being evaluated all the while showcasing how easy it seemed for the

French woman to parade with such volume on top of her head. "Trust me, mon amie, when we're through here you will look like you belong."

She didn't care as much about belonging than what the real purpose of her seeking Claudine out had come to. Her aunt's situation.

"Do you think it will convince the vicomte?" Charlotte deprived herself of the sensation to relax her chin while new weight towered above the crown of her head. The coiffeur added another cushion along with a piece of hair, pricking what felt like a needle into bone.

"The Vicomte de Vantinelle is a hard man to please even if you are from court, so I cannot say for certain, but perhaps it will help if you do not remind him so much of the last war."

"The last war?" Charlotte made the mistake of turning her head toward Claudine beside her, catching a rancid smell of a pomade being applied to her new hairstyle even while cloaked in a rosy scent.

"Oui." Claudine made a spiraling motion with her finger as if providing the coiffeur with silent direction before her eyes pinned back on Charlotte. "The vicomte was in service to the king's royal army. That is where he gets his title."

Charlotte leaned back, if only slightly against the gilded armchair, letting the whole of what she'd done sink further in. The man was a former soldier and she'd said war was a waste of lives. She'd insulted him. Yet, how could he not agree when he no doubt had seen the carnage of war up close?

Whatever the reason, she needed to find herself in his good graces for her aunt. But that begged another question that lingered in her mind.

The smell from her coiffure grew stronger, Charlotte unable to keep her nose from scrunching. She only hoped Claudine and the hairstylist hadn't seen the gesture. "Did my aunt ever meet Monsieur de Vantinelle?

"To my knowledge, they were never introduced." Claudine went over to a window framed with velvet curtains where she proceeded to lift the pane, allowing true smells of roses and jasmine from the home's garden inside.

"Then how did she find him? And why him?" Her tone came out harsh, but Charlotte couldn't help it. She didn't understand. Why do business with a Frenchman who had bad ties with the colonies? The idea seemed unsound even as Charlotte knew her aunt was anything but. Or was Aunt Sylvia really to the point of such desperation?

Claudine lifted her shoulders, the movement somehow graceful even underneath the piling of her own coiffure. "He is well-known in the business community. It wouldn't have been difficult for Sylvie, especially with her connections already here in Paris." She took a few steps back toward a powdered blue paneled wall.

The small retreat took Charlotte only a few seconds to understand why. The hairdresser pulled out a mask and covered her face. Before she could object, puffs of powder swirled around her. When the man finished, the coiffeur retrieved a silver tray lined with pendants, plumes, and barrettes.

"There." Claudine pointed to a fluffy, pink plume out of the selection. The feather was a perfect match to Charlotte's petticoat. "That one will do nicely, I think. Tell me, what is your opinion?" A satisfied smile graced her lips before directing Charlotte's to a gilded mirror.

Careful as to not ruin the coiffeur's effort in what seemed to be a tedious feat, Charlotte managed a balanced turn of her head, stealing a glance in the same mirror that occupied Claudine's antechamber.

Suppressing the gasp that dared to cross the threshold of her mouth, she blinked a few times before peering more deeply into the glass. She hardly recognized her reflection.

Aware of the hairstylist's work, the teasing of her strands and the weight added to the crown of her head, she'd expected her hair to be tall under the cushions, which was certainly the case. But this—the tresses of her head were piled skyward, resembling the shape of a pyramid softened by gentle curls. And she hadn't foreseen something else—the powder applied to her hair made her blonde strands nearly white. She took a closer look at her face, noticing something peculiar about the change. After a quick examination, she quickly realized what that was.

Any scars or natural marks on her face and neck were now covered with the same powder, masking any evidence of life's trials. Adding to the already stunning sight, her newly paled skin held a striking contrast to the bright rouge on her lips.

"It's certainly . . ." She was going to say "different" but had no desire to offend Claudine or the man who had gone to such lengths to style her head. She thought back, too, of the party at Laurent Girard's and what she remembered of the similar fashion she'd seen of the women there. The style certainly wasn't what she was used to, but perhaps the change might suit the vicomte and that's what mattered.

Having not given an answer fast enough, Claudine's lips thinned, the pointed look she gave Charlotte telling her she'd guessed her original thought. "I believe the word you're searching for is 'magnifique'. Trés magnifique, monsieur."

"Thank you, madame." The coiffeur bowed to Claudine before offering his own smile of evaluation. "She is trés belle, now. Don't you think?"

Now? Charlotte stared at the looking glass, the wide eyes of a stranger staring back. She hardly resembled herself. And she might've interjected as much, but she'd been the one to ask Claudine for help for fitting in with the French nobility. And as far as she could tell, between the women she'd seen at Laurent's party and the woman before her now, she certainly looked the part.

Charlotte caught Claudine give a silent nod to the coiffeur. The man responded by gathering his tools and leaving the room.

Somewhat hesitant to move after so much fuss, she turned, if only vocally, to the issue that pressed her the most. "Do you think the vicomte will be at the Opera tonight?"

"It is very possible, but even if he is not, there will be others there who are in his circle." A faint swishing of fabric came closer, Claudine motioning for Charlotte to rise from a chair containing floral cushions and an oval-shaped back. With Claudine's help, she did.

"If you conduct yourself well around them, it will no doubt reach the vicomte, which is much better in my opinion." Claudine gave a slow sigh rimmed with a smile. "And far less work."

Getting out of Claudine's carriage and onto the Rue Saint-Honoré proved to be a challenge Charlotte hadn't considered with her new updo. In all her life, she'd never had to wonder how to exit a horse-drawn vehicle.

She would've tried to mimic Claudine if given the chance, following her teacher's lead, but the driver had opened the carriage door to her side first. The problem left her with no alternative but to somehow contrive a way to step out in front of the opera house with all her ensemble, including her mounded coiffure, intact.

Normally, she'd use one hand to lift her skirts to ensure a secure footing on her dismount while her other hand would take hold of the driver's on the step down. But the recent addition of her pouf and its height gave her reason to pause. How was she going to keep her hair from hitting the top of the carriage door and risk undoing all the hairstylist had done? She murmured frustration under her breath. She needed three hands when she only had two.

Too prideful or embarrassed to ask—she wasn't sure which one won out—she thought quickly, aware the footman and Claudine were waiting.

Gathering her skirts with one hand, Charlotte brought the free one to the top of her head to balance her updo as she ducked under the door's rim. Her movements were slower than she liked, and awkward, her body somewhat contorted while her head remained obstinately straight for the sake of her coiffure.

Making progress, if only a little, she cleared the door with her strands still in place and stepped onto the carriage step, feeling the slightest bit of accomplishment. She relaxed her grip on her skirts and too late realized her mistake.

The toe of her leather boots caught within the folds of her dress while trying to meet its other half on the carriage step. She tried to wriggle her boot free, but her shoe's entanglement within her gown left her unsteady. Her weight shifted beneath her, sending her body and the hairdo she so adamantly tried to protect, downward.

She shut her eyes, not wanting to face the pavement she was about to meet . . . or would've met if it hadn't been for the male arms that had caught her.

"Are you all right, mademoiselle?"

Charlotte opened her eyes, raising them to meet a man of thin physique wrapped in an earthly linen coat. Despite his unimpressive fashions, the man was handsome. His face was sleek, everything about it manicured and clean, yet a strong chin giving a hint to his masculinity.

"It was bonne chance I was walking toward the carriage." He lifted her the rest of the way to her feet, his hair, unadorned by a wig and less powdered than she had seen on the other men making their way into the opera, reminded her of what she'd tried to protect and nearly failed at.

"Mon dieu!" Claudine departed from the last step of the carriage, rushing over to the scene, though looking less pleased than worried. "Mademoiselle Charlotte, we will need to work on your exit from the vehicle on top of your French, I'm afraid." Her eyes went to the man who'd helped prevent the disaster before back to Charlotte. "I see you have met the Baron d'Aubray."

The baron huffed, giving a smirk. "My sister uses my official title to hide her embarrassment of her wayward younger brother."

"Brother?" Charlotte looked between the two nobles, settling on the one she knew better, if only slightly.

"It is not an embarrassment to show who you truly are." Claudine frowned at the man claiming to be her brother in a way that confirmed the connection. "For you, Marc Chazot, that is the Baron d'Aubray—a name that goes back to the Middle Ages. Our father would scold you from his grave if he could."

"He doesn't have to." Marc huffed, a smug smile still on his mouth. "He has you to do it for him."

Claudine didn't say anything, the woman's expression also saying little behind her powdered face and rouge like the comment was unsurprising. Charlotte couldn't tell if such a reaction was because the subject had been touched on before—the comment no longer producing the punch intended or that the woman had something about her, like all other things, that rose above a sharp defense.

Instead, Claudine's attention shifted to two women who'd exited from one of the carriages in the row behind him, their current focus aimed in Charlotte's direction and her less than graceful exit from the carriage. Their fine dresses of satin told Charlotte they were of the same noble class as Claudine and by the way her tutor regarded them—a controlled smile to whatever words were spoken behind decorative puffing fans—Charlotte had an inkling she knew them.

"Marc," Claudine regarded her brother, her tone lacking the sharpness from a moment ago. "Please escort Mademoiselle Charlotte to our seats inside. I must give my greetings to the Comtesse de la Roche and the Duchesse de Clairmont."

"Are those friends of Claudine's?" Charlotte observed the two women welcoming Claudine in the group while thinking of what her tutor had said earlier about appealing to the vicomte's circle to her advantage. "I should introduce myself."

"Acquaintances. And I advise that you don't." Marc took Charlotte's arm, the surprise of the gesture stopping her in her plan. He placed her arm in the crook of his elbow while leading her under a triangular pediment supported by a series of columns to the opera house's grand entrance. "Some have nothing better to do with their lives than find their happiness in other's misfortune. Such are those two." His gaze trailed to the two women with Claudine. "They are only friends to each other as long as they are not in competition at Versailles."

"Competition?" The word felt strange in the current setting as they walked past two men in livery and entered the grand foyer where a crowd dressed in their finest mingled in the room's opulently decorated space. The word evoked nights of playing games with her siblings and seemed ill-suited at the French palace or here at the opera.

"You have not yet been to Versailles?"

Charlotte detected amusement in his question, the smile he gave her telling her he already knew she hadn't. She didn't like it, not knowing the secret he kept hidden under his grin. It made her feel less than somehow. She wouldn't ordinarily mind such antics, caring little about what others thought about her, but to not be accepted into a populace of Paris that included the vicomte when that's exactly what she needed, unnerved her.

She lengthened her neck, half imagining her coiffure swiping against the grand chandelier above as she passed under the candle-lit fixture. "Not yet, but I fully intend a visit."

"Then you will see for yourself what I mean."

His smile grew broader. He was enjoying her ignorance. Why couldn't he just tell her now? Again, frustration mounted at a game she didn't want to play, but the feeling didn't last long.

They had begun their climb up a stairway cut in fine stone, the candlelight from the sconces reflecting a warm glow off the gilded mirrors and statues while the mixture of beeswax candles and floral scents of theatre-goers invited her further in. Her heart began to beat faster, but not in a way she feared, her anticipation climbing with each step taken up the cut of fine stone.

Her boots stepped onto a rich dark green carpet, the plush material under her feet soft and—she gasped, as Marc led her into a private box along the side of the auditorium.

"Is this your first time at the opera?" He gestured to an empty seat, taking the one beside her. "I do not believe I have seen you among the crowd before."

That, she wasn't surprised by—her image in the reflection at Claudine's apartment coming to mind. No one had seen her like this before.

"I saw *Alceste* when I first arrived in the city," but she'd sat down below on the parterre with Abigail and Garrett, her view obstructed by a woman's hat. Here, above the stalls, she had a clear view of the decorated proscenium arch over the wood stage the performers would soon occupy. Which made her consider . . . her seat wasn't positioned only for watching the actors. Apart from the balconies above, her current placement would provide her an eagle's eye view of anyone within the crowd.

She scanned the seating below before realizing her mistake and paying attention more to the boxes at eye level.

"If you are looking for the royals you will not find them here."

She wasn't. In truth, she'd been looking for the vicomte, but Marc's comment made her curious. "They don't enjoy the opera?"

"It is not the opera King Louis does not enjoy. It is Paris."

An attractive brunette claimed a seat in an adjacent balcony, clearly an aristocrat, or perhaps like her, pretending to belong. A shared moment between she and Marc commenced that he seemed to enjoy, the proof curving in his mouth before he reclined in his seat.

"But the art is not lost to him. If he wants to attend the theatre, he has the convenience of one within his palace estate."

"He has his own opera house?" She stopped in the middle of scanning the rest of the balconies. Having never obtained entrance to the palace—a circumstance Charlotte was determined to change—she had trouble envisioning one, especially with its own theatre.

"I was there when the king married his Austrian bride six years ago. The royal family dined their marriage feast on the stage."

Marc's mouth twisted as if he had eaten something bitter from the wedding feast he just mentioned. "I stood with my father, expected to do nothing but spectate as the newly wedded dauphin stuffed his face and his fourteen-year-old wife ate next to nothing of the grand meal."

"You didn't eat anything?" Her mouth pinched, feeling the dry paint on her lips. "You just *watched* them eat?" The idea seemed strange. She had better things to do than watch someone else eat—royal or not.

"It is considered a high honor to be an observer of the royal family in any way."

The inflection in his tone expressed the opposite to the words he voiced. Not to mention she couldn't help observing how differently dressed he seemed compared to the rest of the high-class attendees tonight. The man was handsome and put together well enough, but his choice in such plain fashions confused her, especially considering his title and his sibling. Had the decision to forego such ornate dressings been on purpose?

What appeared like a deliberate decision reminded her of things having foregone back home like fine imports from England due to the war. There wasn't a war here in France, but was there something she didn't know?

Preferring to steer their conversation a different direction, she kept her curiosity at bay, choosing a safer topic. "And you, Monsieur Baron d'Aubray, do you come often?" She looked at how comfortable he seemed, already sure of his answer.

He met her question with a downturned mouth. "Those that know me well call me Marc. Please do me the honor." He kissed her hand, Charlotte thinking back to his flirtation with the brunette in the adjacent box. "I hold a particular appreciation of the arts and count myself fortunate to live in a city where they flourish."

"Paris takes art in different forms." Something she had no trouble noticing evidenced by her first steps within the Tuileries, the city's magnificent architecture, and even Louise's lace. The city was a cornucopia of imagination and creative activity. Which begged the question. "What style of art do you prefer?"

His smile widened a fraction. Unlike the conversation about the royal banquet, this was a subject he liked. "I prefer them all, but painting is what I enjoy most to partake in."

"You paint?" Her powdered eyebrow perched. She had some trouble believing that—the painters she'd seen around the city dressed more commonly, never mind being able to afford a box seat at the opera.

"Oui." He leaned in, over-confidence gleaming in his eye. "I would love to paint you someday if you wouldn't object to it."

A flush of warmth spread to her cheeks, somewhat startled by his forwardness, but she wouldn't let herself be easily flustered. She'd been around men like this last year when her aunt introduced her into society and had learned quickly. No matter what country, it seemed they were all more or less the same—they knew they were rich. And they assumed they could obtain anything they wanted with their status.

"That, monsieur, is a lovely offer, but I don't think I would be wise to accept it without seeing your work first." She stood her ground despite his face being inches away from her own. She tossed him a smile. "There is the possibility that you're not very good."

She thought that'd be enough to ward him off, but to her surprise his grin revealed a nice set of teeth, the message unmistakably clear. He liked the challenge.

"Oui. You are right, mademoiselle." His face moved away from her own as he reclined again in his seat. Something between arrogance and amusement played in his expression. "You should come see some of my work. Perhaps then you can better determine whether it is satisfactory enough to be a subject of it."

She squared her body away from searching the crowd for the vicomte and toward him. The man seemed sure of himself. "Do you get a lot of women to pose for you, monsieur?"

The corners of his mouth stayed in their raised position. "I have had a few, yes."

She huffed. Well, he certainly was honest. She had to credit him for that. But she hadn't seen their conversation going in this direction, especially when he'd caught her like a gentleman outside.

"Marc has completed portraits of some of the noble families and is a student at the Académie Royale." The familiar female voice drew Charlotte's attention, her challenge against the Baron d'Aubray dissolving.

Claudine approached them, an attendant dressed in livery ushering her into their boxed area within the balcony. She took the seat on the other side of her brother. "We can visit his apartment later this week if you'd like."

"Paintings of noble families?" Charlotte eyed Marc, aware her bottom lip had dropped open at her mistake. The Royal Academy? Why had he let her judge him so critically? She hadn't intended to actually see his work, but now she felt she owed him an apology. "Of course. I would like that very much."

"I didn't realize you'd be in attendance this evening, dear brother." Claudine produced a fan from her reticule, her voice light with pleasure.

"I heard the theatre would be less crowded tonight." Marc's smile began to diminish. "It seems the rumors were true."

The cluster of people still making their way inside the auditorium told a different story but having already embarrassed herself twice in front of this man before the show actually began, Charlotte wasn't about to give him the satisfaction of a third. She stayed silent, though continued her search for the vicomte.

"I see." Claudine gave a soft exhale, something dimming in her expression. "I hoped that meant you two had resolved your differences."

"Hardly, Claude." Marc gave a short huff, the enjoyment Charlotte had witnessed on his face when speaking about the arts all but gone. "I don't think Vincent and I are going to be agreeing any time soon. The man is obtuse to change. You'd have better luck getting the king to renounce his throne."

"You shouldn't talk like that, Marc." Claudine's voice went to a reprimanding whisper, the first time Charlotte had witnessed the woman strain. "Under the king, we are the nobility. We have everything we want."

"Yes, *we* do, but what about everybody else in Paris?" Marc's tone was sharp, and Charlotte couldn't help but wonder if it was edged with truth.

She thought of Louise struggling to make enough for her mother's medicine, the underpaid street vendors all over the city, and the overly thin boy she had bumped into in the alleyway. She regarded herself, her head feeling a fraction heavier than it already had been under her coiffure's weight.

Whether it was the overture being played by the orchestra that prevented Claudine from inputting anything further to Marc's stance or something else, Charlotte didn't know. Her French tutor stayed silent, her poignant gaze toward the stage as the curtain began to pull back and reveal a man of fantastical appearance dressed in flowing robes of midnight blue and shimmering silver.

Under a crown made of flowers and vine that depicted his mythical status as king to the fairy realm flowed a white wig and—

Charlotte couldn't look away, transfixed by an illusion that was flawless. Yet it wasn't the magic that held her captive. It was the painted face—so hauntingly like her own.

***

"Charlotte? Is that you?" Louise answered the door to the darkened dentelle, bringing a lantern up between their two faces.

"It's me." She was tired. Though the performance at the theatre was more than satisfying, her head was sore from the burden of her headdress.

She hadn't bothered with the effort to hold her coiffure in place as she exited Claudine's carriage this time, which led to her frustration from her earlier mishap. Her tall tresses had refused to budge from their tightly pinned place at her scalp. Her head throbbed.

"Wow." Louise drew back, the lamplight casting a glow on her round eyes. "You look so—"

"Noble?" That was the look she was going for, after all, but Louise's thinned mouth told her she had guessed incorrectly.

"I was going to say expensive."

She didn't doubt that, still adorned in the dress Claudine loaned her and the pinching ache at her skull serving as a reminder to the lengths taken to achieve her look for tonight. "Claudine thought it would make a good first impression at the opera. What do you think?"

"I think it made an impression of some kind." There was a lack of compliment in Louise's tone.

Louise led her inside and up into the main living space of the apartment—the wooden steps so plain and bare compared to the carpeted stone of the opera house. A single lamp sat upon the table she'd dined at with Louise and her mother the day she'd come into their store.

Charlotte gestured to the two lace patterns still attached to their needles spread out upon the table's surface. "I see you've been busy tonight. Has your mother been working too?"

"She tried for a little while but had to stop. She's resting now." With the lantern still in Louise's hand, Charlotte could see the burden threaded in her friend's weak smile.

Charlotte grimaced, thankful her own expression couldn't be seen in the darkness. She'd enjoyed a night at the theatre while Louise continued working into the late hours, even now. Conviction pricking, like one of the pins the coiffeur stuck into her head, Charlotte took a seat at the table. She picked up the needle and untied where the thread stitching left off, trusting in the memory of her fingers from working with her aunt last year.

"So how did things go tonight? Did you speak with the vicomte?"

Louise occupied the chair next to her, securing a thicker thread outlining a lace design using a series of temporary stitches. The lack of judgement in her tone only amplified the guilt Charlotte felt.

"He wasn't there, but Claudine introduced me to some of the noble families who were, including her brother, Marc."

"What did you think of him?"

Using a thinner piece of thread and needle, Charlotte looped the thicker cord, repeating the action with rhythmic motion as a raised effect against the design began to take shape. "I'm not sure yet, except that he says he's an artist. Claudine is going to take me to his apartment later this week to see his work."

"I know you said your visit at the party didn't go as well as you had hoped, but do you really need all that to speak with the vicomte?" Louise pulled another stitch through. She angled the needle to Charlotte, her meaning perfectly clear.

"It can't hurt." The way she saw it, her English heritage—though proud of her ancestry even as the war might determine a different one, did her no favors with the man she sorely needed to impress. "And it's only a short time. Once I make my apology for my offense at the party, I'm sure things will prove right between us." A declaration she voiced with more certainty than what she felt inside. But she had to try—to do everything in her power for her aunt and family's welfare. If that meant reminding the vicomte less of whatever stain that ran deep from her home by embracing what he knew in his, then she would.

And why not enjoy the adventure of it? Words from her aunt came to her mind's eye, prompting further justification.

While you're young.

Charlotte didn't know how long she had before God claimed her life like he had her mother's. Now was her time to live. And why couldn't part of that living be as a noble, at least for a little while?

Louise continued her needlework with a patience that was beyond commendable, Charlotte feeling the tension of her disagreement within her silence. She appreciated her friend's caution, but she wasn't about to be convinced otherwise. She had a plan, and she would see that plan through.

Charlotte stretched her fingers, already feeling cramping with the tiny movements. "How long are you going to do this?"

"Until I'm tired enough to stop." As if on cue, Louise gave a yawn, but continued working like her body's draw for sleep hadn't phased her. "I like to do as much as I can before the weather starts to turn again.

There's less light during the day in the winter and the cold makes it harder for my hands to work."

Charlotte's brows sunk between her nose. "But there's less light now. It's the middle of the night."

Louise laughed. "Yes, but at least I have the lamplight and I can still feel my fingers."

"So, what happens then—when the weather gets colder?" Feeling a sudden need to continue stitching, Charlotte picked up the needle and thread again. "Does that mean you're out of work until the spring?"

Louise anchored the thick piece of thread with another series of tiny stitches. "A group of us in the trade meet more during the season. The combination of bodies and conversation helps the time go by and takes our minds off the cold while also keeping us warm. We like to keep a fire at our feet, but sometimes that's risky. Just last year, one of the girl's skirts caught and her ankle was burned. Thankfully, that was all." She gave a tired smile. "I'll let you experience it firsthand if you're still here."

Charlotte's needle stopped halfway through the parchment. It was barely fall. The cold season seemed so far away. "You think there's a chance I will be?"

"I don't know, but you said the other nobleman at the party told you the vicomte's displeasure with the English runs deep. If that is true, it may take some time to heal whatever has caused it."

Charlotte pressed her lips, remembering she still had the rouge on them. Could it really take so long? There was no established agreement between the colonies and England that indicated the war's end was on the horizon. She would have liked to stay in Paris with Louise and her mother, but her funds were unlikely to stretch that far, not unless she could give some good news to her aunt of a secured partnership and that needed to happen much quicker than the changing climate.

Louise paused her work, putting her hand gently, but firmly over Charlotte's. The gesture brought an indescribable comfort. "There is no point worrying about what happens later while there is plenty to worry about now." Louise drew her hand back, a fraction of the lamplight helping Charlotte glimpse a grin on her friend's face. "For instance, you might need to worry if Maman wakes up and sees you in such a way. She is bound to have questions and I'm not the one who is going to explain why a noblewoman is living with us, never mind stitching lace."

Pulling the needle the rest of the way through the parchment, Charlotte made another pass while taking in Louise's account. Explaining her situation to Louise's mother wasn't a conversation she wanted to have, not after the woman had offered her refuge and not when she didn't understand the full scope of her predicament. She thought of what her own mother might think. What she was doing felt like deception, yet she told herself it was for the sake of her aunt and family.

Pins still jabbed against her scalp. That, along with Louise's gentle warning sent her to undress. She traded Claudine's elaborate gown for her basic shift and removed the powder and rouge from her face with water from a bucket. She was starting to feel more like herself again, except for one complication—of notable size. The pile of hair still stood tall and erect, presenting a problem as grand as her lofty hairdo.

Because of both the time and skill taken to achieve such a look, Claudine had told her to leave the style in for at least a week. Charlotte had no desire to displease the woman who'd taken an interest to help her, but the image of Louise's mother came around again as well as the complication of sleeping with things as they were. A few minutes later, the cushions and pins were plucked out.

Her body—no longer aching from their strains—relaxed, Louise's bed looking more than inviting the longer she stared at it. Charlotte's gaze shifted slightly to Louise's mother asleep in the bed not built for two, but which would nevertheless occupy that number tonight.

Charlotte liked staying with these women, but she had accommodations elsewhere. Nicholas had said as much in their tête-à-tête in the dentelle and a word from Nicholas J. Edwards was like a bar of pure gold—it held its value. It was high time she be reunited with her luggage and the rest of her finances. She just needed to figure out how to make amends with a man who severely tried her patience.

Chapter 6

"No? What do you mean, no?" Nicholas leveled his gaze at the man in front of him adorned in a long, powdered periwig with curls past his shoulders. Despite his even tone, he heard the impatience in his own voice. He was becoming more acquainted with these rejections than he could tolerate.

"I mean the king refuses to have an audience with you at this time, Captain." The minister handed him King George's signed letter requesting the meeting, dismissing it with a coolness in his tone Nicholas didn't altogether like. "He does, however, invite you to explore the grounds at your leisure."

Nicholas took the letter, seeing the invitation for what it was—a stately way to appease him out of the L'Oeuil de Boeuf of Versailles. His fingers strained to keep his grip light on the paper while he returned the royal correspondence to the inside pocket of his naval coat. Despite the resounding pressure he felt, he reached for a resolve that had been fashioned since the Academy in his youth. "The King doesn't seem too concerned about neglecting an ambassador of England." He eyed the minister, aware of others in the king's antechamber waiting for their chance and lowered his voice. "Does he really want to risk starting another conflict after being beaten in the last one?"

The man curled a smile, looking anything but alarmed by the comment. "Oui." The swift response came out pointed. "You are right, monsieur. His Majesty is not concerned with England." The arrogance in his jaw grew more pronounced. "You see, between the war in the west and the previous one, rumors have spread of your country's financial constraints. I do not believe King Louis is too worried about neglecting King George at all since the English king already has his hands full." He gave Nicholas a look of feigned regret. "I'm sorry, Captain, but you will not be meeting His Majesty today."

The man gave an abrupt turn. He strode past a Swiss guard and through a set of double doors that led to the king's chambers, leaving Nicholas to absorb the impact of his blow. Another refusal. Another failed attempt.

***

Having dropped his letter to King George with a London merchant at the Seine River, Nicholas walked back to where he'd found accommodations in the city.

The general post was off the Rue de Plâtrière, but with the classified information he was entrusted to find out, the public mail system hadn't been the means he'd chosen. There was always a chance the French police tagged him as a person of interest—a very likely outcome given his several appearances at Versailles, especially in uniform. Any outgoing correspondence might as well be delivered to the head of the gendarmes by his own hand. Instead, he'd chosen to be cautious and hired a merchant ship captain who'd agreed to take his letters by sea for a price.

The afternoon light had already produced its deep shades of orange and pink when he'd arrived at the boardinghouse and began the small journey to his room. He was tired, the long hours of waiting in the Bull's-Eye Salon, accompanied with nothing to show but another refusal

75

to see the king again still left him irritated. The only thing that sounded good was tinkering with a design by Joseph Priestley, a carbonated water system he'd been able to get his hands on.

He'd read how Captain James Cook had taken the invention with him on his latest expedition in hopes the product might alleviate scurvy. Nothing yet supported that claim, but Nicholas found the beverage nonetheless satisfying and a glass of the bubbling liquid sounded more than refreshing right about now.

He made his way down the hall but stopped. A glow appeared to be coming from behind the door to the room he had procured for Charlotte, grabbing his attention. The placement of her room had been intentional—far enough from his own to where she'd have plenty of distance for privacy, yet not too far so he could still keep somewhat of an eye on her if he had to.

A scent of mint and something floral reached him from the other side—pleasant, especially compared to the crowded room of the king's antechamber at Versailles. Without thinking, he took a step forward, the wood flooring creaking under his weight.

"Is someone there?"

Nicholas stiffened. Sounds of shuffling inside the room followed by hurried footsteps drew close. Too late to retreat. He straightened like a man who hadn't been caught—knowing he hadn't done anything wrong—though a part of him still felt like he had.

The door swung open.

Charlotte appeared on the other side with a fire poker in hand—aimed straight at his chest.

Chapter 7

"Captain Edwards?" With something akin to confusion and surprise, Nicholas watched cautiously as Charlotte lowered the fire poker from the middle of his chest.

"I didn't realize you were no longer staying with Louise at the dentelle." The floral scent he'd smelled before grew stronger with the door ajar. "I only stopped here because I saw a light coming from the door."

She deposited the weapon beside the doorpost just inside the room when he noticed smudges of ink on her fingertips. "Yes, well, it was time to give Louise her bed back. Not to mention I missed my things." She gave him a relieved smile. "Thank you for bringing back my luggage."

"You're welcome."

She stepped back into the room, allowing the door to fully open. Besides the unpacked suitcase, a handleless porcelain teacup sat on a side table where he ventured the floral smell originated. By the looks of things, she'd made the small table into a makeshift working space—a leather-bound notebook sitting on top and open to reveal the beginnings of intricate drawings.

He took another evaluation of her smudged fingers, putting together what he'd learned at the dentelle. "Are those for the lacemakers?"

She looked behind her as if to follow his line of sight back to the table and sighed. "They're not complete. In truth, I'm just getting started . . . trying to get my thoughts together with what might stand out."

She motioned for him to come in, but he hesitated. He wasn't the sort of man to walk into a woman's quarters, even invited.

"It's all right, Captain." His pause appeared to have put a smile on her face. "I'm quite confident you're incapable of any ill intentions. Normally, I'm set against a man stepping foot in my room, but I'm certain you'll hold fast to your untarnished reputation. I have nothing to worry about."

She didn't, but it wasn't his untarnished reputation on his mind. "I appreciate the trust—" Even in the scoffing way she'd voiced it. "—but I'd like to make sure your own reputation remains likewise. I'll admire them from here."

She gave him a cockeyed look, then huffed. "Really, Captain, I doubt you have one black spec against your character. Are you as perfect as Jesus Christ?"

He frowned, not liking her tone, but also in the way she meant to compare him with a man who couldn't be compared to—out of reach apart from the grace given to him. "Far from it, Miss Thatcher."

She stared at him, her blue eyes penetrating. He thought she might ask him to leave or even shut the door in his face, neither of which would have surprised him. But she didn't. She turned and walked to the makeshift desk, picking up the notebook before returning to the doorway where she'd left him.

Without a word, she handed him the notebook. He read her face, looking for confirmation and she gave a single nod.

The designs were rough, at the beginning stages of their development but had potential. Amazement ran through him, wondering how a woman so bent on blind action could make herself sit down long enough to create such intricate drawings.

He went through the notebook, skimming through the sketches, aware of her watchful gaze on him. "They're good."

"They're a start."

He looked up from the pages to find her shaking her head. "But they're not good enough, not yet."

Something rolled in his stomach. She meant her work, yet those words—*not good enough*—was a constant replay in his head.

Her eyes held a spark of determination. "They'll get there once I fine-tune them."

Despite their vast differences, Nicholas admired the woman's confidence. If he wasn't careful, he'd have to admit it was a quality he liked about her. That was, when she wasn't consistently against him. He returned the lace sketches to her, her eyes meeting his with a mixture of scrutiny and if his own weren't misleading him, concern.

"What happened with you today? You look tired."

He was. She, however, looked freshly changed and alert.

The concern in her expression made him want to tell her more specifics about his day, but he couldn't.

She seemed to read his silence, her crossed arms proof she already knew the answer. Since receiving his orders in Boston, he'd been forbidden to speak of his work in Paris. He didn't like the secrets, but his orders gave him no choice, especially when a war was the cost if he went against them.

"I'm sorry." He heard his tone take on an officialness he didn't always like but came naturally in the scenario. "You know I can't say."

Any regard she had for him disappeared.

"Of course you can't." She frowned, curving her head out the door of her room and down the hall before eyeing him. "And I suppose there's no coincidence your room is a certain proximity to mine?"

"Not at all." He smiled, realizing his plan had been figured out, yet finding a sort of enjoyment that it had. "If you're not going to let me hire an escort for you around Paris, I will at least be able to know whether you are all right each night."

She returned his smile with a small one of her own, though he read something false in the feature. "I didn't know you cared."

"I do." Her insincerity made the truth easy to come by. "But not in the way you might be thinking. You were on my ship on the way over from the colonies, that makes you my responsibility, at least until I get you back with Abigail in London." He looked at the distance spanning their two rooms. "This allows me a way, though not to my entire liking, to do that."

"Honestly Captain, am I expected to hear from you each night?" Her hands balled into fists, not looking pleased by that notion.

"Not necessarily. If I see a light coming from your room, I'll know you're burning a candle and you're there. Now that I know you're settled—" He gave a slight bow before straightening. "I'll be on my way."

"Captain Edwards."

He stopped only a few paces away from his room when she'd called to him.

"There is one place I'd like to have an escort . . . if you wouldn't object."

He turned back in her direction, hearing a slight tremor in her voice. She'd taken a step into the hallway, her chest, though covered by the draping of her shawl, lifted as if she'd taken a breath, not bothering to let the air out again.

It was the first time she'd looked vulnerable to him. Knowing from experience this was a rare occasion, there was something beautiful and striking in the moment seeing her guard down.

He swallowed, remembering what she had asked of him. "Would you like me to hire one?"

"No." Her chest lowered, Nicholas reading what he could only decipher as relief on her face. "I'd like to go with someone I know—even at least partly."

He nodded, but for some reason that fact—one he couldn't refute—stung. They'd crossed an ocean together, yet he knew almost nothing about her. Duty had filled every spare moment—and the distance between them showed it.

He was going to ask where they were going, preferring to know what was ahead of him, but something prompted him not to. Though not explicitly voicing it, in a small way she had asked for his help—his trust. He somehow sensed it was a step in the right direction for each of them and he wasn't going to jeopardize that progress.

Nicholas watched her disappear into her room and waited until the door closed. As he turned toward his own lodgings, he noticed a change within himself.

Though his failure to meet with the French king remained, his irritation over the problem had eased. What was more, he thought he would find himself dreading the same space with Charlotte, even as his duty as a gentleman remained strong. But he admitted, if only to himself, that he was looking forward to tomorrow.

Chapter 8

Charlotte stood in the middle of the Cour du Mai, unable to fix her gaze on anything else. The building in front of her—once a palace and superior in the large courtyard—now crumbled to a fragment of its former glory.

How much destruction a fire could do in a short amount of time. With just a spark, the inferno could consume everything in its wake only to leave its path forever changed, much like the war that had started back home.

She glanced over at Nicholas, wondering if asking him to be here had been a bad idea. She'd wanted to see the wreckage from the fire that had broken out on the Île de la Cité the night she'd met Louise, though she wasn't exactly sure of the reason—her town having been consumed by one last year. One might wager she would rather stay away from the reminder. Nevertheless, something about the aftermath drew her in as if viewing the wreckage here somehow made her feel better about the one overseas.

Part of her felt remorse for the way she'd bruised him the other day, but this place sparked memories of a day in the past. She had no desire to hold on to what happened last October like so many in her town did, but the ashes of what remained were an ever-intrusive reminder, nonetheless.

The destruction of her town administered by the Royal Navy left many homeless, including her own family. But with the unexpected loss came an unexpected opportunity—a door opened into her aunt's life and home.

She had traded the everyday encumbrance of lonely farming for social engagements that appealed to her liking. And she had learned what it meant for her aunt to continue a respectable business after her husband had passed on into the next life with no heir to take that business over. The threshold was one she had happily walked over and was unwilling to walk back through. For that, she had harbored no ill will toward King George's navy, including Nicholas, who'd helped give the order to light the canons that day.

Nicholas stood next to her, outset in his usual blue waistcoat. His thumb flipped at a pocket watch, the lid opening and closing rhythmically telling her that while his eyes were set on the catastrophe ahead of them, his thoughts were somewhere else. No doubt something concerning his assignment or an appointment he would rather be at. The only thing the man cared about had to do with commanding orders and all things Royal Navy. Well, that was his fault. She hadn't demanded that he come, even if she would rather not be alone in the current setting.

"It looks like the chapel fared better than the rest. Most of the damage was to the north." Nicholas closed the lid a final time before disposing of the pocket watch in the interior lining of his coat.

"And the north side of the chapel," she pointed out, but he was right. God's sanctuary had escaped most of the damage.

She scanned the courtyard. Nobody seemed concerned by their interest in the gothic structure. What had once been pristine now lay in disorder—men hauling debris, stacking charred stone and splintered timber onto carts while others raised scaffolding against the wounded walls. And she hadn't come here just to see the devastation from the outside.

She nudged Nicholas, keeping her voice low. "Why don't we go inside? I'd like to take a look if you don't mind."

Without waiting for an answer, she moved toward the chapel entrance and climbed the narrow stairway to the upper level.

Her breath caught as she passed through the double doors. Stained-glass windows towered around her, basking the sanctuary in colored light. Slender columns painted in deep blues and reds drew her gaze upward to ribbed vaulting and an azure ceiling scattered with golden fleur-de-lis.

She felt almost weightless, as if her feet might lift from the ground toward the heavenly canopy above—the strain of her mission and what awaited her back home—but a vapor.

A moment later, Nicholas came up beside her, a muscle in his jaw noticeably flexed. She'd seen the look before when something hadn't gone as planned, like when their ship took on water and the crew had to act fast to stifle a leak.

"I'm not sure we're supposed to be up here."

"I don't see why not." The workers seemed too busy to care if she had stepped foot inside the sanctuary.

"You mean to tell me the crumbled building connected to this one doesn't give you pause?"

Condescension colored his tone, but he made a good point. She hadn't thought about that, though she wasn't about to tell him.

"On the contrary." She had to tilt her chin slightly upward to meet him full on. He was still a good foot above her, but she was determined to appear confident under his skeptical gaze. "I want to find out what happened and sometimes to do that, one has to get right in the thick of it."

As if in direct opposition to her movement, he lowered his chin. "What about the fact I only see a bunch of men managing the aftermath?"

She threw him a reproving look. "You mean to tell me you don't believe there's room for a woman's role in all this?"

"No. I'm saying it may not be safe, even here in God's chapel." His tone was firm but softer than she had expected it to be. "We don't know if the damage from the fire has compromised the building. Even if it's just the one side, buildings typically need all of their foundation to stand."

He appeared to search the room, though nothing in his eyes told her he had found what he was looking for. "I bet they've moved all the relics as a precaution too. If you want, I'll even go check the reliquary to prove my point." He gestured to the east side of the room where a tower stood. A slow smile began to tip at his mouth.

Delighted by both the idea to check the reliquary and what she detected was his indignation toward her subsiding, she almost let him do it. But he didn't have to. She had already read in the paper what was claimed to be a piece of the cross and the crown of thorns from Christ's crucifixion had been moved from the Sainte-Chapelle for the time being.

She didn't know if the relics were real, the possibility of a headpiece made of brambles and ancient wood were at great odds surviving over a century of a changing world, but to her that didn't matter. The tall panes of glass windows in reds, golds, blues, and greens depicting images of the Bible stirred something inside. All the stories she'd grown up hearing from her parents; her mother, were depicted around the room—Genesis to Revelation—as the sun cascaded in from the windows, each one pointing to the light of the world.

Charlotte parted her gaze from the windows of Christ, the lump of sorrow in her throat making its way down when she noticed Nicholas looking at her.

"Are you all right?"

Any hint of the irritation she'd seen earlier in his blue eyes had vanished. She was thankful for it, the moment having surprised her and how easily she had given into her grief.

Maybe it had been a mistake to come here—the place stirring up old memories—she having to sift between ones she wanted to hold onto and others she wanted to forget.

She squeezed her eyes shut, trying to curb her emotion before blinking. "I was just thinking of my mother. She would've loved this place. It's beautiful . . . even in the ashes."

"I'm sure she would've, but I also have the feeling she's getting to see a whole lot more firsthand."

She startled, having had no idea how the man felt about God. The warm smile he gave her reminded her less of his rank as captain and more of a friend. Though he hadn't been there at the time, Nicholas knew about her mother's death, and she appreciated the image he described, giving her comfort.

"Thank you, Captain. And that means more than you know." She fixed her gaze upward at the chapel windows reaching great lengths. Angels on some of them made her wonder if her mother was now among them or somewhere else in the heavens. She couldn't say the feeling was contentment, but whatever good she felt about such a dark time had been thanks to Nicholas.

She closed her eyes, shaking her head, if only to herself. *She* was supposed to be the one making amends when instead Nicholas had beat her to it.

She wiped the moisture from her eyes, finding her countenance again. "You know, I can't help but think we've gotten off to a rocky start." Remembering how the rough terrain of their relationship began, she assumed starting at the onset was as good as a place as any. "My actions on the voyage over here were no doubt unconventional compared to what you are used to. I should've left the creature to the sailors and—" She breathed in deeply, before sending a rush of air out her nose. "I should've tried to reach out about my new accommodations in Paris."

He stiffened and she could see the Royal Naval captain had returned. "You should've come to London with us as planned."

She didn't agree but she was trying to make peace. "The point is I'd like to make it up to you somehow . . . for the inconveniences of my actions."

The look he gave her read doubt that she was capable of pulling the feat off. "Really, Miss Thatcher that's not necessary."

"But it is." She stepped forward with fresh resolve. "And I won't be taking 'no' for an answer, Captain. If we're going to survive Paris together, we need to find some common ground."

His hand reached for the clean-cut hair at the back of his neck, his expression still holding doubt. "Don't take this the wrong way . . ."

Her defenses went up. Usually, when someone started the phrase 'don't take this the wrong way', they had something negative that would follow.

". . . But I don't think we could ever be successful at doing that. There's nothing you and I have in common, and I doubt there's anything you could do to 'make it up' to me, nor do I expect it."

She crossed her arms as if the man had given her a challenge rather than releasing her from an obligation. "The whole time we were touring Paris, you were off doing who knows what for the sake of your orders. The Louvre, The Tuileries, Versailles—surely, there's some place you'd like to see in this grand city while you're here. Really, Nicholas, you'd be the first visitor to Paris to not step foot into the Notre Dame cathedral."

A cool breath rushed in, she realizing she had addressed him so informally. She couldn't help it. This man unnerved her. "I'm sorry. I didn't mean to call you—"

"My Christian name?" His eyebrow lifted and if she didn't know any better, she would have guessed he was pleased by her mistake. "It's all right. I think we've known each other long enough, especially considering you tried to kill me on the *Speedy* over here."

She snickered, wanting to roll her eyes, but refraining. "You're never going to let that go, are you?"

"Something like that has a way of sticking with you."

"Fine." Another gush of air released while she pulled the fichu on her shoulders downward. "Well, you might as well do the same for me. Call me Charlotte from here on out."

He gave a single nod that was as stiff as his pressed uniform. "Noted."

Now that was settled, she wanted to get to the part of her making good on her word. "I've made a new acquaintance recently. Perhaps she can secure her seats for you at the opera."

Nicholas frowned, cutting her optimism short as well as their visit to the chapel. "Thank you for the offer, but I'm not interested." He turned to leave, crossing the room under a blue ceiling with painted stars that mimicked the night sky.

Having seen what she'd wanted to, Charlotte followed. "You mean to tell me that a man in your standing wouldn't appreciate box seats to the Théâtre du Palais-Royal?"

"I think many men in my position would, especially with you by their side, just not me." He boasted a languid smile that made her nerve pinch. "Besides, I'm not here to tour Paris. I'm here on orders."

"Really, Captain. I'm beginning to think there's nothing of interest to you other than your duties as an officer."

His jaw flexed, but she wasn't through.

Having stepped in front of him at the top of the steps to cut him off, she eyed him. "Tell me, what *exactly* are you doing that's so important for King George?"

His blue eyes deepened, nearly resembling the hue of his navy coat. "You know I can't say."

She'd expected as much. His orders didn't allow it. If a secret was meant to be kept, Captain Nicholas James Edwards was the man to trust. She wasn't about to waste her energy trying to pry the information from his iron-clad lips.

He breathed in a heavy sigh, letting air out again before giving her a bitter smile. "Why don't we speak of something else—something that can be elaborated more on?" He looked at her as if wanting to make a truce, but only on his terms. "How did it go the other night at the party? Did you meet with the nobleman?"

Having moved to the side to allow him to move forward again, she stilled a fraction to his question before forcing her foot down the first step. "I did."

"I trust that means your aunt will be pleased."

She took a few steps down the stairway, though less confidently than on the way up. "Not exactly. It seems the vicomte is going to need some persuading. The man is of a fixed opinion on some matters."

"What matters?" He grimaced.

"He's traditional when it comes to the customs of the French nobility, which I don't possess, but that's not the problem." Not while Claudine was her teacher on the subject, anyway.

"What is?"

"My bloodline." She could see he had more questions, but she was running out of answers. Yet she wasn't about to let him be privy to that. She struck her chin upward, a smile of confidence regaining its strength. "But I have a plan to remedy that. I just have to give the man the right perception."

"The right perception?" His eyes narrowed. "What's wrong with the perception you already have?"

"Nothing." Even as the word came out, she wasn't sure she believed it—her colonial fashions serving as a reminder to the slight she had committed against the man and her home he cared so little for. Her foot reached the bottom of the staircase. "It's just not what the vicomte is used to. I'm trying to get a better understanding of that and meet him where he's at. I think doing so might help persuade him."

Nicholas gave her a crosswise stare. "And where exactly are you trying to meet him, if I may ask?"

"I . . ." She stopped, his perusal knocking the words from her mouth. The man had a way of being commanding while somehow polite at the same time.

"Mademoiselle Thatcher. How good it is to see you again, though I must admit, also a surprise to do so in this place."

Though startled, Charlotte welcomed the interruption to Nicholas's constant pursuit, even when the look he gave her conveyed their conversation wasn't over.

"Monsieur Girard."

Laurent Girard had met them at the foot of the stairway they'd just come down. The man's tone today, despite the cordial smile he gave her was decidingly less friendly than at the party. He was accompanied by a gentleman wearing a modest peruke and a coat that matched his waistcoat in a muted shade of green.

"The surprise is likewise, but also a good one. I wanted to see the damage for myself. Is it unsafe for us to be in here?" She looked more toward the man with a leather-bound notebook and readied quill in his hand, an inkling he might have the answer.

"No, mademoiselle." The man she had addressed smiled, pointing the feather tip of his quill at the aftermath. "As you can see, the fire did not completely leave the chapel unscathed, but most of the structural damage is to the north side of the church."

Following the man's quill, she turned her head to the north side where the Grand Chamber in the old palace was located. That made her consider Laurent's reason for being here.

"Monsieur Girard, I'm told you hold a seat in Parliament."

Laurent drew his head back, a gleam in his eye showing surprise to the subject but also pleasure with the mention of the topic. "You have done your research while here in Paris, Mademoiselle Thatcher. Do you hold an interest in politics?"

Hardly on both accounts. Her aunt had disclosed the small detail when describing the party's host in her letter.

"The north side." She tilted her head to a part of the building displaying broken windows, their broken frames above blackened stonework. "That's where you meet. Am I right?"

"In ordinary circumstances, you would be. The Parlement of Paris has met there since the 14th century, but for the time being we will have to move to an alternate location." The clearing of his throat was distinct as he gestured to the man beside him. "This is Pierre-Antione Renaud, the architect hired to provide an assessment of the damage and to propose his opinion to what should be done as far as the fate of the building is concerned."

Charlotte put her attention back on the architect. "And what do you propose, monsieur?"

The man had made a few notes in his ledger before the quill stopped in his hand. "I have not finished my evaluation, mademoiselle, but I do believe the building can be rebuilt with time. I have some modifications to suggest, but these will ultimately be decided by His Majesty." The architect looked down his nose through the middle of his notebook, adding before she could inquire further, "and will be discussed *privately* with His Majesty."

"You must excuse us, but there is still much more for Monsieur Renaud to evaluate before we can take his proposal to Versailles." Even in his polite phrasing, Charlotte heard the same punch to the message by the architect conveyed in Laurent's tone.

Feeling like she'd been put in a place beneath these two men, Charlotte let her silence slip between them. She glanced at Nicholas in his Royal Navy attire, wondering if their mistrust was aimed at her or more at her companion. Perhaps it was simply protocol or the simple fact she was a woman unafraid to make such inquiries of men. It wouldn't be the first time she'd caught the male sex off guard by her boldness to get answers . . . or the last. One thing was clear, these men were ready to part ways, their backs already turned away from she and Nicholas.

Nicholas offered nothing, his prolonged silence telling her he was content to let the men move on. And she would have let the matter conclude there, but there was one more thing she had to know. A venture of resurrecting a building so grand would cost a grand sum and money did not flow from the skies. If it had, satisfying the vicomte and her aunt would be of no consequence.

She cleared her throat toward the Frenchmen. "Of course, gentlemen." The two men turned back to face her, she reading impatience in both sets of eyes. "We'll leave you to your task. But there is just one more question I'd like to ask of you and then we'll be on our way." She didn't wait for them to interject this time. "Does the King of France have the means by which the building can be reconstructed?"

"He has the means, but the course for the project will be set the same way as it always is, Miss Thatcher—" Laurent boasted a confident smile, but not one she liked in this moment. "—by the French people."

***

Leaving the Sainte-Chapelle, Charlotte felt an emptiness inside, like something had been taken away from her. She knew exactly what Laurent meant—the final tipping point that had ignited the war in her own home. Taxes.

Here, she wasn't the one impacted by an increase on tax, but Louise and her mother would be, along with so many of the poor in the city. After the past two years of bad grain harvests and increased cost of bread, the news was hard to digest—her friends helping to fund a project for a building they hadn't and may never enter.

The moldy loaf of bread she'd eaten at the dentelle came to mind. Louise and her mother didn't have enough for kosher food, let alone to pay for a building they might not ever use. The very notion didn't seem fair.

"I can't help but notice you're more quiet than usual since we left the chapel." They were across the bridge from the Île de la Cité when Nicholas spoke, half-startling her from her thoughts. "When we first arrived, I had the impression you were hoping the building could be saved. They're going to rebuild the palace and refurbish the church. Some might say that's good news."

She shook her head, following his line of sight back to the building they'd just come from—a remnant of so much history. "I'm glad the buildings will be restored, just not of the methods that will be used to restore them. It will be harder for Louise and her mother with the added burden."

Nicholas drew in a slow breath and nodded. "I think that's how it's usually done with these things. The people have a shared system—everyone contributes."

The concept seemed fair and didn't at the same time. The people shared in the responsibility, yet not everyone benefited.

Anger stung at the corner of her eyes. "And why not the king? Laurent said he had enough means." She had half a mind to say as much if she ever got the chance to visit Versailles.

"Take it easy. I admire your desire for justice, but you're not going to make anything better for Louise storming into the palace."

And she wanted to make things better for Louise, not worse. Maybe this once, Nicholas was right. She wasn't so sure she could change French policy, but maybe there was a way she could change things for Louise and her mother. She just had to figure out how.

Chapter 9

The woman stared at Charlotte from the canvas, her silk, gray dress draping over a chair to expose only a quarter of its red, velvet exterior. Strands of beading decorated hair arranged in a fashionable pouf reminiscent of, though not to the height as the one Charlotte donned at the opera. Still, the way she was able to extend her neck while looking relaxed was impressive. On her lap was a small brown and white spaniel-type dog equally posed to its owner—both subjects holding an elegant closed smile.

Having spent most of her life on a farm, Charlotte knew the way of animals. Even the trained of them had attention spans that were sure to wander eventually. Couple that with the time she imagined such a portrait took to complete, and it begged the question of whether the final product had come so naturally or if the artist had done the woman and her paired pooch a favor.

"That's the Duchesse de Brienne and her canine friend, Maximilien." Marc came up beside her, glancing at the painting she'd been looking at in his apartment. "She got the dog last year from her husband and is very fond of it. The animal goes everywhere she does. Unlike its owner, the pup is young." A sharp puff of air came out through his nose. "It kept wanting to jump down and go sniffing around the place. Took me four sittings to get the picture how she wanted it."

"I wouldn't have guessed. Every part of it looks perfect." Even the woman's skin held no blemish or wrinkles, making it difficult for Charlotte to determine how old the Duchesse de Brienne really was.

"Good. The duke will be pleased then." He tipped his head, a teasing glint in his eye. "At least about the painting. With all the attention she's giving that little dog, I wonder if he regrets the decision of getting the canine." Dark eyes drew their attention away from the canvas and onto her, his body moving in a way that allowed her to glimpse a word written on the bottom corner of the portrait. No. Not a word. A name. *Chazot.*

"Does it do well to convince you to have one of yourself completed?"

She could hear the flirtation in his tone and thought about the opera when he first threw the idea out, wondering then if he'd truly meant the offer. Now, it seemed he had.

"I haven't decided yet."

In truth, the idea of having herself painted by a local artist, and one with talent at that, was tempting. Beyond obtaining the business deal with the Vicomte de Vantinelle, having her picture captured in such an artistic way would have made the trip all the more complete.

And there was no doubt Marc could portray her well. She casted a subtle glance back at the painting of the duchesse and her little dog— perhaps even better than her true self. But she couldn't ignore the voice inside her head telling her to tread carefully where he was concerned.

Then again, she'd made a mistake—an unfounded assumption of his character. She thought again of their conversation at the opera, wanting to see more of his work. Instead, blank canvases lined the walls.

"What about the other women you've painted? Where are they? I'd like to see them."

"I imagine hanging on a wall in their mansions where they can be easily noticed and gloated upon. They have an annoying habit of keeping themselves distracted from real issues of Paris with their constant need to impress each other." His tone was sarcastic before a sigh dissipated some of his annoyance. "But I respect that you want to see more. I have a few others I can show you. There is one I am willing to bet you will recognize the subject of." He tipped a smile before leaving the room, returning momentarily with another large canvas.

He was right. She did recognize the subject. "Claudine." Charlotte looked back at him. Why this painting had been tucked away roused her curiosity. "But why is it here? Why not on a wall or above a fireplace?"

"Because if it was, my friends would think I was quite in love with myself." Claudine entered Marc's studio with a floral dress less elaborate than Charlotte had seen her in for the opera, but no less captivating on her graceful frame. She was followed by a man in a rich, dark fabric who had opened the door to Marc's apartment upon their arrival. "I already have two and that is more than enough."

"Not when your brother is a painter." Marc snatched a slice of brie from a tray of cheeses and breads the servant deposited on a working table and took a bite. He gave her a closed-mouth smile before swallowing the food down. "As for my other work, not everybody has a taste for it, but you are welcome take a look."

When Charlotte nodded that she would, Marc disappeared from the room. He was gone several minutes when Claudine had stepped out to tell the servant they would require refreshments to compliment the pastries while they waited.

She wasn't alone long when Marc returned, producing several portraits on canvases smaller than the larger one of the duchesse and her canine and also . . . very different.

Charlotte still couldn't keep her mouth from gaping at the sight of each one. Their subjects, Parisians, but not conveyed in the glamour she'd grown used to at the opera and hoped to still see at Versailles.

They were the city's rat catcher, leaning against his long stick where lifeless rats hung like trophies from his day's work. Another portrait depicted the watercarrier, his legs buckling under the weight of two full buckets. Yet another showed the lantern lighter, carrying his ladder and the long pole he used to light the streetlamps at dusk. But it was the image of a woman carrying a tray of nuts and utensils, a child clinging to the folds of her dress, that stilled her heart.

The subjects of these were not elegant or even clean for that matter and lacked every sense of propriety to aristocratic life. But their imperfection—their *realness* summoned emotion within her that hadn't existed when she'd looked at the poised portraits of the duchesse and Claudine.

"Are they real?" She wanted to put her hand out as if to touch them, but refrained, reluctantly shifting her gaze to Marc. "Real people, I mean." She could hardly look away, still feeling moved by their plight and by whether they even realized it was being put down so permanently.

"Very." Marc produced a subtle lift to his chin. "With the nobility I have to be more selective of what I choose to detail and what not to. With these I can paint what I see—what I feel like needs to be seen but is often neglected." His eyes narrowed. "Or even worse, ignored. In the words of Voltaire, 'It is not sufficient to see the beauty of a work. We must feel and be affected by it.' In this way I intend to bring about change in my city—through the means of stirring emotion."

"You like them, no?"

His tone told her he'd already known her answer, but he couldn't have been correct, not when she barely knew for herself.

"What makes you think so?" The paintings were intriguing, but they certainly weren't anything she'd hang up on her own wall to display if given the chance.

"Most of the nobles that have seen this part of my portfolio are appalled by the work. However, their reactions are not driven by desire to help the wretched soul depicted or enact social change, but rather an inconvenience to their expectations." He gave her a pointed look, his tone hinting at satisfaction. "Your reaction was different, more of what I hope to captivate by those who see it. That certainly tells me something."

"To be fair, I'm not a noble."

"No, you are not." Despite the lengths taken to make her look like one at the opera, his expression remained unchanged, telling her the declaration hadn't come as a surprise. "So why the charade at the opera? I am told the colonists do not hold their fashions at such—" His gaze moved to the top of her head where the coiffure from the opera had been replaced by a powdered updo. "—heights as we French like to do."

She felt her guard go up. "Perhaps I thought it would be fun—to partake in French custom." She'd never thought of her night at the opera as a charade.

"And was it . . . fun?"

"I enjoyed the theatre." She let the truth come out freely. The stunning view of the stage and the use of Claudine's borrowed dress were highlights of the evening to be sure. But not all the night's activities had been to her liking. In truth, she still had a burn mark on the back of her head where the coiffeur's curling rod had singed her hair. And even now comfortable enough in her normal set of stays, she cringed at the over tightly strung ones of that night.

Though not fully understanding his aim, Marc's series of questions made her feel like she was being pushed in a direction she didn't want to go. Little did he know she wasn't the type to be pushed around so easily.

"Well, you're right about the paintings." She swept her hand across them, spotting the letters of Marc's signature again. Chazot. "These are my favorite."

"Don't let anyone outside of this apartment hear you say that, mon amie." Claudine's rebuke came through the threshold as she walked back into the studio with Marc's servant trailing behind her again, though this time carrying a tray bearing a silver pot and porcelain cups. The smell of coffee filled the room.

"My sister is one of the ones that doesn't hold a taste for this type of expression." Marc revealed a bemused smile. "Although she didn't always feel that way."

"That is because you were first starting out." Claudine's response came out almost as a reprimand while Marc's servant poured her a cup of the hot beverage. "You needed subjects to pose for you and I didn't have the time to keep being one of them. But now—" Adding a drop of cream, her mouth pinched toward the paintings of the street hawkers. "Despite having a name for yourself, you keep at these pictures when you don't have to."

"But that is where you are wrong, sister. I do have to." A vein along the stretch of Marc's neck became visible. "The poor wretches' voices are not heard by our class's trivialities, so I must tell their story. It is my duty to my country even if fate has assigned me a noble birth."

"All I know is that one day this could get you in trouble if the wrong persons caught sight of what you're doing." Claudine placed the delicate cup on one of the worktables, the movement poised even under her stiff tone. She used a serviette, dabbing the cloth napkin gently at the corners of her mouth where a frown had formed. "Some of the nobles, especially the monarchy, don't appreciate something so radical."

"It's not radical if it's really what's going on, Claude."

Claudine folded her hands gently in her lap while meeting her brother's sharp rebuttal with unflinching dignity. "I just want you to be careful. That is all. Your work could be misconstrued to follow opinions of thinkers like Voltaire and Rousseau. Let me ask you this question." Her tone was soft and measured. "What happened to them?"

Marc returned his sister's concern with a condescending sneer. "I believe Rousseau has since returned to Paris and Voltaire lies comfortably in his estate in Ferney where he uses his sharp wit to advocate for justice and reform."

"Yes." Claudine gave a slow nod, though the depth of her tone told Charlotte she'd hardly agreed with Marc's view of the outcome. "But only after they were exiled from the city, Voltaire even imprisoned for his *sharp wit* criticizing our government and the aristocracy." She raised from the chair, evidently having said as much as she wanted to her brother over the topic. "Come on, Charlotte." Her tone held no room for objection, though Charlotte had none to give. "I believe you have had a chance to see enough of my brother's work to judge whether you would like to be a subject of it or not."

***

When prolonged silence had rattled the inside of Claudine's carriage long enough, Charlotte was the first to speak. "Marc's paintings are excellent. He truly has a gift."

Claudine gave a small, fleeting smile. "My brother has always held a passion for his work. He would do well with what he loves if he would just put his other passions to rest. He is dedicated to the French people—a just cause, but he exclaims their struggles with an untamed tongue." Her last words were pointed, not so much with criticism, but what Charlotte sensed as worry. "I have already had to intervene on his behalf from arguments made among different acquaintances of the nobility, but there will be a day when my efforts to keep my brother out of prison, or worse, will no longer matter." She seemed to study her hands, folded genteelly in her lap before casting a look of caution Charlotte's way. "You would be wise to be careful, Charlotte. Marc holds a zeal when it comes to his cause. He often forgets he comes from a family born of gentility."

The carriage bounced them down the rough city streets, Charlotte having heard the echo of warning in Claudine's tone. Marc's cause was one she agreed to be well-founded if done in the right way. And she had to admit, she could relate with his untamed tongue. How many times had her own words—true as they were and as right as she felt about them—been coarse and bitter rather than gentle and seasoned to taste? She'd been in her fair share of trouble with little to show as far as a desirable outcome was concerned.

Claudine's carriage slowed into a gradual halt. Charlotte glanced out the window where they'd been forced to stop behind a pile of crates that had fallen off the wagon in front of them.

In the time it took for their driver to help reload the crates and return to his post, Charlotte was able to witness an artist who had set up his easel overlooking a double alley lined on each side with chestnut trees. On them, the colors of autumn appeared, the trees beginning to resemble to her a fire of torches lighting up the street both on canvas and in real life.

Her mind's eye went back to her visit to Marc's apartment and the smaller paintings. They were void of any life or beauty of the aristocracy, though she still saw beauty in them—Paris's poor not caring to be noticed, yet nevertheless captured by the artist.

Unlike the street hawkers, and according to Marc and her own experience at the opera, the nobility had an affinity to be noticed, not that she could blame them. She, too, preferred the center stage than the seats of the audience.

Marc claimed their portraits were displayed for all to see, especially by their peers in their lavish estates—Versailles their only superior.

Her breath caught as the idea struck.

Charlotte clung at the velvet upholstered seat beneath her, the thought nearly overwhelming her at what prospect it could bring—what difference the plan could make. Maybe not all the difference, but surely some. The only problem was that she needed to speak with the king and queen of France to make her idea come into fruition.

"Is there something wrong, Charlotte?"

The carriage started moving again when Charlotte noticed Claudine staring at her hands now clutched to the seat, her knuckles having turned white around her billowed skirts. "No, I'm fine. But I was thinking . . ." She released her grip on the cushion, the wheels inside her mind having already turned and come to rest. "When can we make a trip to Versailles?"

Chapter 10

Charlotte flicked at the white ostrich plume as the feather drooped over her eyes and swept across her forehead. Her chest beat at two-fold speed. She couldn't decipher whether to attribute her heart's manic rhythm to nerves or excitement, but both held significant reasons to win out.

After missing her chance on their tour, she was now finally able to see the great palace of Versailles. She had Claudine to thank for that and for the allowance to let her borrow the dress from the night at the opera again. She did, however, decline the long pins that pinched her scalp to accomplish the popular coiffure of French court. She couldn't be distracted by the throbbing on her head when so much depended on today going right.

"Spectacular, is it not?" The Comtesse d'Amboise, one of the women Claudine had introduced Charlotte to at the opera, tamed the sweat that threatened a sheen to the white powder on her face with a quick flicking motion of an embellished fan. Even as the autumn air carried a cool breeze outside, the room with the mass of people congregating in anticipation indoors remained overly warm. "The hall has over 350 mirrors. Quite the expense. Though crafted here in Paris, it is rumored tradesmen from Venice were hired to create them for this specific room."

The one, small and blemished looking glass they kept in their house in Massachusetts did little to compare to such luxury. The Galerie de Glaces—the Hall of Mirrors—appropriately named so, reflected not only the opulence of the gilding throughout the hall and painted ceiling but also the light from seventeen arched windows proudly outlooking an equally impressive garden.

"The king and queen will enter through there." Charlotte trailed Claudine's gaze past the crowd of noble men and women to a pair of gilded doors that presently remained shut. "They'll come through on their way to Mass."

The flutter Charlotte had already been feeling in her stomach unleashed into a full swarm. An opportunity she'd hoped for. If she was to speak with the king and queen about her plan, now was her chance.

Preparing her body for what she was about to do—determined it wouldn't fail her—she tried to breathe in deeply. But the measure of her breath was cut short, Claudine's lady's maid having pulled the stays over tightly against her ribcage.

Another unsatisfied breath escaped without properly refreshing her. She was used to bindings to accentuate her figure, but the way Claudine insisted they were worn at French court was constricting—the whalebone structure pressing into her lungs and chest, while her back remained stiff by the self-restraint.

"Oh, Claudine, we still have time before the procession. You must show Mademoiselle Charlotte the way you glide across the floor." The comtesse brought the eloquent fan to her painted lips, ceasing the back-and-forth snap motion. "Claudine is well-known for her grace in the act. Many argue she does the walk better than the queen herself and Her Majesty was taught by none other than Jean-Georges Noverre, the ballet master."

"Marie Antionette has not had the benefit of a French noble upbringing, that is all. Her childhood was spent in the place of her home in Vienna." Claudine sighed, flipping her fan with less vigor than the comtesse. "But if I must . . ." She gave an expression that portrayed half annoyance, while the other half looked as if she took pleasure by the request.

The comtesse swept her fan in the air over the wood parquet floor, a gesture telling Charlotte to make room while others did the same in the already cramped hall.

Having latched her fan, Claudine stepped out into the cleared space and all maquillaged faces in the Galerie des Glaces watched with delightful expressions as the woman moved forward in both a perplexing and astonishing way.

If she hadn't seen Claudine's slippers put on her feet at her estate, Charlotte would have sworn the woman was on wheels. The feat was one of the most graceful things she'd ever seen—to move with such lightness like she was hovering over the floor—as if the smallest gap of air separated her feet from the surface of the earth.

She had always thought her mother had a grace about her. Every movement—somehow unintentional—was soft and done with a tenderness Charlotte remembered well. But this was altogether new and remarkable.

Claudine's, she suspected, came more from her agility and finesse. The Versailles Glide—the name Charlotte now knew from whispers around her—her tutor made look effortless. Then again, how effortless could it be to make one appear as if they were floating on clouds?

With continued amazement, Charlotte watched as Claudine completed a walk under a long, vaulted ceiling depicting images of monarchial achievements and crystal chandeliers before finding a place again with Charlotte and the comtesse. The crowd, a sea of satin and brocade, applauded, while Claudine relinquished a smile with the most aristocratic satisfaction.

When the nobles rejoined their conversations in the grand gallery, Charlotte was more than ready to give her own compliments. "I've never seen anything like that before. You looked like you were floating."

"That is the idea." Claudine combed the surface of the parquet with her arm before pointing to her slippers underneath her dress. "To look as if one is gliding upon the surface when in fact, it is but a trick of the feet."

Movement took place around them, and the crowd began to separate again, this time the entire assembly of nobles. When the rustling of silk and brocade gowns and men's heeled shoes settled, Charlotte found herself with Claudine and the comtesse by one of the windows of the hallway overlooking the gardens. A strong silence filled the room with anticipation—every pair of eyes drawn to the entryway, including her own.

King Louis Auguste stepped through the double doors first, his tall, stocky frame wearing an apricot-colored silk suit embroidered with gold threading. Merely inches behind him, Marie Antoinette followed, her voluminous set of panniers looking like two large balloons tucked under each side of her hip. A stream of sunlight coming through the large windows made the matching gems to the paler hue of her husband's fashions sparkle in her powdered pouf while the king's own suit dazzled under the chandeliers.

Charlotte might have been transfixed by the pair if it had not been for what followed them.

"Why so many?" Charlotte whispered the question out loud, unable to pull her gaze from the colorful procession of nobles that flanked the royal couple from each side.

"They are all part of the king and queen's entourage. They are there to help."

"To help?" Flabbergasted, she turned to the comtesse, who had been her source of information. "But what could they all possibly do for one person?"

"Some are part of the majesties' morning ceremony for getting ready—their levee. The higher-ranked nobles have the honor to attend. Other nobles have since joined him and there are also the valets and guards." The comtesse made a small nod with her head at each group she spoke of while they proceeded down the hallway.

Charlotte's heartbeat climbed, pounding against the unyielding fabric of her corset. Another effort to breathe in deeply to calm her nerves and condition provided little satisfaction. Apart from paintings, she'd never seen royalty in person, much less occupied the same room as one before. There was no king or queen in the colonies, not yet anyway. And the matter remained uncertain if there ever would be.

She pressed her lips together to prevent them from opening too wide, wondering if she should mask her awe of such splendor. Not so much of the persons themselves—Louis Auguste with his rounded chin and blue eyes that exhibited more of a kind, shy nature than a proud king, and Marie Antionette whose grand panniers were a stark contrast to her petite figure—but at the power these two had over so many. Even in this very room where the richest of France resided, she could sense a reverence while also an earnestness as if hoping for perhaps a glance, or some sort of acknowledgment by the young royal couple.

They were halfway down the hall, the distance between Charlotte and the monarchs shortening along with what might be her only chance. She looked for an opening, though finding none—her only hesitation recalling Claudine's briefing of the ceremony and the expectation to keep a distance from the royal couple. They were so close. A few steps and some maneuvering on her part and she'd be able to reach out and touch the lace trimming at the queen's elbows—an idea she ventured Claudine would be appalled by. Despite not wanting to offend her tutor on court custom, Charlotte felt a corner of her mouth raise. She didn't need to touch them, only to speak with them.

"Pardon, Your Majesties." Certain she'd broken a rule that concerned her stepping out of the formation of nobles lining each side of the hallway by opting for the dead-center, Charlotte remembered to keep her head bowed. Maybe Claudine would give her credit for that. She even curtsied for added measure. In the corner of her eye, a guard hurried toward her, telling her she needed to act.

In her haste, the notion she had picked up from Aunt Sylvia to always look a customer in the eye overruled Versailles etiquette and her gaze met blue eyes nearly the same age as her own in the young queen.

"I was hoping to ask you . . . about the rebuilding of the Palais de Justice and the . . . Sainte Chapelle."

Charlotte tried to take a breath, but the air flow was weak and forced. Not now. She couldn't waste this moment. She had already interrupted the ritual. She might not get another opportunity.

She willed a controlled breath out, wishing she'd left her head bowed to better hide the struggle from her face.

"In fact—" The words faltered as her chest tightened again. "I believe . . . I have an idea . . . that may help the people."

"The people, mademoiselle?"

Charlotte thought she glimpsed a flicker of a smile beginning to form on the queen's rouged lips. Encouraged by the lightness of the monarch's tone, she was about to voice, as best she could, her plan when a force around her arm gripped tight.

The beating inside her chest grew rampant as if trying to break free from her ribcage. The room tilted. Sound around her dulled. She gasped, but the air wouldn't come fast enough as she was pulled backward, away from the royals and the moment she had nearly claimed.

She somehow seized a breath as the stranger's hand continued to pull her into the aristocratic assembly. No. Not a stranger—not entirely.

The Vicomte de Vantinelle kept a firm hold onto her arm, seizing her from the procession as the floor remained unsteady under her feet.

Through blurry vision, she saw the king and queen resume their ceremony down the Hall of Mirrors. And though all eyes should've been on them, more than she liked at this particular moment were now on her, including those of the vicomte.

***

"Ma chère, are you all right, Charlotte?"

As soon as the royal procession was over, Claudine and the Comtesse d'Amboise hurried Charlotte to the palace gardens outside.

"I . . . think . . . so." And she was. Though her waist and lungs remained under their French constraints, her heartbeat had returned to a steady rhythm.

"You nearly collapsed in the middle of the gallery."

Charlotte heard the concern in Claudine's voice quickly melt away.

"As if your other rash display was not enough. What were you thinking in there?" She didn't wait for Charlotte to give her defense. "Speaking to the king and queen of France when not spoken to? I specifically addressed that on our way from Paris, did I not?"

She had, the long carriage ride from Paris giving ample time to cover the rules of Versailles. "You did." Taking in quick, shallow breaths, Charlotte tried to coax the air back into her lungs. "And I'm sorry, but there was something I had to ask them. I was afraid another occurrence like that wouldn't come."

"Let's hope not." Though dignified, the scolding in Claudine's expression and tone was evident. "Well—" Claudine's lips pursed with agitation, the two thin brows above her eyes now elevated. "Did you get your answer?"

Charlotte met her tutor's gaze fleetingly, angry at her body's disobedience. "No, I didn't." She hadn't disclosed her plan before she'd been pulled back into the crowd.

Claudine gave a short song of laughter, shaking her head. "You are certainly bold, Miss Thatcher. To that I give you credit. But see to it you do better to mind the etiquette of French court. I was the one that brought you here so that you may speak with the vicomte, *not* the king and queen." The woman's gaze was penetrating. "Do not make me regret that decision."

Without another word, Claudine slipped away with the comtesse, the two taking a path down the middle of two large rectangular pools, each framed by bronze figurines and without an invitation to join them. Charlotte could hardly blame her. She hadn't thought about how her brazen decision might affect Claudine and her reputation—one she offered to use to not only see the palace but help her in pursuit of the vicomte's favor. And after reading the disproval on the man's face earlier along with the rest of those in attendance in the Hall of Mirrors, she questioned whether his approval was even attainable.

"I see you have already made quite the impression on your first visit to Versailles."

Marc came alongside her where she had forged her own path along a different walkway from where she'd seen Claudine and the comtesse begin their promenade.

"And whatever gave you that idea?" She knew he was talking about what happened in the Hall of Mirrors, but his comment made her look around, only to be disappointed, though not surprised—stares still lingering from her outburst.

"I admit, it is the first time I've seen such a crowd find more interest in someone else other than the royal family."

She sighed, aware of the whispers being exchanged behind embellished fans. "So, how bad was it?"

"If you're asking whether you are no longer welcome at Versailles by the king and queen, rest assured." His friendly candor put her at ease until he took her arm into his own like the night he had done at the opera. It wasn't that she was opposed to the small gesture of kinship, only the way he continued to presume she didn't mind.

"If they wanted you gone, your presence here even on the grounds would not be permitted. Lucky for me, that is not the case." A rueful smile took shape as he led her down a path that opened into a grand fountain. "My sister, however, is who you should be more concerned about. There is a certain image held here at court—an expectation—established by the monarchy predating the one who currently holds the throne."

She could already deduce by his tone that he felt he didn't belong in the same grouping.

He glanced upward at the fountain portraying a mother and her two children receiving shoots of water from peasants and animals below as if they were the only ones worthy to receive the true elixir of life. "Many of the nobles, my sister included, will attest the system is to set us apart from the common French people. And though I admit there is truth to that, I believe it is more for the monarchy to keep their subjects in line—busy worrying about the rules and extreme expense of the fashions so they must continue to be in Their Majesties' good graces to afford such frivolity and acceptance. Just a word or glance from the king can make or destroy one's future."

"For not holding the monarchy with the same esteem as your sister, you still seem to partake in its privileges easily enough." She gave him a daring look, her incident in the hall well behind her. "You're here, aren't you?"

"I come here on occasion because of Claudine. Though, if you have not ruined my sister's opinion of you, I am inclined to come more often." His wry smile slowly faded. "As I said before, there is a certain expectation. If I didn't make an appearance every now and then, there might be suspicion as to why. Stay long enough and you will find word spreads around in court almost as quickly as fire."

"Is that why you paint? Because you're tired of all the magnificent fashions and parties?" She couldn't seem to help the sarcasm from coming out in her tone.

"I paint because I can speak my mind in my work without ever having to say anything with my mouth." She felt his arm tense within her own, his stare boring a hole right through her. "Unlike the Vicomte de Vantinelle you seek out, my proximity to the king is not close enough to declare such opinions. But a picture can say many things, even when I cannot."

The canvases of the street hawkers came into her mind's eye. So much told in their eyes like she could read their story, their plight. She might've asked Marc more about them—if he'd spoken to them on top of crafting their image. But thinking of the street hawkers and their daily jobs brought up a subject she'd heard about but had yet to confirm. The idea of work.

"Is it true you cannot work as a noble?"

"That is one of the 'privileges.'" She could detect a bitterness to the last word. "The law forbodes it. To be seen as dependent on work of any type is beneath a noble's standing."

Words that came out more rehearsed than heartfelt and ones she couldn't say she agreed with either. She hadn't liked working on the farm, true, but that didn't mean she didn't think work was something to be disregarded or an expectation put solely on the lowly. Even with her dislike of farm work, she'd found value in the activity, providing not only food to eat, but purpose.

"What about painting?" She'd seen plenty of Parisians relying on their talent to feed their stomachs.

He nodded as if he'd suspected the question was coming. "To pursue the arts is encouraged for one's refinement and prestige, but to cross the line—out of necessity rather than interest, then yes, even painting can be a cause to the loss of status."

The gravel crunched under their boots as they walked along manicured hedges and ornate marble statues that lined the path. Another question came to her mind and what she was doing here. "Then what about the Vicomte de Vantinelle? If what you say is true, how can he conduct business and not be penalized?"

"It is hard to say if credit belongs to the king or his advisors for the change, but His Majesty made an edict in March of this year concerning the nobility and approved nuances for which they may engage without fear of penalty." His free hand waved in the air as if warding off concern he'd wished to keep at a distance. "I do not know the details of the vicomte's dealings, only that he does not deal with goods or his customers directly. Though involved, his removed position deems the market acceptable by the Crown."

A position she didn't understand and was a straight contradiction to another aspect of Aunt's Sylvia's advice to business operation. To not be engaged with one's customers to better understand their needs and build trust seemed like a poor business venture. How many times had she seen her aunt do just that to form trust with her customers until the war when the colonists' division questioned her aunt's loyalties? Again, the idea for why her aunt would choose such a man for a partnership was beyond her understanding.

The very subject of her inquiry caught her view, walking in step with Laurent Girard along the path. The two men were still several feet from her and Marc, but their closing proximity sent a chill of anticipation up her spine.

She needed to speak with the vicomte—apologize and then relay her aunt's wishes of an alliance. Perhaps now that she had gone to such efforts to remind him less of her homeland and more of his own, he might be more inclined to hear what she had to say. Or, remembering he had been present for her recent scene in the palace, maybe not. Either way, she had to try.

"Monsieur Vantinelle, might I have a word?" Without allowing him opportunity for rejection, she quickly explained. "I'd like to apologize for my words at our last meeting. I promise it wasn't my aim to make an offense—only to speak my mind."

"I believe you accomplished that task quite well, mademoiselle." The vicomte's remark was void of flattery. "From that evening and what I recently witnessed here at court, you seem to hold little regard for restraint."

His face hardened. "I can already see your motivation is to pursue your aunt's lumber business tying into mine. I am an acquaintance of Sylvia. The woman is charming and no doubt commendable with how she has handled her husband's business for all these years since his death, but I have yet to make such a high opinion of you."

Charlotte's throat closed tight, hardly knowing how to respond.

"I take it you are enjoying a respite from the rest of the court's spotlight?" Laurent broke the tension, though his tone lacked any true compliment. There was a gleam in his eye—one telling.

Charlotte understood the man plainly, he was referring to her own incident in the Hall of Mirrors even if he didn't say so outright.

Wanting to squash the flame of her embarrassment once and for all, Charlotte set the conversation on a different trajectory. "Has the king met with Monsieur Renaud?"

Her question to Laurent concerning the architect from the Palace on the Île de la Cité and Saint-Chapelle was met with a dismissive nod. "Oui. He met with the king this morning and the plan has been approved. Once the demolition is complete, the rebuilding will commence and the Palais de la Cité will be returned to its glory."

Emotions inside reared up in opposition. To see the ancient building restored was something she hoped for, but at the expense of Louise and her mother, and all those who fell short of the nobility was not.

She'd missed her opportunity in the Hall of Mirrors to suggest a different plan, and most likely would not get a second one. Except—

That was the thing about opportunity. Sometimes the right moment presented itself without warning. One couldn't always predict when that moment arrived, but they could be willing. So, when the queen of France strolled past them on a parallel walkway with only two of her courtiers as opposed to a dozen, Charlotte didn't think twice.

Chapter 11

Nicholas walked through the city streets of Paris. The letter he had tucked inside his breast-coat pocket earlier felt more like an iron bar sinking into his chest. Another failed attempt with a bonus of his pending defiance. Strange to think that his father somehow held more power with the sway in his decision than the king of all England did.

His hands clenched at his sides as he walked, thinking about what King George would do when he found out Nicholas had re-entered London without completing his assignment. His rank was certainly at stake, but the probable demotion didn't bother him as much as he thought it might. The only part that raised alarm was how his father might view his possible demotion—or worse, how it might affect the man's reputation in the highlight of his career.

Something lurched in his stomach at the idea. Yet, not to go to his father's celebration as his only son seemed far worse for the same reasons.

He was proud of his father, even if their relationship was nowhere close to where he had hoped it would be by now. Perhaps this was another chance to move it in a more positive direction. If he could just do one more thing to prove himself—one more chance—that might be enough.

The freshly painted wood sign of the dentelle came into view and the heaviness in his chest lightened a little. He hadn't seen Charlotte since they visited the Sainte-Chapelle. He could tell by the way they'd left that conversation, there was something on her mind that she meant to get to the bottom of. That was fine. He'd been busy with his own problems, but he had followed through with the plan he'd laid out, making sure she'd arrived at the boardinghouse each night. So far, she had.

"Are you in the market to buy some lace, monsieur?" The voice, rather than the question, further lessened the load in his chest. The pleasant tone he'd normally attribute to Louise was directed at him and he found he liked it.

"It's not just for women, you know." Charlotte smiled at him from across a table where she sat with an opened book and quill in hand. She'd made the remark with a flair he'd heard some of the local women in the city use. Her French was getting better. He would've told her as much, but by the confident twinkle in her eye, he was sure she already knew.

"I'm aware." He'd seen as much at Versailles with some of the noblemen attaching lace to their collar like a cravat, or to their sleeves, sometimes both. "Not really my style."

He glanced at Louise, who was working on a lace pattern while an older woman who shared her coloring was arranging finished pieces around the shop. Though lighter, the weight still in his breast pocket reminded him of the reason he'd come.

"I stopped by to let you know I'll be leaving for London at the end of the week."

"You're going to London?" The quill froze, then dipped, spattering a blot of ink across a page. Charlotte looked at him, eyebrows drawn together, as if wondering if he'd planned to take her with him.

To her credit, he'd thought about it. He could deliver her right to her sister so he could better focus on things here upon his return.

The idea enticed, but considering what she was doing for Louise and her mother, he thought better of the scheme. At least she seemed to be doing some good. He couldn't say the same for himself.

"Relax. You don't have to come with me." He almost added, "unless you want to," half-hoping she'd say she would, but the tight line her mouth had formed earlier stopped him. He settled for a broad grin. "Not this time anyway."

As if obeying his previous command to be at ease—though he knew better—the lace shawl around her shoulders slipped slightly as she released a breath.

She deposited the quill into an ink bottle, her lips forming into a tiny smile as if to say, "we'll see."

"Then what takes you to London, if I may ask?" A single brow perched high with inquisition. "Or is that confidential, like everything else about you?"

He brushed the comment aside for the fact Louise and her mother were present in the room and knowing it wasn't true. The only thing confidential about his life was his current assignment. She was trying to get under his skin. The effort was wasted, his mind more focused on other matters.

"It's not. My father has been promoted to admiral." He slid his hand into his coat pocket to retrieve the letter. "Garrett sent word. According to him, my father is expected within the week from the colonies. A banquet will be held in his honor."

"Oh." The mischievous grin she'd worn collapsed along with the scrutiny in her tone. "I take it that means Garrett and Abigail will be attending?"

"I'm sure they will be. Garrett spent much of his childhood with us after his father died. He almost sees mine as a second."

Charlotte gave a slow nod, her sudden silence making him reconsider asking her to join him. She raised the quill, the point of it grazing her chin along with a small line of ink.

He managed to keep the smile he felt coming bounded. He stepped closer, intending to offer his handkerchief—but she wiped at the mark first, smearing it toward her lips.

The grin he'd worked to keep tethered, came loose.

She caught his expression and frowned, the stain shrinking a fraction in size. "What?"

"Oh, chérie, here." Louise rushed over, pressing a cloth into Charlotte's hand and pointing to the stain. "The quill."

Her eyebrows squished together with lack of understanding before blue eyes went wide.

Nicholas hadn't missed the color rise in her cheeks, enjoying the moment for what it was—the first time he'd seen Charlotte Thatcher embarrassed. The result was strangely becoming.

After several attempts with the cloth, Louise nodded, indicating the stain had disappeared.

"Well, tell my sister Versailles is all I expected the palace to be." She jutted her chin, the blemish and the woman he'd begun to see more of and even like, gone. "More in fact."

"You went to Versailles?" The question escaped through clenched teeth.

She stood up this time, rounding the desk to meet him. "I did." There was a triumph in her tone as if to say, "no thanks to you."

Feeling the muscles in his neck grow tight, he gave a silent prayer, praying God might grant him a longer fuse than the ones used in his cannons. So, she made it to Versailles. Good. Maybe now that she could cross that off her list she wouldn't give him as much trouble when it was time to return to London.

The only part that didn't settle well was that their paths might cross at the palace. He wasn't doing anything wrong. He knew that. But the idea of what kind of conversation they'd have when she found out he'd been to the very place on her agenda didn't sit well.

"Captain Edwards, please, monsieur." The gentle request of Louise drew his attention back. "Come take a look at what Charlotte has been working on." She inclined her head to Charlotte. "Show him, mon amie."

The two women exchanged a glance before Charlotte retrieved the book from the table. He recognized the leather binding and the red ribbon. By her hesitation, he half expected her to show him the same sketches he'd seen at the boardinghouse, but he was wrong.

Curving lines unfurled across the page, some opening outward, others folding inward, blossoms emerging along their paths. Despite their movement, every line returned to a single central motif—one he recognized instantly, especially here in France.

"It's the fleur-de-lis." He raised his eyes from the page, catching a hint of the arrogance he'd seen in Charlotte earlier in her haughty smile.

"I got the idea last week."

He didn't have to guess where. "At Versailles."

"A wonderful thought, no?" Louise beamed, Nicholas detecting enthusiasm in her tone. "To incorporate such a symbol of France. Our customer is sure to love it when the design is complete."

His silence must have made a statement louder than he had intended because Charlotte's hands went to her waist. "What? You don't like it?"

"It's not that." He rubbed his chin, a little surprised his thought meant something. "It's really nice, actually." He meant that. "I just hope your customer is nothing short of royalty." He pointed to the lily that took up precedence in the sketch book. "That flower represents the French monarchy. It's a pretty bold statement they'll be wearing."

Charlotte's mouth toggled into a smirk. "And do you think Her Majesty, Marie Antoinette, is worthy enough for such a symbol?"

"Your customer is the queen of France?" He looked between Charlotte and Louise, hardly believing.

"Oui. That is right." Louise had returned to the work she'd put aside, the needled thread moving livelier than before they'd disclosed the news about their new customer. "The queen has already seen the design and has issued the order. As you've pointed out, the lily is an important symbol of France. Wearing it will help her win the hearts of the people." The movement of Louise's needle slowed, but never ceased. "At least, I believe that is Her Majesty's hope."

"But she's the queen." Nicholas furrowed his brow, his bicorn hat slightly slanting forward on his forehead in result of the movement. "Why would she need to win their hearts? All she has to do is say the word and people have to obey." Experience learned from his own king and his father first-hand.

Charlotte closed the book with gusto, staring him down. "Is that really what you think, Nicholas Edwards, or have you been in the Navy so long you simply take orders without actually thinking about them?"

He wanted to smile—not about the comment where he took orders without thinking about them but that she called him so informally again. He even caught Louise and her mother stopping in their tasks at the outburst, their attention suddenly drawn to Charlotte. Yet the way she looked at him—so mad—made him tuck the smile away.

"Marie Antoinette is from Austria and though perhaps many things according to French gossip, not a dictator." Her words cut the air. "She wants the support of the French people freely, but not all accept her because she is not French born, nor has yet to produce an heir to the throne. Neither of which she has control over. But—" Her voice softened as she turned to Louise, Nicholas reading something shared between them. "Perhaps we can help each other."

"C'est merveilleux. The order that the queen's dressmaker has already placed will keep us busy for a while." Louise's words and bright eyes conveyed more in them than a simple comment. And he hadn't missed a distinguishing glow on Charlotte's face, mimicking the lacemaker's own delight.

How had she managed it? Charlotte had only visited Versailles once, and she'd already gotten closer to the monarchy than he had since they first arrived in Paris. A shadow of failure to his own assignment threatened, but there was also something else there too. Pride. Pride for what she was doing for Louise and her mother.

Temptation prodded. He wanted to ask whether she had gained any insight on how to win an audience with the king of France but knowing where the root of where his motivation lied, he refrained.

"Yes. So, Captain—" Charlotte took her seat again, placing the book back on the table before opening its pages where the red ribbon marked her work. "Unless you plan on buying some lace or have a gift of sewing I don't know about, then you must excuse us." Her tone took on a more businesslike manner, but she held a gleam in her eye. "We have much to do."

Nicholas took a step backward, though feeling a smile of his own tugging. "My apologies, Miss Thatcher. I'm afraid I have no need for lace at present and my knowledge on needle and thread only goes as far as buttons and small tears." He tipped his hat forward, reading the message loud and clear. "I'll let you ladies get back to work."

***

"Nick."

Nicholas was only a few paces from the dentelle when Lewis Talbot approached him. A young man was at his friend's side and if he guessed right, at least a good five years Nicholas's junior.

Lewis pressed a firm hand on the lad's shoulder, his broad grin exhibiting pride. "This is my nephew, Stephen. And this, my boy—" Lewis motioned to Nicholas with his other hand where a copy of the *Journal de Paris* was attached. "This is the Captain Nicholas James Edwards."

The young man's hazel eyes scanned Nicholas up and down as if looking for something that wasn't there. "Captain of what, sir?"

Nicholas felt his smile from the dentelle grow faint. "The Royal Navy for His Majesty—the King of England, Mr. Stephen."

"I wouldn't have known that, sir—not by looking at you."

The young man was direct, like someone else he knew. But he heard no purposeful offense in the declaration, especially realizing why. He wasn't in his uniform.

"Perhaps that's Captain Edward's objective." Lewis swung the newspaper under the crook of his arm, but not before Nicholas caught sight of the headline. "Un Combat pour la Liberté: La Guerre Américaine Passionne la France." A Fight for Liberty: The American War Captivates France.

"Given England's strained relationship with the French over the previous war, a low profile could be an advantage."

His friend's words had truth. Nicholas recalled the looks he'd received from Monsieur Girard and the architect upon he and Charlotte's visit at the Sainte-Chapelle. The same looks registering on nearly every French noble he came into proximity with. They didn't trust him. But the French's view to his naval emblems was not the reason he hadn't donned his uniform today. Though, Lewis's thought was one worth remembering.

Nicholas brushed his hands down the lapels of the simple linen frock he'd packed as an alternative to his formal dress when times called for the occasion. The letter tucked inside his gray breast pocket crinkled with the movement. Despite the unpleasant reminder of the reason for his change in wardrobe and what awaited him, he was able to coax a smile. "Your uncle is very clever and holds an intriguing idea, but I'm afraid the reason for my military coat's absence is far less exciting. There were a few adjustments that had to be made to my uniform before I can go back to—"

"*Captain Edwards.*" Stephen contorted his mouth as if he'd been chewing on something hard and had come to the end of it. His eyes brightened in a way that made Nicholas feel he was being reevaluated with a better opinion. "My uncle says you're very esteemed, sir. Is it true you're being considered for admiral?"

Though not surprised, a dull ache spread within him. The misconception was one he'd grown used to. "You're thinking of my father. We held the same rank for a little while but you're right. The board has been considering his promotion." He forced a smile. "In fact, they've decided on it. I'll be heading to London at the end of the week for the celebration."

"And you'll need your uniform looking pristine for the occasion, I'd wager." Lewis cracked a knowing smile, showing he'd discovered the reason for his less than official appearance.

"Yes, I have it at the tailor's now." Nothing short of pristine would do for the grand event. Noting a tension beginning to develop in his jawline, Nicholas thought it best to divert their conversation to something other than his father. His attention turned to Lewis's nephew whose countenance appeared less bright than a moment ago. "Your uncle tells me you're on your Grand Tour."

"That's right, sir. I thought I'd have to wait a few years, but Uncle Lewis insists I'm ready to partake in the adventure."

The youth looked young for the occasion, but Nicholas had never been a good judge when it came to age. "How old are you, young man?"

"Fifteen, sir."

"Never too young to start learning the proper ways of society." Lewis gave another squeeze to his nephew's shoulder.

"No, I guess not." As far as Nicholas knew, there was no written rule on how old one had to be to embark on such a life passage. He was just more familiar with those who had done so around the ages of eighteen or twenty. "Are you enjoying your tour thus far?" He turned to the lad again who reminded him more of himself when he'd first started the Naval Academy at age thirteen—excited, yet unaware of what the next journey would bring.

"It's well and good, sir." Stephen flicked his gaze toward his uncle, a mixture of annoyance and amusement within it. "But apparently, my lessons in the language are not up to my uncle's standards. We've just come from the printer's. He's put in an ad requesting a new French tutor for me." He thought the young man might've rolled his eyes if good upbringing hadn't allowed it. "Here I thought I would be attending French masquerades and touring the city's most beloved relics."

"It is important for you to become polished in your manners as a gentleman." An opinion Lewis stood by no doubt, traces of his humor somewhat subsided for a parental stance. "The sophisticated language and etiquette of the Parisians will prepare you in your career aspirations and one day as a leader of your household."

"And learning the minuet is supposed to help me do that?" This time the boy's eyes did roll, reminding Nicholas again of the path to maturity the young man still had ahead of him.

"It will help you partake in dancing at a masquerade, which will help you get a wife." Lewis's gaze turned poignant before pleasant. "Dancing, after all, is a favorite recreation among many respectable ladies."

A light shade of red colored Stephen's cheeks.

"Which reminds me." A slow smile reared up. Apparently finished chiding with his nephew, Lewis's attention went to Nicholas. "Did you have any luck with that lady of yours?"

"As a matter of fact, I did." Nicholas pointed out the newspaper Lewis had tucked between the side of his body and his arm. "It looks like I won't be needing to place that missing person's ad, after all."

A belly laugh caused his friend's waistcoat to dance, though not in the style of the minuet. Lewis gave a hearty pat on the back of Nicholas's coat, attracting the attention of passerbys along the street even as they went along their way. "I would love to meet the woman who managed to outmaneuver the son of The Captain."

"Outmaneuver?" Nicholas gave his childhood friend a sideways look, choosing to ignore the mention of his father. "I caught her, didn't I?"

"Did you?"

Something about Lewis's expression conveyed more than he said outright, but Nicholas wasn't about to ask the full meaning with his nephew—cheeks returned to their natural hue—looking only too anxious to discover the same.

Another glance at the newspaper caught Nicholas's eye. He pointed to the *Journal de Paris* still in Lewis's possession, part of a headline getting his attention. "Are you finished with that?"

The large grin his friend wore at Nicholas's expense a moment ago wavered. "Actually, I have yet to read it. But here." His arm released the newspaper, holding the *Journel de Paris* out to him. "Take a look inside if you want. I just need it back."

Nicholas shook his head. He didn't have to. He was able to see the headline that had attracted his attention in the first place on the backside of the newspaper, and the energy that ruptured when his father was involved returned.

He hadn't forgotten Charlotte's remark to make amends for the search he had to conduct to find her. He still had no expectations for the offer, nor did he wish for her to try and go through whatever lengths she had in mind to see that she would. And now that she was in his sights at the boardinghouse, he was no longer bothered by the event.

What truly unsettled him, however—even if he couldn't quite say why—was her assumption that he cared only for the Navy. It simply wasn't true, and he knew the perfect way to prove it.

Chapter 12

"Nicholas, could you please explain why it was so urgent for me to be brought down here to the Pont Neuf?" Charlotte crossed her arms over the flower rosettes of her dress, looking anything but impressed to be standing on the bridge that spanned the river's distance on the Ile de la Cité. She looked down her nose below at a small huddle of women dipping their clothes in the water. "And I hope it wasn't just to watch the women washing along the river."

There were washerwomen, but that wasn't the only thing going on along Paris's river with the daytime hours dwindling. The barges that ran in and out of the river carrying merchandise were either on their way elsewhere for more trade goods or settled for the night into one of the Seine's muddy embankments. Locals who came to the river to swim or bathe were also growing scarce.

"I could—" Knowing she'd rather be working on her project for the queen's lace at the dentelle and hearing a pinch of irritation in her tone, he knew he needed to stall. "—but I have a feeling in the next minute or two you'll figure it out on your own."

There was nothing extraordinary worth noting, at least not on the surface. And he might've even shared Charlotte's opinion if he didn't already know what was coming. But he did know what was coming.

Above them the sun lay to the west, beginning its decent down toward the horizon, allowing a small window of time before the somewhat less bustling streets of Paris realigned themselves with vendors, entertainers, beggars and commoners.

Charlotte sighed with a humph, her eyes dotting different spots along the bridge of the Pont Neuf and riverbanks. "Really, Nicholas. I don't see anything."

"And you won't. Not just yet."

She returned his answer with a suspicious glance. "Will I even know if I see it?"

"You'll know, but you're looking in the wrong place." Reading further discouragement and remembering directness was more of what she preferred, he opted for another method. "Here." He took hold of her arm where the sleeve of her dress fanned out just below her elbow, his touch encountering the smoothness of her skin. Her gaze shot to him from where she'd been searching the Pont Neuf.

He led her to the edge of the stoned bridge for a better view. "Take a closer look down into the water."

Half expecting challenge to his instruction, he was pleasantly surprised when she leaned her body forward over the water. He appreciated how she narrowed her eyes as if to concentrate on the water's surface while keen to another appreciation he felt had taken root.

Her skirts, normally bellowing at her sides, tightened around the backside of her body as she leaned over the bridge, revealing a nicely shaped curve from where he was standing.

He swallowed. He knew he should've been looking at the water, helping her find what he knew was there under the small waves, but his eyes preferred the curves of her back at the moment.

Breaking his focus, despite not entirely wanting to, he shifted it to the muddy river.

"Are you sure there's something down there?"

"I'm sure. Just keep watching."

Another minute and her mouth fell open.

"What is *that*?" Deep blue eyes fixed on something copper and round that had broken the water's surface. The strange object moved along the river toward the right bank, gradually unveiling the mystery of what they'd just seen.

Nicholas grinned, more than satisfied with the reaction he received, and for the ability to be able to view such advancement. "*That* is the machine hydrostatique and its inventor, Dr. Freminet."

Attached to his metal helmet was a leather suit with a large, barrel-like container secured to his back. He was something out of a work of fiction, yet there he stood, fully real and fully remarkable. He slowly walked out of the river and up the bank where another man stood holding a pocket watch.

Nicholas motioned to the man on the bank. "And that I imagine is either a colleague or a companion of his, perhaps even just a safety measure."

Charlotte turned toward him from the extraordinary site, giving Nicholas a sideways look. "Before I ask why you know all that—" She pointed to the diving suit with its equally significant air tank trailing behind the inventor and connected by a hose. "First, tell me what on earth they're doing with that thing?"

Enjoying her enthusiasm, he was happy to oblige. He joined her by resting his elbows on the side of the bridge. "It looks like we got here just in time. Freminet is testing what men wondered about for centuries, perhaps millennia—what would it be like to see life underwater and not have to come up for air." Nicholas followed the scientist from a distance, watching the man's awkward movements as he slowly made his way from out of the water. "He usually conducts his dives in the harbors of Le Havre and Brest, but the paper announced he was in Paris. I wondered if he might take a chance in the Seine while he was here."

"Well, it appears he certainly has." She looked at him less brazen than he was used to seeing her, perhaps even interested. "Tell me, are you one of those men who have wondered such a thing—what it would be like to swim with the fish?" She straightened from the bridge's edge. The humor in her tone lacked anything condescending.

His fingers latched to the stone railing, now more than aware at how very few knew that part of him. "Only since the first time I boarded a ship."

She crossed her arms again. This time there was a gleam in her eye where there hadn't been earlier. "So, there *is* more to you than a tailored navel coat and following orders." Her voice hinted with pleasure at the possibility while she directed her focus back on the inventor. "Tell me, how does it work?"

Liking her perusal on this particular matter, he motioned to the two men again who appeared to be in an exchange, using hand signals as their means to communicate. Freminet's companion jotted something down in what Nicholas suspected to be a ledger or book of some sort. "That large tank Freminet had strapped to his back is a reservoir full of air. On the previous accounts I know of the tank drags behind him in the water, but it seems he's changing things up. The two hoses you saw attached between the reservoir and his helmet are for breathing—one for the inhale, the other for the exhale. He's able to stay down there for several minutes."

As if the inventor could hear their conversation and was aiming to prove Nicholas's explanation correct, Freminet walked back down the bank of the Seine. He entered the water again, the last of his mechanical suit of copper disappearing soon underneath.

***

Unable to look at anything else, Charlotte could hardly believe what she had just seen. The man and his strange suit were remarkable. That was, if everything that Nicholas was telling her was correct. And by the way his explanation had been exhibited with an air of confidence and excitement she'd never seen in the man, she believed he was.

"Freminet proposes his invention for being useful in exploring a shipwreck or to investigate reasons for obstructions and water channels. Both are certainly helpful, but not the extent of the suit's capabilities." Nicholas brought himself standing from his elbows where he seemed to be enjoying the overall spectacle.

She hadn't been oblivious to his change in wardrobe when he'd entered the dentelle earlier, but she was certainly surprised having seen him in nothing else other than his uniform. Normally one to confront such change, she would've asked him about the difference, but then he brought up the subject of leaving—the impact of caring at all about him going to London without her only rattling her with confusion. And now the choice in his clothing appeared irrelevant compared to such an incredible display of novelty.

"His work is a gateway—a precursor for truly seeing life under the water's surface." Nicholas's eyes brightened. "Today, minutes, but perhaps in a not-so-far-away future, hours. Can you imagine?" He breathed in, regarding the man about to dive under again while she regarded Nicholas in a new way.

"I don't think I have to. You're giving me a fine description."

A smile surfaced, one she'd never seen before and liked.

She tossed her chin in the direction of the spot where the man went under. "So, would you ever do it if given the chance—try one of those things on and talk to the fish?"

Without hesitation, the depth of his grin grew more prominent. "Absolutely."

She laughed, enjoying their easy candor, and seeing a side of this man she hadn't known. He was handsome like this. She thought she'd pinned Captain Nicholas Edwards entirely. Now, she was beginning to see that wasn't true. But why keep this part of himself hidden when it was clearly interesting and likeable?

Having been granted an idea, she scanned the water's surface, the only sign that someone lay underneath being a long hose. "If Freminet wasn't still underwater I'd go ask him to give you a turn." A promise she absolutely meant.

"Unlucky for me he is."

"But he has to come back up sometime, doesn't he?" She didn't have a clock to tell her how long, but Nicholas had said minutes. She couldn't imagine that many could take place, even in his suit of armor.

"He does. And as much as I appreciate the gesture, that won't be happening." His eyes angled to the darkening sky. "That's probably his last dive for the night. The window of light is disappearing. He won't be able to see anything much longer, especially down there."

"Then you should at least speak with Freminet about his work."

"What's the point?"

"*What's the point?*" Exasperation settled in her tone, the enthusiasm fading like the sun as the ball of light dipped below the horizon. He was on the precipice of a dream, merely yards away depending on where the inventor was on the riverbed floor. This might very well be his only opportunity and he was choosing not to take advantage of it. If it had been her dream, she'd already jumped into the water.

Heat rose within her. "Nicholas Edwards, you go on about how this man is essentially breaking the threshold for a dream of yours and at a chance to speak with him about his research, you decline because it's *too dark?*" She cut to the river to where the man in discussion still lay immersed somewhere under the water's murky surface. "Apart from one other time, I've never seen those blue eyes of yours light up the way they just did when you were speaking about that man's invention."

Anger burned through her. What was it that held this man back? He may not have been wearing his captain's gear, but she had no problem envisioning the uniform on him. She ventured she'd also received her answer, but she needed to hear it from him. "Why do you not pursue it?"

"Because I don't have the freedom to do as I please." His eyes hardened. "There are expectations I have to follow and none of those include Freminet or his invention. Something you might not understand."

"Nonsense." She didn't buy his excuse or his claim about her. She understood expectations perfectly. As a woman and younger sister of her time, she'd been expected not to amount to much. But bound to her mother's fate, she had too short a life to care for such drivel.

She stared at him. The air cooled as lamplighters began their work along the street, dusk swallowing the last warmth of the sun. She resisted the urge to pull her fichu tighter, unwilling to show even a hint of retreat. "I'm not budging from this bridge until you speak with Dr. Freminet."

He looked at her like he might sling her over his shoulder and drag her back to her room at the boardinghouse. But she knew he wouldn't. His gentlemanly upbringing wouldn't allow such action. Which she saw to her advantage.

"Fine." His concession was terse, but she didn't care. She won the small battle and in time she hoped he'd see it for what it was—for him.

When the top of the copper helmet could be spotted breaching through the water, Charlotte seized at the moment, grabbing Nicholas's hand. She was surprised by how rough it felt in hers. Knowing his station as captain, she'd always assumed he'd given orders regarding the ship's labors, but then she remembered seeing him perform some of the tasks himself on their way from the colonies.

Seeing Freminet beginning to make his slow and cumbersome exit from the Seine, she took off in the direction of the diving apparatus and the machine's engineer.

By the time they reached the bank, a small apprehensive crowd had gathered to see the strange creature that came out of the Parisian river. The man was hardly out of the water and up the bank when Charlotte broke through the crowd.

"Monsieur Freminet." She called to the inventor, making sure her voice carried over the group of spectators. She even waved her free arm in the air for good measure, still feeling Nicholas's grasp in her hand. She didn't bother to look behind her, imagining he might be rolling his eyes at her tactic if he allowed himself the privilege.

Freminet moved with sluggish speed toward his companion who still had the watch in hand. She sniffed, the smell of fish hanging as heavy as she imagined the inventor's wetsuit. Not a single acknowledgment. She stopped and bristled. It wouldn't be the first time a man ignored her.

Charlotte straightened, taking a determined step toward Freminet and his colleague. "Bonsoir, Monsieur." The words came out louder and more expectant. "I'd like to speak with you about your inven—"

"He cannot hear you, mademoiselle."

Charlotte flinched at the heavy French accent. The pocket watch slid into the French colleague's coat before he tapped a finger to an imaginary space around his head. "The helmet prevents it. Without seeing you, he has no idea you are speaking with him."

The colleague's finger twirled in the air at Freminet before pointing to her, the movement causing the man in the suit to turn in her direction. A round glass window in the helmet was fogged, revealing little.

The diver placed his hands to the collar of the strange suit, his companion helping to lift the copper piece to unveil a set of intelligent eyes.

Freminet sucked in a deep breath through his mouth and pear-shaped nose as if the Parisian air mixed with mud and stench was the sweetest perfume.

"This woman wants to speak with you about your invention, Sieur." The inventor's colleague carefully eased the helmet onto the ground while Freminet began unstrapping the leather bodysuit.

"You've heard of my machine hydrostatique?"

"I have—"

His black eyebrows peaked, encouraging her to explain.

"—from a gentleman." She was about to angle her head backward, then realized Nicholas had stepped up beside her, looking far less put out than when they'd left the bridge. "This man here says your underwater breathing machine is a gateway for aquatic exploration."

"I take it your husband here is the man you speak of?" He looked to Nicholas, smiling.

"My . . . husband?" She nearly sputtered the words out, unsure of how the man had acquired such an outlandish notion. Then she understood. She still had a hold of Nicholas. Why she hadn't let go of him leading to this moment, she didn't know. She let go of their grasp, though not before catching the most roguish grin she'd ever seen on the man. For once in her life, she was lost for words.

"And I mean it." Nicholas took a step forward, a small remnant of that grin still showing. He offered his hand to the inventor who had climbed the rest of the way out of his suit and accepted the handshake. "I've seen a great deal of the ocean above the water, but in all my years in the Navy, I haven't seen much of it underneath. What you're doing can help unravel the mystery of the deep."

"I doubt the mysteries of the deep can be unraveled in my lifetime." Freminet gave a good-natured huff again, drying himself with a linen sheet. "But it is my goal to at least begin such exploration and to put the diving suit to good use in whatever faculty that may be."

"Certainly that." At the allowance of both men, Nicholas began to inspect the diving contraption with an almost boy-like enthusiasm. "I could see its usefulness extending to more possibilities. How nice it would be if you had the ability to repair part of the ship below the waterline while still in the middle of the ocean."

"Monsieur, have you considered the idea of letting someone else try your diving suit?"

Freminet rubbed at the side of his cheek at Charlotte's inquiry as if considering the idea for the first time. "The machine hydrostatique is only at its experimental stage. I can but last twenty minutes in the suit before I must return to the surface for air. No one has tried apart from myself, not even Pierre."

"Nor would I." A flat tone came from Freminet's colleague.

The inventor gave an abbreviated laugh. He leaned in toward Nicholas and Charlotte, putting a hand to the side of his mouth as if shielding what he was about to say next from Pierre. "Between you and I, he is not as adventurous."

Pierre produced a hardy grunt, folding the peculiar garment away into a trunk. "I am not so willing to risk my life. If God meant for us to dwell among the sea creatures, then he would've fashioned us with gills."

The man's insistence somehow brought a smile to Freminet's face, a friendship between these two men evident. "Maybe, but he has equipped us with minds and hearts to seek the unknown." He turned back to Charlotte and Nicholas from his colleague. "What is it within us that wants to search this world, but to know more of its Creator?" Charlotte caught a twinkle in the man's eye as if somehow reflecting the unseen stars of that same Creator.

"Speak for yourself, Sieur." Pierre stowed away the breathing tank, latching the trunk closed. "I'm only here to make sure you stay alive."

"Which makes me wonder . . ." Charlotte's glance went to the copper helmet, now sitting on the ground. It had taken both men to lift it off Freminet. She pointed to the protective metal headgear. "Why do you wear that, of all things? Why not another material for the mask? It seems incredibly heavy."

"Oui, mademoiselle. It is very heavy, but that is part of its purpose—to sink to the bottom." One of his palms faced upward, the finger to his other hand diving down into the middle of his hand. "It is also less susceptible to damage from the sea water and suitable to hold the air. Besides, it is only when I am out of the water when the suit becomes cumbersome. Underneath, it is as if the water lends aid, pulling some of the weight off my shoulders." He drew his shoulders toward his ears as if acting out the motion for their benefit. "If it wasn't getting dark, I would encourage you to try, monsieur. As God's salvation is meant for everyone, the diving machine is not to be kept solely for the Frenchman."

"What about tomorrow, then?" Charlotte leaned forward, unable to let her query slip away unvoiced.

"That is certainly a possibility. We have a few more tests we would like to run before we leave for Brest the following day." Freminet turned to Nicholas. "What say you, monsieur?"

"I'd say that would be a dream come true, but—" Nicholas gave her a brief glance. "I'm leaving for London tomorrow. Unfortunately, for something that I can't miss."

"A misfortune. But you never know, we may run into each other again. The city has a way of bringing people together."

By the time Charlotte and Nicholas left the two scientists, darkness surrounded the shadowed city while the early evening lull was replaced again with busy streets.

"Nicholas—" Charlotte declined a woman offering perfume as she walked in step with Nicholas along the Champs-Élysees back to their boardinghouse. The long street was now lit with oil lamplight as they passed booth after booth of street vendors selling everything from food and drink to different forms of entertainment. "Why didn't you correct Dr. Freminet about our relationship, or rather, lack thereof? The man thought we were married for goodness sake."

"In light of the conversation, I didn't think it was important to correct him. And—" There was that grin again. "It's nice to know you can get a little tongue-tied from time to time."

Heat filled her cheeks and she was thankful for the dim lit street that hid the new color of her face.

"Nicholas, look." Charlotte rushed over to an enclosed tent manned by two girls calling out to the public to view what was inside. A wood lantern with a glass slide sat among them, projecting an image of a great pyramid on the side of the tent's canvas, and showcasing their means of entertainment.

"It's a magic lantern show." Nicholas stepped up beside her, appearing less mesmerized by the spectacle, but not at all against the performance.

"Aunt Sylvia told me they were popular in Paris, but I've never seen one myself."

"Then you're in for a real treat." He approached the two girls, reaching into his inside coat pocket.

It was then Charlotte realized what he was doing. "Wait. Nicholas. I can pay for my own ticket."

The soft glow of the lantern light made it easy for her to distinguish a frown. "I'm sure you can. This is just something I like to do."

"No, really. It's all right." Her hand slipped into one of her pockets tied underneath her skirts. She stretched her fingers, feeling for the coin inside, but grasping only linen fabric. Something in her stomach dropped.

"What's wrong?" Nicholas's downturned lips smoothed.

"I . . ." She looked around, seeing only busyness along the Champs-Élysees in the form of shifting shapes and shadows she knew to be people. Nothing caught her eye as suspicious, but she knew her pockets hadn't been empty.

Somehow her glance stole to an image she'd seen before, not one she knew, but recognized. The boy from the bakery.

Before she had a chance to think the presumption through, he fell in step with the crowd. A moment later, it was too late.

She looked back to Nicholas, knowing the boy was gone along with any sense of pride she had at paying her own way. "I think I've been robbed."

Chapter 13

Nicholas unwrapped the silk handkerchief, inspecting what at first glance resembled a pocket watch inside. The face was rounded with roman hour numerals, Arabic ten-minute figures and a repeated, swirled decorative pattern at every quarter hour numeral beginning at the twelve. The detailed craftsmanship was beautiful, but inside the protective case of silver that shielded the white face, laid the real treasure—a brass, highly-engraved mechanism of genius.

Tiny rubies and diamonds were inlaid on the caramel-colored metal of the timepiece, adding not only to the stunning design, but to dually serve in reducing friction of movement as the marine timekeeper became the invention that solved a problem for nautical navigation.

Nicholas inspected the timekeeper, having been polished by the clockmaker earlier that afternoon. The prize in all its elegance was no doubt a suitable gift for a king. More than satisfied with its condition, he wrapped the chronometer back up in the velvet cloth before safekeeping it to the breast pocket of his naval coat.

Stepping inside the great hall of the Banqueting House of London triggered the muscles in his body to grow rigid. He looked around for his father in the large rectangular room filled with Royal officers, noting the tiniest easement in his countenance when the man couldn't be found. He breathed in, somewhat relieved, and also ashamed of his reaction toward the man God had seen fit to raise him.

Officers in uniform and their dates in elegant, practical gowns rather than the excessive volume and brocade of the French court came up to mingle. Nicholas greeted them all with conversation and a smile he didn't feel.

"I was wondering when you'd show."

The familiar male voice brought on a genuine smile—one he desperately needed.

Garrett sauntered over with not one, but two goblets of claret. "When I didn't see you at the apartment today, I thought maybe you ran into some trouble getting back to London. Here." Garrett handed him the fuller glass. "Glad you made it to the party." The languid smile that his friend gave him accompanied by the distinct odor of his breath gave Nicholas reason to believe his friend had already been enjoying the festivities of the night. Good. It was a celebration worth commemorating even if he didn't feel likewise.

Nicholas swirled the red liquid in his glass. "I'm not really supposed to be here—not until I finish things up in France. King's orders."

"So, you had to choose between disobeying the king of England or your father's promotion to admiral?" Garrett pursed his lips in a way that told Nicholas he was weighing his options. His half-empty glass angled toward Nicholas's. "You might want to at least take a sip."

Nicholas huffed, appreciating his friend's humor even with the uneasiness of his decision tottering inside. "This seemed the better of the two choices."

"I'd have to agree. There's at least a chance King George might be persuaded. Your father on the other hand might not be so forgiving."

"No, but at least he'll have some time away from the war while he's here. The man's not used to not having others follow his orders like the protesters in Boston. I imagine he'll be glad for the respite."

Garrett frowned, suddenly appearing more interested in the liquid in his glass. "Your father is leaving for the West next week. I'm sorry, Nicholas. I thought you knew."

Nicholas avoided his gaze from the pitiful look his friend gave him, wanting to focus on anything else but the fact he hadn't known his father's immediate plans. A shot of hope sparked. He had to remember—he hadn't spoken with his father yet. There was still a chance the man just hadn't told him what Garrett already knew.

"From what you said earlier about France, I gather things are moving slower than expected?"

Slower wasn't the right word. It was more like not at all. "I'm going back in the morning." Nicholas sipped from his glass, the liquid wet on his dry palate. He knew the alcohol might ease him for the short-term, but it wouldn't solve his problem. He sat his drink on one of the long banquet tables arranged with silver platters of towering foods and fine silverware. "Any news about the war in the colonies?"

"As far as I know, the plan to crush the rebellion quickly is working. Our forces have driven General Washington out from Manhattan and have taken New York completely. But we're also getting more reports of spy activity." Garrett deposited his empty glass on the table next to Nicholas's. He leaned in. "I heard a man was captured in New York. Hale is the name, I believe. There's a rumor going on the rebels might be looking to recruit allies—France is a likely guess. I hear King George is sending some of our own to do the same."

The increased spy activity was news, but not surprising. Nicholas already had a brief encounter with one at the onset of the war, but last he checked, Abigail and Charlotte's older brother had no more fight in him. Speaking of . . . Nicholas looked at the spot beside Garrett that lay vacant. "Where is Abigail?"

"Home. She wanted to come." Garrett gave a sideways smile. "Mostly to question you about Charlotte, but she hasn't been feeling like herself lately. She'll turn around, I'm sure of it." There was a far-off look in his eyes conveying something wistful yet determined. "I only hope she'll start feeling better by the time we have to sail next week for the colonies. Which reminds me—" He exhaled. "Would you mind looking out for Charlotte while we're gone? Abigail doesn't want to leave her sister behind, but she'll feel better about it if she knows you're with her."

"Of course." He was already doing that anyway.

"Thanks. We know she's in good hands."

Nicholas swept the banquet hall for his father again. A small dense crowd gathered to one side of the room, taking the space of two white columns that extended from the polished floor to the upper level. He didn't have to guess what, or rather who, attracted them. No doubt the man of the hour lay somewhere inside.

He refocused to his friend, Garrett loosening the cuffs to his lieutenant uniform he'd been able to wear again since his reinstatement. "It sounds like the board didn't waste any time to get you back on a ship, but I am a little surprised they're sending you two back to the war knowing your past."

Garrett shrugged. "Why wouldn't they? We could still be of some use. Besides, our mission won't be directly involved in the conflict. We'll strictly be helping the wounded. Abigail's been spending her time at the hospital helping out wherever she's needed, but I know her. She's anxious to get back to working on her own patients. She'll be able to once we're on the ship."

"I take it that means you have some say, then?"

Garrett propped his chin, a more than satisfied smile emerging. "I do. The board's putting me in command of a decommissioned frigate and if all goes well, you might be looking at a captain yet. Though, the last time I was this close, things ended up differently than expected."

Garrett's smile eventually lengthened, Nicholas catching his meaning behind both the words and action. His friend had met his wife in one of the unlikeliest places.

Forgetting his father for at least the current moment, Nicholas laughed. "It seems like it all worked out."

"It didn't go as planned, but I found out my plans are not always what God has in mind. Good thing."

Nicholas read a contentment in his friend he hadn't seen there a year ago, though he didn't quite know how to respond. He had ideas of his own, but never plans. Any plans set before him had been given to him either by his father or the Navy, sometimes each going hand-in-hand.

He was more than happy for his friend, and he had no trouble believing the Almighty had a plan for his life. But he couldn't help pondering if his course had already been laid out before him in the life he currently knew.

He raised his head at the vibrant painted canvas above him, sending a prayer heavenward and feeling a sudden tightness in his shoulders. Like the Almighty was answering his question, the officers and their ladies began to bell out like one of Charlotte's dresses, opening a path and sight to his father.

Nicholas swallowed, almost wishing he'd taken Garrett's advice about the drink. His hand went to his coat pocket where he'd put the chronometer for safe keeping. He felt weight tugging down against the fabric, but he had to be sure. Still there.

Instinct took over, his feet taking advantage of the opening even as his heart raced inside his chest until he came to the man who commanded his attention without need of a single word.

The *Captain*, as most knew him in the Navy, wore a new admiral's coat with added gold trim and gold buttons detailing a fouled anchor with a laurel wreath border. The change made the tall man before him seem somehow more foreboding and distinguished than he already was.

"Congratulations, sir." He wanted to say, "Father," but he'd learned through his youth that "sir" was the appropriate response. Despite the desire for the words to be genuine, Nicholas heard the praise come out empty.

It wasn't that his father hadn't earned the promotion or that a part of him hadn't felt a sense of pride for the accomplishment. No. His higher rank was an honor the man undoubtedly deserved. Nicholas just wished their conversation felt more like he was talking to a close family member than to a superior officer.

"Thank you, Captain Edwards." There was no hint in the Admiral's tone that conveyed he'd been speaking to his relation.

"I have something for you." Nicholas pulled out the silk handkerchief, still neatly wrapped around the timekeeper.

His father accepted the gift with reserved curiosity, his weathered hands unbounding the cloth with slow deliberation.

When the last flap of the cloth had been removed, Nicholas filled the silence. "It's a copy of Harrison's H4 design—much more compact and accurate to his previous models. Captain James Cook used one just like this on his second and third voyages. He gave the timepiece much praise, even started calling it 'our trusty friend, the Watch.'"

Remembering that part of the story he'd read in the newspaper brought an unexpected smile to Nicholas's face even if his father's remained unchanged. "Just think, the ability to determine longitude and improve navigational accuracy all possible in the form and size of a pocket watch." He pointed to Harrison's H4 chronometer, though not daring to take it from his father's hand. "With this, one doesn't have to rely on blind navigation or hear about another tragedy like the one off the Sicily Islands." A loss of nearly 2,000 men when severe weather drove a fleet of British ships off course into the treacherous sandbanks of the Sicily islands.

There was more Nicholas wanted to say about the chronometer—how impressed he was by the invention and how it would likely, perhaps already, change the world of nautical navigation. But the tired expression on his father's face, one he'd seen before, made his dialogue of appreciation come to a rearing standstill.

"I'm familiar with the late clockmaker's work." His father's tone came out acidic, corroding Nicholas's attempt like the way the seawater degraded the quality of a fine ship over time. "Including the board's reluctance to reward him fully for the Longitude Prize citing that his results were sheer luck and by our most senior astronomer who stated the watch to be inaccurate."

In many cases of his past, Nicholas might have let his father's opinion take reign, but he'd given the chronometer as a gift—one he stood behind. He swallowed, feeling the gulp lodge within his Adam's apple at something he'd never done in all his life—challenge his father.

"But sir, the man's invention was successful on the two naval trials it conducted. You can't truly believe luck was the factor to its exceptional performance? King George himself supports the accuracy of it and the man's work." Nicholas knew he was taking a risk, but the inventor had died March of this year and wasn't able to defend on his own behalf. "Surely, you cannot fault a man for taking something that's been dangerous and tedious and making it safer and more efficient?"

"No, I just pity the man who has to rely on such a tool."

Although his father didn't say as much outright, Nicholas couldn't help but sense the retort was aimed at him.

"I and others like me have gone our whole naval careers navigating the waters without the need of such a device. If you ask me, it sounds like a crutch to lean on without the acquisition of a broken leg." His father stared at the timepiece, viewing the shining metal illuminated by the overhead candle lighting as something that needed to be thrown away before looking at Nicholas with the same expression. "I can also see you're quite animated by the business. Between this and what I've heard of what's *not* happening in France, frankly, I'm disappointed." His father closed his eyes, his shaven face moving from side to side. "You're a captain, Nicholas. Put these senseless inventions behind you and focus on your own assignments. Maybe then you'll succeed at what's expected of you."

The inside of Nicholas's stomach concaved. The blow hit hard. It was one thing to knock down his interests, but Nicholas hadn't realized his father knew about his problem in France. And how much the man had been privy to, Nicholas didn't want to ask. Without much coercion, the muscles in his jaw submitted into a strained relaxation like they'd performed the exercise a thousand times in his past.

The father handed the gift back to the son, but there was little else to the exchange. Nicholas returned the chronometer to his coat pocket, feeling the extra weight bearing down inside his chest. And as far as his father's plans from here on out? Not one word.

***

The walk over to the River Thames was unplanned but familiar, like a patch of grass one continued to tread over and again until the piles laid down into a formed path. Except this was different from a field of grass. This was London. Unlike the green patches of earth, the cobblestone streets of the city left no clue of his past visits, even if his memories had.

When he reached the dockyard, Nicholas anchored himself onto a pile of ready-sawn planks that would later be used for building a ship. A sixth-rate frigate was in front of him perched on scaffolds some yards away, soon to be launched into the Thames, while a man under the scaffolds signaled to another who'd been carrying provisions where to load them. Nearby, a small group had come up to watch, including a boy and his father, the boy's expression glowing with youthful wonder.

At once, the tension in Nicholas's back eased while he watched a schooner being held in a dry dock, the reason obvious as to why. A group of labored men worked heedlessly scraping the bottom portion of the ship where an assortment of barnacles—gray and white crustaceans—stuck stubbornly to the hull.

The methodic rhythm of laborers and spectators along the Thames was almost like a melody, Nicholas enjoying his position as a bystander if only for today. He watched alongside the overcrowded river as vessels of different sizes and occupations brought in coastal goods for inspection.

Captains of the boats did their best to navigate around each other—sometimes easily, sometimes less so—as they worked to weave their way to and from the part of the river where trade and customs were managed. In a way, the Pool of London was chaotic, yet everyone knew, or at least seemed to know what they were doing.

It was a mechanism, a system that worked, and for a person that appreciated efficiency Nicholas gathered the system was efficient enough for its time.

"It's good to see an officer show interest in the vessels they take command of." A man came over to him, wearing a tricorn hat that matched his brown coat. His hand gripped a cane Nicholas guessed by the stick's fine carving and the man's upright stance, came more out of fashion than of need.

"When you understand how something works, you start to develop an appreciation for it." The stranger folded his hands over the ivory handle, inviting himself into the space Nicholas had claimed as his own.

Nicholas suppressed a flicker of annoyance at the intrusion but found no fault in the remark, especially when he agreed. He followed the man's gaze toward the river, knowing his own time here at the dockyard along with experience at sea went something beyond his studies at the Naval Academy. Here, he'd observed the mechanics of building and repairing ships, while out there, he'd lived it.

He'd watched ships built piece by piece—caulkers, joiners, carpenters, riggers, sailmakers—each labor joining the next until something remarkable emerged, he and his crew counting their very lives on, whether they'd been conscious of that fact or not.

Like the water underneath a ship gradually becoming deeper as it made its way out from the wharf and into the open sea, his appreciation expanded.

Nicholas considered the man again and his reasons for being here in the dockyard. He had a stance about him that gave him the impression of giving orders rather than receiving them. He might've guessed a captain or admiral, but he doubted a single officer would be brazen enough to miss his father's celebration. Then again, he had.

"You'll have to pardon me, sir, but you don't look like a craftsman." Nicholas took a closer look at the man's hands. They were still folded upon his walking stick, but the lowered view Nicholas had from the planks allowed him to see underneath the man's fingertips. Just as he suspected. Not a single mark or callous.

"Not exactly, though you could say I'm invested in the craft." The man offered a proud but friendly smile, one that told Nicholas he hadn't taken offense but had appreciated the observation. "I'm a shipwright back in Liverpool." He extended one of his unmarked hands, Nicholas accepting the gesture of greeting. "The name's Roger Fisher."

"Nicholas Edwards and you're welcome to join."

Fisher took a seat next to him at the vacant side of the planks. The wood boarding toggled under Nicholas with the added weight.

"What's a shipbuilder from Liverpool doing in a shipyard in London?"

Fisher chuckled. "Traveling mostly. I have a sister here." His hands folded again on the ivory handle of his cane now angled out in front of him, this time Nicholas recognizing the image of Poseidon, the mythological god carrying his famous trident.

"You know." Nicholas rubbed his chin, trying to remember. "I think the *Speedy* was manufactured in Liverpool."

"Then there's a good chance she was built in my yard." Fisher's back straightened from leaning against the planks behind him, his gray eyes brightening. "In fact, I think I remember. After all, it takes years to build a single ship. In that time, you really start to get to know each one. She's a frigate if I'm not mistaken?" He looked at Nicholas as if daring him to contest as much. He didn't need to.

"She is."

"How is she? Is she handling well out there?"

Nicholas trailed his gaze to where the man nodded, catching that his meaning meant far beyond the river ahead of them. He was delighted by the man's genuine interest, as if he'd asked about a person instead of a boat. "I've only been with her for less than a year, but so far she's doing great. She's not as fast as she used to be."

"She wasn't designed to be. Not for the long haul."

No, she wasn't. "But she's steady, able to cut through the seas even in storms and has been able to withstand plenty of fire when she needs to under battle."

"Good. I'm glad to hear it. I take pride in the vessels we build." Fisher's chest lifted under his waistcoat as if exhibiting that very notion. He seemed to look toward the men that continued to grind away the sea creatures from the hull, pointing in their direction. "It's quite something to see just what all can make its way to the bottom of a ship. Wouldn't you say so, Captain?"

A wry smile appeared, Nicholas catching the shipbuilder eyeing the gold lace and nine gold buttons on the lapels of his blue coat, distinctions that signified his rank. "Tell me, do you ever feel those barnacles attach themselves to the bottom of your ship? Or does their skill at being sneaky match their level at being a nuisance too?"

Hearing the color in his tone over a common and problematic topic in the Royal Navy, Nicholas released a grin of his own. "If you mean when they first attach, I wish I could." He shook his head, his lips curling under. "It's not until we have problems with the ship slowing down a knot or two under a good wind when we realize just what the culprit is." He sighed. "But by then, we've already lost time."

Fisher nodded with an aggravated huff that told Nicholas he took the problem personally. "They're quite the pest of the sea if you ask me. Who knew an animal that seems so insignificant could do so much damage? We've tried some things back in Liverpool with some paint we think to be toxic to the sea creatures but haven't had much success yet."

Anti-fouling paint. Nicholas was familiar. Different mixtures and combinations of such had been used for years but proved little to the desired effect.

Extra wood added to the existing parts of the ship had been another idea. Planks could be removed or undergo damage without harming the integrity of the vessel, but that never lasted long without the wood having to be replaced.

Nicholas looked at the men scraping the barnacles off the hull, wondering how many years the same tactic had been used without signs of improvement. "There has to be a different way, a better way." He was almost positive, yet he held no immediate solution to a problem that had existed for centuries. At least, nothing better than what was already in place.

"I'd like to think there is."

Nicholas's head jerked back to Fisher. He hadn't realized he'd voiced his thoughts out loud. But it seemed he had.

"We just have to find it, Captain. If you happen to come across the solution, I'd be most interested to know. Why, if I didn't have to allow the extra time and expense to get my ships docked and repaired so often, trade with the West Indies would no doubt heed an even better profit." The shipbuilder tipped his hat, standing to his feet.

Nicholas briefly watched Fisher go before returning his attention back to the drydock. He guessed from the conversation he had with the shipwright, the man's grievance was more about gain than anything else. Yet, he couldn't help thinking there might also be concern beyond just the means for money. But even if there wasn't as far as the shipbuilder went, the rest of those sailing on the ocean might still yield benefit if something could be done.

A new problem emerged—one that didn't so much rely on his position as captain of the Royal Navy or had the pressure that still burdened his current mission. No, this was one of his own choosing and desire. Not just out of service or given by order. Yet if he could solve it, he could very well affect seafarers on a large scale. A new invention, or even just an idea.

If he could somehow think it through—find a solution to an issue that took time away from missions and left men's hands cut and scraped, he could benefit all that sailed the waters, not just those limited to the country he was born into.

The muscles in Nicholas's neck went stiff. Except figuring out a solution to a problem that'd been around since man began sailing the ocean was bound to take time—time he didn't have with his current assignment. He breathed out, the chronometer moving with his chest, reminding him of his father's disappointment.

His thoughts halted as if someone had suddenly dropped an anchor to stop his momentum from moving forward. Again, duty called along with the years of due diligence under his father's discipline. So, as much as he wanted to change the lives in the age of sail, that would have to wait.

Chapter 14

My Dearest Charlotte,

I wish I had better news to send you, but the state of things in the colonies has escalated and not in our favor. It pains me deeply to say this, my dear, but I've had to resign Betsy to another household, the means to compensate for her service no longer available.

Support for the patriot cause is growing. I might commend that as a good thing if it weren't for the already misconstrued attitudes toward our family's alliances.

Your brother's decision to remain uninvolved in the fight since his imprisonment last year coupled with your sister's marriage to a British officer continues to exacerbate the tension that was once unspoken, but now no longer remains so.

There are some in our once beloved community who still call us friends, but these are few. Others that do acknowledge us, which are the majority, do so through degradation of the Thatcher name and our character, their persecution of insults and threats too vile to put on paper.

My heart grows heavy having to tell you that is not the full extent of our troubles. Your brother has kept to himself and no longer resembles the vigorous man he used to be. In short, your father and I are worried for him. Aside from the torment that seems to rouse him at night, he keeps alone during the day, working the fields and tending to most of the farm. Although we are thankful for his hard work, there is little to show for his effort with hardly a buyer this year from the cabbage harvest. As for the state of my current enterprise, your late uncle's business is as plentiful in profit as Thatcher's are in friends.

I tell you all this not to upset you, although it is trying, but to convey the urgency of making a partnership with Monsieur Vantinelle and quickly. The man is relatively new in the industry, but he is astute in every way and may be the only lifeline to save our family's reputation and our near future of a diet comprising solely of cabbage.

The one piece of news I can give to keep your spirits from faltering is that despite our suffering, Olivia is flourishing into a joyful and curious toddler. Although we are scorned into poverty, it is God's gift of her spirit that helps us find strength to endure each day.

It is my prayer Providence may also supply you strength to endure what is needed of you for such an important task.

With all my love,
Your Aunt,

Sylvia Davenport

Charlotte let the red wax fall from the candle before sealing the envelope. Having penned her reply to her aunt, she was anxious to see her letter sent as soon as the next transit to the colonies allowed.

Her body rocked against the upholstered seat beneath her, trying to grasp the news she'd just received. Betsy gone. The woman had been employed by Aunt Sylvia for close to 20 years. Their relationship had started on the foothold of obligation—one in need of services while the other of finances—but the connection had slowly blossomed into a kind of kinship, each respecting each other in their own right. The fact her aunt had mentioned Betsy's change of employment first meant it was the most wrenching of all the loss.

The rest she couldn't say she hadn't seen coming, though under what she knew to be a gentlewoman's stoic facade in portraying how things truly were, she could only guess they were worse than her aunt wrote them to be.

A shot of guilt ran up her spine, having told her aunt that she'd been in the same social circles as the vicomte and well on her way to their conversation relating to her aunt's business. She'd expressed confidence that the deal would be made, though she'd left out the part about her first encounter with him at Laurent's party entirely. Her reassurance wasn't exactly a lie, but it did feel like one, especially as she reflected on just how little progress she'd made with the man.

But she'd make up for her slight exaggerations by delivering the promise she'd made in her letter. That, she was determined to do. She just had to figure out how.

She puffed out a fraction of air from her nose before taking a sip of tea, the special blend she preferred. The floral scent filled her nostrils as air pulled back in again. She sat the teacup back onto the small table, recalling one of the rules her aunt told her regarding business practice.

According to Aunt Sylvia, a woman's position of sole ownership was preferred, but in many aspects that was not the case, nor the norm. Sometimes bringing in a man was the only way to save a woman's business from floundering. The perception that *he* rather than *she* contained ownership, somehow made society feel better.

Charlotte remembered the advice verbatim, her aunt's strict guidance clear from behind her desk of ledgers.

"If you must bring a man into your enterprise, you must first convince him to do it. If God has not blessed you with looks to persuade him, you must find other means."

When Charlotte had asked what those other means were, she was told she'd have to figure that out on her own, but that her intellect was where to start. Her aunt had leaned over her desk, her eyes sharp. "They will never see you coming, my dear."

When her aunt said "they," she'd meant men who didn't recognize the full extent of a woman's capacities and so far, her aunt had been right. The element of surprise had been to her advantage in life. She would have added her tendency to be aggressive, but she was starting to question that as of late.

She tapped the cup with her fingernail, hearing the faint chime of porcelain. The vicomte seemed unimpressed by her. In fact, it was evident enough that her aunt's choice for a business partner did not like her. She wasn't so sure she could secure anything with the man. But that also didn't mean that all was lost. He wasn't the *only* business merchant, after all.

Lumber, the final product her aunt sold, had historically been used to build ships. That's where she would start.

✳✳✳

"What do you mean there's no shipyard here in Calais?" Like a twig bent to its critical point, something in Charlotte snapped.

She'd spent three days on a cramped public stagecoach and shared rooms with strangers to get here. Now this man was telling her she'd come to the wrong place?

"Oui, as I said before there is no shipyard here, mademoiselle." The dock clerk she'd chosen to seek out scribbled something down in a ledger amidst a cluttered desk full of other account books, manifests, and various writing tools.

"But this is a port is it not?" Her protest carried confidence, yet the man gave her a dismissive look, one that made her doubt what her eyes could clearly see of the docked boats and span of water underneath them.

"That is right too, miss, but no ships are built here. This is a trade port where men take advantage of the fishing grounds."

The combination of the sea breeze and the rank smell around her were a testament to the latter. She scolded herself at her miscalculation. In the colonies shipyards seemed to run the port cities. At least that was her experience, she having seen them firsthand in Portsmouth, Boston, and Philadelphia. Even Falmouth, her birthplace, had a small-scale operation. Apparently, that was another difference between France and the place she called home.

"Fine. Then where can I find the nearest shipyard?" Resisting the urge to drum her fingers on the man's desk as an effort to annoy him into telling her, she folded her hands. "Preferably the closest to Paris?"

"That would be two different answers, miss. The nearest from here is right over at Dunkirk." He pointed his quill north up the shoreline before the feather changed direction to the south. "But the most connected to Paris is in Le Havre about 40 lieues."

A little over four kilometers. She quickly did the math, but it didn't add up. "And how is that closest to Paris?"

"I didn't say it was the closest mademoiselle, just the most connected."

She let the silence do the work for her, only raising her eyebrows to encourage him to go on.

"Le Havre comes out at the base of the Seine River—lots of boats travel that way to get to Paris."

Realization dawned, she finally understanding what he meant by the relationship. The Seine. Paris's main river and where she'd seen Dr. Freminet's underwater diving contraption with Nicholas. That was a direct connection. And from what the man described, a more suitable location from the colonies avoiding the extra distance up north. But she wouldn't be able to make the trip today.

Her funds were too much depleted for the expense of another room on top of the one she held in Paris. Not to mention, she'd already paid for passage out of town. The ride through the night would get her back in Paris in two days' time.

She hated spending her already limited funds for such an excursion, but if things didn't work out with the vicomte—even as she hoped it still would—she should at least have another option. But now . . . she wanted to wring her hands at her wasted effort.

After a small dinner at a local tavern, she was at a hotel called *De la Messagrie* where her means for transportation waited under a darkened sky. The large stagecoach was as big as a small house and fitted with eight horses. Though only six passengers currently resided in the vehicle, including herself, she surmised eight could fit comfortably enough. But just as well if no one else joined them—their absence allowing more space and comfort for the overnight trip.

A sound of murmuring outside the stagecoach made her previous hopes vanish and the new stranger stepped inside to join the rest of the traveling party.

The man with his tall figure had to stoop his head on the way in, the driver's lantern revealing honey-colored strands of hair at the base of his neck where his tricorn hat hadn't covered. And was that a familiar looking pocket watch in his left hand?

"Nicholas?"

The man jerked his head from where she'd called out, his face, she imagined in the darkness, mimicking her own surprise. She couldn't be certain, however, but she felt herself folding her body inward in the chance she was right. Of all the stagecoaches.

The smell of seawater mixed with sandalwood claimed a seat next to her, only giving her further proof to support her assumption, yet his booming silence made her feel like she'd been caught in something she shouldn't have been doing. And she supposed she had with having come to Calais on her own.

Eventually the soft conversation of the others in the vehicle died out as the stagecoach trucked though the night. At first, Charlotte wondered if Nicholas had also fallen asleep among the group, but his shadowed figure stirred, looking anything but relaxed for an activity that required that very state.

"Is there something you want to tell me, Charlotte?" She heard him shift again, along with a heavy breath.

"Not really, no." Her body went still, her voice coming out quiet even in the sleepy compartment.

"You don't want to tell me why you came to Calais by yourself or why this reminds me of the last time I left for London?"

She straightened, hearing a question he no doubt knew the answer to. "I have my reasons."

"I'm sure you do. I'd just like to hear them, that's all." The abrupt way he voiced his request made her believe that was clearly *not all.*

When she didn't respond, she heard a small murmur under his breath, though she couldn't make out his meaning.

"Can you at least tell me what you were doing?" His voice grew calm, the irritation she heard moments ago, though still there, significantly diminished.

"I was—" Her voice shook, feeling embarrassed by her mistake— "trying to find an alternative option for my aunt."

She could hardly make out his silhouette much less his face, but she imagined he was nodding or something similar by the ease in tension she felt in the air. Expecting a reprimand, she was relieved when she didn't receive one.

"Calais is a good port for trade, I'll give you that." He sighed. "But in the case of you and your aunt, you have better options if she's set on a French partnership."

A wisp of air moved between them, agitating the smell of wool along with the musky scent from earlier as something was removed from his head. She could make out the points of his hat on the vacant seat between them, hearing the faint rustling of hair being combed through.

"I'm not in the business of handling goods, but I do know something about war. If France gets involved with the war in the colonies, Calais' short distance across from England makes the town a prime target for interrupting trade. But—" His tone became more irritated, though still remaining calm "—that's something we could have talked about in Paris if you would've asked instead of storming into your next plan."

She could hear what he didn't say—how she'd wasted her efforts, her time and money on such a trip.

"From the time we spent together . . ." he paused, his tone holding a gentleness to it she hadn't foreseen. ". . . and apart, I've come to understand that when you have something on your mind, you tend to go after it. In many aspects I admire that." Still unable to see his face, she wished she could, having thought she heard a smile. "But sometimes it's good to know when a little restraint is needed."

"Like in this case you mean?"

"Yes, like in this case."

She pulled herself upright on the benched seat, a little surprised. Not by his answer, but the firmed kindness in his delivery.

"All I'm trying to say is that sometimes it's good to think about what the fire's going do to you before being too eager about jumping into it."

"Fire?" She blinked in the ebony space around them. The metaphor seemed extreme compared to what she was doing or had aimed to do. "Really Nicholas, it was just a short trip. I simply came to see if I could find an alternative for my aunt's business."

"And did you?"

Not wanting to look him in the eye even in sheer darkness, she looked down at her rose patterned dress. The rosettes were perfectly blended with the rest of the carriage's interior as the night pressed on. "No."

"I'm sorry." His tone had changed, the firmness in his correction of her previous behavior, gone.

"It's all right." She took a shaky breath. "From what you've said, it may not be a good fit anyhow."

"I take you looking for an alternative partner means things are not going as expected with the vicomte?"

She let her silence speak again for her.

"I'm wondering if your problems with the noble have less to do with what you told me at the Saint-Chapelle concerning the colonies and more to do with something else."

"Like what?"

"I don't know. Maybe something we've already talked about tonight. Maybe something entirely different."

More rustling beside her prompted her to do the same. At least until tomorrow she didn't want to think about the vicomte or what else she could do to help improve her family's deficit at home. "How was your father's celebration? Did you see Abigail?" She missed her sister terribly, even though they communicated often through their letters.

"Garrett said she wasn't feeling like herself, but he didn't seem too worried."

She hadn't missed his lack of mention to the party or his father. So be it. She didn't want to talk about the vicomte either. Perhaps that was something they had in common, men in their lives they couldn't seem to appease.

She didn't know a lot about Nicholas's father, but any man who called himself *The Captain* and was known by the rest of the naval community as such, she could take a good guess of just what kind of man he was. And taking into consideration his son—a man she did know who followed orders to their exact degree and clenched his jaw every time his father was mentioned—it wasn't difficult to surmise the kind of relationship the two shared.

Though her relationship with her own father was not a close one by any means, Charlotte still felt Nicholas's situation was one that she could not speak to. Unless the Almighty intervened, one's father could not be changed. But a father was one thing, while a business partner was something else entirely. And as far as the vicomte was concerned, she still had other options.

Chapter 15

Nicholas flipped open his compass before closing it for the eighth time in the corner of the café.

He was running out of ideas to complete his assignment. The war with the colonies was ongoing and there were questions that needed answers. He'd tried everything to obtain the necessary audience with King Louis and appeared to be at a dead end.

"A grand spot to meet don't you think?" Lewis Talbot strode over to the wooden table Nicholas occupied, one of many belonging to the French café.

Nicholas had written to Lewis to let him know he'd made it back to Paris, though half expecting his friend had already taken leave for the next destination on his nephew's Grand Tour. It seemed he hadn't.

"Where is your nephew?"

Lewis settled himself into one of the mismatched chairs in the café, the seat protesting against his friend's weight. "Taking a dance lesson with his new tutor."

"He no doubt has the French culture down by now. You ought to let the lad have some fun before your tour moves on."

A waiter brought them two cups of hot coffee, both of them partaking in the beverage. After the night Nicholas had with Charlotte getting back from Calais, the black liquid did him good. He'd been highly surprised to find she was on the same stagecoach as him headed back to the city and also a little miffed that she had taken upon herself to chance a trip to the port unchaperoned. But something had softened between them. He hadn't expected she'd listen to a word he had to say on the issue, but she had, at least if her silence was any indication.

Lewis blew at his coffee, a faint furrow at his brow. "I didn't take you for the type to care for the frivolities of youth. You never seemed like the sort growing up."

He had been once, before the Navy cut that part and those liberties of his life short. "I'm just saying the boy is young, younger than most who impart on a Grand Tour. At least make it worthwhile for him."

Lewis took another sip, his attention appearing drawn to the diverse crowd of men in powdered wigs and velvet waistcoats who lay huddled in conversation. "Any news from home? I take the fact that you're back in Paris means that lady of yours didn't go with you to London?"

The mention of Charlotte and his friend's taunting tone brought on a smile. "No. She has plans of her own here, but I think we've come to an agreement, or as close to an agreement as we can get."

"You like her." There was an absence of a question in Lewis's tone that left no room for rebuttal.

To say Nicholas liked Charlotte was an easy admission, but the rest remained complicated. His time already devoted to the Navy gave little attention to the prospect of marriage, especially when his desire was to see his wife each night rather than be gone from her months at a time. And his father's attempts at providing a suitable match for him only further deterred that option. But Charlotte—she was challenging, yes, but he had to admit of the women he had escorted to banquets and balls, she was the one that never left his mind. He found he liked the challenge—not someone to be fixed or improved upon, but who was engaging and someone he was starting to fall for while she pushed him to re-evaluate his own life.

A puff of pipe smoke wafted under his nose from a nearby table, bringing him out of his reverie while the constant humming of voices like the ever-present work of a bees buzzed around him. "This place seems to be a hub of conversation."

"You'll find that tends to be the case here." Lewis made a broad gesture toward the other patrons, some hunched over papers while others spoke in animated tones. "The Café Procope has grown into a place of intellectual activity, discussing everything from enlightened philosophy to the latest Parisian gossip."

Not having realized his friend knew as much, Nicholas only now considered this hadn't been Lewis's first time in the café. "And you make it a habit of attending these discussions?"

"I make it a habit of being informed, that's all." There was something defensive about his friend's tone, but Nicholas couldn't place why. "Much of the conversations are debates and theories that tend to be fueled by current events stringing across Europe and beyond."

Nicholas had no trouble understanding what Lewis meant. "You mean the war in the colonies?" His voice dropped to a near whisper. With no plan yet to get an audience with the king and therefore no plan to go to court, Nicholas felt there'd been no occasion to wear his uniform. Now, in light of what Lewis told him about the café and topics of conversation, he was glad that he hadn't.

"Oh yes, you will find close attention is paid to what's happening in the new land." Lewis leaned forward, the tan color of his waistcoat pressing against the edge of the table as the excess bulged at the surface.

"There is an unrest here in the capital among the lower classes that holds a similar ill regard for the French monarchy that the colonists have extended to the English one. I hear our soldiers have taken New York and seem to be squashing the rebellion, but if things take a turn, it will only fuel the unrest here. And those two over there—" His voice took on a more solemn tone, Nicholas catching his eyes dart to two Frenchmen. "They will be the catalyst for it."

"What makes you so sure?" Nicholas narrowed his eyes, pondering the man across from him. "That seems like a strong opinion for persons you don't know."

"Maybe." Lewis leaned back in his chair again, a certainty in his expression. "But I've seen them in here a time or two and have heard their arguments. That man there with the slender sharp face and piercing blue eyes is Maximilien Robespierre. He's a law student, but just won a prized award for rhetoric from the college. The man's tongue is skilled at persuasion, and I've seen him turn the crowd's opinion easily here. But he's not the man anyone should be worried about, having strongly laid out his conviction against the death penalty."

Lewis nodded to the second man. "The one beside him is Marc Chazot, the Baron d'Aubray, and is the more ruthless of the two. He's a two-sided coin. A nobleman by birthright yet a revolutionary by heart. He claims to follow in the works of Voltaire, but I can't help think the famous French philosopher might not have a preference for that aristocrat's rash attitude."

The noble Lewis referenced guzzled down a glass of red wine.

Lewis leaned over the length of the table again. "He doesn't have much good to say about the monarchy. In fact—" His friend's voice fell hushed. "No one will outrightly say for fear that it will cause trouble to the artist, but some attribute *that* to be his work."

Nicholas followed Lewis's gaze to one of the walls of the café. Two pamphlets, the same size and width, were attached to the wall like an opened book.

The first one was a lady dressed in the style of the French court, her headpiece much like the ones he'd seen while at Versailles, tall and decorated except for one striking difference. The artist had embraced the role of hyperbole, the woman's headdress extending to such an extravagant height that her grand wig had managed to get entangled in one of the candled chandeliers and caught on fire. Two servants could be seen trying to put out the flames in the background, while the noblewoman remained oblivious to her dangerous situation, she too preoccupied with impressing her companion. It was hard for Nicholas to say if the picture was meant to capture the queen of France as its aim, but even if not, the attack on French nobility was evident.

The second pamphlet was of two tradesmen working in what resembled a blacksmith shop. One man worked at a forge, his back turned from the viewer. The other worked at an anvil with a hammer in his hand. At first nothing seemed unique about the artwork until he caught sight of a crown on the floor at the foot of the anvil, unnoticed by the man who worked the trade. Putting the image of the crown with the white stockings and highly embroidered waistcoat under a leather apron, Nicholas knew without a doubt this pamphlet had fired on the king of France.

Nicholas smoothed a finger over his lips, his brow furrowing. "The picture of the woman is comical, but I don't understand the one next to it, only that it appears that's the king."

"I doubt I have the best interpretation, but I believe the picture is to signify how the king holds more interest in his passion than to govern his people."

"His passion—as a blacksmith?"

"Not a blacksmith." Lewis shook his head. "A locksmith. The Baron d'Aubray and others in his same class have confirmed the king has a workshop in the palace that he frequently confines himself to. The authorities do not like such propaganda, so many of the pamphlets have been burned. But these have survived." Lewis motioned to the pamphlets on the wall, the movement grabbing the attention of one of the Frenchmen Lewis had warned him about. "I don't know how, but they have."

"You have not heard of His Majesty's hobby?" The man Lewis referred to as Marc strode up to their table, Nicholas catching something spiteful in both his expression and tone. "The big oaf spends a large part of his days working in his palace workshop on his locks while he turns his back on his people."

Nicholas didn't like his attitude, but the man seemed to know information he'd like to find out. "His locks?"

"Yes. An interest of the king. The French court does not acknowledge such, but as you can see, it is no secret." His arms went open as if presenting the tasteless picture to the whole café. "Most of these pamphlets were confiscated and burned by the gendarmes. Somehow, this pair managed to survive." He shrugged, looking anything but ignorant concerning that matter.

"Do you know who made them?"

An overconfident smile revealed an answer Nicholas already suspected. "I do, but I hold that information in the strictest confidence. They are a work of art, are they not?"

He said the word "art" like they were something to behold and in a way they were. They had made Nicholas stare, but not because he respected the artist's talent. He didn't know a lot about art, but he'd seen enough to know when the artist's message was to convey something beautiful and inspiring verses something degrading and most of the time untrue.

"I can't say I'm a man that knows that much about art, but that—" Nicholas eyed the pamphlets. "—doesn't suit my taste. At the end of the day propaganda is propaganda. And in my experience, there is always more that hasn't been told than is."

His honest opinion was met with a scowl. "I suppose that is my own fault for asking an Englishman's opinion over a Frenchman's issue. And you?" Evidently done with Nicholas, the French aristocrat looked to Lewis, an air of evaluation in his demeanor. "I have seen you here before."

Lewis stood to his feet, giving a slight bow as if to try and undo the damage Nicholas had done. "Yes, monsieur. I have been to the café a small number of times and I have heard of your opinions to the state of your country."

"Well, see to it that you do not come again." Casting forth a sour expression, the baron turned on his heeled boot. Whether on purpose or not Nicholas didn't know, but the man supposedly brought up in French etiquette and gentility had just shoved Lewis aside with the charge.

As Marc walked away, he either didn't notice or didn't care about the letter that had fallen out of Lewis's coat pocket during the encounter.

"You weren't kidding. I'll be content keeping my distance from him. Here." Nicholas stooped to pick the envelope.

"No." Lewis scrambled for the letter. "That's all right. I've got it." He shoved the correspondence back into the inside of his coat, though not before Nicholas saw the crimson-colored stamp with the crowned "G" emblem—King George's seal.

Chapter 16

Charlotte breathed in. A pungent smell of wet earth mixed with fish floated around her. There was something familiar about the smell and yet something different from the last time she was here. The lack of the complimentary scents of sea water and sandalwood made her all too aware of what that something was.

Her time here by the Seine River with Nicholas had been marked with fewer pedestrians on the Pont Neuf. Today, people scattered over the bridge, not only to cross from one side to the other, but to make their living by way of two enterprises: entertaining or selling.

The river, too, was within its full activity. A choice that had been deliberate—the earlier hours more suited to her agenda than when Paris returned to their homes to sup before taking to the city again. Dr. Freminet may have been able to use the river's calm waters to conduct his research, but she needed the bustling activity of the merchants and traders to conduct her own.

The once-open quays now teemed with activity. Ships pressed shoulder to shoulder along the docks as workers hauled wine casks ashore and inspectors watched for smugglers among the crowds. Grain barges drifted past while bundles of Lyon silk were lashed tight for transport, the river alive with trade and possibility.

She smiled to herself, feeling a sort of accomplishment before she had actually done anything. A group of men used a system of ropes and pulleys to unload just what she'd hoped to find. Timber.

The workers used the roped system to hoist the logs from the ship's deck before swinging them to the dock. From there, some of the men held a large stick with an impressive, tipped hook as a tool for loading the logs onto a waiting cart.

She went over to the scene, making sure she kept her distance from the men at work and the lumber in their possession. A man stood near them clearly overlooking the undertaking. He barked something in French she didn't understand, yet the workers pivoted by swinging the logs in a different direction that seemed to satisfy the man who'd given the order. A satisfied hum tingled her throat, knowing she'd found her man.

"Bonjour monsieur. Are you the overseer to this operation?" She faced the group unloading the beams while standing beside him.

He didn't look at her, his attention solely on the workers and their progress unloading the ship.

"Oui, I am the foreman."

"Wonderful. I'd like a moment of your time if you have one."

When he didn't give her an answer, she chose to take his silence as a sign to go on.

"Do you by chance know where this load of lumber has come from?" She knotted her hands in front of her at her blue, linen skirt. It was one of her plainer dresses that she'd brought from home, and a crucial reminder of why she was here. The dress was hardly a favorite, but practical—the best choice for being taken seriously in the current setting, especially when she ventured her panniered skirts and piling mane from court would have the opposite effect.

"Yes, mademoiselle. According to the ship's captain who I spoke with earlier, this one's come from Normandy."

Ignoring the annoyance in his tone, she aimed to find out more. "And do you know where this load is destined?"

"No, I don't." His fingers, dirty from work, tapped against his trousers. "My knowledge of what happens to the timber only goes as far as getting it unloaded off the ship effectively and in a timely manner." His tone sharpened as his head jerked to a worker struggling to steady a beam. "To do that, I won't be able to answer any more of your questions, not while my attention needs to be focused on my workers' safety in the job they have to do. What I can tell you is judging by the size and cut of this haul, this wood's bound for a yard until it's ready for use." He signaled to the waiting cart where some of the unloaded beams sat.

One of the workers that had been helping unload the timber came over to them. The worker gave her a single glance before speaking with the foreman, their heads angled toward each other as they spoke in hushed tones, indicating she was not part of their conversation. The foreman gave the other man a nod and the worker returned to the ship, the foreman after him. He was there for several minutes, talking with different men aboard and at one point disappearing beneath the main deck.

When he disembarked the ship again, Charlotte ran up to him. "What's wrong? What are they doing?"

"The wood is rotted—much of it. We didn't see the damage before because many of them are piled below in the hull of the ship, but I have just confirmed it. We'll still have to unload the cargo, but the buyer will not be happy."

And neither was he by his grimace.

Yet, she couldn't believe how perfect this seemed for her. The dock clerk in Calais had told her goods from Le Havre traveled to the capital via the very same river she viewed now. With that in mind, she'd come to the Seine in hopes of finding a potential buyer for her aunt. This could be her chance. She tempered her excitement.

"Who is the buyer?"

The man scratched the stubble on his jaw with his calloused fingers. "He is the owner of the Chateau de la Chênaie."

Nothing she recognized. She folded her arms, considering. "I see. Is that here in Paris?"

"It is in the country—in Fontainebleau."

She sighed. Another journey. And considering the futility of the last trip she'd embarked upon without Nicholas's knowledge, she was hesitant to proceed on another.

The hesitancy was new, she not sure if she entirely liked the change. She knew she didn't need the man, but Nicholas's caring nature when she had been anything but easy toward him made her feel safer somehow.

"Is there something I can be of assistance with mademoiselle?"

The inquisitive voice behind her was more refined than the foreman she'd been speaking with. Given the concern she heard in the male tone and what she was doing—a woman of her class, if only by her aunt's status, speaking with a day laborer—she hastened to reassure him.

"No, no." She flapped her hand in the voice's direction as if to ward him off. She appreciated the gentleman's inquiry to her safety, but it wasn't necessary, or desired for that matter. "This man and I were just talking about his latest shipment. You can move along but thank you for your assistance."

There was a beat of silence, then footsteps that approached closer to her and the foreman.

"I am afraid I cannot, as much as I'd like to." The insistence behind the words annoyed her.

She didn't need this distraction when she was on the cusp of finding a new partner. She turned to the other man so that she was facing him full on. Stutter-stepping backward into the embankment, the hem of her dress became a soggy, muddied green. "Monsieur Vantinelle?"

Her hand went to her chest. At first, she considered how he might be viewing her—out of the tumultuous workings of court attire, opting for the simpler ones from home instead. A home he had less than pleasant feelings toward. But then she remembered. This man might've seemed like her only option before, but he wasn't now.

She dropped her hand from her chest, suddenly not caring about her soiled skirts. "I didn't expect to find you here. I thought men like you preferred the comfort of your salons and drawing rooms." Her tone came out condescending, but she didn't care. The man had already made an assumption about her based on where she was from. She might as well do the same, especially now that she had an edge.

He seemed to scan her form, appearing somewhat shocked, but undeterred. "I am just as surprised to find you here. Yet, here we are."

"Yes, well, don't worry on my account. I just had a few more things to accomplish here and then I'll be on my way." She began to turn back to the foreman, new questions arising that she needed answers to.

"You mistake the reason for my interference, Mademoiselle Thatcher."

She turned back to the vicomte, feeling her brow thicken with flesh.

"I heard the man clearly state that he had many distractions to his work to see to. I do not think he should have to bear another."

"A forbearance? I was hardly imposing on this gentleman here." One look at the foreman told her the laborer agreed more with the vicomte before the nobleman crossed his satin-wrapped arms behind his back.

"May I offer to walk you back to your accommodations while we let this man get back to—" He sighed, glancing briefly at the timber still being unloaded. "—the unfortunate situation at hand?"

She wasn't going to get any further with the noble around. She didn't know why he was here, but it was obvious by his firm stance that he wasn't budging. She'd have to come back and finish her conversation on another day.

She almost accepted his invitation to escort her to the boardinghouse, thinking the time could be well-used to further her aunt's request about the business partnership. The frustrated look on his face and the very notion that she might have to explain what she was doing here at the river made her think otherwise.

"Thank you, Monsieur le Vicomte, but I can manage." She swept past him, already planning her return to the river. If the man thought a firm stance was going to send her away for good, he was highly mistaken.

***

Thwarted from her plan and progress, Charlotte stomped back toward her boardinghouse, the caked mud from her boots and hem flinging in every which way on the journey. There, she could at least sup her tea where besides acting as a medicinal remedy for her condition, always seemed to calm her.

"Charlotte, is that you?"

Hearing the male voice calling out to her, Charlotte's quick and determined stride came to a standstill on the corner of a Parisian street. Only now was she acutely aware that she hadn't applied the rouge and powder that held such popularity by the French nobility, and her soiled skirts did her no favors. She didn't worry over her appearance as much with the vicomte even given his contempt for her homeland, but Marc was a different matter. Viewing her as if under an artist's scope, she wondered what he might think, if only a little.

"Marc." She turned, feigning a smile to mask her surprise and the irritation lingering from her earlier conversation by the Seine. "I thought you would be at Versailles today enjoying the hunt?" An activity she cared little for.

"We would've, if it weren't for my brother's insatiable curiosity to fill his head with radical notions." Claudine and her ever-present fashion sense and refinement emerged from a modest townhouse crammed in the middle of two adjoining homes. She joined her brother on the front steps, the slight pinch in Claudine's mouth telling Charlotte that she disapproved of whatever they had just partaken in. Either that or Charlotte's less than agreeable fashion sense today. Maybe both.

"They're not radical." Marc offered Claudine the use of his arm, helping his sister to descend the steps toward an awaiting carriage. "You've just been behind the mirage of privilege so long you can't see what's right in front of you. We were attending a salon at the home of the Madame de Vatin." His eyes directed to the tall, stacked building she'd seen them come out of. "I would've just come myself, but Claudine insisted I not."

"Because I know your passion is what drives you. Which wouldn't be a problem if you knew when to bridal your tongue. But a loose tongue can be dangerous. You never know what damage it will do."

A loose tongue. The phrase reminded Charlotte of a different occurrence when she'd heard something similar about her own actions. Nicholas had called her a loose cannon. She couldn't help but think that although the two descriptions were different, they still held the same meaning.

Marc shrugged, holding the caution with little care. "The former General of Finances was there to enlighten us with some of the proposals he made to the king, one of which stirred the crowd immensely—equal share of taxes on all French parties." He looked at Charlotte as if he held a piece of knowledge worth its price in gold. "Did you know that nobles are tax exempt? They do not have to pay certain taxes."

"A privilege that you yourself have, brother." Claudine's tone contained a sharpness, though not betraying the gracefulness with which she stepped down the final length of steps to the cobblestone street. "And let us not forget Monsieur Turgot was *dismissed* from his high position. Perhaps keep that in mind if you choose to follow the man so willingly. Consider where his ideas might lead you." Again, the warning of a loved one rang true, though by Marc's unchanged animation, to deaf ears.

"The court no doubt made the decision to dismiss him due to the inconvenience of what it might cost to change things for the better. The man wants to help his people while the nobility only wants things to stay the way they are—lopsided and unfair in the eyes of most of its citizens."

Claudine offered no words of reproof this time. She let out a lengthy breath as if she'd grown weary of the subject. Such a reaction made Charlotte wonder just how often the topic had dominated their conversations.

With the help of her driver, Claudine was the first to enter the carriage, her voluminous skirts squeezing through the less than suitable opening.

This time when the offer for transportation home was extended, Charlotte accepted. She took her place next to Claudine inside the carriage as the driver closed the door.

"Have you heard the news, chérie?" Claudine laid a gloved hand on Charlotte's arm, a poignant smile emerging. "The King and Queen have decided to open Versailles to Paris's local artists. They are hosting a contest to have their work displayed in the halls of the palace." The lines of worry Charlotte could only imagine were under Claudine's make-up would've disappeared in that moment if they could've been seen.

"Admission will be charged to anyone who chooses to come. The money raised is said to be granted toward rebuilding the Palais and Saint Chapelle from the fire."

"For a single day those that come to tour the palace will also take in the grandeur of the paintings chosen by the royal family for their walls." Pleasure resided in both Marc's expression and tone. "All of France who come to Versailles will be sure to see them."

Charlotte's lips parted, but nothing came out, feeling euphoric while also perplexed by the news. "That's wonderful, Marc." Not having missed the diminished respect Marc had for the monarchy earlier, she felt inclined to ask. "That is to say you will be submitting your own work, I hope?"

Her question was answered with an arrogant grin—one that made him markedly less handsome to her, even if happy for him for the occasion. "Oui. It is a rare and choice opportunity."

"I'm surprised you did not know, Charlotte—" Claudine gave her a knowing smile. "—considering you were the one who approached Her Majesty with the idea in the first place."

Charlotte lifted her chin, feeling the full measure of her satisfaction. Along with her idea of the fleur-de-lis for the queen's lace, she'd also approached Marie Antionette about the art contest in the palace gardens on the morning she *temporarily paused* the Hall of Mirrors procession. The conversation that day had been short and to the point, more out of necessity than anything else for fear of a guard pressing Charlotte out. But had her proposal of the contest become a reality?

"But how do you know that?" Charlotte bit her lip, feeling a slight quiver in her stomach. "Her Majesty and I had a private conversation." Or as private as Charlotte imagined it could've possibly been, the queen in constant companion of her courtiers. With only two present at the time, she'd counted herself fortunate for such a nonpublic moment.

"Nothing stays secret in Versailles." Marc gave her a droll smile. "I told you, even in a palace made of stone and mortar the walls are thin as paper."

"In this case, the walled topiaries of the palace gardens." Claudine gave a small laugh with the correction, the sound coming out like a song. She returned her hands delicately to her satin dress, the color of a pink carnation. "But the occasion of the contest is sure to be a grand event." Her tutor's eyes sparkled with delight.

And the opportunity Charlotte hoped for—to truly impress the vicomte.

Having been dropped by Claudine and Marc at the boardinghouse, Charlotte spent the next half hour enjoying a cup of her special tea before retrieving a small sack of French coin. She traced her steps back toward the dressmaker Claudine had recommended, taking an alleyway as a shortcut, but stopped.

A child—thin and clothing disheveled in a way that told a heart-wrenching story—came up to her, the girl's small eyes moist. "Madame." Her voice broke as she addressed Charlotte. "I have lost my Maman."

An excruciating void gripped at Charlotte's chest, knowing what it was like to lose one's mother, though by what she understood by the child's request the little girl's mother was still alive.

Charlotte bent down, meeting the child's eyes and making a promise she intended to keep. "We will find your maman. Tell me, what does she look like?"

The child's lips parted as if to say something and in the middle of the motion, Charlotte felt a light tug near the pocket of her skirts. She glanced in the direction of the pulling sensation, but by the time her brain had connected with what was happening, her body was too slow to react. All she caught sight of was the back of someone's head, possibly a girl based on the braids. The figure seemed to be a few years older and hurried down the alley before suddenly turning a sharp corner, vanishing from view. When she turned back to face the lost child, no one.

Charlotte searched her pockets, digging her fingers deep into them. Her chest burned with anger when they came up empty apart from a loose thread that had torn inside. She fought the beating in her chest, feeling it quicken, her heart threatening to fail her, but she couldn't die in the middle of a Parisian alley alone. *She wouldn't.*

Remembering the tea she had recently and its medicinal effects calmed her, giving her a sense of hope in the midst of her wretched condition. She drew strength in having thought to take it and thankful for the timing. Gradually, her heart began to slow to its normal rhythm, and she could better grip the consequences of what had just occurred.

Her bag of coin was gone. Which meant the dress she had in mind for the day of the contest at Versailles was also gone along with her stolen money. Having to learn what was becoming a painful and trying lesson, she was grateful the bag hadn't contained all of her expenses, but the amount at her current disposal wouldn't be enough to replace what she'd had in mind for the dressmaker, or to buy a new dress at all for that matter. Not at the rate making lace took to obtain her earnings.

Trudging back in the direction of her boardinghouse in defeat, Charlotte saw the sign for the dentelle.

"What is wrong, mon amie?" Louise ran to the door to meet her, her friend's normally bright-eyed expression turned bleak.

"The monarchy is having a contest at Versailles, one I recommended." She knew she shouldn't feel this way over a dress, especially when she considered the sacrifice Louise and her mother took every day just to make sure bread remained on their table and medicine obtained. "I thought . . . I was hoping . . ." She squeezed her eyes tight, unable to face Louise with her frivolous desire yet still wanting it. "For the occasion . . . for the vicomte . . ." Her head slumped forward, her chin nearly hitting her chest, angry that she was feeling this way and only now realizing she still had her mud-trimmed skirt from when she'd been at the river that afternoon.

Looking at her without the judgment she undoubtedly deserved, Louise put a finger to the corner of her mouth. "I have an idea." The finger tapped once, her friend's expression thoughtful before she turned up a side smile. "But you're not going to like it."

Chapter 17

"I wish I could say it was nice to see you, but that would not be entirely true, Captain Edwards." Louis Auguste's advisor stood in front of the doors that led into the king's bedchamber, guarding the tall, gilded gateway much like the Swiss guard behind him. "I presume you are here for the same reason as your previous visits?" To say the man looked displeased was an understatement.

Nicholas gave a smile that did little to improve the man's mood. "If that reason is to have a private audience with the king of France, then yes, that's why I'm here."

"Yet, you come and wait in the L'Oeul de Boeuf for hours and have been denied each time." The advisor's voice held challenge, but it wasn't patronizing, more like he'd grown tired of these meetings.

If that were true, and he believed it was, Nicholas couldn't blame him. He had too, but today he'd changed his strategy.

"What makes you think it will be any different today?"

In truth, he didn't. Not really. This was his last shot—his last chance to prove to both King George and his father he could be counted on. If his plan didn't work now, he was out of options apart from returning to London and facing his failure head-on. Hopefully today, he wouldn't have to.

Nicholas could feel the tightened rise and fall of his chest. Much like the chronometer he'd tried to give to his father, a rectangular box hung low within his coat pocket. "Because I have something for him this time." He patted at his breast, the light thumping of the box shifting the contents inside.

"Not another letter signed by King George as to why you're here, I hope." The natural slope of the advisor's mouth inverted. "If so, perhaps I've been too generous in my assessment of your capabilities."

"Take whatever assessment you like. It's not a letter. It's a gift." Nicholas retrieved the box wrapped in simple brown paper from the inside pocket of his Navy uniform. "It has come to my attention His Majesty of France enjoys hobbies of a common nature. I'd be happy to deliver this myself if you'd just let me—" He made a motion to side-step the advisor, but the man cut him off, the tight curls of his peruke somehow holding fast in place.

"I applaud your effort, Captain, but there's no need. I will be the one to determine whether this *gift* is of value enough to bother the king." He peered down the bridge of his nose at the box and motioned his hand in a way that flapped the lace around his wrist. "Here, let me have a look."

Nicholas frowned, pulling the box away an inch. "I take it you're not a man who appreciates surprises."

The man's chin snapped up, ruffling the tied cravat at his neck. "As a man whose very responsibility is to make sure the king is well-informed—" He rolled his shoulders back, his gaze penetrating. "—absolutely not, monsieur."

The advisor snatched the brown wrapped box from Nicholas's palm. Despite Nicholas wanting to deliver the package himself, he still took that as a good sign. It showed interest. That was already farther than he'd been able to get on his previous visits.

His pulse hitching up speed, Nicholas watched the man untie the small piece of gold ribbon before opening the box to reveal a brass combination and pump lock laid inside. Nicholas smiled to himself. He didn't know King Louis Auguste at all and disliked that the man avoided him at each turn, but he could appreciate the man's interest in useful things.

The top of the lock was engraved with the king's crown and coat of arms, an idea that came from the work Charlotte had come up with for the queen's lace. One side of the shield showed off the unmistakable fleurs-de-lis of France and the other, the golden, interlinked chains of Navarre. At its base, two intertwined L's were forged—the king's monogram.

Already reading the cynicism lessen in the advisor's eyes, Nicholas felt the tightening in his chest loosen to know the pamphlet drawing he'd seen at the Café Procope held some truth.

After taking a moment to study the lock, the French noble met his gaze again. "I see you have decided to choose from the king's *least* coveted hobbies here at court." The corner of his mouth slightly raised, giving Nicholas further encouragement. "Nevertheless, I will take it to him."

"And how do I know my gift will reach the king? What is to stop you from keeping it yourself or selling it?" Desperation coated Nicholas's throat even as he tried swallowing it down. But there was a war that depended on his success.

The king's advisor had been in the middle of retying the ribbon before stopping short of completing the task. The hint of a smile he'd given Nicholas now twisted like he'd been outrightly offended. "Trust me, Captain, if I were concerned with only my own interest, I wouldn't take the time to do either of those things. Throwing the lock away would be much easier. But I can tell you this to put your mind at ease concerning your gift. I will return with an invitation from the king, or I won't. Either way you will have your answer."

Nicholas couldn't say he altogether liked the one-sided arrangement or his chances, but he didn't have much of a choice. This man was his only pathway to the king of France.

With trepidation at the forefront, Nicholas watched the king's advisor disappear behind the set of gilded doors, leaving Nicholas with no choice but to wait.

It was less than half an hour when the same man returned, giving nothing away in his expression of whether the gift had been well-received or not. He made a motion for Nicholas to accompany him to the side of the room, the drumming in Nicholas's chest inching up a notch in speed.

"Congratulations, Captain. His Majesty has agreed to see you."

"Good." Nicholas released a breath he hadn't realized he'd held, but he didn't think the advisor noticed. "What I have to discuss with the king shouldn't take up too much of his time." He took a step toward the gilded doors again where he'd meet the king in his bedchamber—a common practice of Louis XIV evidently continued now in the reign of his grandson.

"Your meeting with His Majesty will not be today." A firm hand stopped in the air between them at the line of buttons on Nicholas's coat.

Nicholas stepped back, preferring the space away from the Frenchman, but not at what felt more like a game being rigged against him. "Why not? I told you. It won't take long. I only need to—"

The man shook his head, the swift movement sending a small particle of white powder into the air of the L'Oeul de Boeuf. "The royal family will be hosting an event, Les Muses de Versailles. The occasion is to display works of Paris's local artists in the palace. The king will see you then and only then, monsieur. After that, you will no longer be welcomed at Versailles *so patiently* as you have been. Do you understand?"

Hearing the finality in the man's tone, Nicholas nodded.

"In the meantime, the king has invited you to explore the royal gardens at your leisure." The message came out clear enough. He was being sent out of the king's waiting room. He was about to ask whether the French king liked the lock, but before he could, the advisor had vanished behind the doors of the king's bedchamber again.

It didn't matter. The lightening of his chest gave room to a deep breath of relief. He'd been granted an audience.

Something between elation and liberation emerged inside as Nicholas made his way back through the corridor of the palace from the king's antechamber. At last he could write some good news to his own king.

The message wouldn't completely satisfy, but the news might suffice until he could get his questions answered the day of the contest.

He'd exited the palace from a pair of tall, double doors that led out into the great gardens where he was greeted by a small gust of wind holding the pleasant scent of fall foliage. A picnic of grand proportions was underway, probably the last of the season due to the oncoming winter. He looked for the queen, surmising the occasion to be for her benefit by the servants carrying trays of different French foods. But nothing gave him the impression she was in attendance, having seen her from afar surrounded by her courtiers like a queen bee cloaked in a swirling hive of gilded, buzzing attendants, each vying for a place closer to her light.

He marveled at the scene, his thoughts going to a woman he was sure would enjoy such frivolity, the thought bringing on an easy smile.

Though he didn't know the vicomte, Nicholas ventured by the man's title and the expectations associated with it that he would be close to the palace. Which meant that the vicomte she sought out was among the gathered nobles.

Nicholas scanned the crowd. He was beginning to understand Charlotte better. If the vicomte was here then she wouldn't be far off. He knew what the man's business cooperation meant to her, at least for her family's sake.

His eyes made another pass just to be sure, but he didn't see or hear any sign of her, something not easily missed. A white lace scarf grabbed his attention, not anything out of the ordinary here where lace was abundant, but he recognized this one. The woman it was wrapped around, however, he'd never seen in his life.

No. It couldn't be. Yet, there she was—Charlotte Thatcher dolled up in all the glory of French court.

***

Charlotte wrapped her fichu tighter around her shoulders with little satisfaction. Though the holed patterns of the shawl did well to show off its beauty and craftmanship, they did little to provide any true warmth. Clouds rolled over the lush gardens of Versailles and the crisp breezes of autumn were starting to cool.

A small group of musicians accompanied them on the Royal Way. The performers started to play a minuet on the large, grassy area of the gardens while the rest of the picnic comprised of France's nobility had their choosing from a scrumptious assortment of cheeses, meats, breads, and French pastries.

The small cake Charlotte had on her plate was coated with a light sugar icing. She took a bite of the confection, trying to appreciate Claudine's preparations for such a picnic even as her stomach jilted in opposition.

This wasn't a feeling she was used to—her nerves jumbled. And though she ordinarily welcomed new things, she couldn't altogether say she liked this sensation.

She swallowed the petite four, hoping to quell the knots in her stomach on the way down. It wasn't that she was surprised to see the vicomte here, but more with how to proceed with him next.

"I didn't realize you invited Monsieur de Vantinelle today."

"But of course. Why wouldn't he be invited?" The Comtesse d'Amboise helped herself to a handful of small cakes from a servant's silver-dipped tray.

"The vicomte is here at the chateau often doing his part to help the king. I would not deprive him of taking a small reprieve from the obligation." Claudine took a sip of hot chocolate, her red lips staining the top edge of the porcelain cup. She gave a tiny smile, looking at the man in a way that hinted at admiration, maybe even fondness for him. "Besides, it looks like music has put him in good spirits."

Apparently so. The man was currently dancing with the Duchesse de Brienne, a woman Claudine had introduced her to. Charlotte hardly recognized her as the same model from Marc's painting. The powder that was meant as a veneer to mask imperfections instead gathered in the deep lines of her face to produce the opposite effect, thereby accentuating her age while her stained pink cheeks had been overwhelmed by rouge.

"Too bad it hasn't done the same for the duke." The comtesse swished her fan to shoo a wayward crumb from her lap where it landed on the green grass.

Charlotte followed her gaze across the lawn at an equally painted male face with downturned lips holding a brown and white pooch in his arms. The duke devoured a stack of cold meat while the pup whined for a treat.

She looked at the vicomte again, somehow feeling encouraged and more ready to face him than she had been by the river when he essentially told her to take a hike. She was still researching other options in case she failed to make a business deal with him, but maybe today she could shift their relationship in the right direction. Dance, after all, required a partnership. It might be a place to start.

The quartet began to play another song, one she didn't recognize but guessed many did judging by those that joined in the dance from their seats on the lawn, and from those who'd paused their walking nearby to partake.

Seeing the duchesse had returned to her dog, Charlotte saw the opportunity for what it was—an opening.

She gathered the skirts of Claudine's borrowed gown before making her way over to the vicomte. That's when she noticed him, the corner of her eye beholding a blue navy coat that stood out among the colors of a pastel palette. Nicholas.

She turned her head fully in his direction just to be sure, and the conversation she'd rehearsed in her mind for the vicomte vanished. Nicholas looked directly at her. The angle of his chin and the way he smirked made her feel like he had caught her in something she'd meant to keep secret. What was more, he seemed to be enjoying himself. If anything, he should have been the one out of place, but as it was, she suddenly felt like she stuck out like a black spot on white silk.

He strode up to her, looking less like the gentleman she knew him to be and more like a vagrant. "How is your picnic going?" The question seemed innocent enough, but that rogue smile of his told a different story.

"Fine." She gave him a look, confident he was holding something back even now. "Correct me if I'm reading you wrong, captain, but it appears there's something else you want to say."

She could swear there was a rascal in this man if she hadn't known better.

"Oh, there's a lot I'd like to say, but to start, I think we're even now in regards of you making things up for ditching London. Other than that, I just have one more question."

"What?" She readied herself for something patronizing.

The gentleman she knew returned, his smile softening a degree. "Would you like to dance?"

At first, she wasn't certain if he was serious, but his glance went to the group on the lawn before back to her again. She'd never seen the man dance before, and it was hard to imagine a navy captain bent on protocol might be willing to partake in such fun. Yet, she had to admit there had been more to Captain Nicholas Edwards than she'd previously believed.

"I didn't peg you for the dancing type."

"Well, maybe there's more to me than what you have pegged. So, what do you think?" His eyebrows raised. "If you don't mind dancing with an Englishman at French court."

She answered by walking toward the group of dancers. The musicians started an allemande, she and Nicholas joining the smooth, flowing movement.

"I take it that's the vicomte your Aunt Sylvia wants a business partnership with?" Having already bowed to each other to signal the beginning of the dance, Nicholas took her hand in his.

She felt a shot of warmth at his touch while seeing his observation had been correct. "How did you know?" She followed his lead, imitating tiny steps that caused the panniers under her skirt to bounce. His hand never leaving hers, he brought it up over their heads, guiding her under his arm while she made a complete turn to the music's rhythm.

"I've been around the palace a few times. You start to learn who's who."

"A few times?" The admittance nearly made her stumble, but the strength in his arms helped keep her balanced. "You mean, this isn't your first time to Versailles?"

"No, it isn't." There was something careful and calculated in his confession.

"And just how many times have you visited?"

"More than I like."

Her skin prickled with annoyance as she made a pass underneath their connection. He wasn't exactly being forthcoming, but she had heard enough to take a guess. "Nicholas Edwards, do you mean to tell me the reason we came here to Paris in the first place was because your orders had you come to Versailles—the one place I'd begged to see?"

"Yes, that much I can say."

A part of her wanted to stamp his foot, but the satin slippers Claudine had loaned her where no match for his boots. Irritation stirred within her. He hadn't said much, only confirming what she had put together on her own. But she could piece the rest together. "If you've come to Versailles, then that means you've come to meet the—"

"King. Yes."

The sequence of the dance had brought both of their hands together as he revealed the truth. The feel of the small embrace sparked something within her even as the news he uncovered made her hands go limp in his grasp.

"The king?"

Realizing her feet no longer moved to the music, he cleared her away from the dance area and the rest of the aristocrats.

"My orders have me here to meet the king. I'm sorry, Charlotte. I wish I could've told you sooner. I'm not sure I should be telling you even now."

His hands were still wrapped around hers. She removed them, stepping back to create a small distance. "Not unless I pry the information from you, you mean?"

"No." He stepped toward her, closing the distance again, his voice firm but holding that same gentleness she'd heard in the stagecoach from Calais. "That's not what I mean. I'm giving you the information because I want to."

She considered that. The man in front of her would take a secret to his grave if he had to. And this one—a matter of great importance when she really thought about it, he had decided to share with her.

Her shoulders began to slowly relax, shifting downward while emotion flowed upward as if filling every compartment inside her body for the trust this man placed in her. "Well, did you get your meeting?"

"Not yet, but I will soon."

He smiled, looking more relieved than happy.

"All right." Satisfied enough not to interrogate him further when considering the weight of the information he'd just given, she retrieved some foods from a servant's tray, bringing back a plate of cold meats, fruits, and a mix of sweet and savory pastries. She placed the foods on a plot of grass, taking a seat nearby as her skirts fanned out around her. "You mentioned you had some things on your mind. What are they?"

"Well, to name the obvious, I'd have to say there's something different about you today. But I can't quite make it out." He rubbed at his square jaw, giving her an exaggerated up and down look, his lips tucked as if he were trying to solve a mystery.

She laughed.

"I hardly recognized you in that costume of yours."

"Costume?" She let a hand flutter to her throat, her lips giving a mocked pout. "I'll have you know Claudine has fitted me with the finest of French fashion."

He swallowed a bite of meat pastry, looking unimpressed. "The dress is nice, but I've seen you look prettier in less extravagance."

She felt a warming in her cheeks. She'd been called pretty a time or two, but from this man it held much more meaning to her. The shock of the compliment diffused her weak defenses, if only for a moment. "Look around you, Nicholas." She waved her hand toward the ornaments of Versailles—the fashionably dressed men and women in their light-colored satin suits and gowns and their overly decorated hair and faces. "You don't exactly blend in here."

"You make that sound like it's the worst thing. But I'm not so sure it is." He leaned in closer to her, his eyes boring into her own. "You mentioned before the vicomte isn't a fan of the colonies, which I'm still not convinced is the case. But if that's true, is that why you're doing this—to somehow change his mind about you so you'll make a partnership?"

His stare was penetrating, making her smugness vanish. Had she been so easy to see through?

He shrugged. "Look, if your aunt wants to do business with a man so bent against someone he hasn't truly gotten to know, she's going to get the wrong end of the deal if he agrees to one. For you and your aunt's sake, I hope he doesn't."

"Excusez-moi, monsieur." The male voice broke the tension but only a little.

Nicholas looked annoyed, like there was more he wanted to say, but wouldn't with the added company. She wondered if that conversation would continue later when they had another moment alone.

With a firm jaw and what she read as recognition in his eyes, Nicholas turned to Marc. "Is there something I can do for you, sir?"

The side of Marc's mouth curved up.

Not sure what to make of the encounter, Charlotte was only aware that a different kind of tension arose. It wasn't between her and Nicholas this time, but something unspoken between him and Marc. Yet she wasn't sure if she wanted to uncover its cause here in the public eye, especially with the vicomte close by.

Having more of a knack for starting trouble than ending it, she reached for any solution to diffuse the situation before it escalated any further.

"Captain Edwards," She made her tone light and friendly, feigning complete ignorance to whatever conflict lay between these two men. "This is Marc Chazot, the Baron d'Aubray and Claudine's brother. You'll find he's an excellent artist here at court. As a matter of fact, he'll be painting my portrait to enter into *Les Muses de Versailles* here at the palace." She forced a small laugh, hoping the humor might lighten the mood. "Perhaps even in my *costume*."

Nicholas's gaze shot to her, his jaw having gone slack and telling her the attempt to humor failed. "He's painting your portrait?"

"Yes, for the contest." Her voice wavered with an unexplained feeling of apprehension. "The winners will have their artwork displayed within the palace walls. And the king and queen are opening the palace that day to all who want to view the selected."

"Yes, no doubt most of Paris will be flocking to the Chateau." There was a glimmer in Marc's eye, the reason stemming, she could only guess, from his excitement for the event. "Those who are able to attend will be sure to spread the word of what they see."

She shared his excitement, hers originating from the chance to be viewed in such a favorable way by the nobility and hopefully the vicomte, but she could see Nicholas didn't hold the same opinion. The man looked downright livid.

Nicholas looked from Marc to her. "And to think I thought being noticed wasn't something you lacked." He stood from his place at their picnic, meeting Marc at his full height. "I'm sorry, sir." His tone dripped with insincerity as he pulled at the bottom of his lapels to smooth out his uniform over his chest. "Where are my manners? Was there something you wanted?"

"I only came to ask the lady to dance."

Nicholas gave a slow nod accompanied by a tight smile. "That, sir, is up to her." His eyes flicked briefly to her again, the undertone of his

words clear. If she wasn't careful, this dance might lead her down a
dangerous path.

Chapter 18

"This is where I'm going to find a dress?" Charlotte stared in front of her, a layer of confidence in Louise's plan evaporating. She'd visited the Place de Grève before, though not on purpose. The image of the rope around the man's neck was seared into her mind though she'd seen him only briefly when she'd taken a wrong turn. The courtyard was certainly not a place she'd ever venture again, and the last place she thought Louise would take her. Yet here they were. She furrowed her brow, not bothering to hide her confusion. "But I thought they held public executions here?"

"Oui." Louise's tone matched the solemness of the place's reputation. "They do, but not today. On Mondays the space is used by the merchants to sell second-hand clothing. There's a chance we might find you a dress suitable for the Muses de Versailles contest."

"A chance?" Charlotte cocked her head at the large assortment of vendors that stretched over the Place de Grève. The tents, stalls, and tables nearly touched, resembling the weavings of a blanket as if trying to cover the awful memories here with something more distracting. "What kind of chance do you mean?"

"A small one." Louise's tone held the slightest morsel of hope, but her eyes seemed eager. "But even that is sure to diminish while we stand here. The longer we wait, the more likely the more tasteful items will be gone."

Not entirely liking her options, Charlotte weighed them. She could wear the dress Claudine had loaned her from her first night at the opera and her visits since to Versailles. But the occasion of the art contest called for something new or at the very least something different. Sadly, a new dress was no longer possible with her finances seriously stripped. The situation reminded her of the boycott in the colonies and her aunt's idea to fashion their own lace when none from England could be had.

Maybe she could no longer purchase the dress she'd conjured up, but she could make do with the materials at hand—in this case, the unwanted fashions of a duchesse or comtesse. Even if they were no longer current in Paris, the tiring trends here were still at the cusp of their prime back at the colonies.

"So, what do you think, mon amie? Are we going in or not?"

Hearing an earnestness to Louise's tone, Charlotte felt her own rise.

"We are absolutely going in."

They were already late to the sale. In the middle of the square, booths crowded together, each claimed by a different merchant. What had once been neatly displayed now lay in picked-over heaps. Still, Charlotte and Louise went through the piles, tossing aside skirts, hats, and mismatched petticoats.

Merchants pressed in around them—one merchant to the point of nearly pushing Charlotte into one of the changing stalls. She didn't like it, but she wasn't willing to call the search over yet.

She sifted through mended shifts, stained aprons, and simple bodices with patched or frayed edges, feeling more discouraged at each pass.

Until she saw the very item she'd hoped to find walking out of the Place de Grève—a ruby, satin gown trimmed with worn lace and not so worn ribbons.

"Louise." Charlotte's voice came out hushed as she patted Louise on her shoulder.

Her friend looked up from inspecting a pile of fatigued petticoats. "Have you found something?"

"I did, but—" She felt a rush of trepidation. "Unfortunately, it's making its way out of the marketplace as we speak. There." She pointed to a middle-aged woman carrying the prized dress tucked snuggly and securely under her arm.

"Oh." Louise popped up from her bent stance over the stack of petticoats, her mouth formed in a tiny "o." When her lips closed again, her brown eyes veered back to Charlotte. "It might not be the only one."

But Charlotte could see by Louise's apprehension the likelihood that it was—all but certain.

"We'll keep looking." Louise nodded with encouragement, moving on to another booth.

"Maybe we don't have to." Not sure if hope or desperation led her cause, Charlotte scurried to the exit of the square of vendors and cut the woman off before she could get out of sight.

"Pardon, madame." Charlotte's hand went to her chest, feeling near winded from the burst of exercise and exhilaration of what she might obtain. "I'd like to purchase that dress from you. I have an urgent need for its use."

"As do I, mademoiselle." The woman dressed in simple brown linen covered by a tainted apron met her gaze straight on. "Unless you can pay me enough for a new one just like it, I'm afraid I cannot hand it to you." Her expression was apologetic, all the while her arm tightened around the robe as if shielding the gown like a small child from danger. "My daughter has just acquired a position as governess to a young noblewoman at court. She will be required to have a suitable dress for the responsibility." Not waiting for Charlotte to respond, the woman quickly and more resolutely than before, stepped out again toward the exit of the Place de Grève.

Charlotte had the nerve to run after her, but a word from Nicholas came to mind about not being pushy. She decided to let the woman go without further conquest.

She returned to where Louise had stayed behind at one of the booths, the same petticoat in her fingers telling Charlotte her friend had witnessed the conversation.

Feeling a sudden ache in her head, Charlotte rubbed at one side of her temple. "What are the chances we'll find another dress like the one that just ran off?"

"I'm afraid the odds are not in our favor." Louise looked toward the Seine River at a long ago risen clocktower. "It is nearly the lunch hour. The merchants would have sold their best pieces by now."

Disappointment accompanied the pain in her head, but Charlotte couldn't say she was shocked. Louise had only confirmed her suspicions.

Charlotte surveyed the number of vendors. There were still several set up. She wasn't sure on the quality of their selections, but they were there, and so that meant there was still a chance. "Let's separate." She eyed one direction of the square, then another, conveying the different areas they should seek out. "We'll cover more booths that way just to make sure. I'll meet you back at this stall in an hour."

Seeing Louise had taken to the suggestion, Charlotte watched her friend go to another vendor who eagerly approached her with a pair of worn-out boots.

Charlotte scrambled through the displays and piles of clothing that had plummeted carelessly to the ground. The task was as tedious as needleworking lace. Each piece required careful sifting, leaving her increasingly frustrated.

At least with lace there was progress, even a reward to be had if someone were to purchase the pieces. But none of that seemed possible here, her reward of finding the perfect dress for her next visit to Versailles looking non-existent by each pass she made through the clothing.

She wanted to give up, yet she couldn't afford to. Maybe her need wasn't as crucial as the woman with the other dress, but her situation was pressing enough. Claudine, as her tutor, would expect nothing short of exquisite court finery and she suspected the vicomte would too.

"Charlotte." Louise ran up to her, her friend's almond-skinned cheeks having turned pink. "Come quickly. I might have found something, but I doubt the merchant will keep it for long." Her words came out rushed with frenzy. "I told her I have a potential buyer, but if another buyer comes, she's sure to sell it."

Charlotte hurried to the stall behind Louise. Thankfully the merchant still had the dress. Without much coercing, she consented to try it on.

The small corner that served as a dressing room was partitioned by a wool curtain. Inside, the furnishings were sparse: a fogged handheld mirror that offered only a dim glimpse of her reflection in the poor light of a single candle overhead.

Charlotte fastened the gown to the stomacher, the dress Louise had found not quite fitting her body as she liked. Though loose in the outer gown and more material than she needed in the skirts, those things could be adjusted with some minor stitching. Not that big of a deal. The dress was certainly less decorated than those she'd passed by at the palace, but the cornflower blue silk taffeta still surpassed her own fashions from home, which was what she needed. This, she could work with.

"How did you ever find this?" With her new dress in tow and elation renewed for the art exhibition at Versailles, Charlotte walked in step with Louise out of the marketplace of the Place de Grève.

"The merchant said it was a late donation. A servant from one of the noblewomen brought the dress along with some old chemises from the servant's quarters." Louise's eyes shined, perhaps over the feat they'd thought was lost. "We were lucky."

Somewhere in the distance, Charlotte heard the faint sound of a chiming bell, making her aware of how much time they had spent at the marketplace and how much time Louise had given up to help on her quest.

Louise's ear inclined in the direction of the river again where she'd first viewed the clock tower, showing she'd heard the ringing too. "I am glad we found you something, mon amie." She gave Charlotte a hug, squeezing her with kindred affection before she pulled away. "But I have a meeting with the queen's dressmaker later this afternoon. I will need to go back to the dentelle and retrieve the samples she has requested."

"Of course." Charlotte smiled, glad that things were taking off with the queen's dressmaker and the queen's satisfaction over her friend's impressive talent. "Thank you, Louise, for taking me to this place. And for your help."

The two of them parted ways, Louise toward the direction of the dentelle and Charlotte back to the boardinghouse. Charlotte's steps bounded with excitement. She would've skipped on the streets like she had when she was a little girl if she didn't have to watch out for horse droppings.

She hadn't gotten far when the weird sensation that someone was watching her sent a chill up her spine. Her gaze shot around the square but came up short. Feeling her pulse pick up speed, she shifted the dress under her arm like the woman she'd confronted earlier so she could check her pockets.

What remained from her recent purchase in her skirts was still there. Attributing the ill feeling to be a trick of her mind and not of the street, she continued to the boardinghouse.

Having ordered her tea service, Charlotte retreated to her room, but not before glancing down the hallway. She hadn't seen Nicholas since the picnic at Versailles and wondered if their argument on the Royal Way was the cause—an argument that still needed to be finished, if she recalled correctly.

Trying on the dress from the Place de Grève again, she took note of the places that would need to be taken in and where the length of the fabric would need to be folded under to better equip her stride. She lacked any talent for dressmaking, but thankfully the sewing that needed to be done for her new gown was something she could manage.

She was almost finished fastening the gown to her stomacher when one of her pins failed to hold. Her breath caught. A stain, half-heartedly treated, was right in the middle of her torso.

How had she not seen it? Then she remembered the less than adequate lighting of the makeshift dressing room.

A moan slipped through her throat. What was she going to do? She couldn't wear this dress to the palace art contest, not like this.

She sucked on the inside of her lip, angry at both herself and the vendor while considering what could be done. Her extra material might prove useful, but she would need Louise's help.

Having finished her notes and pinning the areas to mark where she needed to make adjustments, Charlotte was about to carefully and slowly pull the dress' petticoat up over her head when she heard a knock. No doubt her tea service.

"Yes, thank you. I'll get it in just a moment." With that settled, she gently grabbed the lush fabric again for a second try, but was thwarted when a second knock sounded, this time heavier and more paused in between.

"Charlotte, it's me."

She stilled. Nicholas.

"I'd like to speak with you when you have a moment."

His tone was assertive, implying that he expected that moment to be soon. So, she was right. Nicholas did have more to say from their conversation at Versailles. Well, so did she.

Letting the garment fall back toward the floor, she crossed the space of the room. She opened the door and at no surprise, Nicholas stood on the other side. What did give her pause, however, was the fact that he had her tea surface in his hand, and that scowl she'd pictured him with simply wasn't there.

"I believe this belongs to you." He held the tray of tea out toward her, though not so far as to completely hand it over as if he might be extending a peace offering and was waiting for her to accept the terms.

She didn't, at least not right away. Her acceptance depended on where this conversation was going. "My tea."

"I saw it being prepared on my way in, so I offered to bring the tea up."

"Thank you." She looked at the tray, holding the same porcelain cup and kettle she'd grown accustomed to and decided to let caution lead. "Is that all?"

His mouth twisted as if he might be chewing on something. "No, that's not all."

She steeled herself for battle.

"I didn't like how our conversation ended at Versailles. So, I wanted to change that."

"Change it?" His tone held an apology, but she wasn't going to let him off that easy. "And am I to suppose you mean the comment regarding my *costume* or for having my picture painted for the contest?"

His knuckles tightened around the handles of the serving tray before color returned to his fingers. "For the record, I still don't agree with what you're doing, but no, that's not what I mean. I shouldn't have left in the middle of the argument." His jaw firmed. "But I take your mention of the portrait means you're still intending to have Marc paint it?"

She raised her chin to meet his heighted gaze. "I am."

His mouth held a grimace. "I don't think it's a good idea."

"Why?" She crossed her arms, nowhere near ready to accept his peace offering.

"I just don't get a good feeling about the man."

She recalled the way the two men had looked at each other that day like they knew one another. "You know him?"

"Not in the familiar sense, no."

She threw her arms out, wishing this man would give her more to work with and throwing him a look that she hoped conveyed that very message.

"I just don't know what his intentions are."

"His inten—?" Her arm fell to her waist while her free hand went to her mouth, knowing where this was going and somewhat tickled the man cared as much. "Nicholas, I appreciate you looking out for me. You have more than fulfilled your duty as an upright gentleman and Navy officer, but trust me when I say I can look after myself."

"I don't doubt that you can. I just know you have a way of drawing attention, sometimes the wrong attention, if I may be so blunt." He glanced away, seeming to set his sights on anything but her. "Like now."

"Now? What am I doing now?"

"I'm trying the get a point across." He gave a frustrated sigh. "And your dress is making it difficult."

"My dress?" Still unsure of what he was getting at, she assessed herself through the much less decorated and grand mirror of her room. Her throat tightened as she glanced down, his meaning becoming as clear as the crystal pendants dangling from the chandeliers at Versailles. At first, she'd thought he meant the stain she'd seen earlier, but no. She'd missed a pin or *two*.

The stomacher of the dress had fallen below the top of her stays, not only exposing her undergarment but far too much even for French fashion. She couldn't say if the pins had fallen out while she'd been disrupted in removing the garment earlier or if she'd missed them completely, but the result was the same.

She caught a glance of Nicholas in the mirror, having realized her faux pas. He suddenly seemed more interested in a small table she'd been using as a desk, perhaps giving her a moment of privacy, but she didn't miss the slight upturn of the side of his mouth as he looked away.

Snatching her lace fichu, she quickly wrapped the shawl around the exposed area. She'd presumed Nicholas would have left her to her embarrassment, the gentleman's way of allowing her to regroup, but he didn't. One look at his full hands told her the reason.

***

Nicholas didn't know quite what to do in the current moment. The first thing he could think of was turn his eyes away. He thought of pretending he hadn't noticed but one glance back at the pink climbing up Charlotte's neck and cheeks told him he wouldn't be fooling anyone.

He'd thought about leaving the room—giving her space to collect herself—but that action, too, seemed out of place with the tea set still in his hands. Somehow, knowing what to do during a raging swell out in the open water seemed easy compared with what to do with such a delicate issue like this one.

Though nothing of true significance showed, he'd seen enough that sent his thoughts sailing straight in a direction he hadn't anticipated, especially considering how they'd left things yesterday at the picnic. He felt a heat of his own climb. For being so outspoken, she was surprisingly modest with her dressings. Still, one thing was certain, Charlotte Thatcher was a beautiful woman. And it took little effort for his imagination to fill in what he hadn't seen.

Despite being thoroughly cloaked by the lace shawl now, Charlotte wrapped her arms around her chest, but the action didn't prevent his thoughts from lingering.

"It seems I may have missed a place for my alterations."

There was a small tremble in her voice, and he couldn't resist the urge to grin while also making sure he kept his distance. He'd always taken pride in his self-control, but he wasn't sure how well he could manage that feat when he found the woman both adorable and alluring right now.

"A new dress I take it?" Nicholas noted a few pins sticking out of the light blue fabric.

"Yes." Her arms slowly drew to her sides, evidently beginning to resolve her composure. "I thought the occasion called for one."

Knowing the occasion meant the art contest brought his pleasant feelings to a plummet. "This painting, you act like it's certain yours will be one of the ones chosen. I can only imagine how many entries will be submitted for the royal family to choose from. How do you know yours will be one of them?"

She furrowed her brow. "I've seen Marc's work. I'm sure of it."

That's what bothered him. He'd seen Marc's work too back at the café. Though Marc hadn't claimed authorship of the pamphlets, his snarky attitude had given Nicholas enough of a hunch. Nicholas had seen that kind of attitude from ill-intended officers and crewmen more times than he could count. The man had an agenda. He couldn't say outrightly what that was, but he didn't like Charlotte getting in the middle of it.

Knowing she aimed to go through with her plan, he just hoped he was wrong.

Chapter 19

Charlotte shimmied into the blue silk, feeling the material cling to her in a way that was more flattering to her figure than it had been now that the adjustments were completed. The change felt good. She smoothed her hand across the lace neckline Louise had suggested to create a more modest touch.

She glanced at her elbows where the dress' sleeves resembled a small bell, a new stitch of lace also adorned on each arm. The effect of the added lace gave the dress a more delicate look, perhaps not the frills of Versailles, but she appreciated the elegance of the design. And though the dress she'd borrowed of Claudine's remained supreme in its material and cost, this one by far was her favorite.

She'd worked all night at the dentelle, with Louise by her side, tending the candlelight from burning out and keeping her company. A certain satisfaction filled her, thinking of what they'd accomplished together.

"The dress looks so different now." Louise had come up to the apartment from the dentelle below, a tiny smile breaking through with her entrance. "But after you told me what happened with Nicholas, I think this is a much better fit. Though I can't speak for the captain himself, I much prefer this look to the less modest designs one often sees at French court."

Charlotte evaluated the front of her dress, this time making sure each pin was properly placed and secure. "Oh, I'm not so sure, especially with how we left things."

"How did you leave things after something like that?" Louise straightened a bow on the front of the dress that had gone awry.

"How we always do—apparently in disagreement." She breathed out, trying to get a grip on her feelings that had somehow changed for the man. "In truth, I believe he's grown tired of his obligation." Before she wouldn't have cared, but somehow now she didn't altogether like being thought of by Nicholas in that way. An obligation.

Louise gave her a look as if she didn't agree. "I've never seen a person look at an obligation quite like he does." She traveled her fingers gently over the lace around Charlotte's sleeves, a longing sadness in her expression. "I'm only sorry we had to use your fichu to get the desired effect."

Charlotte smiled, thankful for the change in topic. "It's all right." And it was. She knew that even though Louise had offered, there were no spare pieces of lace she could provide to make the adjustments accordingly—not any that she could afford to give up for her own and her mother's well-being.

A measure of gratitude lifted heavenward, Charlotte thinking about her shawl now, neatly sewn into the neckline of her dress. The skill was one her mother persistently taught her despite Charlotte's desire to do other things. Now, she was thankful for the gentle prodding that allowed her to incorporate this piece of clothing that she treasured from the past.

Feeling the delicate threads now in her own grasp, Charlotte remembered Louise's errand to Versailles. "With all this work getting the dress ready, I've completely forgotten to ask you about your visit to the palace. Did the queen like the lace?"

Louise beamed a smile "Let's just say I hope you have some more sketches for me in that book of yours."

"Louise, really?" Charlotte clasped her friend's hands into her own. "That's wonderful."

"The queen was so pleased with the idea of using the fleur-de-lis that Her Majesty has already put in another order." Louise's eyes glistened. "It is just what we needed. Now, we can pay for my mother's medicine."

Charlotte could read a hope for distant possibilities in Louise's expression that perhaps weren't so far anymore.

"There." Louise stepped back as if she were taking Charlotte in full view from head to toe, her face glowing with satisfaction. "You look like you belong at French court. Your portrait will be a rival to anyone else's in the nobility if the artist captures you right. Which—" She gave a teasing smirk. "—if he is as good as you say, he will."

***

Charlotte sat in a velvet upholstered fauteuil, her chin angled in a way that was far from relaxed. Her hands might have looked as if they rested on the arm of the chair—one on top of the other—if her shoulders hadn't felt so stiff to refrain from slouching. She gathered over an hour had passed and she longed for a reprieve.

She thought about the duchesse and her little dog, now feeling sorry for the spaniel at its young age with trying to hold such a position, not understanding why. Right now, she felt herself more relating to the poor pooch who was no doubt ready to be freed of such restraint rather than its owner who craved the result.

"How is it looking?" Risking the movement if only with her lips, Charlotte voiced the question. She tried to make the inquiry sound like it came without ulterior intentions when she really meant 'how much longer do I have to sit here like this?'

By the smirk that appeared on Marc's face, she knew she hadn't succeeded. "You are not used to maintaining such a regal position."

It wasn't a question. She bristled, forcing herself to sit straighter despite a throbbing in her back. "I was just wondering when I could take a break, that's all." Though she hadn't done any real hard labor, her neck and back ached from the length of time posed in their over-lengthened placement. She wanted to rub the place where her shoulders met her neck but refrained.

Marc laughed behind the canvas, dipping his brush into his palette before adding a stroke of paint. "It is always an honor to be a lady's first experience."

She watched him, catching the slight arch of his brow as his eyes darted between she and the canvas. Having already disclosed as much, she knew he was talking about her having her portrait painted. But she didn't like how alone they were.

Maybe the private setting was what Marc preferred. She could understand his wanting a quiet atmosphere with minimal distractions, but she hadn't expected his servant to be gone as part of that.

A mixture of linseed oil and turpentine filled her lungs, breathing being the only form of movement she allowed herself. "And where did you say your servant was today?"

"Today is his day off." He traded his brush for another, mixing colors on his palate. "He'll be back tomorrow."

"I see." She swallowed.

He peered over the canvas, giving her a condescending smile. "Does that make you uneasy, mademoiselle?"

"No." Her tone lacked the confidence she needed. "I just didn't expect we'd be to ourselves."

"I did not realize you required a chaperone." His tone was teasing as he continued to mark the canvas. "I can send for Claud if that would ease your nerves."

"That's all right. I'm fine."

He swirled his brush in a jar of water before drying it with a linen cloth. "Did you find what you were looking for at the Place de Grève?" He glanced at her, his lips curling as if faintly amused.

Somehow a part of Charlotte froze, despite her already poised posture. "You were there?"

"Oui. I happened to be there the day of the marketplace."

Her fingernails dug into the armchair, the soft velvet bunching underneath their tips. Again, that feeling of being caught surfaced, but it wasn't what she was wearing that bothered her. As the second daughter of a farmer, she was used to getting things handed down to her. But she didn't completely trust Marc and how he might view her situation, especially when she sensed he had his own agenda in mind. And the way he smirked at her . . . there was something cunning in the feature.

When she didn't say anything, he went on. "It is an interesting place, no—the Place de Grève?" He raised his eyebrows, his eyes glinting. "One day it holds public executions and death while another day the square comes alive with commerce. Such opposing sides is a mystery." His sharpened stare caused her to adjust her posture. "A perfect scene for a painting, don't you think?"

That answered the question of what he was doing at the marketplace, but his reason didn't make her feel better. "Yes, I suppose the area does have some qualities about it that induce the creative mind. Did you find something in particular to paint?"

Marc stepped aside from the canvas. Instead of his gaze lingering on his work, it took its time on her. "I was surprised by what I found, but yes, I believe it was just what I was looking for." He viewed the floor of his studio briefly, his face raising again to her.

She suddenly felt small.

"I have to confess, I did wonder which side of you I was to paint today when you requested. You'll have to excuse me if part of me is disappointed."

Her brow creased. "I don't understand your meaning."

"You are a woman who comes from a country that is now fighting for its independence." He sat his brush down. His voice went low and she heard what resembled disdain in his tone. "Yet you would rather choose noble chains all to impress the Vicomte de Vantinelle." He came over to her from behind the canvas, giving her a smile she might've thought was handsome under a different situation. As it was, she felt a tremble inside, but not one she welcomed.

She was still sitting on the armed chair when Marc stepped close in front of her. It was too close for her liking, invading a space she felt was personal.

"This dress is much too modest for French court." Before she knew it, he began fingering the lace around her neckline. She felt a cold shiver within her at his touch. And the way he lingered—even if the directive came out with an artistic tone, she could tell by his darkened eyes he was no longer concerned about the painting.

He leaned in further, his mouth close to her ear. "The last time I saw this dress, it was on a comtesse with much less coverage." His whisper sent her nearly convulsing from her skin.

This was a position she'd never found herself in before—pushed into a place she didn't want to be with a man who had a clear disregard for her welfare. She could see by his confidant expression that he was used to getting his way—a feeling she knew firsthand. But it felt differently being on the other side of things. No. Not different—awful.

She thought of what she might do in a similar scenario to get what she wanted. It didn't take her long to come up with the answer. She'd keep pressing. Her stomach felt sick, not liking that thought now that the roles were reversed.

"I'm sorry Marc. But I'm afraid I've given the wrong impression." She swallowed, wondering how her words would take effect and keeping her voice measured. "My *only* intention for coming here was for the painting." There was a finality she reached for but couldn't grasp.

His hand pulled away from her in an easy manner, lacking the reaction she hoped for. She felt like any sign of his reluctance or alarm would've been a comfort, but his unruffled smile didn't put her at ease.

"My apologies, Mademoiselle Thatcher." Even with the sophistication of his upbringing returned, his apology lacked any real regret. He gave a mocking bow. "It seems you have left me disappointed again."

He took a step back, releasing the tension of his too close presence. Part of her wanted to ask him about the painting—whether it would be finished, but a much greater part no longer cared.

She left Marc's apartment, her thoughts settling uncomfortably within her in a disarray of confusion and frustration. When she finally arrived at the boardinghouse, she went to her room, not bothering to glance down the hallway. Only then did she allow her emotions to break free. She sank into the edge of her bed, permitting herself to do something she hadn't done since her mother died. Cry.

Chapter 20

"What do you think about this one?" Claudine walked toward a painting hanging on a lavish, red-velvet wall of one of the rooms belonging to Versailles.

Charlotte joined her, but her heart was no longer in the festivities of the event. She'd left out the details about what happened at Marc's apartment, only telling Claudine they'd ended their session in an argument. Thankfully, that had been the end of the discussion, Claudine seeming unsurprised by the information.

Faking her interest, Charlotte turned, the excitement she'd anticipated having this evening non-existent, knowing Marc hadn't entered her portrait for Les Muses de Versailles. The only reason she was here now lied in a chance meeting with the Vicomte de Vantinelle.

She glanced at the tables draped in fine white linen, containing foods in their own artforms of elaborate fruit towers, delicate pastries, and candied fruits. The attendees themselves were a spectacle, both nobles and commoners alike, dressed in what she imagined were their finest outfits. For those with the means or creativity to go beyond, homage to the event was paid through their headpieces—extra plumes, jewels, and even larger embellishments. Though she hadn't seen the queen yet, she had heard that Marie Antoinette had led the trend, encouraging her hairstylist to include a fictional muse she named *Plastea*—a gold figure holding a chisel and mallet to symbolize sculpting—in her own elaborate coiffure.

Charlotte stood on the balls of her feet, trying to get a better view of the painting Claudine was talking about and hide any emotion that still tarried from the episode at Marc's apartment. The piece was different from the others, not having the themes of celebration, love, or leisure they'd been viewing thus far. She couldn't say she had an eye for art, but there were certainly some things that she appreciated about this piece.

The artist decided to go with a different color palette, choosing whites, creams, grays, and even blacks at times, rather than the pastel pinks and blues she'd seen frequently in Paris. It didn't take her long to realize what she liked about the painting. It seemed real. Not depicting the characters of playful frivolity and ideal fancy, though there was nothing wrong with that. But these characters—strong, yet simple in form—exuded expressions she found herself relating to.

Charlotte lowered herself from her tiptoes, though now unable to take her eyes away from the painting that clearly beheld characters of nobility, yet also held something restrained in their overall elegance.

"The paint colors are more muted than the others I've seen—truer to life."

She wasn't quite sure how Claudine would take that, the part about the painting being truer to life. But she couldn't help thinking that besides the pastel color dresses she had seen at Versailles and the furnishings the nobility used to decorate their homes, there was a large part of Paris that had a much darker hue.

"I completely agree." Claudine gave a thoughtful inspection of the painting, Charlotte pleasantly surprised by her evaluation. "It's a relatively new style here in France, having its start in Italy, so I'm told. As you've pointed out, the colors are more life-like and the style simpler and more symmetrical than we're used to seeing here in France." Her fingers covered in a pair of lace gloves—compliments of Louise and her mother—barely crossed at their tips. She gave a tiny smile. "It does not blend in with the rest of the light-hearted paintings I'm used to, but sometimes standing out can be an advantage."

Sensing there might be more to her meaning, Charlotte might've broached the subject if the Baronne de Saint-Laurent hadn't greeted Claudine in that moment. The two women talked, Charlotte noting she'd been excluded from the conversation by an odd look the baronne gave her and the way her body turned away.

"Which room do you think your portrait will be in?" Claudine floated up beside her, having completed her conversation with the baronne.

The mention of her portrait commandeered any enjoyment that Charlotte was starting to feel. "I don't think it will be in any of them."

"You don't believe in my brother's abilities?" Claudine's pointed look was escorted with a tone of challenge.

"It's not that at all." Normally not one to fidget, Charlotte had somehow found herself wringing her hands as they walked past sculptures that had also been a part of tonight's showcase. The disappointment didn't hold a candle to everything she was feeling now. She wanted to put what happened behind her, and so she chose to disclose only what was necessary for understanding.

"He wasn't very happy by the end of our conversation, and the painting wasn't finished at the time. I wouldn't be surprised if he decided not to enter the portrait."

Claudine gave a slight hum as if she wasn't convinced of that outcome. "Knowing my brother, he'll enter something. An invitation from the royal family for a chance to view his work wouldn't be an opportunity Marc would toss away so easily." A gloved hand went tenderly to Charlotte's shoulder, Claudine's face soft with sympathy and truth. "I'm sorry, chérie, but he might submit another piece in your place."

Charlotte hadn't thought about that, but it made sense. Just because *she* had thrown away her own opportunity to be seen by the vicomte, that didn't mean Marc had done the same to show off his own talent. She wouldn't have in the past. She made a mental note of the artwork they'd seen so far, taking another glance at the ones in the Salon de la Guerre—the War Room—where they were now. Which one had been his?

No. As if crossing off a list, she crossed off each piece in her mind, certain this time. She may not have a critical eye for such, but she'd seen enough of Marc's paintings to know his style. And the candelabras that illuminated each work provided enough light to highlight their details, particularly one she knew she would easily recognize—his signature.

Charlotte followed Claudine to the next room with equally gilded walls where they waited behind a mixed group of commoners and nobles to view the next piece of artwork. The painting looked much the same as the rest she'd seen—portraying life as carefree and void of worries when she knew differently resided back home.

Growing somewhat bored by the repeated theme of flamboyance, Charlotte thought of the painting back in the Salon d'Apollon, the Apollo Room.

"C'est La folle?"

The whisper of a woman in tangerine satin with grand panniers grabbed Charlotte's attention as the woman passed by with her male companion in a matching tailored coat.

Is that the fool? The question was easy for her to interpret, Claudine's tutorship and the past months in France aiding her learning of the language. Nonetheless, she flinched. Had she heard right? And if she had, why had the woman been looking at her when she'd said it?

Thinking she somehow misread the exchange, Charlotte turned to see if the woman's aim for such a comment was at something else, but no. All that stood behind her were the tall windows to the Hall of Mirrors leading out into a moonlit sky.

She leaned into Claudine, using her eyes to trail behind the woman and gentlemen now departing the room. "Do you know what that was about?"

"I heard it too, but don't have the faintest idea." Claudine's voice matched Charlotte's whisper, her eyes also following the couple out. "Perhaps we will get an answer in the next room."

They started across the open parquet and down the long hallway until they reached the next set of double doors. She couldn't put a finger on why, but an uneasiness began to creep in as the sparse and more comfortable rooms they'd been in became more crowded with each step they took forward.

"Is that her?" Another murmur came, drawing Charlotte's attention again. Though the murmur clearly meant to be shielded by a fluttering fan, the accessory had done little good to hide the inquiry.

Suddenly feeling self-conscious, Charlotte caught several pairs of eyes that seemed more interested in her and Claudine than on the artwork that had been so elegantly displayed and positioned throughout. Normally a woman accustomed to attention, she couldn't quite say she liked the way they lingered. And it wasn't just the stares. Those who had been engaged in quiet conversations off to the side suddenly turned toward her, only to glance away quickly as if they were hiding something. Others, however, watched her intently, as if waiting to see what she might do next.

She caught a few of the attendees' staring at one of the walls in the room before they turned their attention back on her. She took that as a sign for direction and began to nudge her way through the crowd, choosing to ignore the glances aimed her way despite her growing discomfort. Keeping her head, her goal now was to find understanding—not in the matter *that* they looked at her, but *why* they looked at her.

"Oh chérie."

Having rarely seen the woman flustered, Charlotte stopped, hearing Claudine gasp behind her. She didn't take the response as a good sign, especially now that they found themselves in an intensely filled room with what seemed like nearly every eye on them.

She turned back, seeing Claudine's fingers over her rouged lips.

"It looks like my brother entered your portrait after all." Claudine's hand fell from her mouth over the place her heart rested.

"Really?" Charlotte felt her skin bunch at her forehead, surprised at the notion that Marc would still enter her picture in the contest after what happened between them.

"I'm afraid so."

Unsure of what to make by Claudine's apologetic tone, Charlotte made her way toward the painting to get a better view, then stilled.

There, on the portrait, was Marc's signature.

It was then that everything came together—the whispers, the stares that had become impossible to ignore and—she felt the blood drain from her face—Marc's decision to keep her as an entry.

Where they had ended their session in a fall-out, Marc had evidently seen an opportunity and took it. Something she would've done herself. In this case, something she was seeing clearly for perhaps the first time.

Sometimes God taught lessons in life through experiences and his Word. Sometimes, as in this instance, he preferred to use people as his instruments for teaching. Marc had been that instrument.

The walls to the Hall of Mirrors gave her ample opportunity to look at her reflection, but she had no need for the tall, pristinely clear looking glasses manufactured from Italy to see that she didn't like what appeared back at her.

The pounding in her chest that she had constantly worked to subdue quickly mounted, bringing her to her knees. La folle. *She* was the fool.

Chapter 21

"You won't be needing that today, monsieur." A man in a knee-length coat adorned with silver trim stopped Nicholas at the palace gate, eyeing the sword at his waist.

Nicholas put his hand to the butt of his weapon. "I thought it was the king's custom to carry a sword inside?"

"For the nobility, yes, but for you—to be in his presence, His Majesty has made an exception for today."

Seeing the familiar face of the king's advisor he'd grown tired of come strolling up, Nicholas felt his eyebrows peak. "I didn't realize I was such an honored guest to have you greet me at the gate."

The man scoffed. "I assure you, that is far from my intention." He gave a coy smile. "I know you are eager to have your audience with His Majesty, but I am here to make sure things go accordingly." He eyed Nicholas's sword. "Part of that entails your entry without your blade."

Nicholas frowned. "Surely, you don't think I would take advantage of the situation?"

"With an English soldier having a private audience with the king of France? *No.*" The last word came out clear and distinct, the man's eyes ablaze. "Because I have taken steps to prevent such an outcome."

The confiscation of his sword might have annoyed Nicholas if it weren't for the confirmation that the king truly did expect to meet with him today. Until now, he'd only had the advisor's word—not much to go on when he barely knew the man and he served as counsel to one of England's enemies. But here was proof he could feel good about, that this man had been waiting for him to give the message.

Feeling like he had little choice in the matter, Nicholas withdrew his sword from its scabbard and handed it to the servant at the gate. "Anything else?" He looked to the king's advisor, not bothering to hide the irritation in his tone.

The question was repaid with an upward turn of the man's nose as if pointing his snout in the direction Nicholas should follow. "The king is currently engaged, but His Majesty wishes you to partake in today's exhibition while you wait. You will be summoned when he is ready."

Nicholas was led up a marble staircase that opened into a room decorated with tapestries celebrating past conquests of the current French king's great-grandfather.

"I am also to remind you, our king's generous offer to meet will expire after today." Hearing the bluntness in the man's tone, Nicholas already knew what was coming. "Is that understood, Captain?"

He nodded, the full comprehension that this was his only chance already set in his mind. "Understood."

Appearing satisfied enough, the man gave a quick nod of his own. "Navigating Les Muses de Versailles is fairly simple. Each room contains a selection of art chosen by the king and queen to display." He gave an arrogant smile. "Feel free to admire France's local talent for as long as you like, then move on to the next room. You may pick up your sword here at the gate on your way out."

Having already declined the glasses of Bordeaux and Burgendy offered, Nicholas also wanted to decline seeing the paintings. Not that he didn't appreciate art, but the anticipation of his meeting with France's king gnawed at him like a dog biting the last piece of flesh from its bone.

He gave a resigned breath. The king was busy. Fine. Whether he believed that it didn't matter. The idea wasn't outlandish to think he'd make a British officer wait more than necessary with their conflicted past. But how long?

"You're the Englishman." The man's tone had a pompousness to it like the time Nicholas had heard it back at the Café Procope. He instantly recognized a walk that reflected the same manner. His body went taut.

Both times he'd been around this man had ended in an argument.

"I take it one of these is yours?" Nicholas gestured to the two paintings hanging on the opposing walls, hoping he was right. The last conversation he had with Charlotte was him trying to convince her having her portrait done by Marc was a bad idea. Maybe he had succeeded. Then again . . .

"No. But I do have a piece in the exhibit." Marc twirled a finger around an ornate crystal glass, giving a sly grin. "And from what I've heard, it is stirring up conversation as I have hoped."

Though Nicholas didn't care for his overly confident demeaner, it was hard for him to imagine that a portrait of Charlotte could stir up controversy. "I take it that means Miss Thatcher wasn't your subject, then?"

"Not in the way she hoped, I think, but in a way that conveys her in a truer light."

Nicholas's fists clenched. Though not fully understanding, Marc's comment evoked a sudden urge to knock the man clean.

"Did you see the one of the woman in the Hall of Peace?" A woman dressed in French brocade flapped her fan as she walked in the opposing direction Nicholas had come. For whatever reason, her comment had grabbed his attention.

"La folle." She fluttered her fan to hide a giggle, but her eyes gave her away. "Do you think she has seen it?" The question was hardly a whisper, having spoken to a woman in similar dressings as her own.

"I don't know, but I have heard she is here." The woman's companion put a hand to the side of her head as if to balance her overweighted hairdo from toppling. She lowered her arm, producing a pleased smile, perhaps satisfied her tresses remained fully upright. "I don't suspect she is part of the aristocracy. No one would be so bold as to ridicule a noblewoman. Not even a member of our most respected families could be so forgiven for such an act."

"Then she must not be French." The woman he'd overheard first closed her fan; her tone matter-of-fact is if decided on the issue. "Much as the royals would like to divert gossip away from the king's locksmithing and the foreign queen's spending habits, they would not do so at the expense of a French noble. It would only look worse for them to choose such a piece for today." The woman looked around as if only now considering their conversation might be overheard and the fan pulled open again. "But I must say, it is the most memorable one I've seen thus far."

"I think so too." The other woman snickered. "And the title was a perfect choice—La Folie D'une Femme."

Something turned in Nicholas's stomach, seeing a smirk on Marc's face that only confirmed he'd also overheard the less than inconspicuous couple. A Woman's Folly. The whole scenario brought an unwelcomed thought. He hoped that wasn't Charlotte.

Taking the one clue the woman had offered, Nicholas went on to the end of the exhibit, praying his sense was wrong.

It took him more than a minute to capture a view of the picture that hung at the opposite wall because of a crowd that had congregated in the space. His whole body stiffened.

It was Charlotte, no doubt, the lines of her face an almost perfect duplicate to the woman he knew in real life. Marc had even captured one of Nicholas's favorite attributes—the dimple on her chin when she got angry or annoyed. But that's where the admiration for the artist stopped.

A dress hung awkwardly on her figure as if the gown were too large for her petite frame while her hair, done in the common poufs of the palace, was accessorized with undone ribbons, and tilted to an odd angle. Behind her, a mirror with her reflection showed a thirteen-striped red and white flag, a symbol of the colonies and no doubt a reminder of where she'd come from. Unfortunately, that wasn't all that comprised the painting.

A man dressed in noble attire had his back turned to her as if to say she didn't belong, or he wanted nothing to do with her. Knowing who she was trying to impress, it didn't take Nicholas long to deduce that the man was likely the vicomte.

Marc had certainly taken liberties—all for his political agenda, Nicholas was certain.

Nicholas's teeth clenched. He had the urge to march back to the baron and make that thought of clipping the man's jaw a reality. If it weren't for someone else, he'd do it, but he couldn't help thinking of what more the pair of women had mentioned.

Nicholas felt the crowd shift as well as the overall demeanor in the room. People that had gravitated outside into the gardens, enjoying additional tables of rich foods and fountains, found a reason to return to the last place of the exhibit. Murmurs spread around him, and it took him a moment to grasp the reason behind the sudden commotion. Amid it all stood Charlotte.

"Captain, His Majesty is ready to see you now."

Like a ship caught in a windless sea, Nicholas heard the voice of the king's advisor, though keeping his eyes on Charlotte. He wanted to see what she would do—if he should intervene. She didn't move. He shifted his weight from one boot to the other, biting the side of his cheek. Even in this moment, the woman was still too stubborn to budge.

"Please follow me." The advisor's request came out more like a demand, stiff and expectant like Nicholas would be prime to follow. And he would've, knowing what he still had to accomplish here. But that was much harder to do when the woman he had come to love needed his help.

"I'm sorry." He faced the advisor, hoping the man might understand, but doubting he would. "Please tell the king there was something more urgent I had to do."

Walking away from his last opportunity to fulfill his assignment and all the expectations that still weighed heavy on him, Nicholas stepped past the crowd and between Charlotte and the painting. Her skin was flushed, her chest rising and falling quickly under a pressed hand. Wide eyes that had been locked on the somewhat portrait of herself, raised to meet his.

"Nicholas." She gave a weary gasp as if struggling for breath before her body went limp.

Chapter 22

"What's happened?"

Nicholas had Charlotte in his arms when the French woman called out to him. Somehow, he'd managed to get through the crowd in time to catch her before her body completely reached the floor.

He scooped her into his arms, breathing in the scent of lavender. "She's fainted."

"Is she all right?"

He didn't know this woman, but judging from the concern in her tone, he gathered she knew Charlotte.

"I don't know but is there anywhere I can take her that's more private?" With his arms occupied, the only motion he could make was with his head, angling it toward the large group who seemed more drawn to him than the works of art being displayed.

"Oui, follow me." Without even bunching her skirts, the woman in peach silk began to glide across the floor with genteel haste.

Nicholas hugged Charlotte tighter, trying to get a better grip, though being careful not to squeeze her too much. He wasn't a doctor. He didn't know if there was something more going on, but he felt his first line of action was to get her out of harm's way. Bullets might not be flying toward him on the battlefield, but the room did feel like darting arrows aimed at them.

He followed the French woman into a small private room with soft green walls covered in faded silk damask and gold. Nicholas laid Charlotte down on a settee doing the next thing he knew what to do. He watched for the rise and fall of her chest. When that proved little help, he bent his ear down to her mouth, listening.

"Is she breathing?"

Nicholas lifted his head, seeing a man had run into the room after them. He might've thought the stranger was someone from the palace telling them they were unwelcomed to use the room. But the plain manner of the man's coat and simple queue unadorned by a periwig or peruke—even for tonight's occasion—gave him pause. He noticed the leather bag at the man's side, similar to what he'd seen doctors in England carry.

"Are you a doctor?" Nicholas heard the panting in his breath.

Without answering, the man rushed over to Charlotte, discarding his bag on a woven rug.

Nicholas was reluctant at first to let him through, feeling a protectiveness, but stepped aside.

The man quickly removed his frock and rolled up his sleeves. "I saw her fall. Do you know what happened?"

Nicholas's mouth went dry. It was the first time he'd seen Charlotte collapse and he couldn't guess the reason. "No, monsieur. Not really."

The man put his fingers to her wrist, then mimicked Nicholas's action earlier by putting his ear to her mouth.

Remembering he'd had help, Nicholas turned to the French woman, awaiting more of an answer.

"It is not an exact scenario, but I have seen something quite similar happen on a different occasion. Though nothing that resulted in this state." There was a calmness to her manner, but the apprehension in her tone told Nicholas a different story.

"She's breathing." The man pulled his ear away from Charlotte's mouth. "I'm going to check inside her mouth and see if there is any obstruction that might have caused her to lose consciousness."

Banking on the fact the man was truly a doctor, Nicholas watched as he opened Charlotte's mouth, peering inside.

"Nothing is lodged in her throat."

Charlotte gave a shallow breath, her chest rising to a sudden stop as if the breath was forced.

"How is she?" He'd given the doctor room to do what he needed, but Nicholas couldn't help from stepping forward, feeling a sudden fear take hold.

The doctor put his hands along the sides of her rib cage and moved them down toward her waist as if feeling for something. If the man hadn't been seeing to her well-being, Nicholas would've had a second man on his list to knock out. "She has a corset. We'll need to loosen it."

Nicholas thought of the quickest way to do that. His sword, but that was still at the gate.

"But monsieur, I cannot allow that. Her *modesty*—" The woman moved from the side of the room and stood between the doctor and Charlotte.

Nicholas removed his hat at the lady's scolding reprimand. He raked his hands through his hair in frustration. "Look, I appreciate you're worried about her modesty, but I think there's a more important issue here at hand."

"The captain's concern is warranted." The doctor gave his patient a meticulous glance. "She's still having some trouble breathing. Nothing is blocking the airway, but considering her weak pulse and pale complexion, it might do her well to get more air in."

"Fine. Then I will do it." The lady went to work unpinning the gown of Charlotte's dress to unveil the back of her stays. To her credit, the woman was quicker than Nicholas thought she would be, untying each layer of cord.

The doctor did his series of checks again, putting his ear toward Charlotte's mouth and his fingers back on her wrist. Her hand gave the slightest twitch.

With the corset removed, Nicholas watched for signs of change. He saw movement, her chest rising in a more fluid motion this time as if unencumbered. His muscles somewhat weak from the release of built-up tension, he uttered a soft thanks to God under his breath.

The doctor put a hand to her forehead. "She doesn't appear to have a fever and her breathing is growing steady."

He went to the bag Nicholas had seen him enter with and opened it, pulling out a vial of smelling salts from the leather satchel. "I'm going to try and rouse her."

"Now, wait just a minute." Nicholas put his palm up in front of the doctor. "I'm not so sure that's a good idea."

"What do you mean, monsieur?" The doctor's hand was at the lid, but he refrained from opening the vial. His already stern expression held a frown.

"I'm just considering the situation—what it might be like for her when she wakes up. Whatever happened in that room that led to—" Nicholas gestured to Charlotte's limp body, apart from the breath he could now see her taking in and out. "This. It might be better to get her out of here first."

"Yes." The Frenchwoman gave an accommodating nod, a laced finger going to the corner of her neatly painted mouth. "I see your point and I tend to agree. You can use my carriage."

"Thank you. I'll do that." Nicholas turned to the doctor who had put the vial back in his case, evidently convinced enough of his argument. "And thank you for your help, doctor. It came at an urgent time."

"I am happy it was nothing more severe, but I'd like to see how she's doing tomorrow if that's satisfactory to you."

Reading nothing but genuineness in his tone and demeanor, Nicholas was quick to agree. "Yes sir, that will be fine." He wasn't against the idea of having Charlotte looked at again after tonight, but he wasn't so sure she'd welcome it. Though—he looked at Charlotte again on the settee, her face now relaxed as if in a restful sleep—right now, she couldn't say otherwise.

"Now that we know she's recovering, can I ask you something?" Nicholas diverted his attention back to the French woman as the doctor left.

"Yes, of course." She closed the door again, helping to maintain Charlotte's privacy, which he appreciated.

"Before, you said you saw Charlotte have a similar incident but on a different occasion. Is that right?"

"Oui, the first time she came to Versailles." She crossed over to the settee, laying a hand gently over Charlotte's forehead before she shook her head. "She would've fainted in front of the king and queen if the Vicomte de Vantinelle hadn't pulled her from the hall. I thought with her first time at court it was perhaps overwhelming being in the presence of the monarchy, but after today I am not so sure."

Nicholas wasn't sure either, especially when he had trouble picturing Charlotte overwhelmed by anybody or anything. But he was going to find out.

***

Charlotte awoke, raising herself straight up in a familiar stiff bedding. She closed her eyes again, the tension in her head pounding almost as if her heart resided there and not in her—

Bile burned at the back of her throat. Les Muses de Versailles . . . the vicomte . . .

Her hands clutched to her chest. The beating of her heart was set in its natural rhythm. Had the events of the contest all been a dream? Or more accurate, a *nightmare?* But if it had all been in her mind, why was she in Louise's apartment and in Louise's bed of all places? One look beyond the wood frame told her she wouldn't have to wait long to get her answer.

Louise sat at the foot of the bed, a long trim of lace loosely rolled in her lap while she worked on a scrolled section that clung to a piece of parchment.

"Louise."

The needle, having started the journey back through the underside of the parchment, paused. "Oh, mon amie, I'm so glad you're all right." Louise dashed her needlework in the chair, giving Charlotte an embrace at the bedside. "You had me worried."

"Les Muses de Versailles . . . the art contest—" Charlotte used her arms to push herself taller in the bed. "What happened?"

Louise slowly went back to her seat, her friend hardly meeting Charlotte's gaze while she took up her needlework again. "I'm told you fainted at the palace."

Charlotte pressed her lips, her memory not serving her well. "The last thing I remember was the Peace Room and seeing my—" She felt the blood from her face pool to her feet.

It was all coming back. The hope she'd been counting on to impress the vicomte completely turned on her. No doubt he and all the rest of France had seen her completely ridiculed in what Marc so openly declared her folly.

"Oh." Charlotte groaned, clenching her fists tight as if trying to hold onto the victory she'd been so close to achieving.

"Would you like me to get the doctor?" Louise stood as if to leave, mistaking Charlotte's moaning over lost opportunity for pain.

"No. I'm fine." She put the tips of her fingers to her temples, forcing a breath out. "I just have a case of embarrassment, that's all." She didn't need a doctor to tell her that.

Louise's dark brows dipped. "I'm not so certain that is all it is. I think Nicholas would've left if that were so."

"Nicholas is here?" Charlotte flinched, somehow sitting straighter in the bed than she thought possible.

Louise nodded. "He's downstairs with the doctor and Maman. I think they are discussing what happened."

"What happened was that I fainted, nothing more." As far as her health was concerned, anyway. Her reputation at French court was another matter—one she needed to fix.

"In any case, I'll go and let Nicholas know you're awake." The footboards under Louise's feet gave a slight creak as she approached the stairs. She gave a coy smile. "He'll want to know."

It wasn't long after Louise disappeared to go downstairs when Nicholas came into the room of the apartment, but he wasn't alone. From the rounded rectangular leather case the man carried and the deliberate, purposeful stride when he walked in, she guessed he was the doctor.

"I see you've brought company." She batted an eye toward Nicholas before smoothing the coarse sheets that brimmed in her lap. "Really, gentlemen, it's not necessary." She gave them a smile as if to confirm that fact, hoping at least one of them might be satisfied by her effort. "I'm fine."

Nicholas crossed his arms in a way she knew her attempt came up short. "We'll let the doctor decide that."

Hearing a definitiveness in his tone, she shifted her weight backward toward the wool-stuffed pillow behind her. "Fine."

"I want to check your vitals again now that you're awake, Mademoiselle Thatcher." The French doctor sported a strongly angular face and wore a long black frock over a white-linen shirt and a simple patterned waistcoat. He put his palm to her forehead before she could object. Not that she would've with Nicholas giving her a look that said he dared her to. "We'll see if anything has changed."

Feeling somewhat at ease by the calmness in his voice, she allowed the medical man to continue his examination. He checked her pupils and breathing and even had her stick out her tongue so he could assess whether the color seemed to his standards.

"And what of your evaluation, doctor?" She straightened in the bed again, certain she'd done her part in cooperation. "Do I have a case of public ridicule? Or am I well enough to get out of bed, now?"

"Relax, Charlotte." Nicholas held her gaze with soft eyes, even as she heard a rebuke in his voice. "I was the one who asked the doctor to stay until now. I thought in light of your history, it was worth him taking a look."

"My *history*?" Her chin reeled up toward him.

Nicholas gave her a keen eye that told her he wasn't sorry about a thing. "I just mean I'm aware that this hasn't been the first time you've had this experience."

A truth, but not one she'd told him of. Had Louise mentioned her condition while she'd been out?

"There are a few questions I'd like to ask you, mademoiselle, pertaining to your history." The doctor gave her a smile that put her at ease. "Sometimes it can be helpful to know the past, so we can better understand what's happening now."

"I'll step outside and give you some privacy." Nicholas made a step toward the door as if to leave.

"No. It's all right. You can stay." The words came out before she had time to understand their significance. She didn't know why, but she wanted him to stay.

She could see by his half-smile that he didn't mind the intrusion and for some reason that gave her a good feeling. He retraced the step and took the seat Louise had occupied at the foot of the bed.

"Mademoiselle Thatcher." The doctor claimed a chair beside her that'd remained vacant until now, leaving her to wonder if the chair had been intended for him. "Has getting to the point of losing consciousness always been a part of your life?"

"Not always, no. The first time was actually here in Paris, but—" She rubbed the bedsheets between her fingers, looking to Nicholas, then to the doctor. She'd come to terms with her lot in life, but for some reason allowing Nicholas a full view of it made those terms more difficult to accept. "The complications of my heart have been occurring since last year after my mother's death."

"Your heart?" The doctor leaned slightly forward, as if probing her to explain.

She'd read little in Nicholas's expression, his blue eyes fixed and attentive.

"Yes." Her shoulders slumped with having to admit such a fragile part of herself. "There are times when my heart beats rapidly. My chest tightens, and I feel like I'm losing control of by body." She tried to look anywhere but at Nicholas. "My mother suffered from what I was told to be a weak heart and my doctor in Massachusetts indicated the problem was likely inherited." She tried for a smile, hating how weak and exposed she felt in front of a man she had started caring the opinion of.

"Unfortunately, there's a lot still to be learned about the heart." The doctor rubbed at his jaw. "But it's certainly possible. What you've described is very similar to what I have seen in some of my patients that served in the prior war overseas." He nodded as if to encourage her. "Tell me, were you ever involved in the new war in the colonies?"

"Involved?" She gave an emphatic shake of her head. "I was in Cambridge during the Boston Siege for a small part of the conflict, but nowhere near the fighting. Most of the time I was staying at my aunt's estate in Portsmouth."

He gave a hum as if considering something. "I suppose I wouldn't expect a woman to be on the battlefield, though that is strange you have some of the same symptoms as a man that had."

She wanted to tell him that while women might not be the primary soldiers, many chose to support their men by producing homespun goods as part of the boycott or taking their homestead into their own hands. Some joined the camps to help aid the soldiers with laundering and cooking and there were a handful fighting alongside on the front lines, even if she hadn't been one of them.

"Were you offered anything to help alleviate your discomfort?"

She nodded, somewhat expecting the question. "I drink an herbal tonic made from the foxglove flower as prescribed. It seems to work well enough, I suppose. My doctor also recommended I partake in a more sedentary lifestyle so as to not overwork my heart." She sighed. "But I find that harder to comply with." She thought she caught the corner of Nicholas's mouth rise a little, but trying to focus on the doctor, she couldn't be sure.

The physician smiled, his way of doing so reassuring her even with Nicholas in the room. "Would it be all right if I check your heartbeat, mademoiselle?"

Unsurprised by the question, she nodded. "Of course."

Nudging her body forward to allow sufficient room, the doctor put his ear to her back. The action would have normally been a rudimentary procedure added to the evaluation he'd already completed, except for one crucial observation on her part.

Charlotte felt her breath catch at what she'd failed to notice until now—the bones of her stays, normally tight and compressed around her ribcage, no longer served as a barrier to the doctor's examination.

Heat climbed from the tips of her toes all the way up to her hairline. Her body went rigid, despite her wanting to conceal what she'd just discovered to be missing.

The doctor sat back in his chair, his eyes conveying a professional kindness and making her wonder if he could deduce something was wrong. She couldn't make herself look at Nicholas, pretty certain with the recent amount of time they'd spent together, he had sensed her unease.

"I would only recommend the addition, or in your case, the removal of a few things." His French accent suddenly held a strictness that hadn't been there before as he locked eyes with her. "First, a word about your corset, Mademoiselle Thatcher. As a man, I am only vaguely aware of the undergarment women wear so tightly to constrict their torsos. This, in my opinion as a doctor even under the influence of my French roots, is a fashion faux pas. I would recommend alleviating yourself from the entrapment, or at the very least, wearing the garment a little looser."

Charlotte offered no reply, for nothing but the vulnerability in her chemise came to mind.

"The other would be a removal from Paris."

"A removal?" The doctor's recommendation snapped her out of her contemplative state. "You mean to leave?"

"Your condition, for whatever reason, seems to have become worse since you've been here. You yourself mentioned that the fainting spells hadn't occurred until you were in the city." He gave her a look as if asking her to challenge that fact. "I would be curious to see if a departure from Paris and French court would be to your health's benefit."

She shook her head. "I'm sorry, doctor, but that is out of the question. Not when I—"

"It might do you some good, Charlotte."

She hadn't noticed Nicholas approach the bed. He put his hand on top of hers, leaning in toward her. She felt both strength and gentleness from him. He gave her an almost pleading look. The action was both unexpected and endearing.

"I'll let Captain Edwards tell you more on what we've discussed, and you can make your decision." The doctor stood from his chair and retrieved his leather medical bag.

As soon as he left the apartment, Charlotte's eyes bore down on Nicholas for answers. "And *what* exactly have you two been discussing on my behalf?"

"Only what the doctor recommended—that it might be a good idea to change your surroundings." He gave her a kind and gentle smile despite the scowl she imagined she possessed. "I was thinking England."

So that's what this was about—he'd had enough of her just like everyone else.

"You mean to leave France entirely?" She wouldn't have it. Though liking the feel of his touch, she freed her hand from his. "Nicholas, I can't leave Paris now. I know this comes at an opportune time for you to—" Her words fumbled, not knowing any other way to say what hurt, but was true. "—be rid of me, but the arrangement with the vicomte is too important. I have to . . ."

A pained look shadowed his face. "Your wrong over what this is about, Charlotte." His voice was steadfast, assuring. "I don't want to be rid of you. I want to make sure there's a chance to be with you more. And the vicomte can wait, and so can the rest of the French court in my opinion."

She might've perched herself up to make herself taller in Louise's bed but remembering the lack of support around her midsection, she stayed put. All she could do was try to make him understand. "But I *can't* leave. I can't run away. Aunt Sylvia is counting on me."

He closed his eyes, she now noticing small shadows under each. "You're not running away, just taking a break. Between you and me, I think both of us could use it." His hand pulled down the back of his neck while it dawned on her they might be spending that time together. Time with him she realized she wanted. "I'll get you back, I promise."

Knowing he was a man of his word, she believed him. But it seemed like defeat—to leave Paris empty-handed but for the embarrassment she had Marc to thank for.

Marc. Her blood boiled for the damage he'd caused her—the opportunity lost. Now all of Versailles saw her as . . . what? If they'd come up with L'Autrichienne for Marie Antionette as a play on words with the queen's birth country and a female dog, what kind of name had they conjured up for her? She didn't even want to imagine the gossip stirring in her regard.

Yet, somehow, she had to preserve herself, to salvage what was lost, if not in everyone else's eyes at court then at least in the vicomte's.

Charlotte let out a moan that held a mixture of emotion. "It feels like giving up."

"You're not giving up. You're stepping away. There's a big difference between the two and I think we can use that time to clear our heads."

There it was again, the reference to them doing this together, like he needed the reprieve just as much as she did. But why?

Furrowing her brow, she tried to make sense of what happened— not of Marc's ridicule of her, but of how she ended up here at Louise's apartment, in Louise's bed no less, and why Nicholas was here too.

"Nicholas." She angled her head toward him. "Were you at Versailles last night?"

"I was." His tone was quiet, but firm. The tension she'd seen at the base of his jaw disappeared and the deep blue coat on his shoulders dropped a degree.

She faced him full on to better gauge his reaction. "And was your visit in order to see the portraits selected by the king and queen from the contest?"

"It wasn't the primary reason for my visit, but I did see the portraits."

She swallowed, feeling her throat tighten an inch. "*All* of the portraits?"

"No, not all of the portraits, just a few. My business there didn't have to do with the contest."

She let the air escape her lungs, relieved he hadn't seen—

"But—" His chin tilted down toward the edge of the bed, his eyes peering up at her. She didn't like how slow and careful his interjection had come out. "I did see the last one."

"I see." She felt the base of her chin quiver, imagining the dimple on it was easily visible. She wanted to pull the humble bedding over her head, but there were still questions to ask.

Inhibiting her desire from drawing the sheets over her, she worked to steady her chin. "Then, what was the reason you were there at the palace?"

A slow, weak smile appeared. "I was granted an audience with the king. My appointment was scheduled at the time of the showing."

A lump pitted itself against the back of her throat and she had to swallow hard this time to force it down. "And did you make that appointment?"

"No, I didn't."

His admission begged another question as she tried to fit the pieces of the puzzle together.

"How did I get here . . . to the dentelle?" Her hands pressed to her sides on Louise's bed as if reinforcing she, in fact, wasn't dreaming.

Nicholas looked real enough, and he was perhaps the only reason she was glad she wasn't in a state of fiction just now.

"I brought you here after what happened at Versailles."

"You were in the room?" Her hand went to her throat, feeling the heat in her neck. "You saw it? You saw me . . .?"

"I did."

And he'd sacrificed his appointment with the king—his orders, the code he lived by—to help her.

"Oh, Nicholas, I'm *so* sorry." Her voice came out hushed. "I know you needed that appointment."

He gave her a smile that was void of any anger or blame. "It's all right. I'm glad the situation didn't end up worse than it could have."

She wasn't sure she could altogether agree on her end of things, but she caught his meaning well enough.

His arms crossed over the gold fastenings of his coat. "But I don't know if your tonic is doing that much to help, at least not on its own. That's why I agree with the doctor. Maybe it will be good to give at least one of his remedies a try."

His persistence on the matter of leaving for London made her guess that was the remedy he'd referred to. But the mention of remedies reminded her . . .

"That brings up another question I have." She eyed him, hoping the warmth she sensed rising in her cheeks wouldn't betray her. "How did I get out of my stays?"

His smile took on a rogue quality. She would've liked the feature more if the current subject wasn't so sensitive to her.

"Your modesty is safe. I would've cut the contraption off, per doctor's orders, of course." His lips climbed higher toward his cheekbones when her mouth gaped. "Your friend, Claudine, was the one who wouldn't have it. She was the one who unlaced you. Don't worry, I didn't see anything I wasn't supposed to see." There was a glint in his eye she wasn't sure she trusted. "But what I did see, looked like something akin to a torture device and I've seen a few things in my service."

Getting over her fluster, Charlotte wondered if that were true, especially regarding the corset she'd indulged in here in Paris. The garment was much less forgiving than the ones she was used to, but she still appreciated the support and protection she missed now without it. She grimaced. "Even so, I can't say I've decided to follow the doctor's advice regarding its complete absence from my wardrobe."

"Have it your way." He shrugged his shoulders in a way that said he didn't have anything else to contribute on the matter. "What about the other?"

A breath pulled in, Charlotte feeling how easy it was without the constriction of the French corset—her heart beating steady as if nothing had happened the evening before. Maybe London would be a good change. She longed to see Abigail and she had no idea what she would do to earn the respect of the vicomte now that Marc had completely tarnished any smidge she'd acquired.

She folded her hands together on top of the sheets. "Before I give my answer, there's one more question that's come to mind."

Seeing he made no objection, she went on. "Why did you bring me here to Louise's apartment instead of the boardinghouse?"

The shrug he gave her told her the decision had been an easy one. "You've been spending more time at the dentelle since we've been in Paris for reasons I can only imagine have to do with helping Louise and her mother. I thought given the *sensitivity* of the situation, you'd feel more comfortable seeing Louise when you woke up, rather than me."

Her expression softened into a mixture of gratitude and embarrassment at his thoughtfulness over the situation. Perhaps he and the doctor were correct with their suggestions to leave the city.

Her cheeks puffed. She was finished with playing the part of a weakling tucked in bed. "All right, Captain, when do we set sail?"

Chapter 23

The door of the apothecary clicked behind her as Charlotte approached a tall counter that separated her from a vast assortment of vials and jars.

"Un moment, s'il vous plaît." A short man perched on a ladder finished putting away the last of the three jars he had taken from a crate and onto a shelf. He climbed down from the ladder to meet her at the counter. "Bonjour, mademoiselle. Is there something you are looking for or are you in need of a suggestion for something that ails you?"

She tipped one of the scales on the counter with her finger, watching as both sides balanced again. "I'm on a long-term visit here in the city. My doctor back home has prescribed me a tea made from the Foxglove flower. I've run out and would like to purchase another supply."

Pulling the scale out of her reach, he offered a look of remorse. "Je suis désolé. I am sorry, but I do not have the flower you have described and unfortunately I won't be receiving another shipment until the end of spring."

"Spring?" She couldn't wait until then. "Why so long?"

Seeming unbothered by her impatience, the man uncorked a bottle containing coriander, before adding the seeds to a mortar on the counter. He took hold of a pestle and began grinding the seeds down.

"The growing season for the year is over. But once spring comes, the flower can be harvested."

"Of course." She closed her eyes, feeling foolish. Winter was at their heels. The plant she required was already in its dormant stage. As a girl who'd grown up on a farm, she understood that well, but as a woman in need of medication for a condition that impeded her life, she couldn't accept the outcome. She was leaving for London this very afternoon and would need something to subdue her heart in the chance it didn't cooperate.

"Could I ask the nature of the condition for which the tea is to treat?" He continued to grind, the fragments of seeds slowly becoming a dust powder.

"Yes." She breathed in, pulling a warm, spicy scent through her nose. "One pertaining to the heart."

The man nodded as if he'd already suspected the reason for the flower's use. Placing the pestle and mortar aside, he went over to one of the shelves behind the counter and returned with an amber-colored bottle.

Pour apaiser les maux et calmer l'esprit. She read the label again, translating the words. "To ease pain and calm the mind?"

"Many of the doctors come seeking this to help with any heart problems. The syrup has a way of relaxing the body and therefore the heart while also reducing any pain."

The days and nights at her mother's bedside made her at least familiar with the drug. Then, she never asked the doctor its exact application—only that her mother seemed more at ease when she took the elixir. And wasn't that the point for this trip to London—to calm her heart from its frantic spells?

Despite the small voice raising caution, the decision lay settled in her mind. "Then I'll take a bottle of that, please." She pulled the amount from her new reticule that matched the price marked on the bottle, handing the money to the apothecary. Now, with her morning errand completed, she would meet Nicholas back at the boardinghouse where they would depart for London.

Chapter 24

Pounding feet vibrated the old English oak planks around Nicholas's cabin. Shouts came from his first lieutenant, Greer, throwing out orders to prepare the ship for departure while the crew responded with lively clunking of feet and clamoring.

The *HMS Speedy* was a three-masted frigate. Her small size made it easy to hear what went on around the ship, but even without eyes and ears, Nicholas knew her movements and sounds like she'd been an extension of himself.

Another shout from Greer signaled for the ropes to be untied and stored, but the crew didn't need any direction to complete undocking procedures. The scuffling of shoes and ropes pulling against their wheels took on a sound more like music, a song of hurried jubilee. Everyone was ready to step foot on London soil. Everyone except him.

Nicholas flipped open the brass lid to his compass, repeating the action while the faint sound of water lapped against the hull. The journey to Calais from Paris took two days, riding through the night. All they needed to do now was voyage through the English Channel. If weather conditions proved favorable, they'd reach the pool of London in about a day, maybe less.

A knock at his door brought the lid of the compass to a final close. Putting his compass on the desk and expecting Greer coming to tell him the ship was ready to head into the channel, he gave the order to enter. The door opened, but it wasn't his first mate that came through.

A lightness in his chest and limbs brought an unexpected smile.

Charlotte stepped toward his desk, looking happy to see him. Small rosettes on her dress flowed out from her waist with extra layers that he suspected had more to do with warmth than keeping with the fuller skirts of French court. The added volume accentuated her waist, but not to the over-done look of the panniers he'd seen at Versailles.

"Greer says we're leaving port and making our way toward the English Channel."

"Thank you. Did he send you to convey the message?"

"Yes, but I'm happy to."

He believed that, experience telling him Charlotte wouldn't do anything she didn't want to. The thought that she wanted to see him only lifted his heart further.

She went over to the side of the cabin, fidgeting with an apparatus Nicholas had stored there. Priestley's carbonated water machine. "What do we have here?"

He didn't know if she was feigning interest, but she looked intrigued.

"An invention by Joseph Priestley." Remembering the wording on the pamphlet Priestley provided, Nicholas wondered if it might hold any affect on Charlotte. She wasn't a woman easily flustered, which only made him more curious to find out the answer. Deciding to test that theory, he pulled out the pamphlet from the drawer of his desk and handed the document to her.

"Directions for—" Having started to read the beginning of Priestley's title with her typical flourish, Nicholas tried to curb himself from grinning when she fell silent. Her eyes moved back and forth along the page, her cheeks flashing a rosy hue. "—*impregnating* water with fixed air."

The pamphlet dropped from her line of vision with silence before she returned the paper to him. It was nice to know the woman could get ruffled at least a little bit. Though he'd seen a few instances of that now, none of which lessoned his attraction for her. Some had even aided in that regard.

"It's a way of putting bubbles in water." He returned the brochure to his desk. "Priestley calls the product carbonation because the method infuses carbon dioxide." He didn't even try to hold back his smile this time. "I can make one for you if you'd like to try—"

The ship jarred to one side, both Nicholas and Charlotte reacting by grabbing a hold of Nicholas's desk as their feet staggered across the planks.

"What was that?" Charlotte looked at him, her embarrassment gone and replaced by concern.

"We're hitting some turbulence." Nicholas straightened from where his desk had been his support. He was about to help Charlotte do the same, but she was already upright.

"Turbulence?" She looked anything but pleased by the word. "But I thought we were just crossing the English Channel, not the main ocean." She adjusted her cloak where the hood had flown up at the back of her neck from the ship's chopped movement, her tone uneasy. "You said it was only a day trip."

"We are and it is, but sometimes the channel can get a little rough, especially with a strong storm. The weather is often unpredictable." He went to a peg on the wall where his hat rested, placing the tricorn on his head. "Why don't you go to your cabin while I see what's happening out there."

Her body went rigid, the placement of her hands at her hips further drawing his attention to her waist. "Nicholas, if you think I'm going to be one of those girls who just waits it out while the action happens around me, then I'm sorry, but I'm going to highly disappoint you."

Of course she wouldn't. The woman was as stubborn as trying to steer a ship that had been run aground. "Fine." He opened his cabin door, the argument lacking importance over what they were facing outside. "Let's go and see what's happening out there." Allowing her to precede him, they walked out to the quarterdeck in a few short steps.

A strong, cold wind from the north blew against his back, making the hairs on his neck stand up. The volume of skirts to Charlotte's dress clung to one side of her body, her golden strands dancing in the wind across her face. She hugged her cloak tightly against her.

His awareness suddenly heightened, Nicholas felt his heart pick up speed. Heavy, dark clouds hung suspended at the horizon and in the direction they needed to go.

Letting experience takeover, Nicholas shifted his weight, getting a better stance as the *Speedy* rocked against the waves that were quickly building around her.

"Reef the topsails. Lower the mainsail." He shouted the command to Greer, knowing the order was only a formality. His first mate knew what to do.

Greer, a man prime in years in the age of sail, strode with gusto along the main deck repeating the order to other members of his crew already at the top of the rigging to secure the sails and brace for the storm that would soon meet them.

Hearing Greer had already shouted to secure anything loose and batten down the hatches, Nicholas consulted the barometer, a sudden drop confirming the storm was worsening.

He gave a quick order to his helmsman to change their course at the wheel in hopes of riding out the storm, then returned to Charlotte who'd stepped down by one of the ship's bulwarks. "You should get to your cabin. It might get worse out here."

His mouth grew tense when she didn't respond. He half expected her to challenge him again, until he noticed her hands weren't wrapped around her cloak anymore but fiercely gripping the railing. Other than that, she didn't move. All signs of color were drained from her face. The beginning steps to his annoyance quickly dissipated, Nicholas seeing Charlotte in a one way he never had before—silent.

***

Charlotte clung to the ship's railing as if holding on might somehow invoke a strength she didn't feel. She heard Nicholas shouting orders somewhere around her, but the sound of his voice was muffled as if far away. She put a hand to her mouth, her stomach moving against the rocking ship while all her concentration focused on making sure her breakfast from earlier stayed put.

As if testing her determination, the ship pitched to one side. Her shoes stumbled below her skirts as she reached and found something solid she could hold onto, but the effort did little good for her ill state. No longer able to keep a solid composure and no longer caring, her head drooped over the side of the ship. The once-calm, greenish-blue sea was now a foreboding shade of gray and dark blue, the water's chaotic rolls and swells depicting how her own stomach felt.

She turned her head to face the bow of the ship where a wave crashed over the side, drenching scrambling crew members from the surge's point of entry while heavily misting others. Nicholas's voice was somewhere in the wind, commanding, yet trusting.

"Charlotte." It was only after she felt his familiar touch on her back when she realized how close he was.

"I'm all right." Hearing a heaving to her breath, she gripped the side of the ship tighter.

"You don't look all right." His rebuke was tender, holding concern.

She tried to stand upright but couldn't as if keeping herself bent at an angle was helping to prevent whatever threatened to come up. "I'm just a little seasick, that's all."

"Seasick?"

He looked as if he didn't believe her, but she wasn't about to provide him with any more evidence than that. She held back the bitter sensation that wanted to rise in her throat.

"I don't remember you having problems on the crossing over from the colonies." Gently prying her hands from the bulwark, Nicholas put one of her arms around the back of his neck.

"Yes, well, if I remember correctly, you kept your distance from me after the incident." How he'd managed to do that on a frigate in the middle of the ocean still astounded her. Then again, she'd spent a fair amount of her own time in her cabin when the voyage proved too tumultuous for her gut.

"Thankfully, I have a sister that was well prepared for all things related to sickness." She put a hand to her abdomen as if to quelch the reminder. "She gave me candied ginger. It didn't fully abate the nausea, but it did help a great deal."

He frowned before he hoisted her in his arms, she not caring to stop him. "I don't have ginger."

A fact she wasn't surprised by, him having practically grown up on the sea. Though why she hadn't thought to obtain some from the apothecary left her sorely wanting. She hadn't anticipated a simple day's trip over the channel to warrant the precaution. But she did have something.

"Maybe I could sleep it off." Not at all meaning to, she felt herself leaning in to him while he carried her, the scent of his chest smelling like seawater and oak. "The apothecary was out of what I needed for my tonic, but he did give me something that would relax me."

"What did he give you?" His head bent down to hers, his lips holding a stern position. They were so close to her own, she imagined the two pairs might touch. The thought sent a gush of warmth inside her—a thought she would've welcomed if her stomach hadn't been so violent.

"An elixir." She recalled the inscription from the bottle. "Something to ease pain and calm the mind."

"I've never heard of it. Can you show it to me?" Having taken her into the dryness of her cabin, Nicholas lowered her to her feet, his steady hold on her lingering until she stood upright again—something she was thankful for even if she couldn't entirely voice her gratitude at this particular time.

"Yes." Still somewhat unbalanced, she struggled to her trunk where'd she kept her tonic and the medicine, producing the latter.

Uncorking the bottle, Nicholas took a strong whiff of the contents through his nose. His lips formed into a thin line. "I know what this is. How long have you been taking it?"

"I haven't yet." She closed her eyes, bracing herself as another wave hit the ship. "I still have a little of my tonic left but only enough for one cup. I thought it would be good to have something on hand—" She swallowed another unpleasant taste. She was undecided on whether she should be more irritated with her stomach or heart at the present moment. "—in case I have one of my episodes."

"Knowing what this is I can't say I like either scenario." He replaced the cork, returning the bottle to her trunk before looking at her again. "But you're not having one of your episodes."

"True." She put her hand to her mouth, her insides mimicking the rolling motion of the ship beneath her feet. When she trusted herself enough to let go, she brought her fingers down again. "Maybe I just need to lie down."

"I think that's a good start." After helping to remove her soiled cloak from a waves' break, Nicholas guided her into her hammock. It was then she realized she hadn't set up her bedding, not sure she would've needed to, the trip taking somewhere between several hours to one day. At some point he'd arranged her bedding for her, though she didn't know when.

In different company, she might've ranted or at the very least coaxed someone into helping her, but not Nicholas. The man was thoughtful beyond words. Without meaning to, she entertained the idea of what life would be like with him if God decided to grant her a longer life. That was, until reality darkened the thought much like the sea outside of the boat now.

Feeling the netting giving way to her weight, yet trusting the bedding's ability to hold her, Charlotte sunk into the hammock.

"Here." Nicholas touched her head, his fingers caressing just above her hairline in a way that was soothing to her. "Let me go check on things out there and I'll be back."

Afraid something else might come out besides her voice she only nodded.

After watching him go, she closed her eyes, drifting in and out of sleep. The attempt did little to settle her stomach, her makeshift bed swaying with the ship's motion. She didn't know how much time had passed since Nicholas had entered her cabin again, but he hadn't come empty-handed or dry for that matter.

She sat up in the middle of her bedding to keep herself balanced from leaning to one side. "You're so . . . wet."

He laughed, the water on his face providing a slight sheen. "The storm is a little worse. It started raining."

"Well, that explains one question I have." She eyed his hands. "What are you doing with Priestley's invention? I can't say I'm in the mood for a carbonated beverage." The very idea of putting something into her stomach when something clearly wanted out of it repelled her.

"Let me explain and you might change your mind." His smile deepened. "I don't know if there's anything to the prevention of scurvy like Priestley suspected, but I have found his invention can soothe the stomach."

"And you know this how?" She tried to probe him, but she doubted her glare held any power. "I thought a seasoned sailor like you would be used to the sea."

"For one, no one really gets used to the sea. It's always changing. Even when you've been on the water for most of your life the ocean still has a way of catching you off guard. And secondly—" He started setting up the machine in the same manner she'd seen the invention arranged on his desk. "Yes, even seasoned sailors experience queasiness sometimes."

She felt a faint smile, remembering him showing her the directions and explanation for how to use the contraption. Directions for impregnating water if she remembered correctly. She could tell then he was playing with her and won. The man was both thoughtful and surprising. Now in her cabin, she saw no evidence of those directions and no evidence he needed them.

Completing the set-up, he looked at her from the floor, the only place available for assembling. He filled a glass with a bubbling liquid and handed the drink to her. "I think this will be a better alternative to what the apothecary gave you."

She frowned at his presumption to her decision. "What if I don't want to try?"

He didn't look the least bit offended. "Then I'll take it." He removed his naval coat and hat, both drenched from the storm. "As I mentioned, even those who have been at sea for a long time can have trouble."

Still feeling the unpleasant churning in her stomach and not seeing any better solution, she took the glass from him. "All right."

Having no qualms for trusting this man, she took a sip. The water tingled inside her mouth and throat. When the fizzing had reached her stomach, she took in a bigger gulp, ready to speed the process of her healing.

"Not so fast." Nicholas's hand was on the cup before the water tipped into her mouth. "It works better if you slip slowly. The bubbles might help if you take it easy, but they might backfire if you don't. It's a delicate balance." As if to illustrate his point only further, he climbed on the hammock beside her, his added weight in the right position to add stability and lessen the motion of the swing carried on by the ship's to and fro give.

A delicate balance. Something she wasn't used to in her life, but something she was beginning to see the usefulness in.

Heeding his instruction more thoughtfully this time, she took slow, tiny sips. She allowed the first of each one to reach down into her stomach before bringing her lips to the cup for another.

"Nicholas, I realize there's something else I need to apologize for. The incident that day on the ship—on the way over to France from the colonies. I'm … I'm sorry for having nearly shot at you."

He hummed a laugh. "If I remember right, you did shoot me." He leveled her with a lighthearted stare. "And before you get an idea of refuting that, I have a bill from the French tailor that supports my claim."

Charlotte pursed her lips, recalling the bullet barely scraped against his coat. "You know I wasn't aiming for you. I was simply trying to scare the bird off from flying into the rigging. It seemed like the quickest solution to get things moving along again."

"Maybe, but you nearly lost your ship's captain."

"Are you afraid of death, Captain Edwards?"

He gave a confident shake of his head. "I made peace with my maker a while back, but—" He brushed a loose strand of hair from her face, one of many that had come undone outside. "—I'd have to say there's still life I'd like to explore before I meet Jesus face-to-face."

As if the tenderness of his voice somehow also cradled the ship, Charlotte could feel the *Speedy* begin to smooth out, her stomach also settling.

The gentle swaying of the ship made her eyes grow heavy. Her body leaned to the side of her hammock until she felt warm skin, not her own, around her. A strong heartbeat drummed in an easy rhythm. It was so different from her own, especially when she had her attacks. Her body relaxed further into Nicholas's arms and with each thump of his chest, she allowed herself to give in to the sweet slumber.

Opening her eyes again, Charlotte wasn't sure how much time had passed while she slept, but the *Speedy* no longer countered her every attempt to find her balance, nor her stomach to keep from retching.

After trying to pin pieces of her hair back in place from her nap, she stowed away her hammock before venturing out of her cabin and to the main deck to see if her assumption was correct.

A clear, night sky with stars overhead greeted her along with calm water. But that was all that was calm. The storm on the channel was over, but a different kind of outbreak took place.

A mixture of shadows and lantern light moved in various directions along the *Speedy's* deck, unloading the ship's cargo while others worked on her sails. Ropes were tied off in a familiar fashion she remembered from when she'd first arrived at Calais from the colonies, telling her one thing. They'd reached port.

A man came toward her with a lantern, and she felt a smile tug, recognizing him.

"Welcome to the Pool of London." Nicholas held the lamp up between them, allowing her to see him more clearly. His eyes were somehow bright even in the dark sky. "How are you feeling?"

"Better." And she meant it. "I suppose you were right about Priestley's invention."

"Maybe." His tone held a smile as he fingered a strand of her hair that she'd missed while pinning, tucking the wayward curl behind her ear. "Perhaps we'll get another chance to test that theory."

She hoped she would get to, but not by means of another rocky passage across the channel.

"We're almost finished with docking procedures, but I have a few more things to take care of. You're welcome to stay here, or the carriage is over there." He directed the lantern toward the harbor where her trunk was being lifted and secured onto a vehicle she couldn't make out in the poor lighting and fog.

Catching he hadn't suggested she wait this time, she appreciated the gesture for what it was.

A gentle, but cold breeze swept past her, helping her make the decision. Wrapping her cloak more tightly around her, she crossed the gangway.

Nicholas met her in the carriage when he was finished, the horses' clopping mimicking her anticipation to see Abigail after so many weeks apart. The moon overhead was accompanied by an arrangement of stars. The excitement prompted her to look out her window as if she might somehow identify the apartment until—

"Nicholas." The scattered lights she'd seen from the *Speedy* flickered more faintly in the distance. "I think our driver might be going the wrong direction."

"Why do you say that?"

"Isn't that London over there?" She pointed out the window and what felt like the ever-increasing distance between them and the Pool of London.

"It is." His tone came out as if unsurprised by an observation that caused her great alarm.

"We seem to be moving away from the city."

"I never said we were staying in London."

Her head jerked, nearly hitting the top of the window frame before she sat all the way down on her seat. "We're not? What about Abigail and Garrett? I thought—"

"Abigail and Garrett are on their way to the colonies for Garrett's new orders. I'm sorry. I thought your sister might have mentioned it."

She hadn't, then again Charlotte had been so focused on the art contest and the vicomte that she hadn't inquired if she'd received any new letters at the boardinghouse.

"It's all right." Disappointment would have clouded the moment if it wasn't for what she still didn't know. "Nicholas, if we're not going to London, then where exactly *are* we going?"

Chapter 25

"Grandparents?"

Charlotte had taken a bite of Fanny Whitford's toasted bread with butter. The boiled eggs and smoked mutton she'd seen the woman fry over the open hearth was scrumptious especially on the empty stomach she'd harbored since last night's journey. But the full enjoyment of the savory breakfast was somewhat diluted by Nicholas's announcement.

She finished the bite, swallowing the toast down before looking to Nicholas then to Fanny for a telling sign that what she'd just heard was a mistake. The woman's easy smile, edged with lines of age and warmth, seemed assured of the fact.

"The Capt—" Charlotte stopped, remembering that title had since been changed with Nicholas's previous visit to London. "The Admiral is your son?" This time her remark was aimed solely to Fanny since Wesley Whitford had already gone out that morning to see a family in town.

"In a way, Miss Charlotte, but not the one you're thinking of I presume." Fanny offered her a cup of coffee with cream. Charlotte took both. "James is our son-in-law, but no one suspects it on account of how little we see each other. Our only proof of kinship is Nicholas here." She gave a warm smile to her grandson that at the moment, was a fact Charlotte still had trouble believing.

Nicholas had mentioned the Whitfords before, but only in the context of Wesley Whitford being his father's hired butler.

Fanny's gray eyes, bright with wisdom and welcome, encouraged more questions.

"And what about your mother?" Charlotte's gaze darted back to Nicholas who had finished his plate. The small remnants of egg yolk she'd seen him smear with his toast were the only evidence he'd partaken of the meal at all. He also had a cup of coffee in hand, looking anything but flustered at the artillery of questions she had.

In fact, she might say he looked more at ease than she'd ever seen him. He wasn't wearing his naval coat, not that he would need it out here, and a strain he seemed to always be carrying had disappeared.

"She left years ago, so I'm told." Nicholas took a sip of coffee, his calmed expression never wavering as if he'd come to terms with that mystery.

It was at that point that Charlotte realized she had spoken so much of her own mother but had never asked of his.

"Rachel and James were married for a short time before Nicholas was born. Not long after, she went away and didn't return." Fanny put two more slices of mutton on Nicholas's plate. "We had heard of James's reputation of being a hard man, but we had no reason to suspect there was anything foul going on in their relationship. Only that she was unhappy."

She wiped her hands on the off-white apron that hung at her waist covering an earth-colored dress. "Worried, we looked everywhere for her and eventually found her, but it was too late."

The touch of grief in Fanny's voice didn't explain the rest of the questions Charlotte wanted to ask, but it had told her enough. Nicholas's mother was dead too. In the midst of everything different about them, that was something they'd shared all along, she realizing the connection only now.

"I'm sorry." She wasn't sure if the apology came out more for their loss or her, though unintended, disregard.

"It was a long time ago." Nicholas gave a faint smile. "It took some time, but I've reconciled with it." A muscle jerked near his jawline, the first time she'd seen him grow tense since they'd been here. "Though I'm not so sure my father has."

"And may never still, my boy." Fanny put her wrinkled hand on top of Nicholas's. She gave his a tender pat, Charlotte imagining one that radiated the love of a grandmother, not ever meeting her own. "Rejection, at least the way the Admiral sees it to be, is hard to overcome."

Under hooded eyes, Nicholas nodded. "Yes, it is." He cleared his throat. "Excuse me, would you?" Though it was a question, he didn't stay for an answer, not that Charlotte expected him to.

He didn't say where he was going, but Charlotte could sense by the tension she felt leave the room with him that he wasn't hoping for company.

Having helped clean up from breakfast, Charlotte chose to remain with Fanny in the living area, the older woman taking a seat in an old Windsor chair to work on some needlework.

Noticing a modestly upholstered footstool next to the fire, Charlotte took a seat, finding the choice more than satisfactory. She opened her sketchbook and began filling in a line where an outline stitch would go, the heat of the kindling in the open hearth warming her fingers and making her movement more fluid.

She liked this work—the forming of ideas for new patterns in her mind and incorporating them into sketches someone could use—someone like Louise. There were marks of iron gall ink on her fingertips, but she far preferred that than of the calloused, dirty hands of the farm. Again, nothing wrong with the work itself, just not the work cut out for her life, as short of one as that may be.

The two of them sat in a companionable silence, letting about half an hour go by when Fanny stopped her needlework, putting what looked to be the final stitching to a pair of men's socks. "I expect Mr. Whiford to be back any moment now from his visit with the Cadwell's. He'll be hungry, I'm sure of it." Rocking herself forward, not once, but twice, as if to give herself momentum to stand, she rose with some effort. Charlotte watched the woman vanish in the direction of the kitchen, her neat, silver bun giving a slight bob with each step.

Smiling to herself, Charlotte completed the last curve of a rose pattern she'd been working on. Though they'd met hardly a day ago, there was something about Fanny that made her feel at home here even when she wasn't. And not having been home for the past six months, she welcomed the feeling.

"Hard at work I see."

She had dipped the quill again when the male voice she was beginning to recognize so well and liked drew her attention.

Nicholas was eyeing her without the least bit of sarcasm in his tone. The strain in his jaw from earlier was also gone, but there was something about the way he looked at her that made her cheeks flush.

She didn't know how long he'd been standing there, but when their eyes met, he came close. She was glad that she could blame the fire's heat for her reaction, while knowing that was far from the truth.

She straightened, rolling her shoulders to try to loosen a place on her back where her muscles had stiffened. "Feeling better?"

"Much." She read his smile as genuine. "A new design for Marie Antoinette?"

The scent of pine and leather from his boots swept through her nose as he leaned closer to her and the drawing, she enjoying his smell and interest.

She turned the notebook to give him a better view. "What do you think?"

"I think the queen of France is going to miss you when you leave Paris for good."

She offered a faint smile. Though finding satisfaction with the compliment regarding her design, the reminder of Paris brought up other feelings.

Confusion knotted his brow. "Did I say something wrong?"

"No." The notebook fell to her lap. "It just made me think of Aunt Sylvia and the vicomte and . . ."

"Marc." His tone was even, like he wasn't surprised by her confession, but not entirely pleased either.

"Yes." She fingered one of the pages at the corner. "I suppose leaving France didn't get my mind off things after all."

"I never said leaving would get our minds off things, just a chance to clear them." He moved over to the chair Fanny had occupied earlier, reclining into its wood backing. "I still believe that."

She wasn't so sure she did. Their journey to Cairnhaven had been a distraction from her last day at Versailles, but that's all that it was, a distraction. She still felt her insides coil, even now, when she thought of Marc's rendition of her for all to see.

Carefully as to not run the ink, she blew on the page of her notebook to speed up the drying process. "And when is it that we will be returning to Paris, exactly?"

"Returning?" His neck drew back further into the Windsor. "We just got here."

"True, but we've already been away from Paris for five days. Surely, that's enough time." Besides, if she was going to see things in a different light—*a clearer one*, as Nicholas put it—she would've done so by now.

But the only thing that came to mind was that blasted picture of her on the wall at Versailles. That, and what she had in her arsenal to say to Marc upon her return.

"I can't say I agree with you—not if any part for your reason to go back is to get even with Marc."

Charlotte flinched. How had the man been able to read her thoughts so well?

"What he did was wrong, no doubt, but if your mind is anywhere near revenge for the man then you're not ready." He eyed her, but not in the way he had earlier when he first approached. "And getting away from Paris wasn't just about the contest, remember?"

She breathed in, Nicholas's question along with the fall of her chest all working together as a reminder for her. She had to admit, her heart, even now when angry with Marc, was steady. She hadn't tried the apothecary's elixir yet, now completely out of her herbs she'd brought from home, but maybe she wouldn't need to. Maybe getting out of Paris like the doctor suggested had benefited the weak constitution she'd inherited from her mother.

In fact, she felt strong. And if that was the primary reason she'd left—to get stronger, well then, perhaps it was time to go back and finish what she'd started.

Testing the ink with the tip of her finger, she closed the book to her sketches. "Yes, I remember. And I think the change has been good. Actually, I feel much stronger than I did before we left. But that only means I'm ready to go back. As you know, there are matters in Paris that have been left undone and need to be seen to." She pointed the quill to herself then to him. "And I'm not just talking about me."

His eyes deepened, but in a way that indicated that he didn't agree. Fine. She'd get back on her own. Surely there were alternate means to get her back to—

The front door to the Whitfords' small cottage opened and shut again, Charlotte feeling the chill from outside that had passed through even when close to the fire.

"Oh, Wesley, you've returned." Fanny went to the door, her petite rounded figure bouncing almost like the bun at the nape of her neck. She helped the man Charlotte now knew as Nicholas's grandfather out of his wool coat. "How are Tim and Trudy?"

A shadow cast over Wesley Whitford's face as he looked down at his wife through a set of round-rimmed glasses. "They could be much better." His tone was solemn. "It sounds like the mine has been shut down and has put all the boys out of work."

"Oh, the poor dears." Having positioned her husband's coat on a simple coat rack, Fanny went to the hearth to collect a large pan. "Let me cook up a pottage for them. Nicholas, you take it over. I bet Jim would love to see you even with what they're facing. It's been so long since you've seen each other. And he no doubt would want to meet Charlotte now that you have a lady in your life."

Nicholas cleared his throat, but a smile played at the corners of his mouth, telling Charlotte he didn't mind the comment too much. Her own feelings having changed for this man, neither had she.

The way to the Cadwells' was along a narrow dirt road.

Charlotte couldn't say she was excited to get back to their conversation now that they were alone again, but she wasn't altogether certain who to get to take her to London so she could make the return trip to Paris. Wesley's employment to the Admiral would mean he was used to the trip to the city but asking him seemed like a boundary she shouldn't cross. Maybe she wouldn't have to, not if she could find another way to convince Nicholas to take her.

"Nicholas, can I ask you something?" Charlotte walked in step beside him, the wool gloves she'd borrowed from Fanny swinging at her sides.

"You can."

"Why is it that we've come to your grandparents instead of London?" She might have asked why he wouldn't want to visit his father, but his discomfort every time the man was mentioned had already provided her with some kind of answer.

Her attempt to stay clear of the Admiral was a failed one. His walk along the dirt path to the Cadwells' cottage became more rigid.

"I don't know exactly. Fanny and Wesley are easy. Always have been."

She could pick up on what he wasn't saying. His father was not.

Getting away from Paris hadn't been enough for Nicholas. London had also had its fair share of burdens. Cairnhaven had been his refuge.

Upon arrival, Charlotte could easily see the Cadwells' cottage was a much smaller dwelling than the Whitfords'. From what Nicholas had informed her, the family rented from a Mr. Brenton, a landowner in Cairnhaven.

"Why, if I didn't hear it from your granddad, I wouldn't have believed it. Nick is back in town." Jim Cadwell, a man that came up to Nicholas's nose was the first to greet them with an overly enthusiastic welcome.

The man broader in build, perhaps from working in a mine, gave Nicholas a heavy pat on the back.

Nicholas revealed a smile of his own that appeared to come easy enough. "For a short time. And if it weren't for that red hair of yours, I don't think I would have recognized you, Jim." Nicholas cupped at his chin as if pretending to comb over the full beard the man in front of him possessed. "That mine has made a man out of you."

A deep pitched laughter came from Jim. "In more ways than one, but I've heard the Navy has done the same with you." He rubbed at the thick and almost unruly hair that stretched across his jawline and over his lip. "You look good, Nick. Clean and trim-like."

Charlotte let a knowing smile peak, if only to herself. Since they'd left Paris, Nicholas had allowed a patch of blonde to form in the same areas. Though just on the cusp of growth compared to this man before her, it was quite a change, considering the navy officer's face was normally immaculate. Given she'd only seen him clean-shaven until now, she'd always assumed the maintenance had been minimal, but now she knew that was far from the truth. A misjudgment she'd made and a trait she found she liked and wondered if she would see more of.

Jim's gaze met hers, his eyes squinting in a way that already made her feel welcome. "And you must be Miss Charlotte." He stepped into the cabin, allowing she and Nicholas to enter. "It's nice to make your acquaintance. Any friend of Nick's is a friend of mine."

"And ours." A little girl peaked behind Jim's waist with copper-colored hair high in what resembled a bird's nest rather than any sort of true hairstyle.

"Yes, Joleen, *ours*." Jim smiled down at the little girl before looking up again at them. "The whole Cadwell clan."

Charlotte bent down to Joleen, guessing she was maybe six or seven. She lowered her voice as if keeping a secret between them. "Well, I'm glad to hear that. But we brought a pottage from Fanny Whitford as a peace offering just in case." She winked and the girl giggled.

"Fanny's got a gift for cooking and a heart of gold behind it." Jim motioned to the little girl, then to Fanny's dish. "Joleen, take the pottage to Momma."

"Come on in, Miss Charlotte. You can meet my momma and baby Jane."

Before Charlotte could nod her consent, Joleen grabbed for her hand and drug her further inside.

"Momma, look what Miss Fanny made for us." Joleen let go of Charlotte's hand, skipping over to a woman sitting on the floor of the cabin and next to a wood trough. Inside the trough, a baby girl cooed and smiled, watching the face of the woman come close to hers and kiss her nose.

"God bless that woman Fanny Whitford. We'll have it tonight for supper." The woman, she guessed to be Trudy, was younger than Fanny, no doubt, more like the age of her own mother and adorned simply in a brown-colored dress made of linen. She took the baby out of the trough and sat the infant on the floor next to her. "Take it to the table for me, would you, Joleen?" She patted at a thin, straw-stuffed mattress. "Miss Charlotte, come on over and take a seat on Jim's bed. We'll see if Janie is ready to walk this time around."

"I'd be happy to join you for the event." Adjusting her skirts behind her, Charlotte took a seat on the floor, the place seeming more fitting and where she could better view the action.

"Come on, Janie, you can do it. Nice and easy to Momma." Trudy's arms were outstretched, as if ready to embrace the babe upon reaching her at the finish point.

The baby giggled, revealing a nearly toothless grin. She pulled herself up, leaning her little body against the trough she'd just come out of.

"Momma, she'll get it when she's good and ready just like the rest of us did."

"I know, Joleen. But sometimes it's not about the final result." She glanced at Charlotte, giving her a wink that nearly mimicked the one she'd given to Joleen earlier. "Sometimes what's more important is the journey."

If her mother wasn't already gone from this world, Charlotte would have sworn the gesture had been one account of many growing up. A piece of wisdom not intentionally directed at her, but nevertheless for her.

"Where's Tim and James?" Nicholas walked in with Jim. His blue eyes swept across the area of the cabin, an action that didn't take long in the small space.

Jim looked to Joleen who was sitting to the side of Trudy, still watching the babe. "Joleen, why don't you go out back and get a game of marbles set up. I'll be there in a few minutes." He gave the young girl a smile Charlotte recognized from her older brother, Abraham, when he and father had a matter to discuss privately.

With the girl occupied, Jim resigned himself to take a seat on his bed. He rubbed a hand over the top of a patch on his trousers. "They're out looking for work—checking for any day labor if it can be had."

"What happened with the mine? Why did they close it?" Nicholas chose to remain standing, though Charlotte suspected the decision was more out of the comfort for the Cadwells than the refusal of their accommodations. Both men stared at young Janie, though she doubted the concern Charlotte saw etched in Nicholas's face had anything to do with the babe's progress on her feet.

"We're told the demand for copper is low—not worth paying the laborers." Jim's head hung. "They'd rather shut down the mine than keep us."

"Who is 'they'?" Nicholas's brow formed a single line.

"The bank mostly. Lord Brenton is the owner of the mine, but I'm told he has the mine on a loan from the bank." Jim put a calloused hand to the back of his head as if to scratch it. "I tried to speak with Brenton about it—to help him understand all of our difficulties without the work. He was understanding enough." Though his tone conveyed the meeting was civil, the grimace on Jim's mouth, even half covered by his beard, said it wasn't the outcome he'd hoped for.

"And did he say anything to it?"

Jim's broad shoulders lifted from his frame, no doubt a product of his trade. "Only what the bank told him—it wasn't anything personal, just a matter of business."

The huff that came out from under her breath was louder than Charlotte meant the sound to be. Both men stopped their conversation to eye her. Trudy too and even baby Janie seemed to wonder what suddenly grabbed her momma's attention from her amazing performance.

"Is there something you'd like to contribute, Charlotte?" Nicholas gave her a look as if to say, "tread carefully."

She rose from the floor, outraged. "I just don't believe that excuse, that's all. When a person says it's nothing personal, it usually is. That's poor business if you ask me." She could tell Nicholas had something to say to her she wouldn't like, and she felt bad for ruining little Janie's moment to shine. "I'm sorry. It was hasty for me to—"

"It's all right, Miss Charlotte." Jim's mouth twitched into a half smile. "I'm likely to agree with you."

Nicholas gave a single shake of his head, his lips firming. "I'm sorry, Jim. If I hear of anything for work, you'll be the first to know." He put a hand on Jim's shoulder, the gesture conveying both a bond and a promise. "We'll be praying for you too—that God will provide."

"Thanks Nick." Charlotte caught Jim's Adam's apple move before he nodded. "I believe that you will."

Nicholas's arm returned to his side. "Why don't you and the family come over Sunday?" He glanced at Charlotte as if something were shared between them before his attention went back to Jim. "I have a feeling our stay in town won't be very long and I'd like to see you and the rest of your clan again before we go."

A patch of skin creased at Jim's forehead. "You sure Wesley and Fanny won't mind?"

Nicholas offered the young man a smirk like he'd asked the wrong question. "You already know they wouldn't."

"Thanks Nick." Jim nodded, a softness glowing in his downturned eyes. "That would be something to look forward to and appreciated more than you know."

***

Charlotte and Nicholas walked back from the Cadwells in an uncomfortable silence—one much different than the companionable quiet she had with Fanny earlier that morning.

Nicholas studied the compacted dirt road in front of them, his thoughts clearly elsewhere. She figured the Cadwell's predicament was in part to blame, but had her opinion on the matter also contributed?

"I'm sorry about my outburst at the Cadwells'." She took two steps to Nicholas's one stride. "That was presumptuous of me to say when I don't even know Lord Brenton." She'd always had trouble with speaking her mind outrightly more than society meant to groom her to. She'd come to accept that part of her, and even liked the trait at times. But a time to speak one's mind was when one felt confident, assured of the facts, and this had not been one of those scenarios.

Today, she'd spoken of merely her own opinion without any true knowledge—having just met the Cadwells this afternoon and never having met Lord Benton at all. Somehow the thought also brought the Vicomte de Vatinelle to mind even if she altogether didn't understand the connection.

"It's all right." Surprisingly, his tone offered her no indignation. "If I didn't know Lord Brenton then I'd be likely to agree with you in light of what the Cadwells are going through. I'm just not sure if anyone's to blame or if it's a product of something else."

She stopped walking along the path, the hemline of her skirts swaying forward and away from her shoes. "So, you're not mad at me?" Her sudden halt apparently grabbed his attention, his focus on the ground shifting to her.

"Not at all."

She threw up her hands, ready for an explanation. "Then what is it? You've barely said a word until now and we're nearly to your grandparents' house."

"I'm just thinking about something, that's all." His tone gave little away, but she ventured a guess.

"About the Cadwells or the mine?"

"Both actually."

Her fingers squeezed inside Fanny's borrowed gloves, but her irritation lessened, hoping he'd confide in her. "And . . .?"

"And I don't know yet. But it might be better if I show you something."

When they reached the house, Nicholas rounded to the back.

Behind the cottage where a chimney billowed out curls of smoke, stretched a field gently and gradually inclining to meet a small, wooded area. The last traces of a light morning dusting of snow had already vanished, revealing brown grass beneath rows of apple trees. Their bare branches stretched outward and upward against a pale, overcast sky and Charlotte felt a mild disappointment from missing their season to taste the fruit.

She followed Nicholas inside the barn where he'd been sleeping since they'd arrived from Paris, seeing the two stalls that housed the couples' horse and cow. The strong odor she'd prepared herself for was lacking, stifled by the outside cold. A pallet made of straw lay on the ground along the far wall, much too small for Nicholas's tall frame. She felt a smile begin to creep, thinking of him here in his youth before it occurred to her those young years had been the last time he'd been here.

"Your bed I take it?" She lifted a brow, eyes pointed toward the pallet on the floor, letting her tone tease.

"It's where I always slept when I came to the Whitfords'." He put his hand at the back of his neck, twisting his head from side to side as if stretching. "Though, it's stiffer than I remember."

She laughed. "And what is all this?" She motioned to the bed where a wooden box sat and several newspaper clippings hung neatly on the wall by wrought iron nails.

"They're explorations or inventions I've been following since I was young. I've had Wesley bring some of the more recent developments I've procured back here." His face stared longingly at the arrangement as if at a distant past. "It's a safe place to keep them."

Their day at the Seine River with Freminet and his diving contraption came to view. Even from youth, the man had a mind for innovation—something she could deeply appreciate and love.

Not sure if she was ready to express such an admission out loud, she was becoming quite certain of the truth. She was falling in love with this man.

She stooped lower to get a better look, catching the scent of dried grass. There was one clipping about the first-of-its-kind steam engine and another article dated from years later that talked about a newer, improved version to the former. A man by the name of Franklin had come up with the idea of a lightning rod and another clipping focused on something called a chronometer to calculate longitude at sea. She saw excerpts of two voyages taken by a Captain James Cook as well as a third stating his departure to explore the northwest passage, but no end date to his arrival home.

"Never mind all that." He pulled out two newspaper clippings from the wooden box, each a product of the *London Gazette*. "This is what I wanted to show you."

She skimmed the first. It regarded a trial conducted by the Royal Navy of applying copper sheathing to a frigate, the *HMS Alarm* in 1761. The second article concerned a similar trial to the *HMS Dolphin* three years later.

Nicholas pointed to the two clippings. "They both mention the trials were to test the copper to help as an anti-fouling agent."

"Excuse me, am I supposed to know what that means?" Raising herself up again, she gave him a pointed look, to which he grinned.

"To help prevent seaworm and barnacle invasion on the ship." He looked to the articles again. "It reads like the trials were successful."

"Nearly." She corrected him, skimming her finger further down the page. "If you read on the article talks about the bolts holding the copper being corroded."

He nodded, seeming unsurprised. "They react differently, and they should. They're made of iron."

He presented a final article, this one also discussing a very similar trial, with one key exception. The difference was one she could single-out only because of his comment regarding the bolts. The ship's sheathing was fastened with a copper alloy, and held much more favorable results for both the effect of the anti-fouling agent as well as the longevity of the fastenings.

"Well, it seems like a success to me." She looked up at him. He seemed to be waiting for her to say something more.

"What? No challenge this time?" He gave her a wry grin.

She smiled, always happy to comply. She handed him the three accounts. "What I don't understand then, is why I haven't seen a single Royal Navy ship whose hull is sheathed in copper."

He returned the articles to the box he'd taken them from, closing the lid gently. "There are a lot of reasons for that, the primary one is that it's expensive. Copper is rare and until now, the Navy hasn't been in a true need of it, not like I think they might be now."

She bit her bottom lip, the meaning having come to her. "You mean the war?"

He nodded. "The voyage to and from the colonies can be hard on a ship and the amount of time the ship stays in the water abroad, even harsher. It might be a way to—"

"Help the miners." She felt nearly breathless at the prospect and the idea Nicholas had come up with, but she could tell he was holding back something.

He took a measured breath. "I might have a way, but I need to speak to Lord Brenton first about the mine and then decide if . . ." He let the last part of the thought trail off, rubbing the blonde whiskers of his chin.

"If what?" She could hear her tone, imploring him for an answer.

"If it's time for me to pay King George a visit."

Chapter 26

It wasn't until a week later that Nicholas could visit Lord Brenton about the mine.

Nicholas knew Charlotte was ready to face Marc now more than ever, but the miner's plight wasn't an easy fix. To her credit, she had been patient, allowing him time while not pressing they'd return before he could get answers. And he had.

The Lord had been away on a hunting expedition, but Nicholas found out what he needed to and had suspected.

The closing of the mine hadn't been Lord Brenton's doing, or wish for that matter. The mine's unfortunate outcome had actually put him in debt, the loan he'd acquired from the bank forfeited along with all the miner's jobs.

Nicholas sat on his straw bed in the barn, flicking the lid of his compass open and shut with his thumb. The news of Lord Brenton had been what he needed to move forward, yet even as he sat here in the barn knowing what his next step should be, his feet felt anchored to the ground.

The last thing he wanted to do was stand in front of King George with no news from Paris given the fact the lack of information obtained was his fault. The request of sending aid to his grandparents' town on top of that made the visit even less appealing.

"Glad to see that compass I got you hasn't worn out."

Nicholas's thumb hung in the air, having somehow missed Wesley enter the barn.

"Though you keep flipping it like that, I don't know how long the thing will last." His grandfather stood over him in a plain coat with a lightly embroidered vest. Nicholas hadn't seen the man wear the outfit since they'd been in town, but he easily recognized it as being from his father's London apartment. His grandfather looked at Nicholas through his spectacles with soft eyes. "Something is clearly on your mind, my boy."

My boy. Words Nicholas yearned to hear from his father, now spoken from his grandpa. But he thanked God, even for that.

"A decision that might come at a cost." Feeling the tension in what seemed like every inch of his body, he flipped open the compass, closing the lid again.

Wesley managed to find a seat next to him on the small bed, the straw crunching under him from beneath the sheets. "Is the benefit worth the cost?"

"It could be if it worked." Nicholas raised his eyes to his grandfather. "But there's no guarantee it will." There was no guarantee the king would like his plan, especially considering his now tarnished reputation as the reliable officer he'd been made to be.

"Would there be a cost if you didn't do anything?"

Having given up on his habit, Nicholas closed the lid to his grandfather's gift, turning the gadget around in his fingers. He thought about the Cadwells and the rest of the miners, all looking for alternate means of income. There was absolutely no certainty of success with his plan, but if he did nothing, then how long before the jobs in town ran out?

Though Nicholas remained milling the thought, he detected something close to resolve in his grandfather's face. The telling lines around his forehead and mouth indicated the man was about to speak a truth, and he better listen.

"I think your silence speaks on your behalf." Wesley put a firm, but loving hand on Nicholas's shoulder. "Perhaps the Spirit is telling you something."

Shouting more like it. The past two nights were restless over the responsibility—an urge to act coupled with the uncertainty of what doing so might mean, especially in the eyes of his father.

"Nicholas, if you see a need that no one else is fulfilling, then perhaps there is a reason God has shown that need to you."

Nicholas dropped his eyes again, his hand tight around his compass while the conviction and purpose in his grandfather's tone struck at his core. He'd told Jim he'd pray for God's provision. He didn't realize at the time that provision might come through him.

A prolonged silence settled between them until his grandfather rose from the bedding. Occasions like these when Nicholas had been sitting or hunched were the only times he had to physically look up to his grandfather, yet the man stood tall in ways that he aimed and hoped to reach one day.

"Pray about it, son. I'll be praying too." The man lifted a smile Nicholas trusted. He brushed off pieces of straw that had managed to come out of the ticking and through the wool blankets. "I came to let you know the Cadwell clan is here."

Nicholas nodded, stashing his watch inside his coat. "That was kind of you and Fanny to have them over today. I'm not sure what their Christmas would look like with how things are for them."

Wesley shook his head as if the compliment were unnecessary. "We are only fulfilling the invitation you extended. I know you didn't mean today necessarily when you and Charlotte went over to see them last week, but you know your grandmother." His grandfather shrugged.

He did. The woman liked her house full of people and their stomachs empty for whatever dish she chose to provide them.

"I'm glad to be able to spend Christmas with you this year, Nicholas." The man smiled, his eyes moistening behind his wired frames. His grandfather patted him on the back, his voice tempered with an emotion Nicholas could relate to.

Nicholas swallowed, unable to let his own feelings run free, not sure if it was due to his strict upbringing or something else within him that held back. Christmas with his father was never celebrated. The times they'd happened to both be in London together on the day looked much the same as the rest of their time together—estranged. Last year, Nicholas had spent the holiday in the middle of the Atlantic.

He accompanied his grandfather back to the house, his decision regarding the Cadwells still on his mind until Charlotte came into view. Then the struggle all but disappeared.

She was in a light blue dress he didn't recognize—the color of a robin's egg—but somehow looked familiar. Then he realized, he had seen the dress before, but in a much different setting. The art contest at Versailles. If he didn't know the woman better, he might have thought the choice too extravagant for a Christmas at the Whitford's humble cottage, but he did know this woman. She was up to something.

The lace that had been added around the neckline also tugged at a memory of when she'd missed a few places of pinning and he'd seen a little more of her than she meant him to see. He couldn't contain the smile, watching her as she took Joleen to the stool and proceeded to work the girl's normally mangled tresses into what started to resemble a braid.

"I got to say, Nick—" Jim came up beside him and sipped a glass of his grandmother's spiced punch, his eyes too on Charlotte. "I always thought you'd settle for someone of your father's choosing—an officer's daughter maybe."

"I'm afraid I've given the wrong impression. Miss Thatcher is here under doctor's orders, not to attach herself to the Whitfords or myself." The answer came as if practiced, even when his heart hammered inside his chest and his head knew differently.

Jim's chuckle and gleam in his eye said he hadn't been fooled either. "Yet, she has managed to do both."

Jim was right, even if Nicholas wouldn't say as much. He didn't want to make Charlotte feel uncomfortable when the point was to help her relax. But he'd felt a connection with her that he wanted to pursue, though he wasn't entirely certain if she felt the same.

Nicholas swallowed his own sip of punch, clearing his throat and reaching for a way to quickly conclude the topic. "I saw Lewis Digby in Paris."

"Digby, huh?" Jim angled his head, his all too eager smile dimming somewhat. "The last time I saw him wasn't long after you left. I heard he somehow managed to get into law school—that some gentleman in London he met aided his funds, but he's doing more than that. Though, I can't say what." His friend scratched at his beard that he had neatly trimmed for the occasion. "I just don't know any lawyer that travels as much as he does. One of the Clark boys works at the stables over there. He's mentioned Lewis talking about meeting with the prime minister if you can believe it."

Nicholas wasn't sure, having no idea who the Clark family was or if the account held merit. Without meaning to, his glance went back to Charlotte, she sitting beside Trudy on an upholstered couch. The two seemed to be in an exchange of conversation while every so often Trudy would whisper a secret into the infant's ear who sat on her mother's lap.

As if sensing his attention, Charlotte broke her conversation from Trudy, her blue eyes meeting his like they'd shared a bond that somehow linked them together. The brilliant smile she flashed him only cemented the desire that the connection was real. She mouthed something to him, and he instantly returned the smile, then nodded agreeing to her plan. He knew it. She was up to something.

***

Nicholas was waiting for her when Charlotte had ventured outside behind the Whitford's cottage. The smell of minced pies and roasted pheasants wafted in every inch of the small homestead. Even out here in the cold December air, Charlotte could still breathe in the delicious aroma of Fanny's kitchen.

She warmed, glad he'd accepted both her compliment and proposal. She'd meant what she'd said, or rather, mouthed to him from her place beside Trudy on the Whitford's sofa. Nicholas did, indeed look handsome. He wasn't wearing his navy coat, something she hadn't seen him don since they'd arrived to town, but she had thought he might wear the uniform tonight, given the occasion. She'd been wrong on that account, but not at all displeased. The suit, a light beige coat over a hazelnut-colored vest that had been embellished with gold thread made her wonder how often he got the chance to wear the outfit, given his occupation.

They stood there a minute watching Tim and young James, who'd opted to play a game of Quoits in the frigid air rather than warm themselves by the Whitford's fire with conversation. The two were unevenly matched, James the clear winner with the advantage of a boisterous youth and competitive spirit.

"You look beautiful." Nicholas stared at her, his eyes taking their time moving from her head to her feet and making her pulse kick up a notch.

"Thank you." She'd worn this dress tonight for a reason.

"I see you made some changes since the last time I saw you in that dress." He gave her an almost wink and she tried to remember the last time he had seen her wearing—

Despite the cold, her cheeks heated, suddenly remembering.

"I like it." His tone held true before he thumbed the side of his jaw. "But I can't help notice that lace also looks familiar. And I haven't seen your shawl in some time."

She nodded, confirming what she could see working in his mind. "I used my fichu to make the necessary—" She was going to say *changes* but wasn't satisfied with that answer. Another word came. "Improvements. And that wasn't the last time you saw me in this dress." She gave a sigh, viewing her breath before her. "If you recall, my portrait was also done in it."

His brow creased. "Given that painting was only a representation of you, and not a good one in my opinion, I stand by what I said before. Though, I'm a little surprised you'd choose to wear something associated with the event."

She knew he meant Les Muses de Versailles but that was precisely why she had chosen to wear the dress. She loved this dress, both because of the lace her mother helped her construct and Louise's own part in helping to transform it. She wasn't going to let a single event put a stain to that.

She rolled her shoulders back, feeling a resignation over her decision and still happy to see that decision through. "I'm making new memories, better ones."

He gave her a smile that made her heart pound and made her mind wander down a path she knew she shouldn't go but wanted to.

"Want to have a go, Nick?" Jim stepped in beside them, motioning to Tim and James on the plot of open field that had been frosted the night before. It wasn't a white Christmas, but clouds covered the sky like a large blanket. Jim breathed out through his mouth, casting a vapor in the air. "If I remember right, you used to be pretty good at the game."

Nicholas met his friend's conspiratorial side grin with one of his own. "I was decent."

In a language she could only decipher as male, that seemed to be confirmation enough. She watched as the two stepped up to play.

"Do they have Quoits in America?" Joleen tugged at the satin material of Charlotte's dress, grabbing her attention.

"Why yes, they do." Charlotte bent down to the girl's level like she had the day they'd first met. "In fact, there are many games that are similar, if not the same."

The way that Joleen looked at her, like she was from a different world, made Charlotte all too aware of the ancestry they shared, now threatened by a war to divide them.

She felt stuck in the middle somehow. She was seen by those on one side like the vicomte, who distrusted her English connection even when it was perhaps on the brink of being severed, yet also distant from England in the doe-like eyes that looked at her now.

Seeing Trudy had remained inside with Janie, perhaps to keep the child from the cold, Charlotte wrapped her arms around Joleen, hoping the action might do something similar. They watched the new game transpire, Charlotte a little surprised and alarmed at how quickly it did. James was skilled enough in his own right, but it was plain to see his opponent was better. Nicholas won the game, missing not a single available point to be had. If her plan was going to work, she was going to have to beat Nicholas.

She might've ordinarily drawn her gloved fingers to her hips, but at present they were still around Joleen. Instead, her eyebrows sank toward her nose. "I thought you said you were decent, not perfect."

He shook his head, but she didn't miss the glint of the wry smile that appeared. "Hardly perfect, just practiced."

"And how much practice does an officer of the Royal Navy get at Quoits these days?"

His shoulders lifted at her pretense. "Sometimes there's down time while we await our orders. Soldiers don't usually pack much, but you'd be surprised by how easy it is to make a few rings and a stake."

Her mouth went into a small pout, suddenly not liking her chances, yet feeling a need to continue the pursuit of her conquest. "I imagine so. And do you always win so flawlessly?"

"No." He gave her a curious look. "Sometimes I don't win at all."

That was nice to know, especially with what she had in mind. Taking her arms from Joleen, she stood. "Then I'd like to play if there's no objection."

The side of his mouth edged up. "Of course there's not." He went to the part of the yard where one of the stakes was placed, retrieving a set of roped rings before meeting her down the field where Jim had been standing at the other stake.

"But let's make it more interesting, why don't we?" Accepting the set of rings he handed her, she counted four in all.

He frowned and she felt somewhat sorry for the proposition, knowing her scheme was bound to ruin the nice time they'd shared this evening.

"What did you have in mind?"

"If I win, we leave for Paris in the morning."

He didn't look surprised by her notion. In fact, the way his mouth hinted at a smile made her believe she'd misspoken. "I knew you were up to something."

She didn't say anything, only awaiting his answer.

He didn't say anything either at first, his mouth shifting to the side as if he was chewing on the idea. After another moment, he gave a single nod. "Okay, fine." The smile that was hinting earlier reappeared more brilliantly. "And if you don't, we'll stay another fortnight."

Her eyes widened. Another two weeks—hardly a bad deal here in England's charming countryside with people she liked very much. But her confrontation with Marc was calling and she was obliged to answer. She needed to win.

"All . . . right." She looked at the distance between the two stakes where she'd be throwing, guessing ten to fifteen yards stretched between them. "Agreed."

"Ladies first." He bent over in a playful bow before he turned from her and made his way to the other end.

She tossed the first ring. Unfortunately, the ring landed half a foot away from the stake. So much for starting off strong, especially when Nicholas's first turn landed as a ringer. She took in a quick breath, letting the second one fly and to her incredible satisfaction, landed the ring around the stake.

"Nice throw." Nicholas called the compliment out from where he stood on his end, she hearing the genuineness in the remark. He took his second turn and to her chagrin, the rope found its way to another stake.

The triumphant feeling she'd felt seconds ago suddenly dissipated. She tried mimicking her movements from her previous turn, hoping to also mimic the outcome, but the ring fell short, leaning to one side of the stake. She would have to do better if she were to beat Captain Nicholas Edwards, champion of the ring toss game.

Nicholas went again, this time his ring also falling short. A small sliver of hope rose inside her. It was the physical proof she needed that the man could be beat.

They threw their hoops again to take the next series of turns, Nicholas sinking in all four this time to her two. Seven to three. She bit her lip, not at all liking the gap that spread between the scores, especially when taking into account they were only playing to twenty-one.

Two more rounds like the one they just had and Nicholas was sure to take the prize. That was simply out of the question. This had been her idea. She couldn't let it backfire on her now. She'd played the game enough times on the farm to be more than practiced. She'd even tried tricks simply for the fun of it to see if any ways worked better than the others. In fact—

As if a spark had caught on dry tinder and ignited, she remembered one trick that might just work.

"Nicholas, why don't you go first, this time?" She retrieved her rings, letting her tone come out as casual as possible so he wouldn't suspect anything. "That's allowed, isn't it?"

He shrugged, not at all bothered by the change she'd suggested. And why would he be? He had more than a satisfactory lead.

She watched, admiring his concentration all the while hoping her plan might work. Another ring around the stake.

Though somewhat annoyed at the man's precision—mostly because of what it could cost her—she aimed her ring as if to toss it, but instead of letting the ring fly through the air, she bent her knees, whipping her wrist. The ring rolled straight toward the stake before toppling over the target.

She sucked in a more than gratifying breath, smiling to herself. She might just have a chance after all. She straightened, looking up from the stake, only to find Nicholas with his arms crossed and eyeing her with playful scrutiny.

Tim and James and even Joleen offered playful jeering from the sidelines as she went to the stake to collect her rings for the next round.

"What?" She threw him an innocent look, letting her tone follow.

"Still full of surprises, I see."

His grin only encouraged her own. "For now."

He held out the gathered rings to exchange.

"Don't worry, one day I'll run out of surprises. You won't have to run after me anymore."

"I have to admit, not running after you would be nice . . ."

The comment disappointed her. She knew they would go their separate ways eventually, but it saddened her knowing that reality meant less time together she had grown to enjoy.

". . . but I gather the only way that's going to happen is if you become my wife."

The ring nearly fell from her hand. His wife? Now who was surprised? She looked at Nicholas, trying to discern if his proposal was a way to slip her up from the game, but she knew this man too well. He wasn't a cheater, and from the way his eyes remained unflinching even from across the way, she detected he meant what he had said.

She gripped the ring tighter, thoughts swirling in her mind. Thoughts she wouldn't mind exploring under the right conditions. And right now, was no such time. She drew a shaky breath and let the comment pass with difficulty.

They tossed a few more turns, each time her rings falling over a stake. It was her twelve to his thirteen. She was right on his heels. Unless they both completely missed, this would be the last set of the game.

She took a determined breath and rolled, her chest pounding. 19-19.

Nicholas went, his turn ending less than a foot short of the stake. She rolled again but hers missed too. This time Nicholas's hit his straight on followed by her own soon after. Tied again. If each one was to land their own ring around the stake, they'd go another round until there was a winner.

No. It was time to finish the game. Charlotte whipped her last ring, watching with hoped apprehension as the roped circle rolled and landed over the stake. But she didn't celebrate. Nicholas wasn't one to count out.

He tossed and she held her breath as if the game somehow meant life or death instead of just a friendly competition. Her gaze never wavered at the ring until braided rope touched wood before dropping to the outside dirt. She gasped. She'd won.

Exhilaration coursed through her veins, but her celebration was cut short, seeing Wesley come from the house with a quickened pace in his step she hadn't seen the man take until now. He approached them both.

"Nicholas, there's someone who'd like to speak with you at the door." His tone was hushed, though deepened with concern. "I don't recognize the stranger."

They followed Nicholas back through the cottage where a man dressed in a recognizable deep blue coat stood on the other side of the frame. Someone from the Royal Navy was here.

Nicholas straightened in a way as if he'd morphed back into the officer she hadn't seen since Paris. He cleared his throat. "You wished to speak with me, sir?"

The man nodded. "Yes, Captain. I come with news. It's about your father." The officer's voice was low. He removed a tricorn hat from the top of his head, grasping the hat between both hands. His face was a picture more reminiscent of despair rather than exhibiting a command. "Sir, he's dying."

Chapter 27

Charlotte pushed open the door to the Admiral's bedroom. The creek of the hinges against the loud silence signaled her entrance, yet no movement. She curbed the sensation to cover her nose with her sleeve, having accidentally breathed in the stale metallic scent that overwhelmed the room and brought back memories she would've preferred buried.

She stood in the doorway, allowing her eyes to adjust to the dark and where a nearly spent candle was the room's only source of light. The wax pooled at the bottom of the lantern. Its wick emitted the final stages of use and reminded her of the man lying in the bed so near.

Nicholas sat at his father's bedside, the compass he always carried clutched in his palm. He wasn't flipping the lid open and shut like she'd seen him do, a habit employed when something was on his mind, but she knew he had been.

Gentling her footsteps, she went toward him, the sound of anything even moderately loud seeming unwelcomed in the quiet that dominated the room.

It wasn't until she touched Nicholas's shoulder when he looked to her, his only indication he'd been aware of someone else's presence. His eyes were red and dull from lack of sleep.

"Nicholas." She let her voice come out as a whisper, even when she knew the man that lay in the bed wouldn't be privy to their conversation. "It's been over a full day since you've slept. Let me take a turn."

He rubbed at the stubble that had begun to reappear on his chin, then at his eyes. "I appreciate that, but this isn't your responsibility."

She followed his gaze to the bed, the Admiral sleeping soundly under the doctor's medicine. "No, it's not." She looked back to Nicholas. "But this is something I happen to know how to do." Though there was a large part that didn't want to extend the offer, resistant to a past she didn't want to return to, Nicholas had helped her on more than one occasion. He'd even risked his appointment with the king of France for her sake. And . . .

A tingling started in the middle of her chest, spreading outward to her legs and arms, her stomach fluttering. She couldn't stop thinking about what he said during their game at the Whitfords'. To become his wife. A role in life she never thought of playing, but not because she didn't want the part. She just couldn't have it—not when her life was likely to be so short. He deserved more.

She folded her hands in front of her, waiting for him to argue. When he didn't, she felt more convinced she'd made the right decision to intervene. "Wesley's made some tea. Have a cup, then get some rest."

Steeling a glance at his father, Nicholas pulled himself from the bedside and began to walk out. He paused just before the door, casting her a look, and waiting as if to give her opportunity to change her mind. She wouldn't. Seeming to read her silence as her answer, Nicholas let the door shut behind him on his way.

Deciding the current environment wouldn't do, Charlotte drew open the velvet curtains, letting the afternoon light shine through the apartment window. The change was already an improvement, the blackness of the room turning into shades of burgundy on the painted walls and draperies. And the freshness of the new day from the window helped to subdue the murky feel of a cave.

Now able to view the Admiral in a better light, she could see the paleness of his skin, almost transparent. A faint sheen of sweat glistened at his forehead. That, and the steady rise and fall of his chest underneath the fine, linen sheets were the only indications he was still in this world.

She shifted her gaze to the side of the bed where part of the Admiral's torso remained uncovered, but heavily bandaged from a gunshot wound. She'd been told the surgeon aboard the ship had pulled the bullet out, but they never thought he'd make the trip back alive. Yet somehow, he had.

Charlotte stiffened, the frailness of the body, though different than in a setting she remembered all too well, threatened her composure until finally tears opposed her every command, rolling down her cheeks.

She'd left Massachusetts to escape the war, the memory, her past. Yet here she was facing all the sights and smells from last year again. It wasn't her mother that was in the bed now, but the guilt she'd worked to push down deep resurfaced with a vengeance.

She'd made a mistake. She shouldn't be in here.

Feeling the familiar constriction in her chest, she also became too aware of the increasing speed that her heart began to climb to. It raced, pounding against her ribcage as if wanting to break free. She fought for control, trying to steady her body from shaking and revolting against her will, but she failed.

She reached out her arm for something to grasp, something to hold onto as the room circled around her and her knees began to buckle underneath her weight. Not seeing but *feeling* the top of the chair where Nicholas had sat before, she grabbed onto its armrest with all her might, bracing herself for the worst.

Was this it? Was this the moment her life would end?

Desperate to change that outcome, she remembered her reticule. She reached for the bag at her side on the floor, feeling the cotton edges inlay around her fingers as they stretched for the glass bottle from the apothecary. She pulled the bottle free, her hands sweaty around the corked lid. Tugging with the last of her might, she tried to open the cork, but her finger slipped. She let out a gasp before trying again, desperate for relief—for this to end, but on her terms.

"Who are you?"

Her hand was still prying at the cork when she stopped, uncertain if the voice came from the bed or from another place entirely. She heard a cough, one less forced than her mother's while she'd been on the brink of death but accompanied by a struggled moan.

"I said—" Another cough. "Who *are* you?" This time the question, though strained was more punctuated with agitation, and louder.

Collecting what she could of her composure, Charlotte slowly rose to her feet at his impatience with her gaze set on the man in the bed. "My name is . . ." She gasped for a breath, finding mild relief when one came even as small as it was. "Charlotte Thatcher. I'm a friend of . . ." Another breath swooped in, and she was grateful with how deep this one came even as she tasted the sourness of the room. ". . . your son."

"Friend?" Nicholas's father coughed again, the man's eyes somewhat glazed over. He squinted as if trying to make sense of the word or perhaps sense of her.

"Yes." She stood to the full measure of her height, the ground at her feet feeling stable again. "Can I get you anything?"

The question seemed to pique his interest and he looked to her hands, still shaking with the bottle from the apothecary in her grip. She put the bottle next to the bed on the nightstand and folded her hands together in front of her to steady them. "I'd be happy to get Nicholas. He'd want to know you're awake."

"What's *that?*" His tone dipped as he studied the bottle she'd set on the nightstand, lines at his brow and mouth deepening. The look was critical—but far less foreboding than it might have been had he been in full health.

"That for me?"

"No." Realizing her mistake, she quickly retrieved the bottle, stashing the syrup back into her reticule with almost her full strength returned. "The doctor has already given you something. He's due this evening, but until then there is nothing for you to take just yet."

He eyed her, his gaze sharply demanding even from the lowly state of his condition. "Then what are you doing with it?"

So many questions, yet she felt pulled to answer. She let out an exasperated breath, though this time the cause having nothing to do with her latest episode. "It's mine."

He looked to the bottle, now hidden in her reticule then to her, his frown somehow managing to find a greater depth. "You don't look in need of it."

It was then she realized her heart was steady again and her body no longer shaking, not even her hands. In the course of perhaps five minutes, she'd found a full recovery without the need of taking a single drop. The Admiral was right. She didn't need the medicine, not now anyway.

He didn't say anything else to her, leaving a silence in the room that prompted more of a demand than an invitation to be filled.

"I have a heart condition." She motioned to her reticule where she'd disposed of the bottle. "This is supposed to help."

He grunted, shifting his body, and pushing himself against the bed's mattress. It was then she realized he was trying to raise himself up. She made a step to approach him so that she might help, but his stern expression signaled his refusal. "Then you'd be a fool to think it be to your benefit." He coughed again, she a little surprised to hear the mockery that shaded the forced air. "Even when your malady is healed, you'll still need it."

This time she studied him, but not because of his ailment. "You've used it before?"

He gave a huff. "A different kind of heart condition." Even through his raspy struggle to get the words out, there was something prominent about this man she couldn't ignore. "And I know plenty in my line of work who've used the like for other ailments. The stuff works for a time, but only leaves you wanting more—no true remedy."

Charlotte considered the bottle in her reticule along with the Admiral's words. Her mother had been on the verge of death, laudanum given almost every hour as she requested it near the end. Had she truly been in so much pain or had her reliance on the drug become more than what she could handle?

The taste of bitter regret lingered on Charlotte's tongue. She would never know. And the result had been her fault.

Again, behind his bushed graying brow, the man's scrutiny pinned on her even in his sickly state. She felt a need to explain herself, to explain what happened. Was this what it was like for Nicholas all those years? Constantly under an eye of close examination?

She decided she wouldn't give the Admiral the satisfaction, especially when there was someone else she'd rather open up to.

Instead, she offered an alternative line of conversation. "I can go get you some tea if you'd li—"

"You can leave me be." He clipped her off with his tone.

She frowned, though not bothering to hide her own annoyance from him. She might've told him to rethink his attitude, but this was Nicholas's father, and the man was on his deathbed.

Reaching for a lesson from her mother, she grounded herself on grace that she didn't feel and shut her lips tight. She was doing this for the sake of Nicholas, but knowing herself well, she wouldn't be able to stay silent for long while the Admiral remained awake. She'd make a point to come check on him later, hoping Nicholas was still resting. But for now, she crossed the room, not bothering to soften her steps this time, before closing the door behind her.

Thinking tea—even if unwanted by the Admiral—seemed like a nice thought, Charlotte went toward the kitchen of the apartment. She heard the door ring, Wesley beating her to the front door. He led the doctor to the Admiral's room while she continued to the kitchen.

Her tea in hand, she was down the hallway from the Admiral's bedroom when she saw the silhouette of a man she recognized in the parlor.

"Nicholas?" She let her question hang in the air, seeing him inclined in a wing-backed chair, his tea untouched.

He managed a faint smile, having seen her. "I couldn't sleep."

"I see that." She went over to him, catching the sweet, smoky smell of burning birch in the fireplace. His eyes were still red, telling her his difficulty of slumber hadn't been out of lack of fatigue. She knew what the feeling was like—not knowing what to do and powerless to stop what was happening. At least she could offer him news that might give him some assurance.

She deposited her teacup on a mahogany tea table. "I spoke with your father."

"He's awake?" His eyes widened, drawing her attention to the dark circles underneath them. He firmed his jaw before swallowing. "Does he want to see me?"

She ached for him, hearing and understanding the smallest glimpse of hope in his tone. "He didn't say."

"What *did* he say?"

She went over the conversation with the Admiral in her mind, seeing Nicholas's brow furrow when she didn't answer right away.

She could feel his perusal of her as if searching her expression while she took a seat on a settee with wooden arms and backing.

"Was he unkind to you?" There was a protective nature to his tone that hadn't been there earlier, making her wonder if his unease was more for her well-being than the man on the precipice of life and death.

"No. Your father actually did me a favor." Her reply came out swift, wanting to quickly clear any misconceptions he might be harboring in his mind.

"I was about to do something foolish." She felt a sting of embarrassment, reminded of what happened at Les Muses de Versailles and why she was in England in the first place. She corrected herself, though hating it. "That is, I was about to do something foolish . . . again."

He gave her a languid smile, the first one she'd seen since they'd left the Whitfords'. "I'm sorry I didn't take you back to Paris like we agreed."

The mention to the terms of their deal from the game yesterday caught her by surprise. She could tell even with what he was going through now that he meant the apology.

"Don't be." She reclined back into the seat, her hands resting easy on her lap. "It's strange how things work out—how we're faced with situations we'd rather run away from but end up having to face head-on." She took a deep breath in and out, smoothing the front of her skirts. "I just never thought I'd be doing this again."

"This?" Confusion knit his brow.

In another setting she might have laughed. She'd always thought of herself as being direct with how she approached situations and conversation, yet now she couldn't seem to get a good grasp of what she was trying to say. Or was that how it feels when one is vulnerable? It was one thing to feel exposed from the outside in the case of her missing corset and Marc's rendition of her. Those instances were ones others had taken control of. And as much as those things did bother her, they didn't come close to the openness she was about to reveal from the inside.

"In there." She turned her neck in the direction of the Admiral's bedroom even though a wall covered in the same rich wine color blocked the view. "It brings back memories—some good, some not."

"Your mother you mean?"

"Yes." She could hardly voice it, the word catching in her throat. She felt a pull to tell more, though she didn't know if it was the Admiral's coercing from earlier that was the reason or something else— perhaps even conviction from her mother in heaven. Wherever the prodding originated, she could no longer bury the truth inside.

The sting of emotion burned in her eyes, her stomach knotting. "Nicholas, there's something I need to say, to confess really."

"Confess?"

Seeing his arched eyebrow, she shifted in her seat, not wanting to go on, but feeling she'd taken a step off a cliff that she couldn't climb back up. "I hold responsibility for my mother's death."

He sat silent, his eyes, though tired, rimmed with an expectation that was different than the man in the bedroom. She was thankful. Had he'd spoken, she didn't know if she could continue.

"Back in Portsmouth, Lady Allewood, a friend of my aunt's, would sometimes host parties. I was so excited to attend them, and they were so different from the farm in Falmouth." The memory tugged at a smile, if only briefly. "My aunt was just as excited to show me off in silk taffeta, something I'd never worn before, and I was more than happy to oblige."

The smile she felt briefly before, fell completely. "But the parties were also more than that. They were a distraction for all of us in town who wanted to get our minds off the war and onto more joyous things.

My aunt and I went on our own to most of the social functions, my mother desirous to stay behind because of her condition."

Though Charlotte's hands remained folded, her fingers squeezed against each other. She wasn't sure if Nicholas had noticed as her gaze had shifted to the floor. "Mother didn't want to slow us down, 'to interfere with our merriment,' so she would say. But all I wanted was for her to take part, for her to live, be happy, for even a few hours. A reprieve from thinking about her oldest son in the middle of Washington's ranks or her daughter who was among the smallpox in Cambridge."

Noticing the trembling in her voice, Charlotte took a breath to steady herself. She didn't know when Nicholas had come over, but he had, taking a place next to her on the sofa. She breathed him in, something musky pleasantly overtaking the wood from the fire and anchoring her to the moment now rather than the past. Somehow him being near gave her courage to keep going.

"The last party I went to in Portsmouth, I begged her to come. No." She pressed her lips together, remembering the truth of that day, what she'd done. "I *made* her come. Even though she would quickly grow tired, I'd insisted, not taking 'no' for an answer."

She met Nicholas's gaze fleetingly, not able to look at him if she meant to tell the whole truth, something she was set on doing. "Things were fine at first. We all engaged in a game of cards before a small group of musicians played to signal a minuet. Again, I persisted, encouraging my mother to dance with my father, who was also present, but even he seemed wary of the idea. Despite his concern, she got up, no doubt not wanting to disappoint me." Her eyes went tight, Charlotte shaking her head over how wrong she'd been and seeing that much too late. "After that, she never got up again."

The tremor had somehow made its way deeper in her voice. "I can't help but think if I wouldn't have pressed so hard that night, she might still be alive."

"But you don't know that." Sincere compassion voiced back at her.

"No, but I still wonder. I always wonder."

Nicholas produced a handkerchief from the inside of his vest pocket, handing the cloth to her like the gentleman he always was. She felt his hand brush over her skin, his touch both comforting her and sending her shivers. "That's a lot for anyone to carry on their own, even you."

She used the handkerchief to wipe at her eyes, though not understanding. "Even me?"

"Yes, even you." His soft tone and weary smile made her body relax again, though aware of his closeness to her. "You're one of the strongest people I know. You can handle yourself with many things, but what you just told me sounds like too much to bear alone." His thumb brushed at a tear that rolled past her cheek. "Does anyone else know?"

She forced a breath, closing her eyes like she wished she could do to that night—never see the images again in her memory. "Just you and everyone else at the party that night."

He shook his head. "I don't mean about what happened. I mean that you feel this way about what happened."

Tears beginning to dry, she wrinkled her nose. "I don't understand what you mean. What's the difference?"

"A lot." He wiped at a stubborn tear just under her eye, his touch so gentle. "Most likely the people there don't blame you at all. I know I don't from what you told me. And if I were a betting man—" He gave her a slow smile that tipped to one side of his cheek. "Which I apparently am, since our time in Cairnhaven—I doubt your mother would too."

Though appreciating his words, she wasn't so sure. She looked at him pointedly. "Maybe. But you lost that bet, remember?"

"Not from my perspective. The only thing I lost was the game. Everything else, even now, I feel like I've gained." He stroked the side of her face, his blue eyes deepening into a richer hue while his touch made her chest hammer. "Can I ask you something?"

She swallowed, noticing the action had proved more of a struggle than usual. "Of course."

"When exactly did you start having problems with your heart?"

Her throat loosened. That answer was easy. "Shortly after my mother's death. Why?"

"I'm not sure, but it might be something good to let the doctor know about."

"You mean your father's doctor?" She glanced at the Admiral's bedroom door, shaking her head. "I've hardly said two words to the man. I'm not about to tell him such a significant part of my life."

"Fair enough. What about the doctor in Paris?"

"I'll think about it." She would, seeing he apparently thought the appointment necessary. "But I don't see how that could help."

He shrugged. "How do you feel now?"

Taking his question seriously, she examined herself. Everything seemed to be functioning normally—her heart, her breathing. But something else felt different—lighter in fact, as if a hand she'd imagined gripping her heart and squeezing tight had suddenly decided to let go for whatever reason. She might have assumed the sudden shift was temporary, yet she knew it wasn't. Something had changed.

She turned to Nicholas, her shoulders relaxing first while the rest of her body soon followed as if taking in that truth. "Strangely, I feel better."

Chapter 28

"Captain Edwards, may I have a word?"

Nicholas pinched the bridge of his nose where remnants of sleep had started accumulating at the corner of his eyes. The momentary slumber, though credited to Charlotte's doing, brought images of the Cadwells' and the miners' plight. It was no more restful than what was happening while he was awake.

"Doctor." Nicholas raised himself up on the sofa in the parlor, the cushions under him sinking with the uneven distribution of his weight. "I didn't realize you were here." He rubbed at a tender place on his forehead while glancing out the window where the afternoon light had dimmed into evening.

"Mr. Whitford let me in." His father's doctor shuffled into the room. He was a wiry sort of man in both physical appearance and thought, and older in years, but he was the best there was in London. "I'd go just as quietly," his words came out hushed as if he meant what he'd just said. "But since you are the Admiral's son, I think it would be best for you and I to speak."

"Of course." Nicholas looked at the small table that had held his tea from earlier that day, unsure on how to judge the doctor's matter-of-fact tone. Having not been in much of a mood for the beverage before, his mouth now felt dry and parched for something to wet his throat. "Have you been offered anything?"

The doctor gave a nod, his well-worn medical kit swinging at his side, gripped by his long bony fingers. "Mr. Whitford has seen to me well and Miss Thatcher has proved herself valuable. I don't believe this is the first time she's cared for someone so ill."

"No. I'm sorry to say it's not." And he was, trying to imagine what living with that guilt had been like for her. But the fact she had opened up to him over someone like her aunt or sister warmed him immeasurably and gave him hope.

Nicholas made a motion, inviting the doctor to sit, though not welcoming the news that might be coming.

He'd been trying to prepare his heart for this, knowing that this day was likely to happen sooner or later with both he and his father in their military roles. Yet, he'd been throttled all the same.

When the man declined the offer to have a seat, Nicholas wasn't sure what to make of it, only that the doctor's eyes read less of forbearance and more of something promising in the horizon.

"Your father seems improved from the last time I saw him."

"Improved?" Nicholas looked up, not realizing his eyes had been drawn to the carpet and not wanting to face what he knew was coming, or *thought* he knew was coming.

"Quite so." Though darkness had begun to fall in, the man's eyes lit up. "I just finished redressing the wound. There will be scarring, but I dare say the man is likely to have more years with us in this world." He toggled over his cravat, placing a scarf around the necktie for extra warmth. "I'll stop by on the morrow to see if he's faring the same."

Feeling somewhat frozen with the news, even when the fire had been recently rekindled, Nicholas stood to overcome the moment. "I'd like to see him now that he's awake."

"Very good, but I suggest you do it quickly. I've given him some laudanum that will take effect soon." The man made for his father's front door, Nicholas going after him to see him out.

A few minutes later and with mixed emotion, Nicholas stepped into his father's bedroom. He couldn't say elation was part of what he felt, but he did find out his father would survive, and he was thankful for that. But his last conversation with his father hadn't gone well. Having ended with the rejection of Nicholas's gift and disappointment over his assignment, he doubted even near-death would change the man's mind.

Nicholas looked around, noticing something was different about the space—brighter than how he'd remembered. The curtains were drawn back, letting the sunlight and warmth seep in, even as the end of day approached. A window had also been cracked, allowing Nicholas to smell the wintry mixed air from outside. The streets of London didn't hold the fresh scent of his grandfather's cottage, but the air was nevertheless welcomed compared to the stale stench that had crowded the room before. Had this been a part of Charlotte's doing the doctor had spoken about?

Nicholas looked to the bed, immediately drawn to the tall figure sitting inclined in the goose-feathered downing covers. "Father?" The word felt foreign on his tongue. He'd never used the title before. "Sir," yes, but "Father," no. Yet, out the name came, perhaps a deep desire overcoming reason and routine in the moment.

The corners of the Admiral's mouth fell downward, Nicholas's hopes of a different relationship along with it.

Clearing his throat, Nicholas reverted to what was familiar. "Sir." Checking his emotion, he swallowed what wanted to be expressed, but wouldn't. "The doctor informs me you're making a recovery."

"So it seems." The creases of his father's forehead grew less pronounced, his lips forming into a straight line. "No thanks to those rebels."

"What happened?" It had been the question on Nicholas's mind since his father's first lieutenant had sent for him at the Whitfords'. The only explanation—a bullet.

"New York is a powder keg." His father coughed several times, the strain behind each one still present from previous hours, but not as powerful. He took a breath, forced, but not as shallow as before. "First the fire, then that blasted Hale fellow. The great fire brought out the thieves and Hale's execution brought out rebel sympathizers. Both criminal if you ask me." His father's expression soured, Nicholas hearing a low growl in the back of his throat. "Washington's presence in New York, even at his losses, only makes the conflict worse. I'm irritated to say my wound is from a stray bullet as part of the whole disaster."

"Why did you insist on coming to London?" Something else Nicholas didn't understand when the lieutenant had relayed the news. "By accounts, the trip only further compromised your survival."

His father's eyes, a deep shade of gray bore into him with challenge. "By *whose* account?"

"I'm told the doctor aboard."

"That woman, you mean?" The man in bed grunted, his face, normally shaved except for a set of salt and peppered sideburns, formed a scowl under a patch of hair above his lips. There was a slight sheen to his forehead from sweat, but it was new, the thick film of sweat at his brow gone and the rest of his face having been wiped clean. "She was insistent I stay, yet hardly in working condition herself if you ask me."

"A woman?" Nicholas only knew of one that would be qualified. "You were under Abigail's care?"

His father's face contorted, signaling he'd disagreed with Nicholas's choice of words. "Care or not, she was wrong." He lengthened his neck as if completely disregarding the help he'd been given. "I survived."

Nicholas held back the notion that his father's survival could very well be attributed to Abigail's efforts, having seen her in action on the way over from the colonies. But the question he'd asked still lingered unanswered and he wanted—no, needed—to know.

For once in his life, Nicholas met the man's stare, unflinching. "Wrong or not, it was a big risk. You're lucky you didn't die at sea on the way over. Why take the chance?"

"*Why take the chance?* If I'm going to die, I won't tolerate the notion of being buried on rebel soil. And until we win this war, I will think of that land as such."

The insides of Nicholas's stomach squeezed, like someone had punched him in the gut. So, that was the reason—not because his father had a son to say goodbye to. Politics or maybe pride. Either way, the answer wasn't him.

"What?"

Though he'd been trained not to show his emotion, Nicholas suspected his silence gave him away. But he couldn't help it. No words came to him. His father looked at him as if for an explanation, one Nicholas would be expected to give.

"I thought . . ." The words stumbled out, making him feel more like a child than a captain of the Royal Navy. He hated the feeling, but besides his father's hold on him, something else pressed him to try.

"You thought what?" Impatience colored the Admiral's tone not making the effort any easier.

"I thought you wanted to see me—" Nicholas swallowed, trying to work the knot at the base of his throat. His next words came out slowly as if they were too heavy for his mouth to voice. "—if by chance things didn't go as . . . favorably."

A heavy silence filled the space between them, even now Nicholas allowing his hope to linger.

His father looked away, seeming more interested in the view outside the window than his son who implored him. "You were supposed to be in Paris if I remember correctly. Which I've heard has come to naught as

I understand it." His tone was flat, his father looking to Nicholas with a critical eye. "Does His Majesty know you're back in England?"

His hope completely crushed, Nicholas roused a resolve he knew well while also beckoning upward for what he could no longer fake on the inside. "I'm not certain. But if he doesn't, he will soon."

His father gave a tense nod. "See that you go to him and not be sent for. Otherwise, it looks weak." The advice came out more as a directive.

Nicholas found his father's counsel sound enough but unnecessary. He'd already planned to seek the king out, except his motivation differed from his father's concern of weakness.

Summoning an inward strength not of his own, Nicholas squared his shoulders, believing in the calling. "There's another matter I'm considering presenting to His Majesty." His father still wore a frown, but he went on. "They closed the copper mine in Cairnhaven. Many of the miners are out of work, including some close friends of the Whitfords'."

His father's piercing gaze grew more contemplative, telling Nicholas the Admiral was willing to hear him out. Maybe the king would too. "Your proposal?"

"To line the bottom of our ships with copper plates."

"Copper sheathing, you mean?" The bluntness in his father's tone indicated a familiarity with the concept though held no encouragement for the idea. But Nicholas had thought this through. And he had to at least try.

"The strategy has already been done and has proved effective in prolonging a ship's time in the water. The trials I've followed can be replicated with a few minor changes."

"Trials?" His father managed to raise himself up under the sheets, giving a faint wheeze with the struggle. Even inclined, his head towered well past the headboard's height. "Experiments you mean." The lines on his face wrinkled with an irritation Nicholas knew well. "There's a reason nothing came of it, Nicholas. If they had, our ships would already be sheathed in copper." He shook his head as if to completely dismiss the idea. "The notion is too extravagant, especially over a small group of miners. You'd be a fool to suggest such an idea."

Nicholas rubbed his chin where he felt his own stubble returning. There were barriers to his plan, the most critical, cost. The king had already accumulated a massive debt with the war in the West and ships sheathed in copper wouldn't be a small price for England's purse. But if His Majesty approved, this could be a way to restore not only the miners' jobs in Cairnhaven, but elsewhere too. It was what the Cadwells needed. Maybe what others needed too.

"Put the miners out of your mind. They will manage on their own. You've already tarnished the Edwards' reputation enough. You have yourself to think about. Leave the ordeal alone."

The words were commanding, an order he expected to be carried out. Yet, the concept made Nicholas's stomach churn as if rebellious to his father's mandate. Or was it the concept of self-preservation at the expense of others that caused Nicholas's insides to turn over? Whatever the reason, he couldn't let the fate of the miners go. In fact, his father's words only strengthened the conviction that had already been there.

The Admiral lowered himself in the bed again, the sheets rustling with the range of movement. "Now, leave me. I wish to be alone."

It was a way to tell Nicholas the laudanum was taking effect and that their conversation was over.

Having crossed the threshold out of his father's bedroom, Nicholas shut the door behind him as if sealing away a dream that would never be. He went to his father's study and slumped into the desk chair upholstered in rich leather before dipping a quill in ink and beginning to write.

***

It was an hour later when Nicholas finished his letter, sealing it with a red wax. He stretched his fingers, both they and his hands having grown tight around the quill as he wrote. He wasn't sure what bothered him the most. His conversation with his father left a chasm in his heart he didn't know how to mend, and his request of King George was risky, especially when he had no leverage of a completed assignment.

"Nicholas, what's wrong?"

His grandfather's voice came from over his shoulder at about the time the wax had hardened. Nicholas turned from his father's desk, catching the tentative way Wesley seemed to study him while holding a plate with a slice of meat pie in his hand. Nicholas knew the meal was for him, but he hardly had a stomach for any substance even if he needed nourishment.

"I thought the doctor said your father was faring better?" Wesley sat the tray on the desk as his tentative expression morphed into confusion.

"He is."

"Then why do you look as if you've been given grave news?"

Though Wesley's tone was gentled, his words, unknowingly, hit hard to the truth. Because a grave was what described his relationship with his father: cold, buried, dead. The one thing he'd strived to do—to live up to, now crashed down on him like dirt burying him under.

"After everything, all I've tried—" Nicholas closed his eyes as if succumbing to the darkness that surrounded his reality and future. "I've failed the man as a son. He demands perfection." He sighed, looking in the direction of his father's room. "And I'm all out of it."

Despite the heavy burden, his grandfather tried to lighten the load with a small smile. "Nicholas, you can't be perfect. You know that."

He did. Yet he still tried even after he'd said "yes" to the only One that truly was. Now, he could see his mistake—wanting to win the approval of someone just as fallen as he was. Instead, he needed to hold onto the promise that Jesus approved of him to the point of death.

He struggled for a breath. Had that been the reason for his failures—because some small part of him still thought he could measure up? He swallowed the bitterness of his mistake. Well, consider the lesson learned.

"I need some air." Nicholas nearly bounded from his father's chair, taking the note he'd penned with him. "I'm going out for a bit. Would you mind staying with Charlotte?"

"I would, but Miss Charlotte has already gone out—something about fully healing, I believe."

Nicholas paused, his hands still on his coat where he'd been tugging it in place. He'd guessed she'd been catching up on sleep, but it wouldn't be the first time he was wrong. News of healing brought up images of the apothecary that made him wonder if she'd changed her mind about her elixir. He hoped not, their last conversation having conveyed to him a different outcome—one he thought she felt better about.

He was about to step out when he saw the bundle of clothes on a small bench by the door. His father's uniform.

The tension in Nicholas's shoulders climbed up his neck. He looked to Wesley. "You were on your way out?"

"Yes, but it can wait."

Nicholas veered his gaze at the wool coat, normally a deep blue with pristine gold trim, now dulled by dirt and gunpowder residue. "What needs to be done?"

"His coat was badly damaged from the wound. I was going to take it to Felix's to see if he could mend the uniform to your father's satisfaction."

"The tailor? Let me take care of it." The distraction would give him more time away from the apartment—that and the fresh air he could sorely use.

The walk to Felix's shop wasn't a long one, but Nicholas didn't mind. Though his shoulders were still stiff, he could feel the resistance in his neck loosening as the distance grew between him and his father.

The door clicked behind him at the tailor's shop, the scents of wool, linen, and beeswax greeting him inside. On one side of the store, bolts of fabric neatly arranged by shade displayed rich colors of navy, burgundy, emerald and gold. He went over to a large, mahogany counter that dominated the other side of the room and waited while a man in a simple, yet well-tailored waistcoat finished up a client's fitting.

When the customer had left, Felix went behind the counter, putting away a brass-plated measuring tape next to a pair of scissors that had been neatly laid out. "Captain Nicholas Edwards, good to see you, sir." Felix gave him a friendly smile that only punctuated his angular face, especially with hair tied back in a queue. "Tell me, have we won the war in the colonies yet?"

"I hardly know the latest. My assignment has me elsewhere—closer to home this time." Nicholas laid his father's uniform on the counter.

"By Jove, what's happened to your father's coat?" The man's normally steady brown eyes grew wide. "Is the Admiral all right?"

"A bullet wound, I'm afraid. And the doctor seems optimistic he will be."

"Glad to hear." Felix's attention went back to the clothes on the counter, having already started to lay them out as if to better inspect their condition. "Yes, I'll see what I can do. A new coat might be in order, but I have your father's measurements if it comes to that."

"That's fine." Nicholas gave him a forced smile. "Do whatever must be done. I'll take care of the expense."

Leaving Felix's, Nicholas went to the post office to mail the letter he'd penned at his father's desk.

He put a hand to his neck where the top of his spine met with his back, trying to work some of the muscle. The tension in his shoulders remained, but the reason for their rigid state had changed, at least in part. It was only a matter of time before King George summoned him in. His father had made a good point. Waiting for the king's summons might very well make him look weak, creating a bias against his proposal on behalf of the miners. He couldn't let his lack of action jeopardize his plan before he had a chance to present the idea.

As if his body knew the answer before his mind had agreed, his feet began to take steps in the direction of St. James's Palace. The audience would happen either way. But he'd make it on his own terms.

Chapter 29

"You are back, mon amie."

Charlotte turned in the stationary shop toward the familiar voice, the exclamation in her friend's tone rousing her own excitement of a missed reunion. "Louise. Yes, we just arrived a few days ago."

"How was the trip? Are you cured yet?" Louise had stepped in line with Charlotte who'd been waiting to purchase a new quill and a bottle of ink.

"I wouldn't say cured, but I do feel better." Her confession to Nicholas had somehow seen to that, though she couldn't explain why. But the heaviness inside her chest that had been crushing her life short had lifted, even if mildly. It wasn't a cure, but it was a start—one she felt grateful for.

So grateful that she had tried to express her thanks back in London to the One who had granted her healing. A long time had passed since she'd attended church, that hope her mother had always had in the Almighty snuffed out with her life, or so Charlotte thought.

When it was her turn, she handed the merchant three livres and took her things before stepping back out into the street with Louise.

Charlotte breathed in deep, the unique blend of strong coffee and roasted chestnuts adding a sweetened aroma to the city's overused sewer system. Her current surroundings weren't the idyllic countryside of the Whitford's home, but they possessed a rejuvenating quality, nonetheless.

She'd been in Paris for three days and she hadn't had an attack since that night in the Admiral's bedroom. That meant almost two weeks of her body not striking against her. But the positive trajectory of her own health drove her to thoughts of another's.

"How is your mother?"

Louise broke into a broad smile that Charlotte took as a good sign. "She's doing better since taking the medicine again. She's even started working on the lace. In fact, she's helping with your new design. Together with the other girls, we are making good progress, but it would help to have another set of hands."

Ones she'd be happy to lend, at least until she left Paris, which wouldn't be long. Now that the deal with the vicomte was squashed, there was only one more item on her list to see to.

"How is Nicholas's father?" Louise tilted her head slightly, revealing a look of concern from beneath the shadow of her cloak's hood. "I received your letter saying you would be in London for a few days."

"The doctor seems positive he'll make a recovery. Even so, I'm surprised we left as quickly as we did." With Wesley at the apartment, Charlotte knew Nicholas's father would be well cared for, but it wasn't the Admiral's well-being she worried about.

They had left London the morning after the doctor confirmed the Admiral's likely recovery. Nicholas had been quiet on the trip to Paris, voicing only what was necessary to navigate and communicate their passage. She didn't think his distance had anything to do with her, but something was clearly on his mind. She had tried asking him where he had gone to while she had been out, he mentioning an errand to drop his father's uniform for repair. But that didn't explain the shadows under his eyes or what burden he was currently carrying.

Louise cut through a vacant alleyway, Charlotte following close behind. "There is something else you should know." Her tone, once light, became more weighted. "Claudine came by the dentelle while you were gone."

"Claudine?" Charlotte's stride on the pavement became uneven. She hadn't seen or heard from Claudine since the art contest and she hadn't expected to. Charlotte had no doubt that her episode and tarnished reputation at court had seen to that. "Did she buy anything?"

Louise shook her head—dark, loose strands that framed her face escaping from under her hood. "I think she was looking for you. She requested that you go to Versailles tonight."

"To *Versailles?*" The very mention of the palace made something drop to the pit of her stomach. She sneered, tasting a sour tang in her mouth. "I think I've had my fair share of the French court for a while."

Wishing she had something to curb the taste, she went to a street vendor selling spiced, hot wine. She bought two, handing one to Louise, before taking a sip of her own. The taste of cinnamon and cloves of the fermented drink not only warmed her, but cleansed her palette and her mind, helping her remember what she still needed to do.

She let the liquid linger in her mouth before speaking again and holding a finger in the air. "Though, there is one particular noble I do have an inclination to see, but I won't have to go to Versailles for that."

"If you're not going to the palace, then I take it you mean Marc?" Louise cupped her hands around the warm wine, appearing to use the beverage for heating her hands rather than refreshment. Eventually, she took a gingerly sip. "Does that mean you have not forgiven him?"

"Forgiven, yes." As a follower of Jesus, Charlotte knew that was necessary. And though Nicholas helped her see her mother's death wasn't entirely her fault, she knew her actions still harbored some of the blame. Actions that had been forgiven, not by her, but by God. Having felt that forgiveness and the peace dwelling inside her now, how could she not do the same?

But she hadn't forgotten. The man had pressed her, then publicly ridiculed her among the entire French court, including the vicomte. Even now her chest burned, though not from the wine or her history of ailment. She might have forgiven Marc, but forgetting what he had done was harder to do and she wasn't about to let him ignore the charade so easily either.

"And what is it that you plan to do, mon amie?" Louise's question was leading, as if she could somehow tell what Charlotte had been playing out in her mind.

"Apart from giving him a piece of my mind, you mean?" In truth, she hadn't thought further than that.

Louise smiled, but Charlotte could tell she didn't agree.

"You don't think I should?"

"I'm sure Marc deserves whatever you have in mind, but if we all got what we deserved then . . ." Louise studied the cobblestone, letting the thought fade into the smoky Parisian air.

But she didn't have to finish for the meaning to take effect. If Charlotte got what she deserved, what would that mean for her life . . . and death if it had come to that?

Frustrated with the sudden complication, Charlotte felt the crease forming between her eyebrows as if tugging between two sides of her conscience. But how could she simply let this go? She needed to know there was at least some remorse. Perhaps then she could move on.

***

Late that afternoon, Charlotte rapped on the door of Marc's apartment until a man dressed in black and gold livery opened the door to her.

"I'm sorry, mademoiselle, but the master is not in at this time."

"That's all right. I'll wait." Leaving Marc's servant little room for rebuttal, she walked inside as if she deserved to be there. And in her mind, she did.

After a short hesitation, the man allowed her entry, guiding her to Marc's salon before retreating. Charlotte made herself comfortable in a fauteuil, the floral pattern and ornate design of the wood framing complimenting the mint green sofa in the room. The portrait of Claudine she'd seen before in Marc's studio now stared at her from the wall to remind her of the recent invitation to Versailles. The only reason she could think Claudine would issue the summons after what happened would be because she knew the vicomte was to be there—another opportunity to speak with him on her aunt's behalf.

She removed her eyes from the portrait. There was no point. The man didn't like her from the start. How much more so now that the French court saw her as a fool.

A moment later, Marc's servant returned with a plate of small biscuits and what smelled like coffee in a silver pot.

"Would you like a café, mademoiselle?"

"Indeed, I would." She didn't know how long Marc would make her wait, but at least she would take that time to enjoy his refreshments.

The servant left her again. His queue, in the hair color nature had gifted him rather than under a peruke, was wrapped with a black ribbon and gave a slight movement with his steps out.

Charlotte sipped her cup of coffee, letting the strong taste mix with leftover cinnamon and cloves still on her palette from the mulled wine earlier. She looked to the wall again, though not at Claudine's portrait this time. There was a different picture on the opposing wall she hadn't seen—something new and bold.

The picture reminded her of Marc's other pieces she'd seen of the street hawkers and—she felt a muscle in her face twitch—her own

321

admittedly. But instead of being tucked away in Marc's studio, the portrait was here in a room where any guest was sure to find themselves in front of it, especially a noble. Marc had taken a brazen stance.

The woman was dressed in a gown of plush indigo that had somehow been torn while a brooch attached to her chest was engraved with fleur-de-lis. The flowers conveyed the importance of her high position, yet they were wilted with rust. She sat at a table lined with food Charlotte recognized from her picnic at Versailles, depicting images of cakes, fruits, and breads, but each rotten in some way. The background that reminded Charlotte of the well-cut and orderly palace gardens were under stormy skies and had become severely overgrown from neglect. And unlike Claudine's, where Marc's sister held her focus pleasantly to the side to be easily admired, the other woman stared at the viewer full on with what Charlotte only felt as disturbance.

The portrait was a complete contrast to the picture of his sister hanging on the adjacent wall. Yet, both paintings contained his signature on the bottom right corner of each, leaving little to wonder which artist had painted them. She saw, too, Marc had resolved a name for the picture of the woman, once grand in all her splendor in both person and surroundings, now fallen to shambles. *Madame Régime.* In none too subtle a way, Marc made his opinion of the monarchy obvious in a very public setting of his home.

Charlotte pondered whether Claudine had been aware of her brother's actions, but upon recalling Claudine's anxiety over his brash tactics, she doubted it.

Hearing the ticking of the only sound in the room besides her occasional sipping, Charlotte continued to wait. When her coffee had grown cold, she let another half hour pass by on the gilded mantel clock before giving the matter of her visit up for another time.

Securing her cloak around her, she started her way back toward the boardinghouse.

A light snow had begun to fall, dusting the tops of stone buildings and window ledges of tightly packed homes. Heavy gray clouds hung overhead, shielding the sun from any warmth it might provide and drying the thin layer of slush and mud she had to walk through.

She hadn't ventured far from Marc's apartment when fate smiled upon her.

"Charlotte." The sound of her name coming from his smooth bravado enticed the anger she'd subdued since visiting his apartment. His enlarged eyes conveyed surprise to see her, but not dread as part of her secretly hoped. "I heard you left Paris. I hope it was not on account of me."

Reading less than a genuineness in his tone, she managed a smile. She wouldn't let herself get riled by this man, knowing that's what his full intention was. She knew that because she had done that same thing to other people, wanting to get a stir out of them or wanting them to do what she aimed for them to. And having that in full-fledged view in front of her changed her way of thinking, no longer desirous of getting what she wanted at the expense of others.

"It's actually quite fortunate we've run into each other." Knowing his apartment was only a street over and he no doubt headed that direction, she tried to find humor in what they both already knew. She had sought him out. "I've been meaning to have a chat with you."

"A chat?" He feigned a look of innocence that completely shredded any part of him she'd thought attractive.

"Well, more than a chat." She mirrored his innocence, adding on a deep smile.

"We are close to my apartment. Let us obtain the carriage and talk on the way to your boardinghouse."

"No." She didn't foresee an event like the one in his studio happening again, but even with the snowfall, she wasn't about to take her chances alone with him in the tight space of a carriage. "I'd rather walk if you don't mind." She could see that he did, but he didn't say so outright. He gave a sigh, extending an elbow that she took.

"I hope this chat doesn't have to do with a certain portrait." His eyes danced with a glimmer of amusement, though she found no humor concerning the situation.

"It certainly does."

"Good. You may be interested in knowing the king and queen have issued a special ball tonight. A masquerade." He gave a broad smile, one she wanted to wipe off his face. "Fitting after the spectacle our painting caused, no?"

Our. She fumed inside. As if she'd been part of the whole charade when—conviction pinged. She had, hadn't she? At least in part, trying to win over the vicomte's favor.

She cleared her throat, not wanting to gloss over the small detail he mentioned. "You said the masquerade was special. Why is that?"

"The monarchy has selected a portrait from Les Muses de Versailles which they aim to present at the ball." His tone was apathetic, but she wasn't so sure she believed his disinterest. "It is said the one who painted the chosen portrait will become the official artist of the royal family."

She bristled. "Don't tell me you believe that despicable rendition of me is going to get you the position."

He scoffed. "No, nor would I want such a position at the court." His lips clamped in a way as if he spit on the very idea. "My portrait of you was submitted out of anger, but also to make a point."

She didn't need any clarification about the anger, remembering what happened in his apartment all too well.

"A point?" She wanted to dig her fingernails into his arm to make her own point, but both a thick wool sleeve and Louise's counsel from earlier prevented her. "You mean other than embarrassing me and making sure my deal with the vicomte never happened?"

He sniffed as if a bull ready to charge, yet his pace remained at an easy walk. "Believe it or not, even in my dislike of the Vicomte de Vantinelle, my action had nothing to do with the man other than his affinity for his social class."

"Then what was the point of your actions, exactly?" Against her better judgment, she was trying to understand this man, seeing a part of who she was, or had been.

"The vanity of court. The French monarchy and his nobles claim to help the people all the while he either turns his back to them or is ignorant of their suffering."

As if to further strengthen his claim, a man hovered on the steps of a church they were passing by. His face was unkempt and dirty. He looked to be a former foot soldier, dressed in a gray military coat that, like its wearer, had gone for many months—perhaps years—without proper care. His left leg was missing at the knee and wrapped with a bandage that sorely needed to be changed.

The man reminded Charlotte of her brother, Abraham, and his time spent in prison. He didn't have the outwardly scars this man obviously did, but she knew scars weren't only manifested on the outside.

Her heart went out to the man, though still aware of the unfinished conversation she was having with Marc.

Needing distance, she let go of his arm. "Yet, I'm the one you singled out in your stance." The title of the picture wrote itself as if in front of her. *A Woman's Folly.* "*I'm* the one you called foolish."

His look told her she wouldn't be receiving an apology. "Which you were and still are if you believe pretending to be something you are clearly not is the way to win over the vicomte." His tone was critical, though she sensed it held truth. "It is worse than being an Englishman, even one who killed his son. That may be the only thing the vicomte and I can agree on."

"The vicomte has a son?" Charlotte stepped back, creating further distance between she and Marc, but not out of anger this time.

"Had." His correction held weight. "Oui." He bowed his head, the first time she'd seen the man show any kind of remorse. "Lost to the English in the last war."

Lost. Gone from this life like her mother. The construct of her conversation the first night she'd met the vicomte bored into her mind's eye. 'I cannot believe it is a waste of life to lay down one's own for his country.'

The vicomte hadn't just been talking about the war. He'd been talking about his *son*. And she had said his son had wasted his life in his death.

Bile rose in her throat over her uninhibited speech, her rashness. Marc had been right to call her a fool. It hadn't been her ancestry's fault. The fault was hers. She'd gotten in her own way. But the worst part— her grave mistake wouldn't be limited to just her own undoing.

Feeling a deep sense of failure, Charlotte did the one thing she could do to make a difference for someone, even if small. She took two sous from her reticule and tossed them into the soldier's hat that sat next to a walking stick on the ground. Her arm was outstretched as the coins dropped in when she felt the small tugging at her side. The slightest give to her skirts was quick and discreet . . . familiar.

A series of unfortunate lessons finally proved useful, she not taking precious time to look around or be confused about what had happened. Instead, her feet went flying. "Stop! Arrêt! Thief!"

The boy didn't stop, nor did Charlotte expect him to, not having to be reminded of their previous interactions. But Charlotte wasn't about to give up the chase despite Marc calling after her to do just that. It was time she and this boy also had a chat, and she was going to see to it that they would.

Charlotte continued to follow past the gardens of the Palais-Royal and down alleyway after alleyway, her shoes and dress soon becoming drenched with the muddy slosh of the Parisian streets she'd tried to avoid earlier with Louise and again with Marc. Although sneaky with his hands, thankfully, the boy wasn't fast. He tried darting around a corner, but Charlotte stuck close to his heels even when her extra layers of petticoats became weighted at the hem.

She reached out her hand, hoping to catch him by the shoulder and jar him into stopping, but as soon as her body leaned forward, her foot hit a stone slick with ice, and she went toppling over.

She raised herself up to see the front her dress had been caked with a mixture of wet snow and that the boy had stopped, evidently confident of his advantage. His hazel eyes gleamed at her from beneath a tawny cap. And that's when Charlotte realized—the boy was not a boy at all.

Chapter 30

"Let me walk you back."

Charlotte flinched, not expecting Marc to have followed her through the small passageway she'd seen the girl turn into. The buildings that had walled her in, opened into a large space filled with ramshackled houses and makeshift tents.

The wintry mix nipped at her cheeks and while the cold did well to mask the typical stench of the city, a putrid odor filled her nose and stung at her eyes.

She watched people swarm in the area containing overflowed trash bins that had spilled into the streets. The air was pungent with filth and urine, and something else she didn't care to name.

"This is no place for a woman." Marc's tone beside her was decidingly less confident than it had been earlier and hushed.

She agreed. No, it wasn't. Yet, there they were, several women in fact, among the group in obvious states of poverty. And even children like the girl she'd run after, and some still younger.

Unable to refrain any longer, Charlotte put her hand to her nose. She still wasn't exactly sure what she was seeing, except that this was a part of Paris she hadn't ventured to, nor would want to on purpose.

"What is this place?"

"It is known as the Cour de Miracles." Marc's hand reached out as if he were leading her through a doorway while he gave a mocked bow. "Welcome to the slums of Paris, mademoiselle."

She knew what slums meant, places where the poor resided, often neglected like what she saw now here. Which is why the name Marc had given the place sparked confusion. "The Court of Miracles?" Though strangely captivated by what lay before her, she looked to him for an explanation.

"It's called that because of its reputation. The people who live here fare the worst under our king's rule, mostly because they are the forgotten of Paris." His eyes darted around different parts of the poor vicinity. "As you can see, forgotten but not absent, so they do what they feel they must to live. Many try to make money by pretending they have an ailment they really don't possess." He discreetly pointed to a man wearing an eye patch before removing the bandage as if his sight was supernaturally restored. "When working, they might be blind, but they come here and all of a sudden they can see." His brow raised as if to ask if she caught on. "Quite a miracle, no?"

She understood. "And the lame can walk."

The soldier she'd seen in front of the church steps made his appearance, his amputated leg now miraculously cured. He gave them a courteous bow mixed with mockery as two abled feet strut past them that made her unsure if the gesture had been gratitude for her contribution to his purse or to signal a finality to his performance.

"It appears so."

She wrapped her cloak around her, the dampness of her dress from her recent fall growing cold against her skin. Yet, she felt odd with the attempt to warm herself, a large majority of the crowd's clothing here inadequate for the winter cold. "I haven't seen this side of Paris before."

"Neither have the king and queen and most of the nobles, and they've lived in Paris much longer than you." Marc crossed his arm in front of her as if preventing her from stepping further into the slums. "Forget your money. Let me walk you home. You don't belong here."

Charlotte looked at the array of people again. The Court of Miracles seemed like a complete opposition to the Court of Versailles. So many in hardship compared to the so few privileged. Her stomach reeled at the choice foods and confections she'd enjoyed on the palace gardens and her fleeting concern over her gown for Les Muses de Versailles.

Marc turned from the Court of Miracles, taking a few steps in the direction leading away from the slums, but she didn't follow. She did belong here, or at the very least had a reason for being here.

A thin figure emerged from a building that leaned against another, threatening to collapse at any moment. The tawny cap was missing, but both the hazel eyes and tawny hair unmistakable.

Having been told all her life by both her parents she'd possessed a stubborn streak, Charlotte gathered that much was true. She also imagined God knew that about her, the All-Knowing choosing a way to grab her attention by a means that she couldn't ignore—in this case a girl who'd had the upper hand in pickpocketing.

The girl met her gaze, confirming what Charlotte's heart told her she must do.

"Just a minute, Marc." She might've let him continue on without her, not caring for his company, but considering where she was and how the day was starting to take a shift to night, she didn't want to risk getting lost. "I would like to take that offer of you walking me home. But there's someone I need to speak with before we go. Give me a moment, would you?"

She didn't wait for his response, her eyes locked on the girl who'd made her way into a nearby tent constructed of mixed tufts strewn together. Charlotte watched the girl pull out the small parcel that she'd stolen from her reticule and hand the bag of coin to the soldier who'd been miraculously healed.

Giving a sharp exhale, Charlotte pushed the ill feeling of being used aside while a higher calling beckoned.

"With how many times we've bumped into each other," Charlotte's mouth tugged into a smirk, knowing full well those bumps hadn't been accidental. "I think it's time for you and I to formally meet, don't you agree? You can call me Charlotte. And you might be?" She extended her hand in an offer of good will, her tone carrying expectation she hoped would be fulfilled.

The girl hesitated. No doubt untrusting of what this stranger would do.

Seeing she'd somehow grabbed the attention of others in the camp, including the down-trodden soldier, Charlotte let her voice carry. "Don't worry, I'm not going to report you to the police." She gave the girl a stern glance, paying particular attention to her dirt-stained hands formed into fists at her sides. "That is, as long as you don't steal from me again."

"You want your money back, mademoiselle?"

Having been prepared to receive a look that resonated more with contempt or pretense like the soldier had given her, Charlotte was pleased to find one that resembled more of willingness.

"No, though I wouldn't mind if you and your friends would stop stealing from me in the future." Charlotte crossed her arms, meeting various gazes, but settling swiftly on the girl again. "Either way, I'd much prefer to know who you are."

The girl hesitated again. "Sophie." The name came out low and soft, but Charlotte caught it.

"Well, Sophie." Charlotte took a satisfied breath, eyeing the girl's fingers having been wrapped in worn cloth, but nowhere adequate for fighting off the chill. "You're obviously skilled with your hands. And you seem to have a knack for repetition, at least as far as thievery goes." She chose to keep her smile, but her tone was firm. "Let's see if we can put that into better use. Have you ever worked with lace?"

"With lace?" The balled-up hands released at Sophie's sides, the girl giving Charlotte a somewhat blank expression on her unwashed face. "What do you mean, mademoiselle?"

Thinking of how different she'd imagined this moment to be—confronting her thief only to extend an opportunity—Charlotte laughed beneath her exterior.

If only Aunt Sylvia could see her now. She wasn't doing anything that would benefit her family back home. She'd failed in that matter. But she could still help Louise and her mother's business here. That very thought made her smile peak. "I mean, Sophie, we have business to discuss."

Chapter 31

Charlotte tossed one of her petticoats on the top of her trunk, closing the lid with a finality that brimmed in her bones, but not one she welcomed. She took a bitter glance at the letter her aunt would receive in advance of her empty-handed arrival and breathed in a breath laced with regret.

"Are you sure you don't want me to take you back?" Nicholas leaned against the framed doorway of her room, his hands at the side of a more casual set of breeches than the ones he wore while in uniform.

It was late, but she'd purposely left the door open hoping he might come by. Her heart jumped to see him.

"Something tells me I may not be needed for a while with how things are going on my end, too." Though a weak smile surfaced as if to cut the tension in his tone, the lines under his eyes conveyed the bold truth. Something was still heavy upon him. And had been since they'd left London.

She did want him to take her, but she couldn't help thinking that whatever was on his mind needed to be dealt with. Her own experience regarding her mother's death confirmed that necessity.

She stood from where she'd been leaning over her trunk and had flipped the latches secure. "Thank you, but I've arranged for transportation. A privateer ship arrived from Pennsylvania while we were in London. I've acquired a place on board. I'll be leaving . . . this evening." Her throat suddenly felt constricted, not wanting to completely go through with her plan.

He nodded but didn't look pleased. She hoped for the same reasons she'd felt. She was going to miss him terribly.

"In that case I'll go ahead and give you these." Removing a hand from inside his coat pocket, he pulled out a parcel wrapped in parchment and tied with a white ribbon.

"What is this?"

He handed the small package to her while she looked up at him, giving him a teasing smile she hoped might lessen the current ache of soon being apart. "You got me a going away present?"

"Don't get too excited." His expression mirrored her own, as did his playful tone. "It's not Priestley's carbonated water, but I figured it might come in handy for the journey."

Intrigued, she untied the ribbon and looked inside the parchment, discovering a pile of amber-colored morsels with a distinct spicy scent. "Candied ginger." She met his gaze again, smiling. "Thank you, Nicholas. It's perfect." She was sure by that rogue smile he gave her he was thinking back on their trip to London while on the *Speedy*, but she didn't mind. The man was considerate beyond words. She considered his token to her, her smile fading more at who she would miss than her lack of thoughtfulness.

"I wish I had something to give you. I feel like we've been through a lot together."

"Oh, you don't need to get me anything." He cupped his hand over hers while she still held onto the ginger. The candy almost slipped from her fingers, the gesture, though small, igniting a yearning for him.

"You have a way of being remembered." There was a slight tilt in his tone that made her laugh. "Besides, I'm not counting this as the last time I see you."

"You're not?"

"I was serious back in England, Charlotte."

That didn't tell her much. The man was serious most of the time, especially since they'd seen his father, which made the lightness from their conversation earlier all the more satisfying. Though right now she could've sworn his blue eyes were a shade deeper than usual.

"Serious about what, exactly? You'll have to be more specific." She put the ginger in her reticule, making sure she really wouldn't drop the candy and putting it aside for when she'd need it. She turned to meet him again. "There were a lot of serious moments, if I remember correctly."

"You're right. There were." His hand moved to her face, smoothing the area where her temple met her cheek. That rogue smile she loved played at his mouth. "Since I know you like to get down to business, I'm talking about the moment that has to do with you becoming my wife."

She stilled. There it was again. His wife. "You mean marriage?" Her mouth nearly fell to the rug beneath her feet.

He laughed, though she found no humor in the subject. "Honestly, I was hoping for a slightly different reaction." He closed the small distance between them looking not at all flustered by her response. She couldn't say the same for herself.

"I—" She didn't hate the idea. In fact, what scared her the most was the warmth that spread throughout her body thinking of the notion. Except— "Nicholas, let's not forget the obstacles here." She leaned away from him, taking a step back and feeling as if they'd somehow switched roles—she the now calculated one and he the daring. "You're a captain of the Royal Navy. I know it's been a while since we left, but there is a war still going on between our homelands."

"It's been done before." He stepped toward her, erasing the progress she'd made away from him.

She knew what he meant. "Abigail and Garrett are a rare exception. It's unlikely we'd have the same outcome."

"Oh, I think we could . . . with your stubbornness."

Her mouth dropped. She would've elbowed him if she wasn't trying to see clearly for them both. "But my condition . . . I may not live . . ."

"You seem better and even if you didn't that's not something that matters to me."

That very thought touched her deeply. Knowing Nicholas Edwards gave his all in everything, she had no problem envisioning he'd do the same in marriage, even one cut short.

"Look, what you're saying is all true—" He gave a scoundrel of a grin, the mere inches between them quickly vanishing. "But I didn't hear you say 'no'."

No, she hadn't. And she wouldn't have in that moment even if she'd had the power to voice it, which she didn't.

She swallowed, trying to loosen the tightness in her throat, but failing. His eyes once underlined with burden, now darkened with desire. He leaned in, her pulse quickening at his scent that brought both comfort and longing. She felt his breath on her skin and a shiver ran through her catching a hint of ginger on his breath. His gaze dropped to her mouth briefly before his lips finally pressed into hers, shooting what felt like a jolt of lightening up her spine. She stepped toward him, fully embracing the kiss. The warmth she felt earlier heated, reaching from the top of her head to the tips of her toes and sending her thoughts to what it would be like to claim more of this man than just his lips.

When the kiss ended too soon, Nicholas broke the physical bond between them, leaving her breathless and wordless.

"Just give the idea some thought."

She felt his breath in her ear and another shiver ran up her spine before he took a step back.

After a kiss like that she wasn't sure if she would be able to think about anything else. Her heart still pounded. Though not entirely wanting the moment to end, she was thankful he'd taken another step away from her. She needed the chance to gather herself—to pivot. And doing so wasn't easy with him still looking at her like that.

She swiped a finger behind her ear, having managed to collect some of her composure. "I do have a favor I'd like to ask if you wouldn't mind." Her voice came out somewhat shaky. Apparently, a kiss with Nicholas Edwards had a lasting effect on her.

"Of course." His eyes had returned to their natural blue but had squinted in a way that told her he'd been pleased with the result.

"There's a package from the dentelle——an order that needs to be delivered to Versailles." A very different image came to mind, threatening to hijack the previous moment. She retrieved a box depicting a floral motif from the table she'd used for letter writing and creating lace sketches. "After everything, I can't bring myself to take it. I would be truly grateful if you could . . ."

"Say no more." He took the package from her hand. "I'll be happy to make the delivery. I need to finish my own assignment, anyway."

"Thank you." Relief washed over her, though she wasn't oblivious to the shift in his tone as if the burden he'd laid aside for their intimate encounter earlier had been taken up again. "Any ideas of what you're going to do this time?"

"Not yet."

She saw his struggle and her heart went out to him. Reflecting on what had just occurred between them, she made her own small token of affection, taking hold of his hand. "Maybe something will come to you."

His mouth made a weak curve up. "Let's just hope it comes soon. King George is patient enough, but he has a lot on his shoulders with what's happening in the colonies. His patience will only go so far."

"Charlotte—oh, mon amie!" The desperation in the French woman's tone grabbed for Charlotte's attention, especially considering from who that desperation had come from.

Claudine had rushed into Charlotte's open room with a look of panic Charlotte had never seen before on the woman's face.

"The lacemaker said you might be here." She panted as if out of breath.

"You mean Louise?" Charlotte's brow bunched. "You were at the dentelle?"

"Oui. I have been looking for you. It is urgent." The desperation in her tone returned as Claudine's hand went to her chest where the front of her robe à la françiase held silver threads of embroidery over a royal blue brocade. There was a fast rise and fall of movement under her mitted palm.

"Why don't you take a seat, madame." With their moment ago all but vanished, Nicholas wore a stern expression. It was one she'd seen several times in his uniform. He went over to Claudine, guiding her to a modestly upholstered straight-backed chair. "Take a minute to catch your breath and then tell us what happened."

Claudine hesitated, casting her glance between Charlotte and Nicholas before deciding to take his advice. "Marc has been taken as a prisoner by the gendarmes for treason." Her eyes glistened. "He was arrested at the ball tonight."

"The masquerade?" Charlotte had forgotten, or rather, had worked to put the whole of Marc's announcement out of her mind. She was still angry with him despite their conversation and even after their encounter at the Court of Miracles. Marc had made his intentions quite clear—he had a message to get across no matter at who's expense. But treason?

Charlotte shook her head. Having been like him at one time, she knew Marc. She would've never risked herself in such a way and neither would he. "Marc holds certain opinions about French court, yes, but I can't imagine he would go so far as to commit any act directly against the king."

Claudine batted her head as if agreeing. "I don't think so either, but the circumstances are not in his favor. When the curtain was drawn back at the ball to reveal the winner of Les Muses de Versailles, the portrait was Marc's."

Nearly stumbling backward, Charlotte's hand reached and found something steady. Her gaze met Nicholas's realizing her fingers hadn't grabbed a chair or table, but him. She managed to choke out the title. "*A Woman's Folly?*"

"No, mon amie." Claudine shook her head, a somberness to her expression that carried its weight in a tear down her cheek and made a stained pathway down her powdered face. "A different one he would never present at court. He knows it would be an act of pure defiance to do so."

Charlotte felt a tension forming in her jaw at Claudine's hushed words. "What painting?" Her own question whispered out as if the truth too horrible to say outright.

"*Madame Régime.*"

Charlotte sucked in a breath as Claudine's head dropped to her hands. The painting she'd seen in Marc's salon earlier that day.

"Before they took him away—" Claudine's explanation came quickly, as if scrambling for words. "Marc pleaded for me to seek you out. He said you were at his apartment this afternoon and must've seen the painting."

"I was." Charlotte had never seen the woman like this, so vulnerable. She refrained from looking at Nicholas, hoping he wouldn't get the wrong idea. She'd set things right later in case he had. "I stopped by for a much-needed conversation. The portrait was hanging on the salon wall of his apartment. It was still there when I left."

"But that was this afternoon. The ball wouldn't have started until this evening." Nicholas brow bent. She knew he and Marc didn't get along, but she also knew this man and what he was really aiming at. Marc would've still had time to get the painting to Versailles.

"You think my brother could've done this, monsieur?" Claudine rose from the chair in a more composed manner, her dress' brocade falling to her feet. Her usual elegance and poise were accompanied with a sharp defiance. "It is a death sentence."

"I'm not saying he did, and I'm not a detective, but—" Nicholas met Claudine's low and edged words with careful sobriety. "—you'll need more proof. From Charlotte's account, there's still time for Marc to be able to move the painting to the palace before it was revealed at the masquerade."

The already white veneer coating over Claudine's face paled. "Oh, mon dieu." She put a gloved hand to her mouth before lifting her chin to him with parted lips. Her gaze seemed transfixed in the distance as if looking into a dismal future. "You are right."

Feeling a nudge to prevent her friend any more anguish than necessary, Charlotte put her hand in the air as if to stop Claudine's spiraling of thought she'd imagined taking place. "He would have had time, except I was with your brother until this evening."

Claudine turned to Charlotte, her eyes widening. "You were with Marc?" Hope dangled in her tone.

"I was." Charlotte glanced at Nicholas. He was quiet, standing more like a statue from the years of military training. She didn't like how this conversation about Marc was going, but she aimed to clear any misconceptions given the next chance. She allowed her confession to come measured, but full of truth. "I don't think he would've had time to get the portrait to Versailles, let alone set up for its announcement."

"Oh, ma chérie, then there is hope." Claudine clasped her hands toward heaven after wiping another streaked tear from her eye. "You must come to the estate of Monsieur Morat and give your account." Her hands cascaded to her sides. "That is where the Parliament is meeting since the fire on the Ile de la Cite. Please, chérie. I beg of you."

It was a face of Claudine that Charlotte had never thought she'd witness. Even under the powder and rouge, a sister's angst for her brother was evident. The scenario did little for her own advancement, which is how she would have evaluated it in the past to get her own way like Marc would've done. But she tried to put herself in Claudine's place, which wasn't hard when she remembered her brother's imprisonment last year. What would she have done to get him back from enemy lines?

She hadn't completely forgiven Marc for his actions concerning her self-portrait, mostly because he never offered an apology. Even when she understood his point, and perhaps agreed with him on some grounds of his argument, he had still pushed his agenda at her expense. Surely no one could blame her for feeling more than a little bruised over the situation. The fact that Marc was now in trouble almost gave her a sense of vindication. Almost.

A much better and wiser voice spoke softly inside her heart, telling her to act against her reasoning. She knew what she had to do.

"I don't know how much of my account the French Parliament will accept, especially in light of my reputation at court now, but—" She closed her eyes, not believing or wanting to say what she needed to next, but knowing it was the right thing. "Of course, I'll go."

Chapter 32

"You're certain you want to do this?"

Charlotte paced across the floor with her hands to her hips, asking herself the same question Nicholas had given voice to. She stopped her pacing over the marble surface, viewing him in front of a large set of double mahogany doors that towered over him. "You mean face a room full of nobles who most likely know me as the fool of France and saw me faint at my own image?" She shook her head, pinching her fingers to her temples where pressure had built. "I can't say I'm exactly looking forward to the reunion."

"You could change your mind." He didn't smile, but she caught the light teasing in his tone. "Leave now before they call you in."

She wanted to, but that was the issue about doing the right thing. It wasn't always easy. Of course, he knew that.

She stared down a carved-out image of a lion's head in the solid oak—one of two that pillared the closed doors. "Marc might've been wrong in his actions, but he was also right in his convictions." She turned to face Nicholas again who stood adjacent to the doors. "You were too. I've been going about things the wrong way. Maybe I needed a blunt reminder of that." She sighed. "Even if it was in plain view of all of Paris."

"Glad to see Marc and I can agree on something." She detected a hint of sarcasm, but also truth in Nicholas's statement.

"About Marc—" She cleared her throat, wanting to also clear things up between them.

"You're doing a good thing." He stopped her, his tone holding assurance while he leaned in closer to the door. "It sounds like he needs you in there."

She stepped forward. "What are they saying?"

His mouth tightened in a way that already conveyed what he was about to tell her. "Nothing good."

Though she appreciated Nicholas's honesty, the news wasn't what she wanted to hear.

"I don't know if it will make a difference . . ." She raised her chin at the overwhelming door and the members of French Parliament beyond the barrier. She swore the thing had doubled in size since they'd been waiting. ". . . me going in there."

"And I wouldn't count on it doing so, mademoiselle."

She might've mistaken the male voice for Marc's with the confidence that accompanied it but she knew better. Marc was currently behind the heavy-set doors, and she imagined feeling less confident in his current predicament.

Laurent Girard approached them wearing a black robe and a smug smile on his face.

Charlotte pressed her lips, not confused by the man being present for the meeting, knowing he held a place in Parliament, but by his tone. She offered him a smile, hoping she would at least have one vote on her side. "Monsieur Girard. I hope you can help me clear this misunderstanding."

His laugh was iced, yielding no trace of the assurance she'd expected. "Not many have forgotten about last week's spectacle at the palace. I doubt the nobles or the king are able to overlook such a display of both your portrait and behavior." His lips formed a thin line, giving her a dismissive glance. "And it will be hard to take your testimony seriously, especially coming from a woman."

Sweeping his comments about her aside for a greater good, she hoped, she proceeded to implore the man. "But you're a member of Parliament. Perhaps you could help persuade them?"

He adjusted his cravat, the same shade of white as his powdered wig, looking more interested by the state of his wardrobe than her cause. "That I also doubt, especially when it goes against my priorities of keeping this city's traditions." He humphed. "To suggest that the nobility start paying taxes is an absurd notion and I will not see our city be overrun with radicals that promote these kinds of ideas. It is just as well Marc has condemned himself." He gave her a look that lacked all sympathy, but she wasn't done trying.

"But Monsieur Girard, surely you don't believe Marc would do such a thing?" The words echoed Claudine's own petition in her room at the boardinghouse, her friend currently waiting in her normally stoic fashion on a bench against a wall.

His shoulders raised with indifference. "There are rumors of his involvement in certain radical meetings, and he does little to conceal his opinions of the monarchy. It wouldn't be hard to believe. But you have to excuse me, mademoiselle. I will see you in just a moment." He side-stepped past her toward the door. His chin angled high over his cravat at Nicholas. "You, monsieur, will have to wait out here. The room is only permitted to the French Parliament and those under oath."

A few minutes passed when a man in similar fashioned robes as Laurent emerged from the enclosed room. Charlotte froze, feeling her feet sink at the invisible line she'd created with her walking back and forth along the marble floor.

"I'll wait for you outside with Claudine." Nicholas's mouth peaked. "You'll be fine."

She knew what he was trying to do—comfort her at a very critical moment. But the fact Marc's life might hang on her sole testimony didn't give her much comfort. She prayed for the right words to come, if not for her own reputation, then for the life she could possibly help save.

The man in black ushered her past the lions at their post and under the towering doorway. Though her muscles twitched with every step forward, she couldn't help feeling a sense of reverence being guided into the inner sanctum of power.

She turned her head back, watching Nicholas and what felt like her anchor disappear behind the closing fortress doors.

After a few steps inside the meeting room, the man who had escorted her left her side.

Men in mostly black and red robes with long, curled perukes stared at her from where they swarmed around a large, rectangular table. She didn't know the reason for the different colored robes, only that those in red held a seat at the table, making her believe they somehow outranked the men standing.

The room's high ceilings and tall windows would have normally made the area feel spacious if it weren't for the thick curtains made of rich burgundy velvet that covered them, blocking out any light and unwanted observers.

She felt like she was a part of a production at the opera—she a performer while these men resided as spectators, waiting to be entertained. But she wouldn't be entertaining alone.

Her throat went dry, seeing the man beside her, the only one not fashioned in a powdered white wig. "Marc." She threw a whisper at him.

"Charlotte." He gave her a weak smile, the confidence she'd seen yesterday wiped clean from his face. "I must admit I am somewhat surprised to see you." There was a heaviness to his tone as his eyes drooped with the same burden.

"You're not the only one. In truth, I'm still a little shocked I'm here at all." She folded her hands together in front of her petticoat, trying to prevent them from shaking, though not sure if her nerves were due to her position here today or his own. "I thought my day in front of the French nobility was quite over." She might've added, 'thanks to you', but the comment felt wrong in the current moment.

Marc stared blankly ahead, the area under his eyes swollen. He was wearing a waistcoat of fine, dark velvet with gold embroidery—far more elaborate than his simple daily dress and telling her he hadn't slept in his own bed last night if he had slept at all. And his hands—bound in front of him and in a similar position of what she had done with hers freely.

"Where did they keep you?" She whispered again while a man in black lowered himself to a man in red and spoke something in his ear.

He slumped his shoulders as if the weight of his shackles bore down more than just his wrists. "The prisoner's quarters of the Palais de la Cité was part of the damage from the fire. I was lucky enough to avoid it. Instead, they kept me in the Bastille." He gave a hollow chuckle before turning to her, his lips pressed into a faint smile. "It is a turn of things, no? My art is for my own free expression, yet now it has condemned me."

"Did you replace the painting to be revealed by the monarchy with your own?"

He met her question with a terse look. "Of course not. I do not have a death wish."

She figured as much but had to make sure. Which meant someone else had condemned Marc. But who?

Narrowing her eyes, she looked about the room, aware a prominent figure was missing. "Where's the king? Isn't this case pertaining to the monarchy?"

He sniffed, rolling his shoulders forward. "He does not attend the meetings but delegates his administration of justice to his chancellors and ministers for representation."

She leaned toward him, though watchful of the red robes at the table, looking for any clues that might divulge that information. "And who are his ministers and chancellors?"

He scoffed. "You know one of them."

She followed his line of sight to a man in black and she sucked in a breath. The Vicomte de Vantinelle.

"Thank you for being here." He glanced over to her, his tone genuine. His cravat moved as if moving something down his throat. "No matter what happens to me."

Charlotte gave him a weak smile, glad she had come. "You're welcome, but don't thank me just yet. I don't know if my testimony will do any good."

"We shall see. In any case, it is the only one I have." His chest lifted as his brow did the opposite and furrowed. "If I survive this, that man will have to deal with me face-to-face instead of sneaking around like a coward."

Marc's voice dipped with contempt as he shot a glare across the room where she'd followed his gaze earlier. The vicomte stood next to Laurent Girard, their heads close together as they engaged in what seemed like a heated debate, the vicomte apparently losing by his clearly displeased expression. She couldn't determine the subject, her distance too far from them to hear any true dialogue. Despite the chatter of other members of Parliament surrounding them, their intense exchange was palpable, if to no one else, then at least to her.

She'd known Marc and the vicomte didn't get along, but had he had something to do with Marc's conviction? Her stomach rolled at the thought and how desperate she'd been to win his partnership.

Evidently feeling her stare and perhaps judgement, the man she held in question shot her a fierce glance and she got her answer nearly a moment before the knocking of a gavel brought the room to order.

Chapter 33

The royal crown at the top of the golden gate loomed over Nicholas like a foreboding omen as if daring him to pass under another time. Seeing no alternative but forward, he crossed through the gilded Palisade of Versailles with Charlotte's package in hand.

He hadn't made the trip for King George despite his continued orders, even if his last meeting with his own monarch back in London over the miners hinged on his completed assignment in France. He still had no idea how he'd obtain an audience with the King of France now that the opportunity at the art contest was gone.

He had lost his only chance at the monarchy for someone else. It was a choice he didn't have the slightest regret on, but it was one where he would not get a second turn, especially when the first had been so difficult to come by. Not to mention the French advisor's words echoed in his head as if sealing the door to that opportunity permanently shut. The king would see him only at Les Muses de Versailles. He was no longer welcomed at the French palace, yet here he was, determined to keep his promise to Charlotte.

Taking a straight path from the palace gate to the grand château, Nicholas breathed in deeply. Cold air hit his lungs and sharpened his senses. He had an urge to flip his pocket watch open and closed inside his coat, but Charlotte's package occupied both hands. He counted the obstruction as an advantage, guessing the restless movement might not do him any favors today, especially when the goal was to blend in.

Small groups of French men and women passed by him on their way out in pastel colors typical of the aristocracy. He didn't own anything close to such fashions but knowing the array of individuals that came to visit Versailles each day, he didn't need to. He just made sure the clothing that had distinguished him—his uniform—was not part of his wardrobe today.

"Monsieur, I told you, I cannot allow you in the château."

Having stepped inside the palace after passing unnoticed by two Swiss guards, Nicholas couldn't help but be drawn to a man's dilemma and accent at the palace gate behind him.

An older man with a portly but stately figure appeared at odds with the palace gatekeeper. "But sir, I must be permitted entry. I have come to seek the king's audience over a matter of great importance."

Appearing to ignore the earnestness in the Englishman's tone, the Frenchman stiffed his neck like the wrought-iron boundary he guarded. "I'm sorry, monsieur, but I cannot allow you inside as you are. Versailles holds a strict etiquette for formal fashions."

"Formal fashions?" The older man looked down over his plain, brown suit that completely lacked any of the embellishments coveted by French court, then back to the guard. "Monsieur, I can assure you my clothing is of little consequence compared to the matter I have to discuss with the king of France."

"It is the king of France and tradition that upholds this practice, monsieur. And your current state of dress is disrespectful to His Majesty. Whatever the subject is that you must discuss, you will not do so as you are." The gatekeeper wrinkled his nose at the man's understated wardrobe coupled with a fur cap, possibly made of otter or beaver, on a gray head of hair. "As a foreigner you are not expected to follow the French example in its strictest sense, but you must exhibit the equivalent of court attire. Many Englishmen have passed through in such a way."

"But I—"

"I'm sorry, monsieur, but that is the way things are here at Versailles."

Seeing one of the Swiss guards had been called to escort the Englishman away, Nicholas exited the palace to return to the palace gate. He didn't know why he was drawn to this man, only that he could relate to the man's plight.

"Excuse me, sir, you can borrow my coat." Nicholas approached the man who'd been denied entry. It was then he realized he'd misjudged the Englishman's height by a few inches, the top of the older man's head meeting Nicholas's nose. "It won't be a perfect fit, but you'll at least be granted entrance."

"I don't understand." The man adjusted a pair of small, rounded spectacles bridging a broad nose that reminded Nicholas of his grandfather. "You're allowing me the use of your coat?"

"Pardon me for my overhearing." Nicholas gave him a look he hoped conveyed an apology before motioning to the palace entrance. "But it sounded like you need to get in there."

The man gave a resounding nod, his fur cap shifting forward in a way that almost covered his eyes. "It is of a critical nature, a matter of business that might tip the scales of the future if all goes well."

"That sounds important." The man's mention of business brought images of Charlotte to Nicholas's mind and the package in his hand he still needed to deliver. "In my experience the French nobility can be tricky to conduct business with." Memories of his times waiting in the king's antechamber resurfaced. "Then again I'm not a businessman."

"Nor I. I'm a printer by trade." His round face held a kindly expression Nicholas also read pride in. "Though I also dabble with experiments—some of which have proven useful for easier living."

Nicholas's interest peaked. "You mean inventions?"

"Yes." The man's intelligent blue eyes lit behind his glasses, looking both shocked and delighted. "Are you an inventor?"

Nicholas smiled. "No, but you could say I have an appreciation for them—maybe something even beyond that."

"An admirer then." The man pointed a finger in the air, his round face casting a warm glow.

Though wanting to ask more of what types of inventions this man conducted, Nicholas detained the notion. No doubt the man's reasons for requesting the king's audience pertained to something about his work in some way, but he didn't have time to find out. He'd already made the offer to help this inventor, something he would follow through on. But he also needed to deliver Charlotte's package.

Reminded of the parcel still in his possession, Nicholas sat the box down on the black and white stone below his boots, giving his hands freedom to remove his coat. "Here, let's see if this change gets you in the door." He tried handing his coat to the Englishman, but the man frowned.

"I cannot let you do that, sir. You would be denied entry yourself."

The inventor waved him off, but Nicholas insisted. "I'm here on a delivery run, not to speak with any nobles." He eyed Charlotte's package, still on the ground as if to convey his proof. "I'll meet you out here on the courtyard when you're done."

There was a hesitation before the Englishman put his arms into the sleeves of Nicholas's coat. The man bowed his head with appreciation, exposing the bottom of gray hair that hung near his shoulders. "Sir, you have my sincerest thanks."

As he approached the gate again, Nicholas watched the gatekeeper give a sweeping glance over the man he denied earlier now in a different coat that held modest embellishment compared to French court. The gatekeeper showed little interest to how or when the inventor had obtained one, only signaling a nod that he'd been satisfied.

Watching the older man step past the Swiss guards and into the doors of the palace, Nicholas retrieved Charlotte's package from the Royal Courtyard. No longer in possession of a coat that was deemed appropriate, his original plan to enter through the palace front door would have to change.

He scanned the courtyard for other options, settling on an entry point near the palace's outer perimeter that a horse had stopped in front of. The rider, wearing a dusty brown cloak, dismounted before unbuckling a leather satchel strapped to the saddle. A guard at the entry point gave a brief inspection before the man disappeared inside with a package, all done unbeknownst to the nobles entering and exiting the main gate. That was his way in and one that offered little attention.

"Nicholas."

He'd taken only a few steps toward the entry he'd seen the courier go through when he'd heard his name. In light of what he was trying to do, he might've ignored the call over to him, except he knew the voice and he had questions he'd like answers to.

Turning from the entry point, Nicholas saw Lewis waving him down from a line that had formed at the gate—no doubt a product of the inventor's delay with his fashion mistake. His friend was easy to spot in his muted green suit among the vibrant colors of the Frenchmen among him.

Nicholas took a place beside him in line, though having no intention of trying to enter the palace by this method.

"I see you made it back to Paris. How was the trip home?"

The reminder triggered the vivid memory over the conversation that had occurred between him and his father. He forced a smile, trying to make his current conversation more pleasant. But then he remembered the real reason he'd left Paris. Charlotte.

The smile came more easily. "Not what I expected, but I think the trip served its purpose." Maybe not for him, but he thought Charlotte had benefitted.

He wasn't sure if the doctor in Paris was on to something, but Nicholas had sensed a difference with their time away. She'd been vulnerable with him in London, trusting him with a piece of information she'd been keeping hidden since her mother's death. It didn't matter that he didn't think she had any blame in the incident, but he did wonder what a burden like that could do to someone over time.

Nicholas looked past Lewis, realizing only now the man was unaccompanied. "Where's your nephew?"

"He's already beat me inside." Lewis shook his head, though a smile held his lips. "The lad's hoping he'll get a chance to meet the king."

There it was—Nicholas's lead into the conversation he'd intended to have. "That makes the two of us."

"Oh?" Lewis raised an eyebrow, pulling his head back as if studying him while an inflection chimed in his tone. "I didn't realize the French monarchy made such a significant impression on you."

Nicholas chuckled. The king's refusals had certainly made a significant impression, but not in the sense Lewis intended. "It has a way of doing that, but that's not what I mean." He lowered his voice. "I've had orders to meet with Louis XVI."

"Orders?" Lewis leaned in, his own volume quieting. "To meet with the king of France?" His gaze narrowed on Nicholas, but not before taking them both out of the line and into the middle of the Royal Way where they were out of interested ears. "That's why you're in Paris then?"

Seeing the man's desire for distance as a sign Nicholas's guess was on the right track, he decided to come clean. "Yes, but I only mention that because I have a feeling that I'm not the only one among us who's here on a mission." He eyed his friend, hoping Lewis might see the action for what it was—an invitation.

"You mean me?" Lewis inclined his head away as if shocked by the insinuation.

The man was feigning innocence, but Nicholas was almost certain. He gave Lewis a slow nod, letting his friend know he was unrelenting on this issue. "I do."

"I told you," Lewis straightened, wiping off what appeared to be an imaginary piece of dust from Paris's streets. "I'm here as a chaperone for my nephew while he's on his Grand Tour."

"And I believe that much is true, but I also think that's not the only reason you're here." Nicholas leveled his gaze, bent on the man leveling with him. "I'm not here to derail your assignment, or to even ask the details, only to acknowledge there is more than you've let on."

After giving Nicholas a hard stare, Lewis gave a resigned sigh, apparently ready to give an explanation. His friend veered his gaze around them as if making sure they wouldn't be overheard. Satisfied enough, he leaned into Nicholas again. "There's a man I'm looking for." His voice was muted. "Rumors have pointed to him coming to Paris from the colonies to gain France's support for the war. He goes by the name of Franklin."

"And you're sure he's in Paris?" Nicholas wrinkled his brow, his question answered with a slight nod.

"I've been scouting to find out if the claims have merit. Turns out they do, at least about him making the trip here. According to my sources, he made a spectacle upon his arrival while you were in London. Frenchmen call him the 'noble savage,' adopting a modest style of dress that deliberately stands out and charming the salons with his wit and stories of the New World. The French are starting to embrace his rustic appearance and what they are deeming his virtue."

"What are you going to do with this Franklin if you find him?"

Lewis glanced briefly away before back again. "I'm obliged to bring him to my overseer, whom I cannot name. If the rumors are true, he'll likely face consequences for treason for rebellion against the British government. Likely he'll hang."

"You're a spy." Before Nicholas had time to register the words, they were out. It wasn't exactly what he'd guessed, but it made sense now that Lewis had laid everything out for him along with what he already knew.

Lewis shifted uncomfortably as if he'd been exposed somehow. "You put that together easily enough."

"I like to see how things work." Nicholas shrugged his shoulders, the weight of Charlotte's package bearing little on his arms. Whatever was inside was light. "I suppose that means I also like to put things together."

"Okay." Lewis gave him a look that probed for his own explanation this time. "So, what gave me away?"

"A few things." Nicholas smiled when he saw that answer warranted a frown from his friend. "For one, your nephew is a little young to embark on a Grand Tour. Most go at twenty-one."

"That's not unheard of."

Nicholas met the challenge in Lewis's tone with an easy smile. "No, but it's not typical and you've been in Paris for months. That gets expensive, especially with a private French tutor and a lawyer not meeting clients. My guess is someone else is paying, at least in part—perhaps even a certain benefactor who has the means to pay for law school and a way to get out of the mines in exchange for intel."

Nicholas watched Lewis for anything telling, but if he was right, his friend didn't say. "Though that alone wasn't enough to rouse my suspicion. Your obsession with the paper each time I saw you reminded me of a tactic I'd heard of in Massachusetts last year. I knew a former spy there. But it was the king's seal on the papers you dropped and what Jim Cadwell said while I was away that made everything fit into place."

Lewis rubbed his jaw as if trying to make sense of the clues himself. "What did Jim say?"

"You were meeting frequently with the king's prime minister. I don't know a lot about law, but I do know the prime minister happens to oversee spy activity in England and I don't imagine he needs a lawyer from a small mining town like Cairnhaven when he already has one from London."

"You haven't told anyone have you—that lady friend of yours, even?" Lewis swallowed, looking like a man who'd been found guilty and awaiting what came next.

"Your secret's safe." Though nowhere in view, Nicholas gestured in the direction of the palace where Lewis claimed his nephew had already entered. "Does Stephen know?"

Lewis shook his head once from side to side. "I thought it best not to say anything unless I catch Franklin, then I suppose I'll have to. And you—" His gaze went to Charlotte's package. "Does that have to do with your orders here?"

"No. This is more of a favor." Nicholas wasn't sure, but he thought he sensed the gatekeeper looking at him before whispering something in one of the guard's ears. The action, even if in his head, started an imaginary time watch in his system like a ticking clock. Seeing the guard disappear into the palace instead of approaching him only heightened his alarm.

He turned to Lewis, patting the box in his care. "I need to make sure I deliver this. If I don't see you in there, good luck catching your man."

Lewis followed Nicholas's motion to the main entrance. "Thank you. I feel like I'm close—like he might very well be within those walls."

His eyes drew up and down Nicholas's frame with evaluation. "I take it you're not planning to enter through the main gate without the proper fashion protocol?"

Nicholas eyed the outer entry point where he'd seen the courier walk through earlier. The guard was still at his post, but nothing gave Nicholas caution to differ from his original plan. "I don't need to, not for what I have to do."

"Very well." Lewis raised a brow but didn't inquire further, perhaps hoping Nicholas would return the favor. "Perhaps I'll see you on the other side."

Having watched Lewis return to the gate, Nicholas went the opposite direction. He stepped up to the guard. He hadn't been close enough to hear the exchange of the courier he'd witnessed from before, but he mimicked the man's motions, presenting the package Charlotte had given him. As far as instructions went, Charlotte hadn't given him much, but she had given some.

"I need to deliver this to the dressmaker." The man gave him less than a nod, Nicholas taking the silent affirmation as a sign to move forward.

With a measured breath, he stepped into the palace, but he didn't get far.

"Sapristi! Heavens! I did not believe it when the guard informed me." A loud clacking of a man's heels clipped from down the hallway as if echoing their wearer's displeasure. The voice filled him with dread.

"You have audacity, Captain Edwards. I give that to you—intelligence I'm not so sure." The man Nicholas knew as King Louis' advisor was headed straight toward him, his wig flouncing with each step. The man didn't look pleased. In fact, he looked downright outraged. "In light of your absence at the meeting you requested so urgently during Les Muses de Versailles one has to wonder if you would be so bold as to request another. His Majesty was not amused."

"It wasn't on purpose. That, I can assure you. I had no intention of displeasing the king."

The noble gave a snorty scoff. "It shouldn't have happened at all. And if you are here to apologize, I would not waste your time."

An apology wasn't something Nicholas was opposed to, but the sentiment would have to wait. He rubbed the back of his neck. "I'm here on an errand, actually."

"An errand?" The man pursed his lips before giving him a disdainful up and down look. "I suppose this is the reason you have no respectable coat among you, then?"

Not caring to go into details about his missing coat, Nicholas presented the box still under his protection. "I was told to deliver this to the dressmaker."

"La couturière?" The powder on the advisor's forehead wrinkled. "Let me see." His tone cut short while his palms faced up as if demanding proof.

Nicholas hesitated, knowing Charlotte trusted him to make sure whatever lay inside the package ended up in the right hands. After a moment longer and considering the man might have rejected him otherwise before he had a chance to make the delivery, Nicholas handed the box over.

"I see." Having removed the lid to the box, the advisor lifted a piece of linen. A sliver of a smile tugged at his cheek, the change in his demeanor catching Nicholas off guard. "You are not out of tricks after all, Captain. It seems you have made friends with a lacemaker." The man replaced both the paper and the lid before returning the box to his possession. "Perhaps I have misjudged your intelligence."

Having no idea what this man referred to, Nicholas wanted to ask for an explanation, but he didn't. Not when it would serve him and Charlotte better to keep quiet.

The advisor waved over a servant dressed in livery. "Take this man to the Grand appartement de la Reine. It seems he has a gift for the queen."

***

Nicholas stood a few steps in from where he'd entered an elaborately decorated room with a gilded canopy bed. The queen? He didn't know much about Marie Antionette other than the fact she was born Austrian and married into a French monarchy, and by the looks of the pamphlet he'd seen at the café, wasn't favored by everyone.

But she was a queen, the king's wife. It was no coincidence Charlotte had asked him to make the delivery.

A slow release of warmth filled his chest. He looked down at the box again, considering his current situation, or rather, *opportunity*, and the woman he would have to thank for it.

"This is most unusual, sir." The woman a few yards in front of him sat poised on a highly ornamented armchair, Nicholas recognizing her through her poor representation from the café pamphlet. Her ash-blonde hair was the only true likeness aside from her slender frame. She looked at him with a liveliness he hadn't anticipated.

"Madame tells me you have an order from the dentelle in Paris, but she has no knowledge of making it." She turned to a woman standing beside her he'd guessed to be the dressmaker. "And I confess, neither do I."

Her tone was light, any seriousness she meant to convey overshadowed with something playful in it. Even so, Nicholas's hopes of what he might still be able to achieve plummeted.

"I'm sorry, Your Majesty." He gave a slight bow, aware of both a servant and guard also present within the queen's chamber. "I was only trying to help a friend to deliver this to the palace. It seems there's been

360

a mistake." He felt the box grow heavy in his hands despite how light it was. "Forgive me for my intrusion. I'll be happy to take this back to the dentelle."

"May I see it?" The queen lifted her pale chin as if she was trying to peer into the box from her distance away. There was a kindness in her tone as if making a request, but he knew better.

The servant in the room retrieved the box from his hands, the queen nearly ripping the lid as she opened the package. Finding a piece of paper, her blue eyes scanned the contents of what appeared to be a note.

"It is a gift from the lacemaker and her artist, specifically designed for me." The rouged corners of her painted lips drew upward, Nicholas's hopes rising again at the pleasure ringing in her voice.

The queen handed the box to the dressmaker, who took out a pair of lace gloves. The dressmaker stretched the gloves out carefully as if to evaluate their craftsmanship. "They are flowers, my queen."

"Magnifique!" Marie Antionette put her hand to her chest. "They are not just flowers. They are roses. My favorite." She looked from the gloves to him, Nicholas catching something glistening in her eyes. "Monsieur, I am quite moved by such a gift."

"I'll be glad to convey the news." Having heard a genuineness in her tone, Nicholas felt pride for both Charlotte and Louise. "I only wish my friends were here to witness your delight to their hard work themselves."

He understood Charlotte's reasons for not wanting to come to Versailles. But to miss this? To see her design so clearly cherished by the queen of France . . .

"According to the note accompanied with the gloves, they were hoping for as much and have made a request if I feel it should so please me." Slipping her fingers into each section of her new gift, the queen folded her laced hands in front of her.

"A request?" He searched her face, thinking he'd misunderstood.

"You are wanting to speak with my husband. Is that so?" There was a twinkle in her eye, her question dripping with temptation.

Resisting the urge to walk across the room and read the slip of paper she'd sat on top of a side table, Nicholas stood in place, keen at the guard still watching him. But what all was in that note?

He nodded. "Yes, Your Majesty. I've been trying to get an audience with him ever since I first arrived in Paris."

"How long ago?" She put one of her gloved fingers to the base of her chin.

A bitter smile broke free that he hadn't intended on showing. "Longer than I care to admit, Your Grace."

"You are an English soldier, no?" Her expression held confusion rather than the judgement he'd received from the French advisor as she glanced him over. "Though you do not look the part, I admit."

He gave a slight bow, hoping the confusion wouldn't be seen as an offense. "My apologies. I didn't think I'd be playing my role as an officer today."

The smile she gave was one like she understood the feeling completely, and as an Austrian woman having to fit into French customs of Versailles, he surmised she did.

"My origins might be from Austria, but I am quite aware of the tensions between France and England." Her gaze trailed to her hands. "However, I cannot ignore such a wonderful token you have delivered to me. I will talk to the king on your behalf and—"

Her eyes seemed drawn to something behind him. Before Nicholas could check his surroundings, the servant in the room brushed past him and ended at the French queen's side. Bending level with her ear, he whispered something Nicholas couldn't make out.

"Oh?" Her mouth opened, genuine surprise laying in her response, but the downward shift of her tone bore ill news he could sense was coming. "I'm sorry, monsieur." She regarded him again, but with something more ceremonial in her countenance. "It seems I cannot help you on this matter even with the gift you have delivered to me. My husband's decision has been made."

Empty-handed in more ways than one, Nicholas was escorted back to the royal courtyard of the palace.

Grieving more for the effort on the part of Louise and Charlotte and the chance they'd given him, Nicholas made his way to the entrance gate. He knew Charlotte would want to know if their plan had worked to get him through to see the king. And though it hadn't, he loved her for what she had done for him.

"Sir, sir."

Nicholas had crossed through the gate to the next courtyard when he heard an English accent from a distance.

"Sir, your coat."

The voice grew louder, though strained with each word. The mention of a coat prompted Nicholas to stop walking, realizing his own was missing. Lifting his chin from the view of the cobblestone, he saw a familiar beige frock flying with difficulty toward him.

The inventor waved at Nicholas from the other side of the gate before passing through. The man's ample cheeks, pinked more from the combination of the frigid air and his run over than typical Versailles make-up, puffed into a smile.

Despite his own difficulty, Nicholas couldn't help returning the gesture, feeling something contagious in the man's beaming image and certain his meeting went better than his own. "I take it you had no trouble inside?" He eyed his coat draped over the side of the inventor's arm.

The inventor returned Nicholas's coat, adjusting his furred hat that had significantly shifted from his scamper over. "Apart from an unusual ceremony of watching the royals eat and a nosy advisor, no real trouble. My meeting went quite well, I believe. I'd say things back home are looking brighter—" His eyes conveyed that very thought. "—especially now with France's assistance. In fact, the king has invited me back to Versailles on another occasion."

Nicholas paused from putting his second arm in the sleeve of his coat. "You mean, you did meet with the king of France?" He knew the man had meant to, but in Nicholas's experience with Louis Auguste, meaning to and *getting to* were quite different outcomes.

"Indeed." The man closed his eyes, bowing. "My country and myself are indebted to your beneficence, sir. I only hope one day I can repay you for such an act of kindness." The hand he put to his simple waistcoat dropped to his side and he took a step toward Nicholas, his blue eyes more animated. "I beg of you, who are you that I might put a name to your generosity?"

"Nicholas Edwards." Nicholas stuck out his hand, forgetting until now they hadn't spoken of names. "And you, sir? I have a feeling I'll never forget this day."

"Franklin." The inventor accepted his hand, giving his palm a firm shake before letting go. "Benjamin Franklin. And neither will I." He clasped the front of his waistcoat, his chest raised. "It has been to my greatest fortune to have met you. If you're ever in Pennsylvania, I'd be happy to show you my workshop." He tipped the fur hat forward. "Good day, sir. I hope the day is as bright for you as you have made mine."

Thoughts circling, Nicholas watched Benjamin Franklin walk through the gates of the palisade. Franklin. The man he was almost certain Lewis was hunting. His childhood friend would want to know he'd been closer than he thought to finding him. Yet, Nicholas didn't like the possible ending to that scenario for the man he'd just spoken with.

Feeling torn between a friend's loyalty and what felt like casting judgement in an area he had no jurisdiction, he was unsure what to do.

The only thing he was sure of was that he didn't need an audience with the king of France anymore. Franklin had given him the answer he'd come to Paris to find.

Chapter 34

"Mon amie, are you sure?"

Charlotte handed the leather-bound notebook to Louise. She'd always planned the exchange to occur but seeing the way her friend's mouth dropped made the decision even more satisfying. "I'm certain." She pressed the notebook further into Louise's palm as if affirming that outcome. "These will be a lot more useful here. I want you to have them."

"But these are your sketches, *your* designs." Louise's mouth gaped, her tone fervent as if imploring her to reconsider. "Surely, you would want to take them with you back to the colonies?"

Charlotte had thought about that. Now that things had come to an end here in France with the vicomte, she wasn't sure what to do once she arrived home. She'd apologize for her failed attempt to acquire the business deal her aunt so desperately needed, but what after that?

Farm life after Paris wasn't on the top of her list, though farm life had never been a part of that list even before she'd left the colonies.

Taking inspiration from her aunt, the thought of opening her own shop came into mind, if only briefly. She was well-suited for drawing, but she was slow in the lace craft and her needleworking was lacking, especially compared to Louise's skill at the dentelle. Besides, if the opportunity did somehow arise, she felt sure she could come up with more patterns back home while Louise needed them here, at least for a little while.

"Just think of them as something to remember me by." She let her voice soften to a whisper, eyeing the small group of women sitting in a semi-circle a few feet away needleworking lace. One in particular with tawny brown hair held her interest. "How is she doing?"

"They are perfect. And she is doing well." A sad smile spread across Louise's face, her eyes sweeping over the group of women at work. "She is catching on quickly with the needlework."

Charlotte had noticed. Where it took her a few days to complete one repeat of a simple lace motif, Sophie had completed the same pattern in a single afternoon. She was a quick learner and didn't give up easily—maybe reasons she'd been able to survive in the slums of Paris so well. Here, she was already becoming an asset—an extra pair of hands and wit Louise and her mother would benefit from as the speed of finished pieces quickened and the affordability of regular medicine became more attainable.

Louise hugged the notebook, a tear trailing its way down the apple of her cheek. "But I will miss you, mon amie."

"I'm going to miss you too." Hearing the break in her own voice, Charlotte swallowed. Louise had been one of her constants, keeping her grounded during her stay in Paris.

"Are you all packed?"

Charlotte nodded, forcing a knot that had lodged itself in her throat and seeing her friend through blurry vision. "I have preparations to depart in the morning. My ship leaves in two days' time." After Marc's trial had kept her an extra day, she'd had to make new arrangements.

"My mother would like to see you before you leave. I know it." Louise gave a smile colored with sadness that made the present pain of departing only more bitter. "What about Marc?" Her voice went hushed. "Have you heard anything from the ruling?"

"I haven't." Charlotte closed her eyes, shaking her head.

"It's been three days since you went on the stand to testify. What are they waiting for?"

Charlotte went silent, wondering the very same thing. She didn't know why the verdict was taking so long, but the time had also left her with an ill feeling as if a bad omen. She cupped at Louise's elbow, leading her further away from the group of girls in the dentelle. Though Marc wasn't her favorite person by any means, she felt his current condition, especially when death could be the outcome, should remain private.

She kept her voice low, leaning into Louise even when the judged distance from others seemed sufficient. "I was wondering if the delay was meant for a public hanging. Marc's trial was on Saturday and traditionally there are no punishments given on Sundays. After you told me about the market on the Place de Grève on Mondays, I went there yesterday to see."

It was an admittance that felt strange, guilt settling in her stomach like a heavy stone. Even if she hadn't gone to be a mere spectator, waiting to see if Marc might be brought out on the scaffold felt like a betrayal to him.

"And . . .?" Louise brought her hand to her mouth.

"He wasn't there." The answer came quickly. In fact, she'd been thankful there were no executions that day at all—a gift for a sight she might not ever be able to unsee.

The door of the dentelle clicked open, drawing Louise's attention first, then Charlotte's. A sharp gust of wind blew over Claudine's perfectly pinned coiffure, though leaving not one strand out of place.

The door shut again, the girls in their semi-circle having paused their chattering and work to gaze at the fine noblewoman that had come to grace them with her presence. Though flushed, Claudine's expression was otherwise indecipherable, Charlotte unable to read if her face warranted bad news or good.

Not daring to speak, as if the slightest puff of air could alter the tension one way or another, Charlotte held her breath.

Claudine took a breath for her, the woman's eyes brightening as they met Charlotte's. Her footsteps quickly swept past the girls in the semi-circle until she reached she and Louise.

"Marc has been ruled innocent." She gave an abbreviated laugh, a slight tremor holding in her voice. Claudine kissed Charlotte on each cheek, a French custom Charlotte had seen among women embracing each other. "You did it, chérie, you and your account."

Hardly deserving of such praise or Claudine's sign of close affection, Charlotte stepped back. "I only told them what happened."

"But you made a decision to tell the truth and I know what that cost you."

Claudine had no way of knowing the full scale of what Paris's parliament had asked of her. Yet, Charlotte couldn't help but feel the woman had been privy to some part of the meeting.

In short, they wanted to know everything, even what happened at Marc's apartment when he started painting her portrait. Only then was she grateful for Nicholas not being permitted into the room.

Claudine untied a set of ribbons that secured a hoodless cloak around her shoulders as if the shawl bore something greater around her neck than just warmth. The action made Charlotte mindful of the weight she'd imagined the woman was carrying for her brother. "It is thanks to you that my brother is alive."

That couldn't be true. Charlotte felt her jaw go slack, her gut caving inward. "Surely there must've been more witnesses, or even accounts in favor of your brother's character?"

"My brother's character is not deemed so favorable in the French court with his current views. As for other witnesses—" She withdrew the garment from around her neck, allowing it to rest on the back of an empty chair as she closed her eyes. "None came forward."

Charlotte's throat went tight as if an invisible noose needed loosening. To think Marc's innocence may have relied on her sole willingness to come forward. And even then, she hadn't expected her testimony would do much for him.

What had Laurent told her? Parliament would struggle to take her seriously—especially a woman. He didn't seem to think so either, so why would she expect differently in a room with over a hundred men in powdered wigs and robes? The question warranted answers.

"As relieved as I am your brother is safe from the gallows, I'm still skeptical I had anything to do with how that came to be."

"I take it you mean Monsieur Girard's comment about your credibility as a woman?" Claudine's tone contained ice. She strode over to one of the tables of lace, picking up a piece as if to admire the pattern, one completed by Sophie. "Though I hate to admit, he was right. It wasn't enough alone. According to the Vicomte de Vantinelle, the very notion was brought up in resounding unison throughout the room."

Charlotte folded her arms, noticing Sophie had stopped her work in the semi-circle to view Claudine's interest in her finished product. "Then how . . .?"

Claudine's gaze fixed to Sophie before back to Charlotte. "It was argued that the likeliness of you saying anything false to defend my brother was an outlandish notion after his public ridicule of you at Les Muses de Versailles. In fact, the very idea of you testifying at all on his behalf surprised many. For that, they deemed the testimony trustworthy."

Charlotte's arms fell to her sides. Then Laurent was right about that too. They hadn't forgotten. Strangely, this time it had been to her benefit and to Marc's too.

"What was the vote count?" The question escaped before Charlotte could bar it. Only the outcome truly mattered. She knew that. There was no good reason for why she wanted to know, only that she did.

"72 to 71." Claudine returned the lace piece to the table she'd lifted Sophie's work from, eyeing the child another time.

"So close." Louise let out a gasp. "Who was the deciding vote?"

"Someone you have made quite an impression on and held several conversations with." Claudine tipped a smile in Charlotte's direction.

The first clue wasn't much help, considering she'd made such a sour impression in French court, one she'd have to live with and would rather not. But the second—she'd had many conversations, but only two people that would fit in the categories of being a member of Parliament and someone she'd spoke with more than once. Neither made sense.

"Monsieur Laurent Girard?" Charlotte hadn't felt as confident about his vote toward Marc's favor after seeing him before the trial, but maybe he'd changed his mind.

Claudine huffed, her eyes blazing. "Try again."

Then that left only— "The Vicomte de Vantinelle?" Her lip dropped in disbelief when Claudine's smile resurfaced and confirmed she'd correctly guessed this time.

"But I thought you said he hated Marc?" Louise's voice, aimed at her, was filled with as much confusion as Charlotte felt.

"The vicomte does not hate anyone. That, I can assure you." Claudine stood tall, resuming the poise of aristocratic grace Charlotte was used to seeing. She walked about the dentelle again, seeming oblivious to the circle of girls who tried not to stare, but were most definitely watching her with admiration.

"I came to tell you the news and also to invite you this evening to my estate." Her boots, much more suitable for the outdoors of the city than the marble and parquet floors of Versailles, still managed to glide across the dentelle floor as if she were wearing her slippers. "We shall have a grand celebration and I have a surprise for you." Claudine veered her attention from Charlotte to Louise. "You must also come, mademoiselle."

"Me, madame?" Louise's brow lifted as she pressed the notebook still in her hands into her chest.

"Oui." She looked to each of them. "You two will be my honored guests." A twinkling grin emerged. "And please extend my invitation to that captain of yours. He is also welcomed to join."

"But madame—" Louise stepped toward Claudine, her mouth nearly gaping. "I do not know what I have done to deserve such honor."

Claudine brought her cloak around her shoulders, fastening the two silk ribbons. "I am not so ignorant to the beauty you have shown to Paris, both in and out of the French court." Her grin softened at Louise, though her eyes hinted pleasure. She swept her gaze around the room at the various lace before setting her sights on Sophie who was in the middle of a chain stitch. If the girl caught the hint related to her, she hadn't shown it.

"Oh, merci, madame!" Louise clutched at her throat, elation in her tone. "I do not know what to say."

Having finished tying the ribbons in a neat, little bow, Claudine took both of Louise's hands into her own. The difference of Louise's calloused fingers from lacemaking in Claudine's unblemished ones was striking. Even still, there was something significant about the moment. "Say that you'll come." When she'd received a nod affirming as much, Claudine made for the door. "In the meantime, I have preparations to make."

High-pitched squeals rang from the girls in the semi-circle, including Louise when the door closed, but Charlotte couldn't quite join in. Marc had been freed, a celebration worth commemorating and one she'd be happy to attend, but what did Claudine mean by a surprise?

An unease settled in her chest. The last surprise she'd been a part of was her near undoing, thanks to Marc. Claudine was nothing like her brother, but after everything at French court, she couldn't help but feel torn between welcoming and fearing the idea.

Chapter 35

Charlotte rapped on the door to Nicholas's room at the boardinghouse. When no answer came, she went back to her own room and scribbled a note with the necessary details of the evening before cutting through a quaint courtyard. Her breath went out from her lungs as a fogged vapor until she returned back inside the boardinghouse and into the common room.

Not a soul resided, though that wasn't surprising given the late afternoon hour.

The smell of something savory grabbed her nose from the kitchen, telling her she wasn't alone. She waited a few minutes to see if anyone had heard her come in. When it became clear no one was coming anytime soon, she made her presence known.

"Excuse me, is anyone here?" She gave her voice volume, and though asking, she let her tone hold expectation.

No answer.

Not about to be done, she marched over to a nearby door, almost certain the help she needed was on the other side.

She knocked hard, making sure she was heard. Instead of asking this time, she made her demands plain.

"Excuse me, I need to leave a note for someone." Her voice carried again as she leaned into the closed door. The smell of beef, onion and spices grew more pronounced.

Feeling the impulse to charge through, she fought for restraint. She needed to get this message to Nicholas. She'd somehow managed to keep her body from charging, but her mouth had other ideas.

"He's a guest staying here. Captain Nicholas Edwards."

Thinking of her captain, and not knowing what else to say, only that she wasn't about to move on without seeing her request attended to, the next words slipped off her tongue without much thought as to how they might sound out loud.

"He's about a foot taller than myself." She closed her eyes as air went out through her nose, realizing the comment was unhelpful without her being in the same space as the person she was talking to.

She tried again, envisioning Nicholas like he was there. She saw him as he was back at the Whitfords', out of his uniform and even unshaven on some days, but wholly relaxed.

The thought of him warmed her. It was a side she'd seen of him that she'd like to see more of, but not an accurate description of the Royal Navy officer she knew was necessary during his time on duty in Paris.

"He'll be in a blue uniform. He's handsome with a nice, clean cut for both head and face and striking blue eyes under a prominent blonde brow line."

There. She was satisfied with her description, but not the fact no one had come to answer her call. One last time before she was going through that door.

"Please." The expectation in her tone was peppered with supplication this time. "It's quite important that he receives this message while I'm gone. I'm sure you've seen him. He's—"

She heard a clearing of someone's throat behind her. "Here to get your message."

Charlotte froze, then turned. "Nicholas."

A mixture of feelings emerged, seeing she hadn't been completely correct in her description. His face was shaved, but he wasn't in uniform. She was glad to see him and to know her note would get to its intended recipient, but what all had he heard?

She gave him a scolding look. "How long have you been standing there?"

"Long enough to know that message is for me." He gave her that grin that told her enough, making her face grow warm before the heat spread to the rest of her body.

"It's nice to know you think I'm handsome. I was starting to wonder. Now that I'm here"—his chin dipped to the paper in her hand—"why don't you tell me what's in that note and leave who's trying to get dinner ready tonight alone."

Feeling like she'd been caught, because she had, she angled herself away from the door, taking a step back from the kitchen. "It's an invitation, actually." Her eyes dropped to the note, then flew up to his face, finding consolation she'd been at least correct with some of her description. His eyes were as blue as the sea she'd sailed across with him.

"Invitation?"

She pulled the envelope Claudine had given her at the dentelle that morning from her reticule. "Claudine is having a formal party at her estate this evening."

"And I'm invited?" He glanced at the invitation before raising an eyebrow.

"We all are. As a matter of fact, you'll be dining in excellent company. She pulled her shoulders back, looking at him more directly. "Louise and I are the honored guests."

His smile gentled before returning to the invitation. "I'm glad Louise gets to partake. I also take the cause for celebration means everything went well with the trial and Marc is okay."

"If you mean well enough to where Marc is alive, then yes." She placed Claudine's invitation back into her reticule, wondering if things had gone as she'd hoped for Nicholas. If they had, he gave no indication. "How was Versailles?" She made herself look as if searching for the box she'd given him, though fully trusting he'd completed the task. "Did you have any problems making the delivery?"

"Problems, not really. Surprises, yes." His smile tipped to one side as he looked at her like she'd been caught in a game of mischief.

She played innocent again, but this time taking more steps away from the kitchen door and joining him at the end of a large, communal table. "Oh? What kind of surprises?" She plopped her chin onto her knuckles like a silly girl, but she couldn't help her excitement.

"The royal kind. Of which I'm to express the queen's gratitude for your gift." His gaze remained steady on her, filling with what she read as appreciation. "And my own for what you and Louise did for me by getting an audience with Her Majesty."

Charlotte leaned in, her stomach in a flutter of anticipation. "Does that mean you were able to meet with the king?"

"No."

Though softened, the smile still on his face confused her. Had she heard right?

"No?" She searched for an alternative explanation. "Then the queen spoke on your behalf to him?"

"No."

Her hand slammed down on the table's surface, infuriated. "I was so sure it would work."

"It did."

"But you just said you *didn't* meet with the king."

Glancing at her fingers spread out on the table, he took them into his. "Which is true. It turns out, I didn't need to." He brought her fingertips to his mouth and kissed them, his lips gentle on her skin while a chill shot up her spine. "I got the answer I came for, just not in the way I planned, thanks to you." His tender expression held for a moment before his mouth upturned reminding her of something bittersweet, the bitter part now winning out. "Unfortunately, because of that, I'm leaving for London tonight."

"Tonight?" If Nicholas was leaving tonight, this moment might very well be the last time she saw him. She felt a void she hadn't experienced before. Her only salve was that she viewed the same tension in his jawline that she felt in her chest.

"The information is urgent and overdue. King George needs to know. I have a responsibility to make sure he does. Not to mention, I need to follow through with the Cadwells. I need to get that all behind me."

A feeling she understood completely. What awaited her in Portsmouth—namely her aunt's sore disappointment and the impact of her family's tainted reputation, was also something she wanted behind her.

The journey ahead seemed so long and not just because she would spend months on the ocean to get there. Aunt Sylvia had put faith in her—a thread that tied good news from elsewhere to her family's well-being. But with her plans having come unraveled with the vicomte, she felt as if she were clutching frayed fragments that were dangerously close to snapping. And what would she find when she got home? Suddenly the two-month voyage didn't seem long enough.

She was glad Nicholas could look ahead to a brighter outcome. He'd carried the burden of his assignment longer than she had for her aunt's business deal. Now it was time for some of that burden to come off, though questions arose.

His fingers coaxed the inside of her palm, making those questions even more difficult to voice. "I know you can't give me the details, but do you expect you'll be returning to the colonies?"

"As soon as I can."

His lack of hesitation and the promise she heard in his voice gave her something she held tight to.

The smile she loved returned and he kissed her lips, she breathing him in. His lips brushed hers tenderly before pressing firm against her own with a longing she felt too.

It was a good thing they weren't alone—not caring to take the moment they had before them, yet not having the temptation to go too far.

When they released, a mild burning in her calves told her she'd raised to the balls of her feet to meet him—a sensation she could get used to if given the chance.

"I know you haven't agreed to marry me, and I think I understand why for now." He gave her a knowing glance, one that told her he aimed to change that outcome. "But would you mind if I wrote you?"

"Would I mind?" She looked up at him, her tone feigning an edge. "Nicholas, I expect nothing short of it, especially from you."

That brought on a smile. "Good." His smile sobered. "And there's something else—something I'm not ordering you to do, mind you, but asking."

She felt she would do anything for this man, he already having done so much for her. "And what is that?"

"To see the doctor before you leave."

She resisted the urge to break away from him, knowing how little time they had left. "But Nicholas, I feel fine."

"And you seem fine, which is why I'm confused. Not that I don't mind the outcome, but I'm a person who likes to understand how things work. If the doctor can figure out what's behind those attacks of yours, then maybe there's a way to stop them."

She didn't stop herself from rolling her eyes, but his reasoning was sound. "Fine."

"Good." Triumph stretched across his face. "I'll be leaving for Calais shortly. There are a few things I need to take care of before then, but is there anything I can do for you before I go?"

"No. I'm meeting Louise at the dentelle to get ready for this evening. You carry on."

This time she feigned a smile. She'd wanted to whisper "stay" but didn't, knowing that decision would cost him, and she didn't want to become a debt in his life. But saying goodbye to this man, even as she knew she would see him again, was more difficult than she realized it would be.

***

"I still can't believe I am here." Louise took in a breath. Their current view was at an elaborate grand staircase with an iron balustrade that curved upward to the next floor.

"And why not?" Charlotte fell in step with Louise as they followed Claudine's concierge further into the vast estate. "You're an honored guest, after all."

"I suppose." Her friend stepped slowly, her gaze wandering at the same pace over intricate paintings that adorned the walls of the hallway as if capturing them to her memory.

They crossed a polished marble floor until they were led into the grand salon.

"C'est magnifique!" Louise's mouth fell open at the warm glow of a magnificent crystal chandelier above them that not only served as the center point of the room but illuminated the light blue paneled walls.

Having already seen this room from the first time she'd attended the opera with Claudine, Charlotte could only feel a certain admiration since her visits to Versailles. The room's interior was not as opulent as anything she'd seen at the grande château, but there was something sophisticated and stunning about the space that Charlotte suspected reflected the room's designer.

"I'm glad my honored guest approves."

With hardly a moment to fully appreciate the elegant space, the two women turned to face their equally elegant hostess adorned in an emerald green, velvet robe à la française.

"It is as lovely as you are, madame." Louise gave a deep curtsy, no doubt sincere in both the compliment and the action.

"And it is an honor to have you in my home." Claudine returned Louise's gesture before she looked to Charlotte, giving a slight frown. "But where is your captain?"

Though she knew the inquiry was coming, the mention of Nicholas still sent pains of longing inside. Charlotte forced a smile, not wanting her thoughts of Nicholas to cloud tonight's celebration for both Louise and Marc. "On his way to London."

"No doubt he has news to deliver." Claudine gave a serene nod, turning away from the salon. "Come, the other guests will want to know you have arrived."

"Other guests?" Louise took a step backward into the salon as if seeking refuge in the exquisite surroundings, the rubied color of Claudine's borrowed dress swaying with the movement. "You mean besides Marc?"

"Why of course." Claudine's easy tone was matched with an encouraging smile as if to tame any worry Louise might be feeling. "They are anxious to meet the lacemaker of Paris who has so stirred the queen's appreciation with her masterful craftsmanship these past months, and especially her new lace gloves."

"Then they must also be anxious to meet the designer." Appearing less anxious than a moment ago, Louise stepped forward again and put a hand to Charlotte's elbow.

Knowing her friend was including her, Charlotte felt grateful for this kinship. But she didn't need the recognition and here in France it did her little good. She'd be leaving Paris soon, but for Louise and her mother at the dentelle, tonight was a big accomplishment, perhaps life changing.

Claudine gave a graceful turn of her neck, drawing attention to a green stone matching her dress perfectly. "Yes, in time." Her gaze rested on Charlotte. "But first I must ask Mademoiselle Thatcher to wait here in the salon. This room is much more suitable to a private conversation."

There was something in Claudine's expression that Charlotte couldn't decipher.

"After you have finished, you may join us in the grand salon where the rest of the guests are gathered." Taking Louise's arm into her own, Claudine walked out the door, Louise soon falling in step beside their hostess until the two women were out of sight.

A private conversation? Charlotte retraced her steps back into the salon, having watched the women go. The only person that came to her mind was Marc. But she'd relayed all that she needed to the day of his arrest. There was nothing more to add, not from her, anyway.

A chaise near a kindled fire seemed inviting enough, but Charlotte preferred to stand, feeling she should be somewhat on guard for her upcoming conversation with Marc. A portrait above the mantle of a young man with his hair tied back in a neat queue apart from a curl nearing the corner of his eye caught her attention. She was certain she'd never met him, yet he looked familiar somehow, someone she knew in a younger face.

She squinted, inspecting the painting on the wall from her place on the floor. His high cheekbones, his steadfast eyes—the resemblance uncanny and bringing up questions she'd have to address with Claudine when given the chance. "Is that . . .?"

"Victor."

Charlotte snapped her neck from the painting of the youth to the man she least expected to see at a dinner party held in her honor.

"Monsieur le vicomte de Vantinelle?" She blinked, not certain her eyes weren't deceiving her. When the supposed trick of her mind didn't depart, she braced herself for what might very well become an unpleasant conversation. "I must admit, this is a surprise."

"I think that was my sister-in-law's intention." He offered her two things she hadn't anticipated. One, a smile that heightened handsome features in his older age and two—

"Your sister-in-law?" She slowly put the rest together. "Claudine is your relation?"

"Oui."

Yes. The one word confirmed the connection. His face turned down the hallway Charlotte had seen Claudine and Louise go with a look that conveyed devotion. "Like Victor, my brother, Andre, was also killed in the last war. We have both helped each other pick up the pieces of the past."

Reading the truth in the man's overall demeanor, Charlotte chose that moment to take a seat on the chaise.

"I am sorry to have kept our relationship covert, but we wanted to know more of who Sylvie's niece truly was before committing to an enterprise with her." He walked over to the couch where she remained dumbfounded, his face missing the hardness she'd become used to seeing. "And Claudine mentioned you were already set on seeking her out at the party of Monsieur Laurent Girard." He gave a shrug as if to say the opportunity had been available for the taking.

"Yes." Finding difficulty with keeping her attention focused on the man who'd rejected her offer, Charlotte was drawn again to the painting of the young man. The likeness of the youth held no room for doubt.

"And Victor—" She turned to the portrait, remembering the name the vicomte had used and sensing from that same moment something spoken out of a father's pride. "He's your son." And whose memory she'd mistakenly defiled in her comment about war at their first encounter.

A smile laced with years of loss confirmed what was unmistakably clear to her now.

"His mother passed away years ago, long before his own death in the colonies." He sucked in a breath, held back emotion betrayed only by his voice. "I'm glad you get to see him. More people should have had the privilege to know him." His view remained fixed on the painting. "That was one of Marc's first."

"One of Marc's?" Her mouth nearly fell open with disbelief. "And *you* bought it?"

To hear the man laugh, even in the pit of heartache, was something more foreign to her than the high coiffures of Versailles, but she welcomed the change.

"Marc and I don't always see things from the same view, but he is family as you now understand. We have very different methods of expressing our opinions to the current problem in our country, but we hold to the same opinion." His face darkened with determination. "Something has to change, and will change in time, whether from a declaration of His Majesty or an uprising of the nation. The people of France, especially the working class, will no longer stand aside after being pushed too far and I'm afraid the war we are soon to find ourselves in will only spur a movement we cannot ignore."

The bows lining Charlotte's stomach from top to bottom straightened out at the word she couldn't seem to get away from, though not fully understanding. "France is at *war?*"

"You have not heard?" There was nothing condescending about his expression like she'd envisioned in a conversation with Marc, the latter man withholding information only to tease her. In fact, the vicomte looked content enough to tell her what she wanted to know.

"The king has effectively signed an order to offer France's aid to the war in the American colonies. Soon the cries of liberty and justice will be heard in the ears of Frenchmen." A quiet intensity laced his words and she couldn't help think about how differently Marc would view that outcome.

"That seems like something Marc would be proud to boast about."

The vicomte only nodded. "I foresee so too, which is why he is not here."

"He's not here?" She stood, trying to make sense of what that meant. Had he been taken prisoner again, or perhaps not been let go after all? "But I thought this celebration tonight was for his release?"

"Which certainly is the case, no thanks to Monsieur Girard."

The man didn't snap, his noble upbringing reminding her much like Claudine's in refusing to allow the behavior, but he'd come close just now.

"But under the circumstances of the trial, we thought it safer for him to stay outside the city with some relatives of ours, at least for the time being." A smile brimmed at the corners of his mouth again. "As for the occasion, Claudine has spoken true. Tonight is for you in making his release possible and for commemorating a new business partnership."

She opened her mouth, closing her lips again, her interest about Marc suddenly fading. Had she heard correctly? "A business partnership?"

"Your war overseas has now become our war. As such, the need for building and repairing French ships both here and across the Atlantic will be great." His tone was unemotional and straightforward like the business meetings she'd attended with her aunt. He didn't look like a man who enjoyed the outcome, but he did look like a man who knew how to make an opportunity out of it.

"It will be good to have an ally there and is a good business decision. That is why I have decided to offer a contract between your aunt and myself."

Hearing her breath catch, she worked to curb her elation. "Monsieur Vantinelle, on my aunt's behalf, I am certainly grateful for the opportunity, especially that this agreement benefits both parties."

She could learn from this man if given a chance, but she wasn't so sure she deserved that chance.

She put a hand to one of the bows lining her sternum, treading carefully, but truthfully. "But given your obvious dislike of me and your excellent reputation in the area of French business, I can't help but be a little surprised you didn't go another route. There are more lumber yards in the colonies you'd be able to take your pick from, all of which wouldn't include me in the process."

He gave a slow, single nod, Charlotte hearing a light hum in his throat. "As with Marc, you and I certainly have our differences. That is true." The gold threading of his waistcoat rose and fell with a deep breath. "But you have also shown an incredible amount of your character, mademoiselle. I have seen your boldness. When not disrespecting French etiquette but directed in a useful way, that boldness is a great advantage. And I am not ignorant of the lacemaker's shop you have been working at, nor the way you helped Marc despite his inexcusable conduct at Les Muses de Versailles."

He gave a smirk accompanied with a pointed glance. "Or the fact you spoke with my foreman, inquiring about his employer for another option."

She recalled the day she'd seen the vicomte by the Seine River and had spoken with—

Her mouth went dry. "That foreman was . . . *your* employee? But I thought he said his employer was the owner of the Chateau de la Chênaie?"

"He is correct. I own a small estate in the country where I usually spend the warmer months."

"Then the letter I sent to the owner of the Château de la Chênaie was . . .?" She winced at how much she had missed.

He presented an opened letter written in her own hand. "I was eager to visit the sender of this letter after what happened that day on the Seine. You can imagine I was quite surprised to find the address belonged to a boardinghouse in Paris and the sender having left for London. Even more to discover who'd stayed in the room at the time the note was written."

"I'm sorry. If I would've known I wouldn't have tried to—" She stopped, realizing what she was about to say wouldn't be true, not at that point in her life.

"You were trying to help your aunt when I had refused you." Fine lines formed at the edges of his eyes, she reading a kindness in his expression that told her he harbored no ill will. "When you first approached me about the contract, I did not know you. Between what Claudine has informed me of and what I have seen with my own eyes, I know enough." His chin raised in a way as if to solidify that very notion. "And I am choosing to take a chance on you, Miss Thatcher."

Chapter 36

The grand doors to the Council Chamber of St. James's palace shut behind Nicholas with a loud thud. Nicholas surveyed the room as several pairs of eyes darted back at him.

A man in military dress was at one side of the table, leaning over a map spread out upon the table's surface, and by the look of things, had held the room's attention until Nicholas walked in.

"Captain." The king in a richly embroidered frock of red wool and gold braiding was seated at the head of the table accompanied by a group of advisors. His chin rose from its resting place on his fist. "I take it you have news for me."

Doubting his news would be of any real aid by what he'd walked in on—the strong hinting of a military meeting—Nicholas stepped forward. Even if his findings had come late, he would still be expected to give his account.

"Of great importance, sir." He bowed his head, feeling a respect for not only the leader of his country, but for what this man had the power to do.

"Good." The king gave an expressionless nod. "I've heard rumors France is backing the colonies. Does what you found out support this claim?" A motion of his hand told Nicholas to take the place at the opposite side of the table where the officer over the map took a seat in an empty chair beside him.

"I'm afraid it does, Your Majesty." Nicholas recalled his run-in with Benjamin Franklin, the American ambassador, and his audience with Marie Antionette. "A diplomat from the colonies has not only captured the popularity of the French aristocracy but Louis Auguste's purse as well."

Silent expectation from each person in the room, especially King George, probed him to go on.

"The colonists are receiving financial aid and possibly arms, though there hasn't been confirmation of troops as of yet."

"News we shouldn't be surprised to hear given our history with the French, Your Grace." A man in a black frock less ornamented than the king's red and gold coat spoke.

"No, but not welcomed nevertheless." A muscle in the king's jaw twitched. A tension in the room grew heavy as if King George were speaking to all present instead of the man who had just spoken.

"King Louis knows our military is the best in the world on both sea and land. He won't send troops until he's confident of a victory." The man in a scarlet military uniform who'd been leaning over the maps on the table rose to speak. "Right now, they are executing their revenge from the previous war by aiding our current adversary. A sting from a bee—a nuisance, yes. Painful, but not fatal."

Nicholas felt a tension grip his shoulders. No, not fatal. But still a warning. The British had taken New York over the winter, but the colonists were proving over and again they were a formidable foe. Henry Knox had surprisingly arrived in Boston last year with a large artillery of cannon to take the city and the colonists had even formed a navy of their own. Not to mention their less than structured tactics on the field were earning them advantages. What would happen if France did end up sending troops?

The king put a fist up to his mouth, his fingers just below lips that thinned in the flickering candlelight. He gave a slow sigh despite the encouragement from his general. "We might be in this mess longer than I anticipated."

It wasn't news Nicholas hoped for—not when a longer war meant an amount of debt that continued to pile from the previous one and pull from the pockets of England's people. The Cadwells came to mind—already feeling the effects of life's hardships and not needing the extra cost of what was happening overseas added to them.

"Unless we pulled out from the war." Nicholas's thoughts broke free before his naval training kicked in to keep him silent.

"Pull out?" The king's chest rose against the Garter Star on the left side of his red coat as if to challenge the idea. Echoes of the same question came from around the table.

"Your Majesty," The man in the black coat stood, clear opposition in his expression to Nicholas's proposal. "To abandon the conflict will only give rise to further challenges over our dominance in other territories. If we allow the Americans to have their independence, we could weaken our own credibility as supreme."

King George signaled for the man to lower himself into his seat. For a moment his eyes, though alert to the current dilemma, seemed drawn to one of the paintings in the room of a man on horseback in military dress. "We'll have to watch the French closely." He nodded to the man in the dark frock who'd taken his seat again. "If they do decide to join the colonists' campaign in personage, we'll need more soldiers of our own. That will require more ships, Captain Edwards."

The king looked at Nicholas like they'd shared a mutual understanding, but whatever that understanding was, Nicholas hadn't comprehended.

The thought of the Cadwells' hardship and the impact upon his countrymen clouded his mind. And him? His own fate already written, much like it had been all his life—bound on a ship back to the colonies in due time. Not the way he'd planned, but at least he'd have the consolation of seeing Charlotte again.

"Ships that will require longevity in the chance this war lasts longer than we hoped." The ruler in the room gave Nicholas a pointed glance while his hands drew together in a steeple-like position. "I had the pleasure of speaking with a Mr. Fisher while you were in France—a shipbuilder in Liverpool. The Naval Board brought a letter of his and another to my attention."

His fingers folded into each other, showcasing a sapphire stone in gold mounting. "Interestingly, he also encouraged the idea of copper sheathing as you first presented. His reason, however, stemmed less from the miners' plight in Cairnhaven and more from tactile advantage—not just with the length added to a ship's lifespan, but with how many ships can be built when a crew doesn't have to tackle against marine life in the process. Both perspectives hold much benefit to our nation, especially in a time of war. To your luck, Captain Edwards, Parliament appears to agree and so do I. The copper mines in the Parys Mountain are being excavated for the project and the mines in Cairnhaven will be reopened to add to the effort. Mr. Fisher has wholeheartedly agreed to oversee the plating of the first fleet."

The king gave a regal nod, a hint of a smile barely surfacing at the corners of his mouth. "Congratulations, Captain. It seems you have not only a mind for the sea, but also innovation. You've done the Crown a great service with both your news from France and with our ship industry. The question is, what will you do now?"

Nicholas swallowed back his shock. He'd been told nearly all his life what to do, expectations that held fast like an anchor gripping the seabed, unyielding to the current's strength. But now, the man who had more power than his father was asking him a question he'd never thought he'd hear.

"Thank you, Your Majesty." He bowed low, gratitude lifting his neck again as if snatching a weight from his spine. "If my service in the Navy has led to such satisfaction, I'd like to make a request concerning the nature of it." He glanced at the other men in the room, both the news and commendation granting him a renewed resolve. "In a private setting please, sir."

Taking another bow, Nicholas found to both his satisfaction and relief, the king gave another nod. "Very well, Captain." He lifted his chin, rounded, but balanced with the rest of his face, to the men in the room already reading the signal by raising from their seats and gathering various items from the table. "Give us the room, gentlemen."

"Another request to improve upon the nature of the Royal Navy, no doubt?" King George's mouth curved into a languid smile when the room had cleared.

Despite the good humor he'd read in the king's expression, Nicholas's body went taut again. "No, sir. One to leave it."

"To *leave* it?" The smile upturned as skin bunched at the top of the king's prominent nose, Nicholas reading confusion rather than anger in the change. "Your father is an admiral, and you are on your way. Are you sure you want to leave such a legacy behind?"

He was. The Navy was his father's legacy, not his own. Like Charlotte, he wasn't interested in war. He'd seen enough to know there was more destruction than good that came as a result, and he'd had enough. Though he believed God could make the best of humanity's worst, Nicholas wanted no part in the desolation. Rather, his desire was to bring about restoration and improvement and not just for the country he was born into but to all humanity if he could.

***

"You're doing what?"

With a resoluteness driven both by naval experience and conviction, Nicholas stood at his father's bedside, fully expecting his father's terse reaction. "I've been commissioned to explore innovations around the world." Feeling pride with his new assignment, he found difficulty stifling a smile.

"*Inventions*, you mean." His father spat the word out like such vocabulary didn't belong anywhere on his tongue.

Refusing to yield on this matter, Nicholas kept his feet planted on the planked flooring as if preparing for battle. But his stance, though firm, wasn't as a navy officer preparing to fight, only defend if need be. "There are a number of great minds outside of our country that England can benefit from. Who knows what we can learn from each other?"

The Admiral grunted, raising his torso from a pillow supporting his back. "Nicholas, there's a certain way of doing things—a certain expectation. The world isn't ready—"

"The world is ready, Father, even if you're not. Change is coming and I want to be a part of that, but not in a war." Nicholas added another log to the fireplace in his father's bedroom to stifle the cold prick in the air. Though he doubted the added heat would be enough to truly warm this atmosphere.

"I suppose you're responsible for our newest change then—the copper plating project they've begun?"

Straightening from poking a log, Nicholas met his father's arrogant tone with narrowed eyes. "I was under the impression that news wasn't out yet."

"I'm on the board, remember?" A hard jutted jawline thrusted upward in Nicholas's direction.

Nicholas crossed his arms, perhaps a first in his father's presence. He eyed what was in plain view, his father still under sheets of bedding. "Yes, but you're also bed-bound, if only temporarily."

The attempt of a huff was interrupted by a small series of coughs. His father reached for a glass of water on his bedside table and took a sip. "More a nuisance than an obstacle." He cleared his throat seeming to have found his voice again. "You'd be surprised what a letter can accomplish even bedside."

"A letter?" The king mentioned there was another letter from the Naval Board, but Nicholas didn't think to ask. The extra letter hadn't seemed important in his conversation at the time, but now . . .

"You wrote to the board about my plan?"

His father took another gradual sip of water, his face lined with disinterest. "I merely mentioned the plan for review. Little did I know you already had the workings of one nearly settled through the shipbuilder in Liverpool and His Majesty's support." He shrugged. "Doesn't appear my input was needed." The man never smiled, and he didn't now, but Nicholas could have sworn he heard one in his father's tone.

Feeling a thickness in his throat, Nicholas struggled to recover. "It was." Maybe not for the fate of the miners in Cairnhaven, but for him.

His father held his gaze for a moment, Nicholas feeling something start to shift between them. "Over there." His father quickly veered his attention to a mahogany wardrobe in his room. "Check my coat pocket."

Opening the cabinet, Nicholas saw the familiar blue inside. "Your old uniform." But it wasn't in the condition he expected it to be. The tailor had managed to get some of the blood stain out, but there were no signs of attempts at stitching the hole where the bullet had hit his father.

"I assume Felix couldn't salvage it."

"No. He's making me a new one, but it will take a few weeks. I had Wesley retrieve this one when I found out it was gone."

"Why keep it? Felix would've gotten rid of it for you. I'm sure." The man wasn't known to be sentimental. And even if he was, he doubted his father would want to remember the time he'd been shot so close to death.

"There was something I left inside, and I'd be cross if the tailor would've lost it." His current expression revealed that very truth. "Thankfully he has sense to check the pockets before tossing unusable fabrics." Even terse, Nicholas heard a compliment to the tailor.

"The doctor tells me I'll be living a more sedentary lifestyle because of my injury. He isn't keen on the idea of me stepping aboard a ship, so I'll be leading the rest of my naval career as a more active member of the Naval Board. Perhaps you could find better use of it." His father gave a resigned sigh, eyeing the tarnished uniform.

Intrigued, Nicholas reached into the inside breast pocket. His fingers grasped around an object that felt familiar, then let go. He took hold of the round carved metal again, hardly believing while his heart drummed inside his chest. Harrison's chronometer.

He felt his mouth open, but nothing came out, Nicholas wanting to acknowledge to his father what this meant to him. He had returned the chronometer to his father's apartment that night after the party, but never thought—

His father had kept his gift all this time. Again, words failed to come. Instead, a silence lapsed between them, the silence speaking more than words could ever convey over his whole life.

"I take you have a place in mind for your new commission?" His father spoke first, breaking the silence while flapping open the *London Gazette* that had been folded on his bedside table.

The sudden about-face for his father to put the topic back on Nicholas's current assignment broke the moment that changed everything for Nicholas regarding this man. But that was okay. He didn't need the moment to last any longer. Not when he had given up on this moment coming at all.

He did have a commission, one he was eager to carry out, but the headline he read on the backside of his father's newspaper now told him he needed to visit an old friend in Paris.

Nicholas's palm squeezed around the chronometer before he put Harrison's invention in his own coat pocket. "Yes, the colonies." But he was going to have to make a detour first.

Chapter 37

Portsmouth, Massachusetts 1777

Charlotte sat in a Queen Anne chair in her aunt's parlor, her breath short. Her heart galloped but not because of her ailment, her last episode having been months ago back at Les Muses de Versailles. She couldn't take her eyes off the small babe in her arms—a girl with chubby cheeks and despite being only a few weeks old, a thick head of dark hair that ran to the tiny nape of her neck.

"I'd ask how your first year of marriage has been, but I think I have my answer." Charlotte managed to pull her attention away from her new niece long enough to notice Abigail's cheeks had turned a guilty shade of pink. "Are there any other surprises I should know about?"

Her older sister sat across from her alongside their Aunt Sylvia on a settee while her youngest sister, Olivia, now well-over a full year old, played with a wooden rattle on the Persian rug.

"You already know about the medical aid we're giving the soldiers on both sides, so no." Abigail's tired eyes that also reflected pure joy stared back at her. "As far as Garrett and I are concerned, she's all."

Abigail said the word "all" like the most extraordinary thing wasn't cradled in her arms. Her older sister—a mother. And that wasn't the only thing she was doing. She and Garrett had managed to stay out of the fight while still playing a vital role in the war, treating the wounded.

Headlines of the *Continental Journal* her aunt was currently reading depicted how difficult such a mission would be to carry out and served as a present reminder of what Charlotte had been avoiding.

"What's that like for you on the ship?" Charlotte read the headline as her aunt flipped over the page. "Victory at Trenton: Washington Surprises the British and Boosts Patriot Morale."

"How have you managed to be so close to the conflict without having to engage in it?"

"Convincing King George was not a difficult task. He is also not ignorant to the fact I aided Washington's camp last year or how Garrett and I met." Abigail poked a needle through two pieces of fabric that would one day soon be her daughter's keepsake blanket. "The decision to have us offshore as a medical ship benefits all involved. Garrett gets to continue doing what he loves—serving the Royal Navy. And I get to continue treating patients while the king has been provided aid to his wounded soldiers." Her sister's needle came back through the fabric, the string gradually unbunching until the needle came down again. "I only wish we could tend to all the injured instead of just those on one side."

A thought Charlotte wasn't surprised hearing from her sister, but one she doubted King George would commission given the rebellion against him.

"And what do you call this little one?" Charlotte stroked her finger at the girl's hairline in the most careful way she knew how while breathing in the smell of fresh life and chamomile.

"Elizabeth."

Elizabeth. Tears welded up at her mother's memory and now namesake. She felt love and tenderness rather than painful regret thanks to Nicholas—and she suspected—highly more to God's healing.

Through blurred vision she smiled at her new niece again, then to her sister. "Where does she fit into all of this?"

"Where's she's supposed. With us, of course." Abigail's gentle response came naturally enough, small creases below her eyes sloping upward.

"On the ship—while you're in the middle of doctoring soldiers?" Something protective unleashed within Charlotte for the babe, though her sister had always been the more responsible of the two. Still, her stomach unsettled when she thought about the sick and injured soldiers around something that seemed so fragile.

Her sister brought the needle through the two materials again, taking her time and looking completely content. Abigail's patient reaction was a stark reminder of how different Charlotte and her sister truly were.

"Garrett takes her when I can't and if there's someone sick on board, we bring her to Aunt Sylvia's. It's been challenging, but it's worth it. We like having her with us." Abigail beamed in a way Charlotte knew that last sentence was an understatement.

"And—" Abigail put the blanket aside to reach under the settee where a rattle had rolled away from Olivia's reach on the floor. "—she'll have to get used to it, anyway. Even after the war ends, her father will still be in the Navy. It's in his blood. Now that he's a captain, he'll need a physician."

Charlotte didn't have to wonder who that physician was, but the news of Garrett's new rank gave her cheekbones height. "Give your husband my sincerest congratulations."

"Thank you. I will." Abigail took up her sewing again on the velvet couch, continuing to draw her needle in and out of the pieces of cloth.

Their aunt still had her eye on the paper, but Charlotte knew better. Aunt Sylvia would also be keen to every subject of the conversation.

"So, how did it happen, his promotion?"

"Garrett has always talked about Nick looking out for him like an older brother." Abigail brought the needle taut, her lips curving faintly with warmth. "It seems he still does."

"Yes, Nicholas does have an annoyingly altruistic way about him." Though in the past she might've thought the characteristic irksome, this time she only felt pride.

"Nicholas?" Her older sister paused in her sewing. "I've never heard you call him by his Christian name before. Has something changed between you two?"

Something had changed. Charlotte met her sister's inquiring gaze head-on while not missing the glimmer in her fatigued eyes. "A great deal, actually." She took a sip of her own coffee, working to soothe the agitation in her stomach while anticipation climbed for what else her sister's news might bring. "If Nicholas helped with Garrett's rank, does that mean he's in the colonies?"

A trumpet of geese above them sounded from outside signaling the birds' return from winter. Her view went to the window, feeling a yearning she couldn't seem to rid herself of nor cared to if Nicholas was close by.

"No. He's not here." Abigail's uplifted mouth crumbled, Charlotte hearing the same effect in her tone. "At least, not that I know of. We received the news about Garrett's rank from Admiral Graves. Orders directly from the king of England."

Charlotte reached for a smile that wouldn't come, trying to focus on the good news of her brother-in-law's promotion and dream made true.

Her niece stirred in her arms, making a sucking motion with her mouth.

"She's getting hungry. I'll go feed her." Abigail rose again from the settee and picked her daughter up from Charlotte's lap. Her sister nuzzled the babe's nose on the way out of the room.

Though her new niece deserved credit for much of the amazement, mostly because she hadn't known she existed, Charlotte couldn't help now but direct her gaze downward at the Persian rug. It seemed like only yesterday when she'd set out for France, yet there her little sister was, embarking on her own adventure with a new phase of life.

Olivia was taking steps to Aunt Sylvia, her small feet somehow managing to keep her balanced. She reached out to her aunt, her tiny voice commanding what she wanted with raised arms. "Up."

Not a woman normally so willing to give into demands, Aunt Sylvia laid the newspaper on a table in front of her, close enough for Charlotte to view a heading in bold type. "Franklin Woos the French: Speculation of French Support Grows."

"I can't believe how much has changed."

"You were gone for some time." Her aunt lowered her arms to Olivia, bringing the child beside her on the couch.

Guilt rose inside, her aunt simply speaking the truth. "I know. I'm sorry."

"Don't be, dear." Her aunt offered Olivia a cookie spiced with coriander, which her sister eagerly took, nibbling the sweet treat with delight. "Trust takes time, especially with the vicomte. The man has been through a serious hardship with the English and the matter of his son. In truth, I wasn't sure he'd accept the partnership with such history."

Aunt Sylvia wiped a piece of cookie and drool from Olivia's mouth with a napkin before placing her sister on her lap. "As for the rest of us, I'm glad to see hostilities from the radicals have lessened with the rumors that the independents are seeking out France's support." She eyed the *Continental Journal* and the headline Charlotte had read minutes ago. "Our family's new partnership overseas has people talking—this time in our favor. Your father should have a better return for his crops at the next harvest."

Though breathing in the good news, Charlotte hadn't missed the small detail her aunt included. She leaned forward in her seat while inclining her ear, not certain if she'd simply misheard. "*Our* family's partnership?"

"The Vicomte de Vantinelle was very clear concerning his stipulations to our contract."

"Stipulations?" Her aunt's pinched tone made Charlotte's stomach clench. The man hadn't mentioned any terms the last time she'd spoken with him. She scolded herself for not being more thorough. "What kind of stipulations?"

"The kind that makes you our business liaison, my niece." Her aunt pushed up a slow, gradual smile. "He will have no one else." The woman's gray eyes hinted at pleasure, even as her tone remained pragmatic.

"You mean I'll be overseeing trade between your company and the vicomte?" Charlotte's head lowered from her aunt to Olivia. Her sister cooed in her aunt's arms with heavy eyelids as Charlotte tried to digest the news.

"The vicomte was very impressed with your resourcefulness, citing examples of such while you were in France. Though he suggests refinement in your tactics—" Her tone held correction. "—he believes if any problems arise, you will be able to either find your way out of them or use them to your advantage. And I agree."

Hearing a measure of confidence in her aunt's words and still hardly believing the result, Charlotte had no words of her own.

"That is, if you want to." Her aunt stroked her sister's small torso as Olivia drifted into an afternoon nap. "I have already known the farm is not what you want, but is this?"

Not having pictured the scenario, Charlotte didn't know what to say at first. Her aunt was right concerning her feelings about the farm. But she'd never considered the idea of making travel a way of life. Yet doing so would allow her the opportunity for not only adventure, but to see Louise again—no doubt ample opportunity between trips to continue working on her sketches for the dentelle if they'd desired. She wasn't sure if she believed the vicomte wouldn't have anyone else, though part of her liked the idea if that were truly the case. Nevertheless, the call beckoned, and she wanted to answer.

"When do I leave for France again?" Her body rose in her seat, her wool skirt giving a soft sound with her change in position.

"The winter will break in a few weeks. It will be preferable for you to arrive when it does." Though her aunt's voice remained calm, Charlotte could hear the earnestness. The message didn't need to be outspoken to be understood loud and clear. Charlotte would need to leave right away.

A mixture of feelings worked their way through her, disappointment and elation finding themselves entangled together. This calling suited her, every piece of the venture ahead promising excitement. Apart from one crucial thing. While she would be on her way out of the colonies, it was very possible Nicholas would be on his way in.

Chapter 38

Paris, France 1777

Charlotte's carriage rode past the Hôtel de Beauvais as the driver pulled the horses toward the direction of the Marais district.

It was too soon to expect funds from their new partnership to supply her stay at the grand townhouse she'd first lodged at Paris, but maybe in time she might again if all worked well in their new arrangement.

Having secured a room at the boardinghouse, she ordered her tea service, paying the small fee that came with having the tea delivered to her room rather than at the large table in the common area. A small price after being aboard a brig for months on end with a crew of men for company.

Once alone in her own solitude, she removed her wool cloak and mittens. Her way to Paris from the port city of Le Havre contained sights of budding trees and workers preparing their fields for sewing new crops. A sure sign that spring had arrived, but the air was still chilly. She changed out of her Brunswick, a new traveling gown her aunt had made by the seamstress to commemorate her new position, and one that was tired from the trip.

She sipped her tea, the taste and smell of mint different than the tea she'd consumed for medicinal purposes in the past, but still satisfying in her room without a fireplace. Pulling her notebook from her trunk, she opened its pages where she still had a few pieces of blank paper to use. She retrieved her quill and ink and started to pen Claudine a note relaying her arrival to Paris.

After sealing the envelope, Charlotte put the finished letter in her reticule along with her notebook consisting of several new sketches before stepping back out on Paris's cobblestone streets.

On her way to deliver her letter for Claudine and the vicomte, she passed a boy waving this morning's newspaper around for someone to purchase. A small ache surfaced, Charlotte catching a glimpse of what she'd remembered seeing in Sophie's life.

She couldn't altogether say the boy wasn't really selling papers secondhand from a real vendor, but with the sun now setting and the papers in his hand looking as if they'd been tossed or stepped on in the city's muddy streets, she ventured a guess.

Feeling the prod to do something, even if small, she gave the boy a livre in exchange for one of the papers, though keeping her eyes firmly on her reticule.

She continued to the dentelle, her steps enlivened with excitement over her reunion and for Louise to view her drawings. She barely thought about the newspaper tucked under her arm until her boot hit an uneven cobblestone, causing her to stumble forward. Having caught her balance, she stooped to the side of the road to retrieve the paper. The name that stood out in the headline brought an instant smile to her face. Freminet was back in Paris.

The article simply stated the inventor and his colleague were back in the city conducting new trials with his underwater breathing machine. She looked to the sky again, the sun on its descent in a glowing twilight.

Tucking the newspaper back under her arm, she changed course away from the dentelle to the Seine River.

The scene was strikingly similar to the one she'd witnessed last fall. She could almost see Nicholas on the Pont Neuf that day, until she banished the thought, knowing the man was either on his way to the colonies or already there.

She took a place within a crowd that watched from the river's edge, their size having grown since the last time. The river, normally alive with activity, was now mostly cleared except for the occasional boat. A merchant ship was on its way over to dock into a quay while a group of washer women sat on the opposing bank of the crowd.

She spotted Freminet and his colleague along the same bank she'd last seen them with Nicholas. The two men sat under a poplar tree, Freminet's colleague holding a watch and eyeing the time as if with precision.

"Mademoiselle, you have come again to watch my machine hydrostatique at work, no?" The inventor stepped toward her, extending a warm greeting with a kiss of her cheek as she stepped under the poplar tree.

"I saw you were back in Paris." She held up the newspaper containing the headline she'd seen. She angled her head to the small crowd that had gathered along the bank. "But it seems I'm not the only one interested this time."

"No, certainly not." He gave a hearty laugh, his tone energized by what she deciphered as the increased support around him. "Our popularity has started to grow as you can see."

"That I can. Congratulations."

"Thank you, mademoiselle." He gave a slight bow before turning to the river's edge. "Would you like to try the diving suit as your friend has done?"

"My friend?" She looked around, but saw no one she recognized, not that she was expecting to. She was about to request more of an explanation when Pierre, if she remembered his name correctly, held the watch up in the air.

"C'est l'heure!"

Time.

"Excuse me, mademoiselle." Freminet quickly stepped away from her, taking hold of the hose attached to the machine before tugging the tubing back and forth.

"Wait." Charlotte followed the length of the hose until the tube disappeared into the river, realizing the machine was at work, but its inventor was not inside the suit. "If you're up here—" Freminet began to pull at the hose, Charlotte staring blankly into the water. "—then who's down there?"

Whether the inventor hadn't heard her question or was simply ignoring her, she wasn't sure, but she didn't want to interrupt as Freminet and Pierre struggled to pull the hose out of the water. The two men worked to gather the tubing over and again until she saw the top of the copper helmet break the river's surface.

Gradually, the shoulders, torso and legs of the diving suit also emerged.

The two inventors went to the diver, each taking an arm of the suit over their shoulders to help the unknown figure grappling with the suit's weight to reach fully onto the bank.

Charlotte felt her pulse quicken, not fully understanding, but wondering to the personage as additional assistance was needed for the diver to take off his metal helmet that had fogged sometime underneath.

Little by *agonizing* little, the two men proceeded to help with the rest of the unfitting of the suit.

Exhilaration pumped through her veins. She couldn't see the diver clearly, but she didn't need to. She would recognize this man anywhere, even if she could hardly believe he was here. "Nicholas."

The elation she read on his face when the helmet was fully off and he had taken a breath of Paris's air, suddenly changed seeing her. He looked as surprised as she felt, but then the grin he gave her mirrored her own joy.

As if needing to prove he was real, she went over to him, her mouth still gaped. "How? I thought with your assignment finished here that you'd be going to the colonies for the war?"

"That's partly true. My next assignment is in Pennsylvania, but I won't be involved in the war effort from now on."

There was something different about him, something less rigid. He accepted a linen sheet from Pierre, using the fabric to dry the sweat from his forehead. He smelled like leather and fish, not his most pleasant scent, but she didn't care. Not when she had him in her life again.

"Not involved in the war?" Her mind reeled as if playing out every possible outcome even when she knew he was bound to tell her.

She hadn't received the letter he'd promised yet, but she couldn't fault him for that, her own turn-around from the colonies having been swifter than she had anticipated. Had something gone wrong in London? She wanted to ask but wasn't sure if this was the best place. Even if the crowd was of little consequence, she didn't want to risk exposing bad news in front of an inventor Nicholas esteemed. She only gave him a look she hoped conveyed her lack of understanding.

"I'm still in the Royal Navy and I'm still a captain, if that's what you're wondering." He offered a steady smile as if to temper any of her concerns and she swore he looked taller from the last time she'd seen him if that was possible. "But my mission has changed. I'm leading expeditions to investigate progress and breakthroughs around the world."

"Progress? Breakthroughs?" She looked to the inventors with the diving suit, considering what she'd just seen and what she knew about this man. Her heart lifted with full comprehension. "You've been commissioned to investigate inventions."

A smile confirmed she'd figured it out.

"Nicholas, that's wonderful! But I thought you said you were bound for Pennsylvania. What are you doing in Paris?"

"I saw some old friends of ours were going to be here." He gestured to the inventors, Freminet now in the diving suit apart from the helmet still needing to be secured. "Since their work is part of my commission, I thought I'd come to Paris first before crossing the Atlantic and follow your advice."

"My advice?" She shook her head, the memory absent. Much of her "advice" in the past had been forcing her opinion on others, and she no longer liked that approach.

"Pursuing a dream, if I remember our conversation back on the Pont Neuf last fall correctly." He veered his gaze to the bridge connecting the left and right banks of the river to the Île de la Cité where'd he'd first shown her this part of himself.

Her heart swelled. The man was making his dream come true and he was giving her credit in the process. "Well, I'm glad to have been some assistance."

He frowned, something she hadn't expected. "Yes, well, I'm not through just yet. I'm looking for a partner."

"A partner? For what exactly? You have a crew at your disposal and if I remember correctly, you're an excellent researcher for locating breakthroughs."

"True, but you and I both know there's a difference between being a captain of a crew who has to obey your orders, and people who don't. I need someone who's not afraid to make connections. Someone who's daring when they need to be." There was that scoundrel of a grin she missed so much. "My commission to explore these advancements doesn't come without caveats." He tucked at the white lapels of his blue jacket, the gold buttons lining up in a neat row down the front of his tall frame. "But there's a chance what I find can benefit everyone, not just England."

Her thoughts churned, wondering if she was picking up on what he was asking. "To be clear, are you asking me to be this partner—to obtain contracts with these inventors?"

"I am." He took a single step toward her. "But there's a stipulation."

A stipulation. What was it with these men and their stipulations? She gave him a sideways look, except she couldn't hold onto her annoyance, not when he was looking at her like that. Her body felt weightless as the ground between them disappeared. "Which is?"

"To marry me."

The words cut her breath, yet she wanted nothing else in that moment. "Fine." She tried to push down the quiver in her voice—one raptured in a longing finally fulfilled. But she didn't have to try hard.

Her feet hovered over the muddy embankment, Nicholas having wrapped her into his arms. His lips pressed into hers with tender passion and a desire she also craved.

Though out of the diving suit, she felt the dampness of his clothes against her own, but she didn't care. She no longer held concern if she looked a fool or not. She loved this man, and he was going to be her husband.

When Nicholas lowered her back onto the river's bank, she felt unsteady but exhilarated. Yet she had one more plan to see through. "I do, however, have a stipulation of my own."

He caressed the back of her neck, kissing her forehead and appearing unbothered by her terms. "Of course, you do. Which is?"

She thought of the surprise of her niece upon arriving at her aunt's estate in Portsmouth, enjoying the opportunity to get even with her older sister. She grinned. "Not one word of our engagement until we reach the colonies."

Afterward

Dear Reader,

Thank you for embarking on Charlotte and Nicholas's journey with me in *A Heart's Charade.*

The story would not be complete if it weren't for the contribution of others. I am indebted to both Anne Donnell and Monica Futrell for their time and dedication in not only editing *A Heart's Charade*, but the provision of their critiques and suggestions for making this book a better experience for you, the reader.

My heartfelt thanks also goes to Victoria Cooper for her exceptional cover design and to my wonderful husband who contributed his own talents to further enhance the design.

Paris holds a special place in my heart as I was fortunate enough to visit with my husband on our honeymoon many years ago. The city is rich with history and when the end of Abigail's story in *Love Beyond the Ashes* aligned for Charlotte to be there, I knew I had to revisit the location, even from afar.

No story set in Paris during this time period would feel complete without mentioning the great Palace of Versailles, a marvel to me, especially prior to the notorious French Revolution that would come a little over a decade later. I don't know if I'll be able to visit the city again, but after delving into research and reflecting on my honeymoon those years ago, I welcome a return with a changed perspective.

As already mentioned briefly, a good sum of research has gone into the workings of this book to be true to the historical context. Nonetheless, the story you have just read is a work of fiction crafted from my imagination and should be thought as such. Key figures in factual history make an appearance like King Louis XVI and Marie Antoinette of France. Likewise, all the inventors and inventions Nicholas followed were real. Even Mr. Fisher, the ship builder from Liverpool, held his account in history with his advice to the Naval Board to utilize copper sheathing on ships for prolonged life at sea.

Apart from those aspects and the landmarks of Paris that were there at the time, the rest is pure fiction. This includes Cairnhaven, the miner's village near London, to make the story flow in the way I designed and hope it has.

Medicine at the time of Charlotte's story wasn't as we know it today. Little was known about anxiety or how to treat the panic attacks Charlotte suffered from. Thankfully, modern medicine has come a long way and because of the resources and education available, you and I have at least a basic understanding there could be more going on than simply a "weak constitution." Anxiety touches countless lives in countless ways, but there is hope. Jesus—the very essence of peace—offers calm amidst the storm.

Thank you, Reader, for your attention. Knowing how precious your time is means so much that you have allowed me to occupy this space in your life.

With loving gratitude,

Jill

www.ingramcontent.com/pod-product-compliance
Lightning Source LLC
Chambersburg PA
CBHW020330010826
48973CB00005B/1199